# THE FATE OF THE TALA

## UNCHARTED REALMS – BOOK 5

by

Jeffe Kennedy

*An Uneasy Marriage, an Unholy Alliance...*

The tales tell of three sisters, daughters of the high king. The eldest, a valiant warrior-woman, conquered her inner demons to become the high queen. The youngest, and most beautiful outlived her Prince Charming and found a strength beyond surface loveliness.

And the other one, Andi? The introverted, awkward middle princess is now the Sorceress Queen, Andromeda—and she stands at the precipice of a devastating war.

As the undead powers of Deyrr gather their forces, their High Priestess focuses on Andi, undermining her at every turn. At the magical barrier that protects the Thirteen Kingdoms from annihilation, the massive Dasnarian navy assembles, ready to pounce the moment Andi can no longer sustain it. And, though her sisters and friends gather around her, Andi finds that her husband, Rayfe, plagued with fears over her pregnancy, has withdrawn, growing ever more distant.

Fighting battles on too many fronts, Andi can't afford to weaken, as she's all that stands between all that's good in the world and purest evil.

*For Andi, the time to grow into her true power has come. . .*

# Dedication

To Grace for helping me sort the fruit of ten thousand apple
trees into one basket

# Acknowledgements

Many thanks to Marcella Burnard for an emergency read when I needed it most. Also to Sage Walker for, dare I say it, sage advice, as always. And to fantastic assistant Carien, for happily reading as soon as I send. Your support during the writing of this book meant everything.

Evergreen thanks to all of my wonderful writer friends who brighten my life and enrich my world: Amanda Bouchet, Grace Draven, Jennifer Estep, Megan Hart, Darynda Jones, Katie Lane, Kelly Robson, Veronica Scott, Minerva Spencer, and many others.

To all the faithful readers of this series, many thanks for your patience and all the messages of enthusiastic support during the extended wait for this book.

Thanks to Rebecca Cremonese for her stellar production editing skills, and for being generally awesome.

Awe and gratitude to Ravven for the absolutely incredible cover. Your images bring my characters to life and give me much-needed inspiration while writing. I could look at this cover forever.

Many thanks to my family, especially to my mom, who worried this book would drive me crazy.

Love to David, first, last, and always.

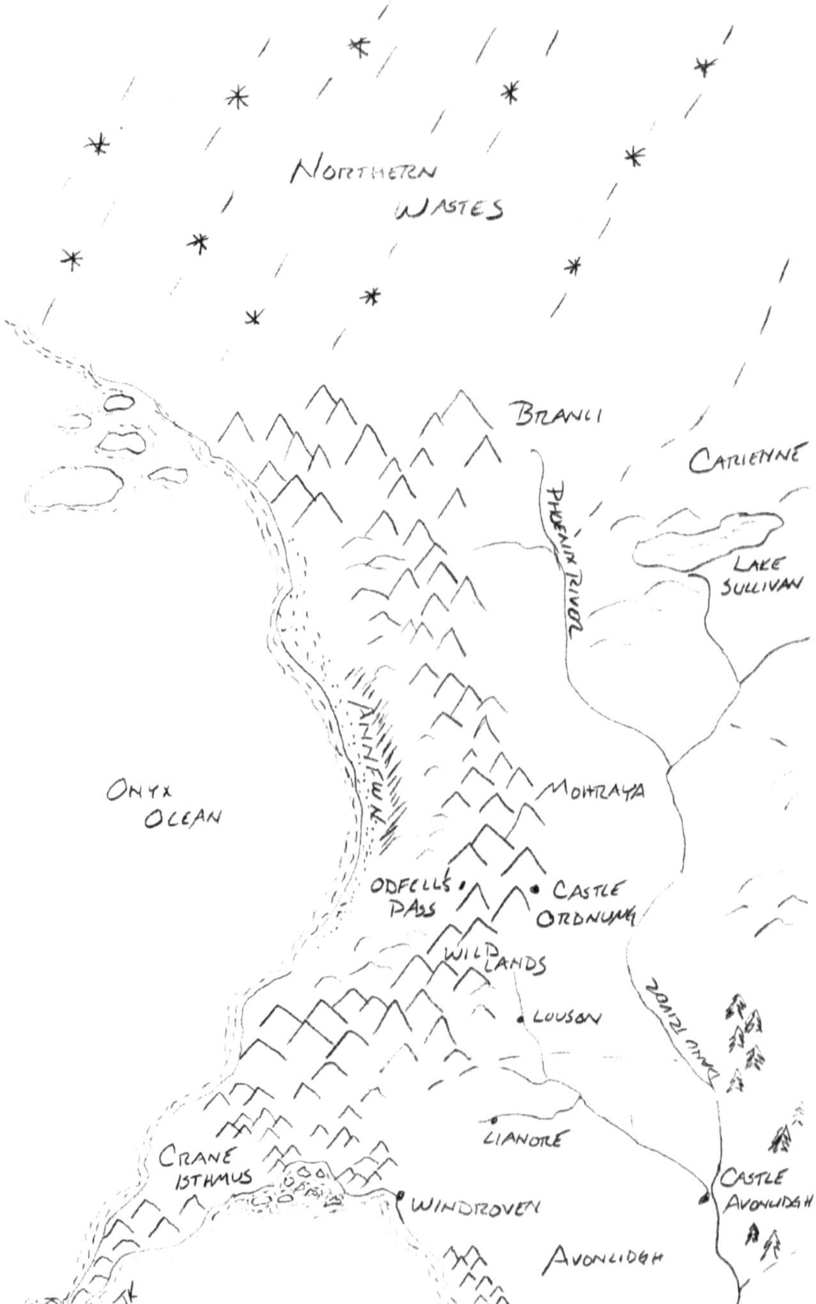

Northern Wastes
Branli
Carienne
Phoenix River
Onyx Ocean
Annewn
Mohraya
Lake Sullivan
Odfell's Pass
Castle Ordnung
Wild Lands
Louson
Onyx River
Lianore
Crane Isthmus
Windroven
Castle Avonlidgh
Avonlidgh

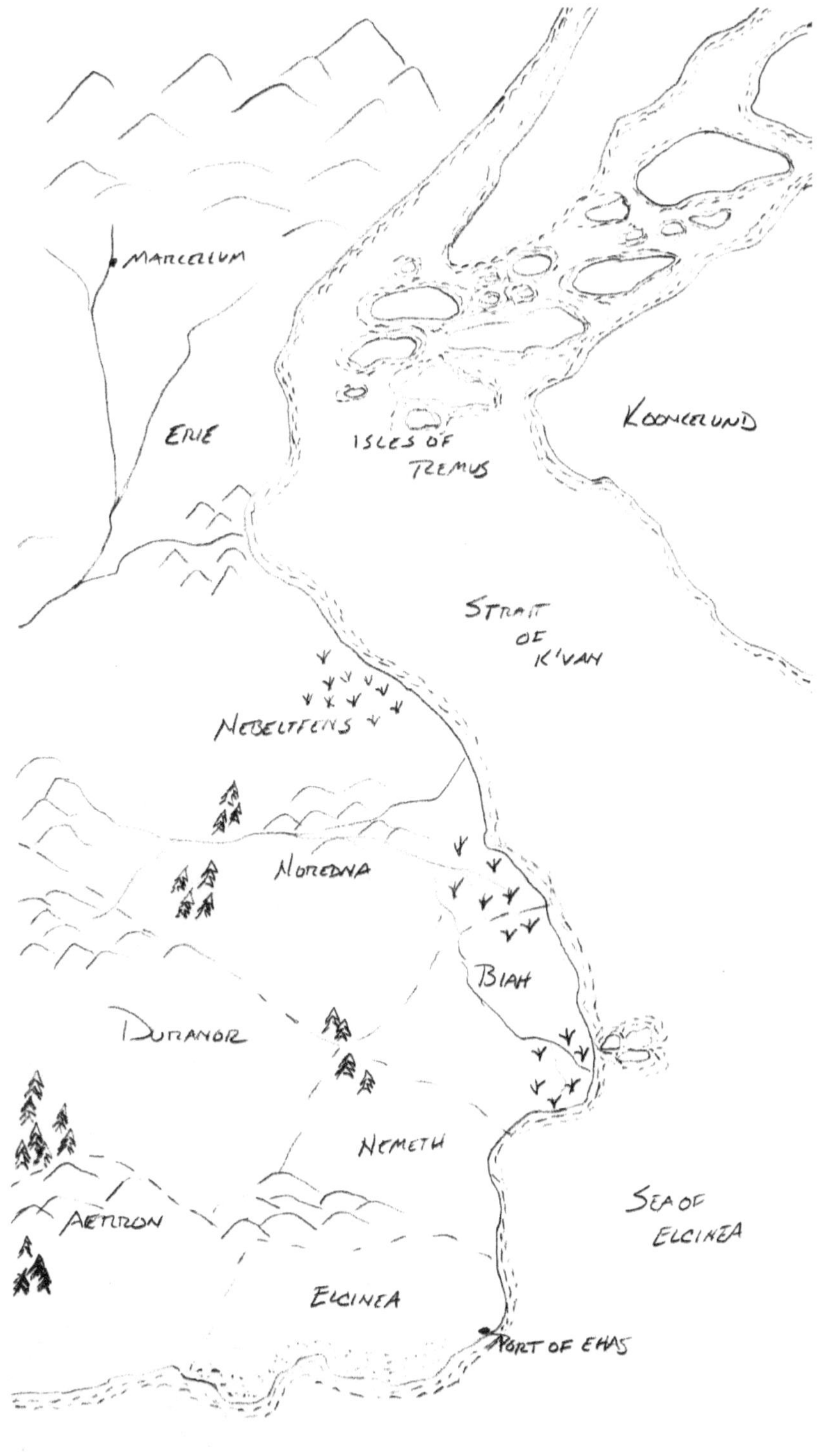

MARCELLUM
ERIE
ISLES OF TREMUS
KOONCELUND
STRAIT OF K'VAH
NEBELTFENS
NOREDNA
BIAH
DURANOR
NEMETH
AETRON
ELCINEA
SEA OF ELCINEA
PORT OF EHAS

DASNARIA

TO JOFARSTYRR

THE
SENTINELS

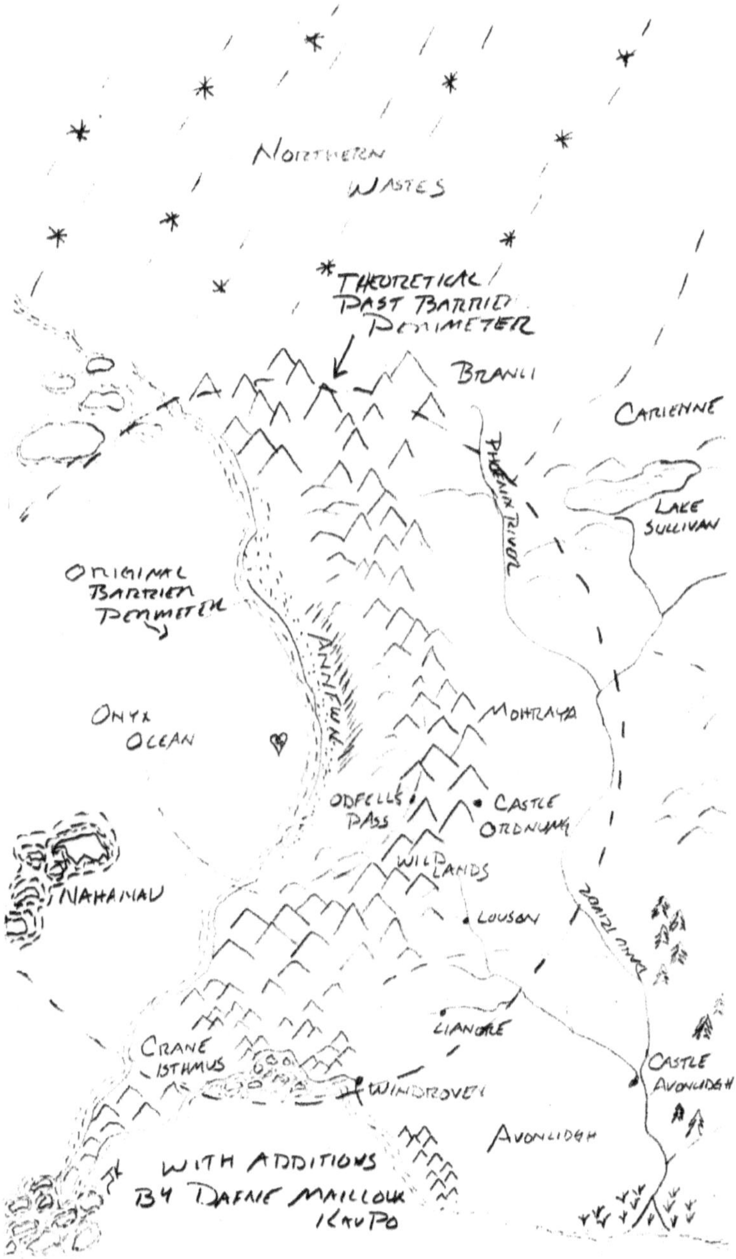

NORTHERN WASTES
THEORETICAL PAST BARRIER PERIMETER
BRANLI
CARIENNE
PHOENIX RIVER
LAKE SULLIVAN
ORIGINAL BARRIER PERIMETER
ONYX OCEAN
ANNFWN
MOHRAYA
ODFELL'S PASS
CASTLE ORDNUNG
NAHAMAU
WILDLANDS
LOUSON
LIANORE
CRANE ISTHMUS
WINDROVER
AVONLIDGH
CASTLE AVONLIDGH
WITH ADDITIONS BY DAFNE MAILLOUX KRUPO

# The Fate of the Tala

by Jeffe Kennedy

## ~ 1 ~

T HE ELEPHANT REARED, its trumpeting loud enough to distort the vision. A tanned woman with white-blond hair clung to its back with athletic grace, sticking easily despite the surprise on her face. More elephants—a few I could see in the narrow frame the goddess allowed me, far more outside its scope—also trumpeted, making a deafening chorus. A lean, dark-skinned man with silver-streaked dark hair tied back at the nape of his neck staggered as the ground undulated beneath him, then caught himself, gaze snapping up to the colorful waves of magic ripping open the sky.

The woman looked, too, the black beads in her braid catching the sun, her pale hair reflecting the cobalt, emerald, and rose lightning. Thunder rolled in bass counterpoint to the elephants' warning calls, the grasses on the low, rolling plains in the distance rattling, and a great river churned an unnatural shade of violet behind them.

The magic storm moved on, and they calmed the beasts, speaking to each other in a language I'd never heard. A young woman, brown-skinned and with amber hair, in fighting gear and daggers in each hand ran up on foot, yelling a question. The man spoke reassuringly, his voice authoritative, using a clear hand signal that she should sheath her blades. The ivory-haired warrior woman dismounted and cupped the young woman's high-cheekboned face, kissing her forehead with maternal care.

Then the blonde looked at me, her unknown watcher. The deep blue of her large eyes dominated a startlingly beautiful face—one that triggered a sense of recognition. She spoke a few words, a twist of accent also oddly familiar.

As quickly as She had seized me in Her grip, the goddess Moranu released me, withdrawing Her presence along with the vision, restoring me to my own time and place.

I sagged against the stone lion head on the breakwater. Sweat-drenched, I uncurled my folded legs to dangle my feet in the cool waves that lapped at the rocks I sat on. Around me, the pristine sea of Annfwn gleamed with serene beauty, a few shades lighter than the cloudless sky, and richer with crystalline depths. The harbor teemed with over a thousand ships, mostly Tala, bright sails and pennants catching the light breeze. High above, the magic barrier shimmered clearly to my eyes, glowing strong, but not rippling with lightning and violent color as it had in the vision.

No, the barrier had only looked that way one time that I knew of: nearly a year before, when it expanded, extending its reach to lands familiar and foreign. The place the vision showed—and the people—had looked very foreign, indeed.

Out of vigilant habit, I traced the arc of the magic barrier with my mind, testing its strength, checking for cracks, and following it all the way to the western boundary where it met the sea—and where the Dasnarian navy paced its outside edge, restless as starving wolves.

Drawing on the Heart of Annfwn, I reinforced the barrier there, something I did several times a day. Ursula, my elder sister and High Queen of the Thirteen Kingdoms, reminded me often to do that, but she hardly needed to. It was unlikely I'd forget to pay attention to the one thing that kept the Dasnarian Empire from sweeping in to overrun our small kingdoms.

Once I'd done that, I followed the barrier northward to the next section I habitually visited, one that felt like a rotten tooth, an aching abscess in the clear magic of Annfwn. The peninsula of Dasnaria penetrated the circular border of the magic barrier there. I'd thickened the barrier at that point—once our people had identified the problem—and made it impermeable to any crossing at all, even the animal life the barrier normally admitted. A bit like closing the stable doors after your expensive breeding stock had run off, since the practitioners of Deyrr had taken advantage of the unwholesome portal to send their creatures inside the barrier to plague us.

We still had sorcerers out there working to cleanse the seas of Deyrr's foul presence. The stench of it had faded somewhat—I made myself taste the magic of that section, despite the revolting flavor and feel—but that piece of land had been so thoroughly possessed by Deyrr that it might never become wholesome again.

Reassured that nothing of note had occurred at the barrier while the visions gripped me, I gathered my consciousness back to my immediate surrounds, sweeping my mind's eye over the cliff city and verifying that all remained quiet.

Well, as quiet as it could be with so many of the Tala concentrated in such a small area. It had been more than a month since Rayfe called the Gathering, and while some of the Tala had dispersed somewhat from those initial days, the population of the cliff city remained at easily four or five times the usual. Crowding the fierce and half wild Tala into close quarters, forcing them to wait for the brewing, war made for quite a bit of tension.

Even though Rayfe had taken a contingent downcoast to clear out a plague of sleeper spies harassing one of our more remote communities, most everyone else remained here, where the first major battle would occur.

Soon. Very soon.

But not yet. For the time being, we could only wait, and do our best to prepare.

Satisfied that all was as well as it could be, I took a moment longer to contemplate this most recent vision. A new one for me, and thankfully not another of us losing the great battle. I wasn't so irreverent as to question the goddess of night and shadows, but sometimes I'd like to tell Moranu She didn't need to show me that particular future anymore. I understood our imminent doom. Each time that vision assaulted me, I ended up gutted and despairing, with no new useful information to show for it.

This new vision must be relevant, as Moranu never delivered anything that didn't turn out to have import. Unfortunately, I often didn't recognize the significance of the visions until the events came to pass—or well after, if I wasn't personally involved. The visions I was able to identify as the past tended to be even less helpful, as I only ever connected those long-ago events with current ones much later. So, this new one might be relevant, but how?

The warrior woman had the look of Dasnaria about her— that ivory blond hair, intensely blue eyes and those high cheekbones—but she was no one I knew, either from my own eyes or looking through the eyes of others. The land she'd occupied had not been Dasnaria, however. No doubt of that, especially as they'd been riding elephants. The only elephants I'd ever seen were Tala shapeshifters. The natural animals lived far from Annfwn and the other twelve kingdoms. Wherever that land was, it was inside the barrier, and something had shifted. They were involved in this war somehow, but on which side?

Almost certainly Dasnaria's.

That meant more enemies inside the barrier. Wonderful.

It would be terribly helpful if Moranu would show me solutions along with the problems. Would that be too much to ask? Apparently so. The goddess didn't do my bidding; I did Hers. Up to a point.

Since all remained quiet for the moment, I cast my mind out to the vast blank area where n'Andana should be. Where I *knew* it was and still couldn't detect anything more than ocean and air. Zyr and Karyn had found the lost continent using the ancient mapsticks. I'd mentally followed Karyn with a magic tether, and even sent Zynda and Marskal to rescue them using that tether. And *still* I couldn't find the place again. Zynda and Zyr could fly there, following physical landmarks, but sending our people to n'Andana posed a grave risk.

How the high priestess of Deyrr managed to do this—and why I couldn't crack her enchantment—worried me greatly. It spoke to her enormous ability that she could hide herself—and an entire continent—from my sight, inside the barrier and not far from the seat of my own greatest power.

Why she hadn't yet launched the devastating attack that loomed so large in my visions had us all guessing. Zyr and Karyn had seen her massive, horrifying army. They'd verified that the high priestess had mentally enslaved probably the entire population of n'Andana. She'd even managed to reincarnate her god, Deyrr. The last time He'd walked the earth, the n'Andanans had nearly destroyed themselves to stop Him.

And here we sat, waiting for them to finish amassing their resources in order to crush us.

Not that we wanted to be in that position. Ursula had agreed that attacking our enemies first was the smartest plan, strategically thinking. However, we couldn't be sure that the Dasnarian

Empire was our actual enemy. Amassing a navy implied war, but they hadn't declared anything. And we didn't know if the emperor had allied with the Temple of Deyrr, who *had* attacked us, multiple times, but never all out.

Even if we decided to go after either Dasnaria or Deyrr, none of the visions indicated we could win. Quite the opposite.

Thoughtfully, I dug in the pocket of my gown for the topaz jewel Karyn and Zyr had stolen from around the high priestess's neck. The focus stone for her magic. Holding it in the palm of my hand, I let it roll across my skin and absorb both my body heat and some of my ambient magic. I'd removed it from its pendant setting, so I could more easily keep it with me when I shapeshifted. A perfectly smooth sphere, though smaller than the Star of Annfwn, the topaz glowed with light in the same way. I'd put the Star inside the Heart of Annfwn for safekeeping, as I didn't dare risk the high priestess getting hold of it.

She'd been able to work more powerful magics than I ever could with this smaller focus stone; I couldn't bear to contemplate what she might be able to do with the Star. So far, though she'd tried for it many times, we'd kept it out of her grasp. She had access to other stones—Karyn had seen the junior priests and priestesses, the high priestess's minions all wearing them—but this had been the largest and likely the most flawless.

It had also been fouled. If I held it too long against my skin, I'd start to smell Deyrr's odor, along with oversweet jasmine. I'd been leery of communing too deeply with it, the way I did with the Star, but perhaps the time had come to risk more. The sense of impending doom intensified daily. I couldn't afford cautious inaction.

To prepare, I took a deep drink from the Heart, then disconnected from it, just in case. I didn't want the high priestess accessing the Heart of Annfwn through me. Steadying myself, I dipped into the jewel, sliding my magic through the focus point…

I jerked in reflexive panic as something seized me in its grip, yanking me out of my body like a hawk's talon abruptly pulling a hapless fish into the air.

"Andromeda," a sweet voice crooned. "At last we meet."

The lovely, lethal face of the high priestess filled my vision, overwhelmingly large. We occupied a nebulous place, not anywhere physical, but an ethereal realm of her making. She'd caught me by surprise and jerked my consciousness into it, and now attempted to frighten me with tricks of perspective.

*Oh, I don't think so.* I wouldn't be her prey. I was the Queen of the Tala, and a sorceress to be reckoned with. I wrested free of her grip and took control of my side of the ethereal realm. She frowned as I pulled back my perspective enough to see her full form, until we seemed to be two women of equivalent size facing each other in a cloudless space.

The high priestess appeared as she did in physical form. I'd seen her before through the eyes of many of my friends— including in Ursula's memories from when the high priestess nearly killed her—but never with my own. Petite, slim, blond, she was very much a classic Dasnarian beauty, except for her matte black gaze. Illyria, the priestess who'd wreaked such havoc at Ordnung, had eyes like that. The mark of Deyrr. I'd grown considerably in my abilities since that brief glimpse of Illyria before Ursula killed her, so I recognized the numinous quality to their lightless depths.

The presence of the god showed in those unsettling eyes. Not pits at all, but the physical expression of Deyrr, the god of corruption, starvation, and immortality through living death. As Karyn had guessed, the high priestess had indeed been born a long time ago, but her body had died before her twenty-fifth birthday. Deyrr animated her, keeping her preserved like a doll made of wax.

"Nothing to say to me, Andromeda?" the high priestess purred, pouting prettily. "Or should I call you Andi? I understand everyone does. I've been so looking forward to meeting you. A conversation between colleagues, if you will. I wish I could say between peers, but you and I both know you can't come close to my level of power and expertise. I hope you won't allow your understandable jealousy to come between us."

"And you are?" I asked blandly.

She giggled, wagging a finger at me. "Don't pretend you don't know perfectly well who I am, Salena's daughter. I knew your mother, by the by. Dreary person. Depressed *and* crazy. A waste of all that delightful talent. I certainly hope you don't take after her."

When you're a manifestation of your own consciousness, lying—or hiding reactions—becomes terrifically more difficult. Still, I managed. I raised an eyebrow at her. "I meant your name."

"You can call me high priestess."

"No." I hadn't loved my despot of a father, and I didn't miss him in the least, but I had learned a few things from him. Titles have power. I wouldn't allow her to force me into a subservient position by using hers.

"No?" she echoed. "But that's the only name I have."

"That's a title, not a name, and you serve no deity I recognize. You are no priestess of mine."

Her visage clouded with annoyance, though she tried to plaster a serene smile over it. She couldn't lie either. "Oh, but He knows you, Andromeda. Deyrr can crush your pitiful moon goddess under His heel. Now would be an excellent time to abandon that misguided loyalty and come over to our side. You know we're going to win. I'm sure even with your amateur training and paltry gifts you've seen the future as clearly as I have. And there are many things you don't know. You may believe you've won a few small skirmishes, but you haven't—" She choked on the words.

"Ah ah ah." I waggled a chastising finger at her. "You should know better than to try to speak a lie in this space."

She glared, lips firmly closed, then spat at me. "It was you then."

"Me?"

"You stole Karyn's mind from me. She won't do you any good. I got to her too late. Those men had crushed all her interest in being more than a handmaiden to their desires."

"Is there a point to this conversation?" I asked, not having to fake boredom. "If service to Deyrr makes everyone this tedious, I'll pass."

"You knocked on *my* door," she snapped, then narrowed her awful eyes. "Which means you have something that belongs to me."

I summoned an image of her topaz jewel. "This trinket? It's so tiny, I forgot I had it. I was about to throw it away."

"Where's the Star of Annfwn?" she demanded, thoughts arrowing like knives into my mind to flay it open.

It hurt—but not enough to devastate me as she'd intended. I'd been expecting some sort of attack like that. Mentally ducking, I pulled on my own magic—thankful I'd had the foresight to disconnect from the Heart—and snapped back into my own body. I shielded my mind, hastily wrapping the topaz in a fold of cloth, and braced for her to follow.

Nothing happened for long moments. I sat on the reassuringly solid rocks of the breakwater, relying only on my physical senses to assess the world around me. Normal sounds of sails catching wind as ships trained in mock battles. The voices of children on the nearby beach echoed over the water, along with soldiers shouting orders as they drilled. The sun shone warm, waves lapped cool on my feet, the scent of salt spray and sweet blossoms filled the gentle air. Gradually, I extended my mind beyond my body, checking for anything else amiss.

All was as before. It seemed I'd successfully extracted myself. But had I learned anything useful? It would be interesting to—

*"AlertAttackDefend!"*

# ～ 2 ～

---

T HE ALARM CALLS rang out, human and animal voices overlapping through my mind and echoing over the water, resonating in my bones and blood. Calling for me.

With Rayfe downcoast, the responsibility to guard and govern Annfwn fell solely to me. Willing away the noise of my people calling for me, I gathered my thoughts, connecting again to the Heart's bolstering strength and the Star's clarifying focus within it. Shapeshifting would forever require concentration from me, would never be the instinctive reflex it was for other Tala. I had to take a long moment to execute it carefully, lest I make a mistake in haste. Especially after that unnerving encounter with the high priestess.

*Concentrate. Focus.*

I became a great blue heron. Once I had the form solid—only a matter of moments, but I hated losing even that much time—I shot out across the harbor, then over the white sand beaches teeming with people in human and animal form. A squadron of staymachs in raptor form, the queen's guard, joined me in protective formation, and I honed my senses, combing the chaos to pinpoint the source of the alarm.

The sea gleamed calm, mirror bright, and pure turquoise. No sign of the churning that accompanied the Deyrr sleeper spy attacks, no oily stench of their undead minions. For once they weren't coming from the sea. Moranu save us, the alert was coming from inside the city. Had the high priestess engineered some new attack while she had me distracted?

The bright silks and draping flowers of the cliff city flew past as I pumped my wings, scanning with eyes and mind, following the shouts of alarm, and the internal calls of the Tala that tugged at me mentally. This made thirty-seven attacks in forty-five days, and despite all our planning and drilling—despite my own sorcerous vigilance—Deyrr's sleeper spies caught us by surprise every time. And in each attack, they lost all of their creatures, killed a few of us, and wounded more.

They could afford the losses. We couldn't. And they'd nibble us to death before the actual war even began.

I sent Rayfe a thought—a warning and reassurance combined, that he should be able to understand, though the distance was too great for us to communicate in words. He couldn't arrive in time to assist. Still, if I didn't send the reassurance, he'd sense me fighting and worry.

Not that anything I could do would stop him from worrying. The man practically made it into an art form.

The calls came from high above, near the top of the cliff face, and I strained my wings to climb, striving to compensate for my ungainly weight. The pregnancy of my human body didn't exactly translate to being egg-heavy in heron form, or so I understood—shapeshifting magic didn't lend itself to much logical analysis—but it sure felt like it sometimes.

I caught a lucky convection current of warm air that accelerated me to the cliff top, pushing me over like a friendly hand.

The sight before me chilled my gut.

A rampaging warthog—three times the size of the normal animal, with wickedly curved tusks and mad scarlet eyes—reared and stomped at the dense shrubbery wall around the training arena. It was going after our children.

Moranu curse it—I hadn't even seen this possibility. Deyrr always came from the sea. Always. How did they get this far in without any of our scouts and perimeter patrols detecting them? Worse, why hadn't I felt it? The high priestess had tricked me, and I had to do better.

The Tala children who'd been practicing in the training arena, supposedly the safest place in Annfwn, were mostly in their First Forms, the ones they easily, or instinctively, took when startled or frightened. Some, those still struggling to shapeshift at will or at all—or with only aquatic forms that couldn't survive on land—were in human form. All were huddling in the far corner backed by a rock escarpment. Their teacher, Meg, in the form of a large black bear, stood on all fours between them and the warthog, head shaking and teeth bared, her growl rolling like an earthquake. It was an excellent defensive form, which is one reason we'd appointed her as teacher in Zyr's absence. But that monster beast far outweighed her. Once it broke through, she wouldn't last long. Not without substantial reinforcements.

A few more Tala had flown in to assist. More were running up the winding cliff road, which would take a while. We needed help immediately. I sent a narrow call for anyone else in the vicinity to make all haste. I really needed one of our flying shapeshifter/human fighter pairs. Unfortunately, most of them had flown off with Rayfe. We were on our own.

The barrier gave and the warthog crashed through.

The bear roared. Children screamed. All manner of animal and human voices shrieked in fury. The hog charged, at least two Tala in human form clinging to its back with daggers dug into its thick hide. Tala in various bird forms flew at its eyes, raking and pecking. It waved its tusks, fighting free of the clinging shrubs, tossing branches and bodies in a flurry. Some smaller animals dashed at it, Tala children ready to fight.

Such brave children. Such foolish, reckless children.

The giant warthog barreled on, undeterred, and Meg rose onto her hind legs, massive clawed paws ready, her belly exposed to sacrifice herself for the kids. Not while I had breath in my body.

I landed between them, my guard spiraling around me in a defensive whirlwind, and I took the excruciatingly long moments to shift back to human form. *Concentrate. Focus.*

The warthog filled the sky as it charged, growing larger by the moment, like a meteor of doom hurtling at me, scarlet eyes like burning suns.

Most of these kids could shift circles around me, but I had sorcery—in human form—and I had the Heart of Annfwn to draw on. Once my body settled into place, I hit the monster with a pulverizing blast of magic.

Nothing. The magic dissipated like soft rain on hot rocks. I had no time to try again. Mouth slavering, it lowered tusks to impale me. Not something my human body could absorb well. If only I could work magic in animal form.

*Concentrate. Focus.*

Exploding into lioness form, I leapt straight in, aiming lethal claws at the mad eyes glaring from beneath protective ridges. I wasn't fast enough, and one tusk caught me in the hind leg, making me sprawl across his snout, but I dug in and held on. I bit down. It wasn't an ideal position—no real lion would do something so ungainly—but I took what I could get. Its fangs sank into a fold of my hind leg, agony pouring through me. Vising down on the warty bridge of its muzzle, sinking my own fangs with desperate strength, I prayed to Moranu this magic wouldn't fail.

The great hog's skull collapsed under the might of my jaws,

the oily taste of Deyrr's undead filling my mouth.

Leaping free, I left the blinded, staggering thing for the others. Humans, Tala, some of Ursula's Hawks she'd detailed to Annfwn's defense, and other warriors from outside Annfwn, swarmed the thing to dismember it. Deyrr's creatures weren't alive anymore. They'd been animated by black magic and implanted with simple missions that they kept trying to execute until they couldn't ambulate. To stop them, we had to chop the creatures into pieces and then burn them to ash. Even then, I worried about the pieces finding each other, the perverted magic relentlessly drawing them back to their purpose.

Worse, the bits of ash retained fragments of the souls trapped by Deyrr and kept in the temple's possession. No matter how finely we burned and scattered them, in a very real sense those particles could never truly die. Few people could sense that reality, but my sorcerous gifts showed it clearly, the shattered bits of life standing out like a phosphorescent glow. The legacy of sorcery my mother left me gave considerable advantages, but brought a heavy burden also. There were things I'd rather not know.

I scanned for more of the enemy. Surely this wasn't the only sleeper spy dispatched for this particular attack, not here where we taught our children, deep into our cliff city, uncomfortably near the king and queen's suites. Rayfe's head would likely explode when he found out how far past our defenses Deyrr had penetrated. Lifting my muzzle, favoring the wounded leg, I sniffed the air for more beasts, mentally casting my magic out in waves to detect what physical senses could not. I could do that much in animal form—using magic to extend my senses beyond my body—just not any of the offensive tricks.

Methodically searching for anything strange, anything even vaguely off, I paced the arena, keeping one eye on Meg, who was rounding up the kids. She herded them away from the still-twitching undead warthog, corralling them back into their safe corner of the arena, putting the steep slope of comforting rock at their backs. Meg had kept her head well enough, but I couldn't help wishing Zyr had been here.

He'd had to give up teaching the children, as we needed him more elsewhere. He and Karyn had become a formidable team, her lethally accurate archery complimented by his deft aerial acrobatics. The two of them had taken on training other shapeshifter and mossback warrior pairs. The combination made for an excellent offensive and defensive squad. We also had to hold Zyr in reserve, since only he and Zynda could replicate the journey to n'Andana—should we decide to attempt it.

Something tickled my awareness, subtle, shielded, but unmistakably Deyrr. *Aha. I've got you.*

These Deyrr sleeper spies were cats of some sort, like my current form, by the mental feel. And … Moranu take them, sneaking up on the children from the rocks. That showed a disturbing level of strategy for the notoriously mindless Deyrr creatures. Something to think about later.

I sent a pulse of alarm through the Heart, along lines of magic that connected all Tala, doing my best to point to the fall of rocks that should've been a good corner to back the kids against. It wasn't proof against agile felines, however—nor the venomous reptiles I soon also detected emerging from crevices, slithering toward the Tala children trapped in vulnerable human form.

This was an ambush, the worst attack so far. I could only hope it wasn't the vanguard of the final battle. The timing wasn't right, but the future shifted so constantly that foresight could be dangerously deluding. I really hoped I hadn't been wrong in not recalling Rayfe and his team. But then, they couldn't get to us in time to save us anyway.

I needed to handle this, and I couldn't fight this kind of attack as a beast. This called for offensive magic, which mean yet another shift back to human form. *Concentrate. Focus.*

Human form hurt, the blood from my wounds immediately soaking through the simple shift I could reliably manifest in. If I could heal when shifting, if I could come back to human form wearing fighting leathers, I absolutely would. Alas for that.

I shouted for Meg to move those kids. The bear responded with alacrity, but the frightened children didn't obey so easily. Even though they appeared to be human, they'd stopped thinking like people and moved into more instinctive, animal behavior. Leaving their safe-feeling corner went against that instinct.

Sending out mental commands to the arriving Tala warriors, I ordered my people to flank and circle behind the encroaching sleepers. I pulled hard on the Heart, and magic, pure and shimmering, flowed into me, making me feel as giddy as if I'd drunk several carafes of sparkling wine. *Moranu, make this one work.* Instead of blasting the Deyrr creatures, I created a shield, a miniature version of the barrier, keeping them from advancing further. It wouldn't last forever—not without draining me—but it would last long enough.

Multiple voices gave reports and asked questions, mental conversations overlapping. I fielded as many as I could at one time, feeling much like an octopus wielding a different tool with my many mental arms.

I limped into the group of panicking children, holding their attention as best I could with one arm of my attention, the lion's share of it on fending off the encroaching attackers. Unlike its permanent cousin, the enormous barrier rooted in and powered by the Heart of Annfwn, my temporary barrier anchored only to me, shifting with my attention. None of my fighters could get through it until I dropped the shield. They moved into position, the Deyrr creatures flinging themselves against the invisible barrier with ferocious intent.

This would have to happen fast. I'd have to drop the barrier and hope my people could stop the lethal Deyrr attackers before they reached the kids. I didn't like the odds, but what choice did I have?

*"Andi. We're incoming."*

Zynda's mental voice slashed across my mind like bright fire. With a rush of gratitude, I grabbed on. *"Are you in dragon form?"*

*"Yes."*

*"Thank Moranu!"* I sent her an image of the rocks behind the arena. *"Wait for us to move the kids, then burn, baby, burn."*

Her mental laugh of anticipation fueled my own flagging spirits. Moranu, but I was grateful for their unexpected arrival. My leg felt like fire and ice at once, my body exhausted from so much shapeshifting, sorcery, and fueling that mini-barrier. I ignored all of that and held out my hands. I raised my voice and reinforced it with magic, the kind that let me speak to anyone with enough Tala blood. Fortunately, no matter how panicked, the kids knew to obey their queen.

*"Listen and obey,"* I called over the cacophony. The children stopped their noise. Wide eyes peered at me through tangles of dark hair. *"Come with me."* They launched themselves at me, like frantic puppies and kittens, some literally crawling up my body, nearly taking me down. I managed to hold firm.

Like a great ship laden with barnacles, my staymach guard flying patterns around us, I waded torturously across the arena. With a mental warning of Zynda's approach, I simultaneously sent orders for the fighters to be ready to handle any attackers that escaped my barrier—now weakening as I moved away from it—and for the others to pull back to avoid dragon fire. Meg lumbered ahead of us, alert for more Deyrr creatures. She reared up on hind legs to roll away the stone gate, letting us escape from the arena, and bellowing at her charges to follow. Some obeyed. Others weren't thinking clearly enough. It takes practice and concentration to maintain human rationality in animal form—something still beyond many of these kids.

I filled their minds with my commands, too. *Follow me. Come with your queen.* Holding their clinging obedience with a strong arm of attention, I made my way to the open gateway. My staymach guard flew at my charges, herding them into a tight group. Birds swirled around my head, four- and two-legged creatures of all kinds clung or danced around me. One child had wrapped her little arms so tightly around my neck she nearly throttled me, her face buried in my hair.

Zynda's vast presence swept overhead, her dragon form both the essence of magic and a cool space in the middle of it. *"Clear?"* she asked.

*"Stand by."* I sent out the call to retreat, pull back. I could only hope they'd be smart. Adult Tala, too, got swept up in the animal drives to fight to the death. My dragging steps set the timing, a slow countdown as we exited the arena. Birds streamed overhead, animals leaping the shrub fence, children breaking free of my hold as they made it out the gate, galloping on human and furry legs, screaming, sobbing, and howling. My temporary barrier thinned to brittle instability.

Shouts of alarm and mental pictures showed three of the sleeper cats breaking through to bound into the arena, leaping after us. We were out of time. I let the rest of the barrier fall. *"Now!"*

Dragon fire scorched my back, and it seemed I felt my hair curling with the searing heat, burning smoke filling my nose.

Forcing my aching leg, I ran with my remaining burden, flinging us down the path I'd first seen on a peaceful day, traveled by no one but me and merrily trotting goats.

That was the Annfwn of the past, however. One that seemed doomed to be lost forever. And it would be all my fault that I hadn't saved it.

~ 3 ~

"YOU REALLY SHOULD be more careful, Your Highness." Healer Vanka channeled her healing energy into my thigh with renewed intensity. It prickled painfully, and I fancied she deliberately made it more uncomfortable than necessary. She wasn't my favorite healer, and she wasn't fond of me either. Over a hundred years old, Vanka remembered my mother, and still resented Salena for leaving Annfwn. In her mind, my mother had abandoned the Tala, and I'd forever be an upstart interloper, part-blood daughter of a faithless queen.

"I'll do my best," I replied drily. Quite a few of the Tala old guard still suspected my loyalties and feared that I'd fail to protect Annfwn. It used to bother me more than it did now—except that every glimpse of the future only verified that they were likely correct. I didn't see any way to save Annfwn, and all the world would know that soon enough.

"You must do better, Your Highness," Vanka insisted. "You carry the future heir of Annfwn. You cannot be capricious about this pregnancy."

Somehow I just didn't see battling Deyrr's sleeper spy attacks as capricious behavior, but I swallowed my sarcasm, struggling to hold my leg still for the treatment, determined not to show how much it hurt. To distract myself, I gazed out the window at the stubbornly empty sky, reaching out to check on Rayfe's progress. He was close, but not quite home yet.

"I know you don't understand our Tala traditions," Vanka continued, "but we follow them for good reasons. You should be in seclusion, resting in peace and quiet."

If only I hadn't sent Kelleah to be Healer for Ursula at Ordnung. Kelleah had understood my reasoning for not going into seclusion and had supported my choices. But, no, I'd had to be all foolishly generous. It had been the right thing to do, as Kelleah possessed enough spine to out-stubborn Ursula and enough flexible thinking to live among non-shifters. But that decision stuck me with Vanka, to my everlasting misery.

But Rayfe trusted Vanka and whatever I could do to set *his* mind at ease made my life easier in equal measure.

"A Tala pregnancy is a rare gift," Vanka insisted with a renewed burst of healing energy. "But you're acting like it's nothing. One might think you flaunt Moranu's will."

Gritting my teeth and pressing my tongue against them, I managed not to hiss at the pain, wishing I could heal myself when I shapeshifted, like other Tala could. I'd tried and tried to master that aspect of shapeshifting and had gotten pretty much nowhere.

I was tired of thinking about it. Truly, I'd done thrice-damned well to be able to shapeshift at all. When Rayfe had first brought me to Annfwn, a foreign princess who sacrificed herself to marriage with the demon Tala king in order to stop a war, they'd all—all but Rayfe, who never lost faith in me—called me too old to learn to shapeshift. I might've been born with the Mark of the Tala, but growing up outside of Annfwn—outside the barrier and in a land bereft of magic—had nearly leached the magic out of me, too.

But I *had* learned to shapeshift. I'd even mastered nearly ten forms. Many Tala only ever had their First Form, and some—

particularly those part-bloods born outside Annfwn like me—couldn't shift at all. Even Rayfe stuck primarily to a couple of preferred forms. I'd never match a prolific shifter like Zynda, but I'd mastered sufficient forms to access the Heart, and that's what mattered. I'd accomplished far more than traditionalists like Vanka had believed possible.

I'd also had plenty of Moranu's will. Having a goddess thrust visions into your mind and guide your steps into a doomed future wasn't exactly a pleasure ride on the beach.

A frisson of blue-black energy rippled through me, the familiar mind-scent of Rayfe approaching, and I nearly cried out in my relief and gladness. In the form of a black eagle, he flew through the arched open windows of our rooms, and my heart actually skipped a beat. With an implosion of magic like the popping of a soap bubble on my skin, he took human form.

Waving black hair still settling around his fine-boned face and shoulders, his midnight blue gaze found mine and the moment of connection hummed between us like unheard music. I caught my breath at the delight of seeing him. Even after all this time together, Rayfe still overpowered my senses. The sheer presence of him, magnetic, feral, and profoundly magical, dizzied me. I craved him in a way I'd never expected to want a man, blood calling to blood still, even though his seed had taken and sprouted.

If Vanka hadn't been practically sitting on me, I would have thrown myself into his arms. I settled for extending my hand, giving him a welcoming smile in the hopes he'd come to me.

He didn't return my smile, however. Instead, he glared daggers. I mentally sighed for it and braced myself. "You're hurt."

*No, I'm Andi,* I very nearly replied. "Not badly, and it's almost healed now," I said instead, dropping my hand. "And, hello, darling. I missed you, too."

He bit out a sigh, and scanned me thoroughly as he advanced. "How is she?" he asked Vanka.

"Well enough, King Rayfe," Vanka fawned, beaming at him. "She'd be doing worlds better if we sequestered her, though. She's endangering our heir with this nonsense. It's not right, her being out and about like—"

"Thank you for your assistance, Vanka," I cut in, not at all in the appropriate temper to listen to this complaint yet again. "It feels like you've finished?"

"Yes, but—"

"Then leave us so I may speak with my lord husband." I'd take a certain amount of her disrespect, but she'd passed my limit. The Tala didn't observe much in the way of formal hierarchy, and I'd never wanted to be in charge of anything, so I rarely pulled rank, but occasionally it was good to be queen.

With a sharp glare, a sour press of her mouth and a cursory nod for me—and a pointedly elaborate curtsey for Rayfe—she became a robin and flew out the window. He didn't seem to notice, intent gaze on me. "You truly are all right?"

I added my other leg to the chair, crossing them at the ankles. Elevating my feet always felt good these days. "Yes. I truly am, and so is—all is well," I corrected myself, seeing him flinch as I nearly mentioned the unmentionable. "But this was the worst attack yet."

"Tell me exactly what happened, in detail, beginning to end," Rayfe demanded, as I'd known he would. That wasn't sorcerous foresight either; I'd simply come to know my husband very well. He poured a mug of cooled fruit juice and handed it to me. I drank it gratefully, then gave the breakdown of the attack as he paced the room. I did not mention my metaphysical encounter with the high priestess. Rayfe might think I'd taken too much of a risk, and I still hadn't decided if it could be useful. I did know that I wanted to retain the option to contact her again, and that would be easier if Rayfe didn't forbid me to do it. Not that I had any problem disobeying his edicts, but I made a policy of never lying to him. At least, not outright.

"They're getting more direct," he commented when I finished.

"Yes, and strategic. These creatures didn't just mindlessly stumble along one trajectory. They held forces in reserve, and adjusted according to our movements. Also, I tried to blast the warthog and my magic bounced off."

He paused in his pacing and frowned at me. "What do you mean it 'bounced off'?"

"I can't describe it better than that. I've never seen anything like it. I had plenty of power, because I was already drawing on the Heart. Since I placed the Star inside the Heart, the magic is even easier to focus. The beast should've vaporized, but the magic had no effect."

"We've theorized that the mindlessness of the Deyrr creatures is a result of the high priestess being too far away to implant more than simple instructions," Rayfe said slowly, thinking. "Could this mean she's now guiding them intelligently from n'Andanda, perhaps also protecting them from sorcery?"

Glumly, I nodded. She'd grabbed my thoughts the moment I knocked on her door, as she put it. She was in close proximity to us metaphysically, if not in actual physical space. "I think that's probably accurate. What about the infestation downcoast—I'm guessing it wasn't as bad as we'd been led to believe?"

He tipped his head at me, as if awarding me a point in a game. "No, it wasn't. I suspect more strategy, this intended to draw us away from here, to leave the children undefended."

The same thought had occurred to me. Had my encounter with her right before the attack been a strategic distraction also?

We seemed to share similar gifts—a commonality that often unsettled me and occasionally frightened me—so had she glimpsed a future where I contacted her and planned accordingly? In that case, her abilities to sort the possible futures probably outstripped mine. She had the advantage of centuries of practice, which meant she could be many steps ahead of me at every turn. The headache, temporarily eased by Vanka's healing, began to creep back in around the edges of my vision.

"At least we outsmarted them in that the children *weren't* undefended." I sounded more weary than I'd meant to. "We saved them all and none of them were seriously injured."

"At great risk to yourself," he shot back, brows lowering.

"Marginal risk to myself," I corrected. "I'm perfectly fine."

"Are you *sure*?" He prowled toward me, blue eyes intent on me. Not in a sensual way, either, alas. Ever since my belly had begun to obviously swell, Rayfe looked at me with that penetrating gaze entirely to ascertain my health—and the condition of our unborn child, which he avoided mentioning directly. "You have to remember your condition, Andromeda."

"It's not something one forgets, Rayfe."

He hissed in frustration. "You seem to sometimes. Vanka is correct in that. Like today."

"It's my job as queen and protector of the Heart to defend our people. That's why you went to such lengths to bring me to Annfwn, wasn't it?"

"Don't start with that." He turned away, pacing to the table to sort through the pile of missives that had arrived for him in his short absence.

I took a breath. It drove me crazy the way he'd begun to treat me, barely touching me—sex was not up for discussion— asking after my health all the time. I'd known going into this pregnancy that the Tala in general, and Rayfe in particular, would be obsessively protective and paranoid about it, but I'd long since passed finding it charming and had moved into boiling irritation. My frustration—emotional and sexual—simmered under pressure, with the least thing likely to set me off.

The sex had worked between us before anything else did. Rayfe and I had connected physically and subconsciously through sexual intimacy, that blazing passion there even when we couldn't seem to communicate any other way, or agree on anything else. Now we'd gone from an active, passionate sex life to nothing. And, as if losing that connection had ripped out the foundation of our relationship, we seemed to have only arguing left.

I didn't blame Rayfe for not finding me attractive. Moranu knew I was swollen in all the wrong places, sometimes sick to my stomach, and often moody. Worse, to ally the fears of everyone watching my pregnancy with strained hope and dreadful anticipation, I had to appear serenely happy no matter how I felt.

Still, even when we were strangers to each other, Rayfe had shown sexual interest in me. In fact, he'd been the first man to *see* me. These days, he looked past or around me in a way that threw me back to being miserable, invisible Andi again. Losing his regard eroded my confidence bit by bit, with every passing day. Instead of invisibility being my shield, it felt like a trap I couldn't escape.

Nor could I help thinking about how Ursula had insisted from the beginning that I would only be a blood pawn to Rayfe and the Tala, a queen in name only, acquired to breed the next generation that they couldn't. Rayfe had convinced me otherwise, that though he and Annfwn needed me for my sorcery, he did love me. And I had believed him.

Well, I still believed that he loved me, but this pregnancy had changed how we interacted so much that Ursula's words had crawled back to slither round my mind.

"Here's one from Ordnung," Rayfe said, handing me the scroll with Ursula's stooping crimson hawk seal.

It suited me fine to let Rayfe change the subject, so I broke Ursula's seal, and started reading. Stopped. Went back to the beginning and read again. "Holy Moranu, Ursula and Harlan got married."

I angled the parchment to the midday light to make sure it really was my older sister's terrible handwriting, and that I'd understood correctly. This time I reread the opening lines aloud for Rayfe.

"Is that really such a surprise?" he asked. "After all, they've been mated all this time. Surely a mossback marriage simply formalizes that existing truth."

"This is Ursula we're talking about," I said. "High Queen of the Thirteen Kingdoms, born with a law book stuck in her throat."

"I know who she is," he replied with a grimace. My sister and my husband had reached a reasonable détente in their political rivalry, but it was a peace between two predatory natures and monarchs of their realms, ones who faced a greater common enemy—for the moment. I had no doubt that, if we managed to survive this war, then Rayfe and Ursula would again be fighting over borders and autonomy. And me.

That was trouble for the future, however, and right now the possible futures I could glimpse past this annihilating conflict were too splintered to follow. The imminent war acted like a huge dam across the river of time. The many resulting channels radiated from it with so many fine ripples and new channels that it gave me a headache to try to think about them, much less track each potential outcome.

But this… Maybe it explained why Moranu had sent the new vision this morning. This marriage would've shifted the probabilities significantly. In some futures, we battled only Deyrr; in others, we fought both Dasnaria and Deyrr. Sometimes they acted as one force; other times as two. In some futures Dasnaria seemed to be allied with us. The possible futures shifted so often and with so many variations that I hadn't tried to track them in a couple of days. Clearly I needed to look again. I rubbed my temple, dreading that prospect.

"Do you have a headache?" Rayfe asked with quick concern. "Maybe you should lie down and have a nap."

"I don't want to lie down." I tried to keep my voice measured, but I sounded cranky even to my own ears. Vanka had wanted me to take a nap, too. I shook the scroll at him. "What I want is for you to listen to me. This supposed 'formality' isn't simple at all. Ursula is the High Queen of the Thirteen Kingdoms. She just married a former mercenary, brother of the Emperor of Dasnaria, the man behind the navy massing outside the magic barrier, preparing to descend on Annfwn."

"Yes," Rayfe replied with exaggerated patience, "I know who Harlan is, too."

I managed not to growl at him. "Right, but listen to this: *Emperor Hestar offered me a treaty, one hundred years of peace, if I married his…* I can't read that word. Mind-allied brother?"

Rayfe peered over my shoulder. "Mind-addled, I believe."

"I don't know why you can read my own sister's handwriting better than I can," I grumbled.

"Probably because all of your written language is equally impenetrable to me," he replied with a bit of a smile, then waved a hand at me to continue as he prowled back to the window. He wore black, as usual, and the sleek leather clung to his lithe body. Rayfe had a liquid, feline physique, and I savored the sight. Not that it did me any good these days, but at least I could look.

With a sigh, I returned to the letter instead. "…*if I married his mind-addled brother. So I'm informing him that I'm already married to his brother Harlan, and fortunately Kral was in Ordnung to see the contract witnessed and executed according to Dasnarian law, too. We'll send a copy of the marriage contract and offer to sign the treaty under those terms.* Hmpf. See? The woman loves laws." Except when she flouted them by lying so outrageously, and to the Emperor of Dasnaria, no less. And she'd given up a possible treaty that could've tipped the balance of this war. So out of character for Ursula to do something this… impulsive. And sentimental. Romantic, even.

Unforeseeable, really. I began to get a very bad feeling.

"Kral was at Ordnung?" Rayfe asked, breaking into my reverie. "I thought he and Jepp were at sea on the *Hákyrling*, guarding the barrier."

"No," I replied absently, skimming the rest of the letter for pertinent information. "While you were downcoast taking care of that sleeper spy infestation, Jepp and Kral sailed in and asked Zynda to give them a ride to Ordnung. Apparently this missive from Hestar, delivered to the *Hákyrling*, was the reason for their urgency. They might've told me."

"*You* might've told *me*." Rayfe had finally stopped pacing to lean against the window ledge, arms folded and gaze sparking with irritation. He really hated not knowing things. "I didn't see the *Hákyrling* in the harbor."

With the sea breeze tossing his wild, dark hair around his face and shoulders, the sun highlighting the blue glints, he looked unbearably enticing. That didn't stop me from scowling back at him, or maybe the unsatiated craving for him made me scowl more. "You *just* now returned." I waved a hand at the window he'd flown in. "And you didn't see Kral's ship because Shipmaster Jens took the *Hákyrling* back out to monitor the

Dasnarians."

"All right. No need to bite at me," he replied with measured patience. "Finish reading the letter."

"Eh, you heard the important part. The crux is that they—including Kral, apparently—are going to lie to Hestar and claim the marriage predates his offer, and they're going to ask for the treaty anyway, on the grounds that they're already family."

Rayfe cocked his head. "Didn't Harlan's horrible, power-mad relatives disinherit him a long time ago?"

"Why, yes. Yes, they did. Ursula seems to be hoping that whatever reasons prompted Hestar to ask for the treaty will be compelling enough for Harlan's family to re-inherit him, so they can have the treaty that way."

"I don't know that word in Common Tongue. 'Re-inherit'?"

"Because I made it up. Whatever the concept would be."

"She doesn't say what Hestar's reasons were?"

"She doesn't want to speculate in writing, in case the emperor is operating without the Temple of Deyrr's knowledge. Instead they're all traveling here to discuss in person, rather than risk a message being intercepted."

"I see. And 'they' are all traveling to Annfwn… who?"

I glanced at the letter. "Ursula, Harlan, Jepp, Kral, likely additional entourage—via horseback. Zynda and Marskal are already back in Annfwn, of course, as they helped drive off the attack on the training arena and also brought this letter, along with others."

"You have a knack for deprioritizing critical information," Rayfe grumbled, eyeing me. "You could have told me that we're expecting visitors. When will they be here?"

I set my teeth. "I'm telling you now, mere moments after I discovered the information myself, and by this evening."

"That's hardly convenient timing," he mused with considerable annoyance. "We're overcrowded as it is and are already hosting several armies of hers."

"Reinforcements," I reminded him. "Sent to assist us."

"So far they've been a nuisance. Were they any help to you today? I bet not." He answered his own question before I could. "Besides, Ursula can't just stomp over the border any time she likes."

I waved the letter at him. "She did give us forewarning, and she is our High Queen, I might remind you. She can visit any of her subsidiary kingdoms with or without notice."

"The hell you say," he growled, sounding like his wolf First Form.

"I do say. I'll add that, with this 'formalization' of their relationship, Harlan could be considered High King, and your liege."

Rayfe gave me a black look. "Not funny, Andromeda."

"You're right, and it's not important." I rather doubted Ursula and Harlan would go that far. He'd been content to be her consort and had no interest in ruling, not like my husband who had a tendency to want to control everything. I sometimes wondered at the fate that had tied us together as mates, with me so slippery about being controlled by anything. "What is relevant here is that, whatever Harlan's status, this marriage has shifted things. If the Dasnarians were waiting on this treaty and decide not to accept the altered terms, then they're ready to attack as soon as the barrier fails and—"

"What do you mean, as soon as it fails?" Rayfe pounced on my words, eyes flashing with feral emotion. "I *knew* it. Moranu take you, Andromeda—sustaining the barrier is too much of a strain on you with everything else. You're spreading yourself too thin. In your *condition*, you simply cannot—"

"Stop right there," I replied with considerable ire, my temper fraying in sync with his. I knew exactly what he'd been about to say, not because I could read his mind, which I tried not to do without permission, but because we'd had this exact conversation so many times I could rehearse it in my sleep. "I misspoke. *If* the barrier fails, it will be because the high priestess of Deyrr is a more experienced and effective sorceress than I am. Which she is." After that morning's encounter with her, I couldn't delude myself about that any longer. I sighed and cast the letter aside, giving into the throbbing headache and rubbing my temples. "I'm just not the sorceress my mother was. I can't—"

"Andromeda." Rayfe knelt in front of my chair, gently clasping my wrists and easing my hands down to my lap, lacing his long fingers with mine. I regretted betraying my fear, but at least Rayfe was touching me. I savored the feel of his skin on mine like a drink of cool water in the Aeron desert. "Salena was powerful, yes," he said, searching my eyes. "And no one knows better than I do how hard it is to follow in her footsteps—but you have the Star and the Heart. And you've grown so much in your sorcery since you came to Annfwn."

"For a part-blood raised among mossbacks," I said with a wry smile. "Maybe if I'd grown up in Annfwn, I could've overcome the mixed heritage, but learning too late—"

"Not too late." Rayfe replied, releasing my hands to thread his fingers through my hair, combing the wild tumble back from around my face. The sea air of Annfwn brought out curl I'd never had growing up at Castle Ordnung, in the mountainous foothills of Mohraya. I'd grown to like leaving it loose in the Tala style, but that meant it tangled and tumbled of its own accord. I leaned into his touch with such intense gratitude I could've wept from it.

"My queen, you're not giving yourself enough credit for all you've accomplished."

"I try to give myself credit." I weighed my next words. I'd needed this, needed to be able to talk to him, to trust in him, my one true confidant. His consuming fears for me, for our unborn child, had pushed me into a position of protecting his feelings—which meant I'd stopped confiding my own fears. "But I also have to face the truth. We can't afford to underestimate the severity of this situation or to ignore my limitations. From what Karyn discovered during her time as a captive, the high priestess is ancient, with centuries to build her skills. With her god walking the earth again, accessing that magic could make her as powerful as a goddess." My breath hitched in my chest, cold sweat dripping down my spine despite the tropical warmth of the day. "I'm so afraid that I'm not sorceress enough to battle that."

"You have Moranu guiding you, and She is surely greater than any Dasnarian demigod," Rayfe scoffed with a smile.

I tried to give an answering smile, but I felt the wobble. Moranu thrust visions upon me, but the goddess didn't seem to actually help me in any way. Of course, being the goddess of changeability and trickery, Her version of assistance could look like anything. Regardless, I couldn't count on divine intervention to make up for my lacks.

Sometimes I wondered if even my mother, the famously powerful and long-seeing Salena, would've been sorceress enough to win this war. In my more bitter moments, I speculated that the complex plotting that had resulted in our current predicament had been partly to foist the responsibility for this fight onto her daughters entirely because she knew she couldn't do it. It felt like a disloyal thought, and yet…

"You're not alone in this," Rayfe said, gently and firmly, probably sensing my deep uncertainty. His fingers stroked through my hair, then gently cupped my head, while he kissed me, sweet and lingering. "We're all in this fight together," he murmured against my lips.

"Thank you," I said with fervent gratitude. I'd needed to hear that from him as much as I'd needed to be held like this. I sank into the kiss, drinking him in, my irritation and anxiety falling away if only for the moment. I wished our lives could be entirely this, that I could enjoy the beauty of Annfwn and the touch of my husband, anticipate the birth of our child with joy. I wished the timing of this pregnancy wasn't so terrible. Everyone had seemed so sure I wouldn't conceive easily, and then—even if I did—that I wouldn't carry the child long, with all the shapeshifting and magic-working. It had been easy to be lulled by that fatalistic certainty. And then, even with Zynda's draconic ability to stabilize magic, this pregnancy could still go terribly wrong. No matter what I did.

The Tala had been suffering for decades or longer with the devastating rates of miscarriages, birth defects and infant mortality. So much so that the Tala superstitiously didn't refer to pregnancy or babies, studiously averting their gazes from my obviously swollen belly. Rayfe was a perfect example: he hovered, incandescent with anticipation over the prospect of being a father, and also refrained from mentioning the child, simply referring to the pregnancy as my 'condition,' as if it were some sort of skin disease.

I needed the physical release of sex, and I missed the intimacy with Rayfe, missed the physical expression of his love. So I leaned into the kiss, deepening it, sliding my hands under his shirt to touch his hot skin and the lean muscles of his shoulders. "Please, Rayfe," I murmured, opening my mind so he'd feel my desire. "I need you."

He pulled away, however, changing the kiss to a chaste peck, then removed my hands from under his shirt and set them in my lap with a soothing pat that had me balling them into fists. "You know we can't, Andromeda. I won't do anything to jeopardize your health."

"Healer Kelleah says there's no danger if we're careful, that it would even be good for me."

His expression shuttering into obstinate refusal, he shook his head, as he stood and moved away. "That's not Healer Vanka's opinion, as you know. Besides, it's not traditional to—"

"Oh, blast Tala tradition! We're already going against it with me not going into seclusion." I took one look at the uncertainty in his eyes, caught the leaked edge of a thought. "Or have you changed your mind about that?"

"Andromeda…" His fear welled up in a palpable wave, chill, damp and fetid. "It's not safe here. The cliff city will be the focus of the worst battles. You've said as much. Maybe you should go upcoast. Just until… after."

A bit more of my confidence eroded away, rocks falling into a turbulent sea. "Not long ago you said that if I left you'd come after me, because you didn't want to be apart from me, ever."

He wouldn't meet my eyes, his mouth turning in an unhappy line. "I just… I hate seeing you injured."

Needing to get a grip on myself, I got up and went to the window. I leaned out, letting the sea breeze cool my skin, aware of the tight skin of my stomach pressing into the stone ledge. The baby squirmed at the pressure, and I laid a hand there. I turned to face Rayfe. "The baby is moving. Why don't you come feel?"

I was breaking our tacit rules by saying the words, by asking this of him, but we couldn't keep going this way. Our marriage was crumbling under the pressures of this pregnancy and the looming war.

Rayfe didn't exactly step back, but he withdrew from me

mentally, staying where he was, gaze focused over my shoulder. "Andromeda…Please don't ask that of me."

"Rayfe."

"Yes?" He kept carefully looking past me. I blew out an exasperated breath. "It's not bad luck."

Now he looked at me, a hint of panic in his dark blue eyes. "I never said it was. The Tala just have certain customs. And… reasons for them."

For a wild and lawless people, the Tala's superstitious observation of those customs bordered on obsessive. I blew out a breath, trying to be reasonable and not let my heartbreak show. "I can't go upcoast and sequester myself. What's coming will happen before our baby is born."

He flinched at the words, but I plowed on.

"I have to be here—yes, at the focal point of the war—because that's my duty. Not just as the Queen of the Tala, but to serve my mother's legacy. I have a responsibility to that, and to all the world."

"I know." But he looked angry and miserable. "I do know that. Of course you should be here. You're needed. We can't win this war without you."

I flinched inside at the slice of those words. Nothing about him wanting to be with me. He would be happier, I realized, if he could put me and this pregnancy out of his mind. I turned so he wouldn't see how he'd hurt me, and looked out the window again at the sparkling turquoise sea, the busy crowds and colorful awnings of the bustling cliff city below. So many happy lives, so many people counting on me. "I know," I said. "Annfwn needs me."

It had been one of the first things he ever said to me. A courtship—if you could call his relentless pursuit of me by any such gentle word—and marriage driven by vows my mother made long before I was even conceived. I'd been born with the Mark of the Tala, and because of that, I'd been destined to wed their king. Neither of us had chosen the other. We'd made a reasonably good marriage, considering that we'd both been forced into it by forces much greater than ourselves.

I didn't regret those choices. The relentless cascade of events since provided one verification after another that I'd followed the path Salena had foreseen, that Moranu herded me into. I was what I was destined to be. Queen of Annfwn. Sorceress. Guardian of all that Deyrr wished to devour.

None of those roles required that I have a happy marriage. Salena hadn't had one. Her marriage to my father had so soured that she'd gone insane and he'd finally murdered her. When I wed Rayfe, I'd wondered if that would be my path, too. For a while it seemed I'd escaped that curse. Now it seemed a very possible future. Some days I wondered if my sanity might be crumbling at the edges.

I found myself desperately envious of Ursula. She'd married Harlan, her grand passion, out of defiance to the fates. Ursula, who'd always put the throne and duty first. How bitter to find myself the obedient daughter, the one who'd caved to duty and sacrifice. I loved the husband my marriage of state had brought. I loved Rayfe with a desperate, sinking, and heartbreaking passion. Which only made this rupturing chasm between us carve more deeply.

"Andromeda." He spoke from closer behind me. "I didn't mean that like it sounded. Annfwn needs you, yes, but… You know that I need you, too."

I swallowed against the tears. "I miss having you touch me."

"I touch you. We kissed, only a few minutes ago." He set careful hands on my shoulders, warm on my bare arms. "I'm touching you now."

"That's not what I mean," I managed to say, and my voice wobbled.

"Don't sound like that. I just meant that we shouldn't… We cannot afford to take chances. The price is too high. Sequestering is not an option, but we should consider observing a certain… distance."

"How much more distance do you want? Do you want me to move into the spare bedchamber?" I asked, throwing it out as a challenge.

"Don't be silly," he said to my vast relief. He squeezed my arms and dropped his hands. "I'll move into it. This was your mother's bedchamber. It should be yours."

I only nodded, unable to trust my voice with the tears welling up. More the fool I for making the suggestion. Never ask a question unless you're prepared to hear an answer you don't like.

I hadn't seen this coming either.

## ~ 4 ~

RAYFE SUMMONED SERVANTS immediately, and they began moving his things into the other bedchamber with daunting speed. To save myself from the depressing sight—and to restrain my acid comments on how relieved he must be not to have to share a bed with me any longer—I retired to the bathing room. There I soaked in a hot bath, getting the last of the blood and ichor off me, and even washed my hair the old-fashioned way. No sense using energy to shapeshift any more often than necessary at this point, and soaking helped relax muscles gone tight from the battles—physical, metaphysical, and emotional. I even fell asleep for a bit, which *did* make me feel better, Moranu take it all.

"You look nice," Rayfe said when we met in the sitting room between our bedchambers. He cleared his throat awkwardly.

"Thank you," I replied, just as painfully polite.

He studied me, his thoughts shielded, and he seemed to be searching for something else to say.

"Shall we walk down to the gate and greet our guests there?" I suggested, when he hesitated too long.

"Good idea," he agreed with obvious relief, and offered me his arm. I rested my hand on his forearm, a formal gesture, but the physical contact nevertheless had me wanting more. I managed not to beg him to pay attention to me again. And I somehow held back all the hurt feelings, bottling them up deep inside.

Instead, we conversed about matters of government as we walked, mostly updating each other on news from the last few days. We returned the greetings of the people we passed, stopped here and there to receive reports and make decisions. Two co-rulers moving through their realm. There was nothing wrong with that.

There was everything wrong with it. And, as with all the doom crashing toward the present moment, I seemed unable to alter the raging river of it as it carved an ever deeper channel.

We reached the Gate of Annfwn, which we'd had built at the point where the now broad and smooth trade road to the other twelve kingdoms entered the civilized portion of Annfwn. Truly, by the time anyone crested Odfell's Pass, they were in Annfwn proper. The Tala who chose to live in those high peaks and forested hills enjoyed dwellings far less recognizable to moss-backs, whereas the cliff city and many structures along the coast were similar enough to make the non-Tala more or less comfortable.

We called it a "gate," but it was more of an arch. Wizard artisans had grown it in place, coaxing the wood into the elaborate patterns that emblemized the Tala—a mélange of animal shapes morphing seamlessly from one to another. With no flanking walls or physical door to close off the archway, the gate served a symbolic purpose for most. I'd worked with the artisans however, layering in magic connected to the Heart like hooks deep in the wood. With minimal effort I could "lock" the gate, preventing anyone from passing through or around it.

Rayfe and I had designed the gate together, and it worked in both directions. Most of the Tala believed I'd use it to prevent incursions from the other twelve kingdoms, in case anyone became impatient—or rapaciously greedy—for the food and other goods we exported to the more impoverished realms on the other side of the mountains. And I could and would do that, if it became necessary.

That would be far future, however, not the immediate one. I worried far more about Dasnaria and Deyrr overwhelming Annfwn, and then overrunning the lands past us. We would not be the threshold they crossed to take over the remaining twelve. That was something Rayfe still didn't understand about me. I was a child of two worlds, whether he saw it that way or not, and the people of the other twelve kingdoms were mine to protect as well.

Zynda, back in human form, and Marskal were waiting for us at the gate. I'd known Marskal since my girlhood at Ordnung, since he'd served at the castle in Ursula's elite guard, the Hawks. A quiet man with a somber mien, who came from a large farming family, he'd always seemed a conservative sort to me. So it still bemused me that he'd fallen in love with—and won the heart of—Zynda, our most talented shapeshifter, and a woman quintessentially Tala in her wild, independent spirit.

And yet, they seemed to be making it work. They fit in a way I'd never have predicted. Marskal had proved adept at riding Zynda's dragon form. With her brother Zyr equally determined to take the form—though not yet successful—that would give us two dragon shapeshifters, a considerable edge in the coming war. I hoped we could also count on two more dragons—the permanent variety, not shapeshifters—as allies. We'd need all the help we could get.

"Your Highnesses." Marskal bowed, greeting us gravely, and Zynda smiled cheekily with typical Tala irreverence for authority.

Then she gave me a long look. "How are you feeling, Andi?"

"Fine," I said, crisply enough to cut off further conversation.

To no avail.

"She's exhausted, moody, and her head aches all the time," Rayfe, the traitor, reported.

"Is it the pregnancy, the sorcery, or the visions?" Zynda asked me quietly, with frank calm. As my cousin, she shared many of the same sorcerous gifts that Salena's blood bequeathed our line, though she'd escaped the main burden. Zynda could work some magic, especially if she had the opportunity to prepare spells, but her greatest gifts lay in shapeshifting. All the fun and none of the onus. She did, however, receive occasional glimpses of the future, and understood better than most how wearing they could be.

"All of it," I confessed to her in the same tone.

Rayfe, unabashedly listening, got that *look* on his face and opened his mouth. Zynda quelled him with a glance, a talent I envied. They'd grown up together, and she was a few years older. He still habitually obeyed her from the days she'd been in charge of corralling the wilder Tala children.

"Marskal." Zynda brushed a kiss on his cheek and he smiled at her, slow, warm, and surprisingly sensual for the dour soldier. "Why don't you tell Rayfe about our recent battle at Ordnung and what we've discovered about Deyrr?"

"What happened?" Rayfe demanded, rounding on the other man. I could almost see his wolf hackles bristling. With the sleek subtlety of long practice, Zynda put her arm through mine and guided us a few steps off to the side, so deftly Rayfe didn't seem to notice my departure, or the change of subject.

"How can I help?" she asked, leaning her head against mine.

Zynda smelled of the flowers of Annfwn, sweet and warm, her unbound hair silky on my arm. Maybe it had to do with her core-deep independence and love of life, but Zynda had a knack for listening without judging. She claimed to be terrible at listening to other people's problems, but she loved discussing magic. And, of anyone I knew, she came the closest to understanding how foresight and sorcery mucked with your perceptions.

She'd also had her own encounters with Moranu and knew how demanding our tricky goddess could be. She'd also been working with the shamans since girlhood, a group I'd been leery of. Early on Rayfe had warned me to stay clear of their semi-fanatical ways, but lately I'd begun to wonder if they—and their leader, known only as "Shaman"—might have insight into how I could solicit Moranu's help.

I didn't know much about dealing with a goddess, myself. Uorsin had been an atheist. Or, more accurately, he hadn't believed in any power greater than himself. He'd propped up Glorianna's worship as the gentlest and prettiest of practices to keep his people calm and unlikely to look to closely at the true corruption beneath the surface of his rule. My younger sister Ami, universally acclaimed as Glorianna's avatar since her birth, had done a great deal to purge the Temple of Glorianna and restore Her true observances, mostly centered around love and nurturing. And Ursula looked to the warrior goddess, Danu, who demanded clear-eyed justice.

Both of my sisters seemed to have drawn much more straightforward goddesses than I had.

I sighed, taking advantage of Rayfe's inattention to rub my temple. The rejuvenating effects of the nap had already worn off. "Flashes of the future come at me all the time these days. A constant barrage, and so much of it is…"

"Horrible," Zynda finished softly. "I'm getting some, too. Nothing on your scale, so I can only imagine."

"Yes. I don't know why Moranu sends half of them, what I'm supposed to understand from them. And then I'm missing huge things. This morning's attack on the training ground. Then I didn't see anything about Harlan and Ursula marrying." That bothered me a great deal, that I'd entirely missed that. Rayfe hadn't understood the extent of my shock, and how lonely I'd suddenly felt.

"Hmm. They made the decision quickly, within the space of a few hours. You know how it is when people make sudden choices, especially ones out of character for them. Those decisions can alter the flow of the future in ways impossible to foresee."

"Even for a goddess?"

Zynda smiled, laughing low in her throat. "If the goddesses could control what people decide, I'm sure this world would be far more orderly."

"True. But I still feel like I should be able to use this foresight more effectively, particularly with events like this that divert the stream of the future so dramatically. I've been spending so much time and effort studying the future, following out all the thousands and millions of branching possibilities that—"

"Hold a moment." Zynda turned to face me, her eyes like Rayfe's, a blue as deep as the center of the ocean. "That sort of pursuit is incredibly draining. No wonder you're tired. No one can sustain that kind of effort."

"Salena could do it," I countered. "Somehow, she saw all the way to this future, probably beyond, and planned for events accurately. If *she* did it, I should be able to."

Zynda didn't argue, or tell me something soothing. Instead she looked thoughtful, lips pursed in a considering moue. "So, let's say she did. And I could point out some things I think she predicted incorrectly, but let's say for the sake of argument that Salena saw all of this and planned for it. Andi, she'd have studied the currents of time over years and years. She had decades to do that, and she did it as an experienced sorceress in the fullness of her power, before she left Annfwn. That's a considerably different project than you, a young woman with not even two years of practice, trying to do the same thing over the course of a few months."

"We don't *have* decades, or years—or even weeks." I said it with sober intensity, and she stilled, giving me a keen look.

"How long do you think?"

Casting a surreptitious glance at Rayfe, I rubbed my temple again, though it did little to ease the ache. "Days, maybe. We're almost out of time to prepare. Worse, I think Deyrr has even more of a jump on us. I tried the working you taught me to blast that warthog this morning and it just… dissipated. And I was pulling the Heart, so I should've had plenty of magic behind it."

She sharpened at that, perplexed and concerned. "I wondered why you didn't try that."

"Did. Failed."

"What about your new trick? Where you sever the animating spirits from the creature's bodies."

I grimaced. "I didn't try that. I was out of time, running low on personal resources—and that really kicks me hard every time—and… I really worry about the repercussions of doing it."

Zynda was nodding. "I know what you mean. But if the sorcery I showed you didn't work, we're facing a big problem."

"You don't have to tell me," I bit out.

Shaking off the grim mood, she smiled with good cheer. "Any time you want someone to point out the obvious, I'm your girl."

"I'm wondering," I ventured, and she sobered at what she saw in my face, "if you would arrange for me to speak with Shaman."

She raised her brows, eyes widening. "Of course I *could*—and will if you're serious—but… Shaman is not a comfortable person to converse with."

"I need advice on interpreting Moranu's will."

Blowing out a breath, she nodded. "Well, Shaman is the one to ask. But I have to warn you that Shaman will extract a high price."

"Higher than losing all the world to Deyrr?"

Her lips twisted in wry acknowledgment. "Point taken. Just be prepared to be raked over the coals. You might come away feeling pretty bruised."

"I already have a husband for that."

Zynda glanced with me to be sure Rayfe hadn't overheard, and she guided me another few steps away. The man had the ears of a wolf. "The pregnancy is hard on him."

"And here I thought I was doing all the work in that arena." I realized how ungenerous I sounded, and scrubbed my hands over my face. "I take that back. I know it's hard on him, on all of you, to have to look at this." I smoothed a hand over my hard belly, the baby inside moving in response.

Zynda watched in fascination. "May I?"

"Yes." Unexpectedly, tears sprang to my eyes, one leaking clear. What a wreck I was. "I would love to share this with someone."

She set gentle hands on my belly, some of her dragon magic coiling through my light gown and skin, cooling and fresh as a sea breeze. The baby moved again, and Zynda glanced up sharply, expression effervescent with delight. "That's incredible. He feels strong and healthy."

"Yes, thank Moranu, he does."

"You knew?"

"I've known he's a boy for a while now, yes."

"Does *he?*" Zynda tipped her head in Rayfe's direction.

I lowered my voice even more. "No. *He* would have to be willing to have a conversation about the baby, instead of referring to my 'condition,' for me to impart that information." I didn't want to revisit the fight I'd had with Rayfe, and it felt somehow shameful to admit to her that he'd moved out of my bed. It especially felt inane to complain about that in the same breath as discussing our coming destruction at the hands of Deyrr and Dasnaria. But Zynda had raised a brow at me, amusement quirking her lips, clearly expecting more explanation. So I added, in a very low voice, "I know it's hard for him, but he won't even look at me, much less touch me."

She smoothed her hands over my hard belly, the touch rejuvenating. The absence of magic her dragon form gave her brought a cool release of pressure. I'd felt it when she was in that form, of course, as I'd been the first beneficiary of her stabilizing magic, but that hadn't been with her touching me like this. And so interesting that it emanated from her even in human form.

"You think you understand, but you can't. Not really," she murmured. "And that's nothing against you. I've tried to explain this to Marskal, too, and though he's a lovely, sensitive man, he doesn't quite get it. I'm not sure anyone who didn't grow up here could really understand. It grinds you down over time, the grief, and the pain. Losing child after child after child, and along with them not only our futures, but our mothers, sisters, daughters, and friends. Sharing that sorrow and fear almost makes it worse, because the losses start to accumulate over time. One death you can spread out over many in a family and in the community. Everyone can carry a little piece of the sorrow. A few deaths and each person carries more, but it's still distributed. After decades and generations of death, we have more dead to mourn than living to shoulder the loss."

She looked up at me again, her deep blue eyes reflecting the bottomless grief of thousands. "Seeing you, like this, carrying our next king—and with him so many hopes we haven't dared to nurture—it adds that much more weight to an already unbearable load. As King of the Tala, Rayfe will feel it more than anyone, even if it wasn't you, his beloved, at risk."

I blinked back tears at her words. I wanted to believe I was his beloved still. "Do you think I should've sequestered myself, if I could have?" I braced myself for her reply. If Zynda said yes, then I didn't know what I'd do.

"Absolutely not," she replied immediately, and to my intense relief. "It's a horrible custom. All that's accomplished is shoving our suffering into a corner where it festers. Just give him a little room to be awful. It's taking everything in him just to hold himself together."

I took a shaky breath. "Thank you. That helps."

Her smile turned wry, and she lowered her voice. "I'll count on you to return the favor, because I'm not going to sequester myself either, even if Marskal could stand to let me, which he never would."

My breath stilled and I put my hands over hers. "Zynda. You're...?"

She nodded and gripped my hands, making an exaggerated face of shock and terror, like the little white-faced monkeys in the fruit trees.

"How didn't I sense this?"

"Don't look like that. You haven't lost your sorcerous edge. I'm using the dragon magic to mask it. I've only told Marskal, and now you."

"Are you afraid?"

"So much," she whispered. "But we have to keep going,

despite the fear, yes?"

"Yes." I squeezed her hands, beyond glad to share this with her. "I won't tell anyone."

"I think that's best. You know how the Tala are, so superstitious." She winked saucily.

I laughed, smothering the sound with a cough, but Rayfe glanced sharply at me, then quickly away. He nodded at something Marskal said.

"What's this about a battle at Ordnung?" I asked Zynda. "Ursula's missive didn't mention that."

"No, she didn't want to put it in writing. That's part of why she's traveled here. They should be here soon."

"Yes," I replied, looking through the Gate of Annfwn to the road winding into the forest beyond. "Momentarily, in fact. I felt them cross the border several hours ago, and now they're just a short way up the road."

"You still sense the border crossings, even without the barrier in place?" she asked, face alight with curiosity.

"I do. I can even sense you in dragon form," I added, just to see how she'd take it. As I suspected, she frowned, not angry, but annoyed.

"Dragon form is anti-magic. You shouldn't be able to feel me."

"I can feel mossbacks cross the border and they aren't magic," I pointed out.

"But they simply lack magic. Dragons absorb and nullify magic."

"I can feel Kiraka, too. You both feel like…kind of a deep hole that moves."

She studied me. "Hmm."

"Don't be annoyed. You dragons can't have all the power. It's only fair for us sorceresses to have a few tricks on our side."

I impulsively squeezed her narrow wrists. "Thank you for listening." I raised my voice. "Our guests arrive."

Ursula's entourage came in to view, rounding the bend between the giant trees that also served as homes for the Tala whose First Forms made them more comfortable among leaves than stones. They passed through the gate, the spells I'd installed there reporting that they were who they appeared to be. At least that sorcery worked fine. I had a similar passive scan on all the borders of Annfwn, which is why I could sense Zynda's movements. It created a slight drain on me, but anytime someone entered Annfwn, I wanted to know about it.

Unfortunately the sleeper spies seemed to have been planted before I took those precautions. Or, more concerning, the high priestess cloaked their movements using the same tricks she employed to hide n'Andana from my sight.

Ursula's steely gaze fixed on me as they approached, and I studied her in turn. She looked healthier than a month or so before. She'd regained some of the vitality she'd lost to her near-mortal wound and looked strong, lean as her sword, and just as sharp. She'd also gained a calm radiance, an almost joyful aura. Harlan, smiling at me from his horse, had the same look. I was happy for them, I truly was. Still, Harlan was such a nurturing sort, I knew he'd never shy from touching Ursula. I managed to avoid looking in Rayfe's direction, though I sensed him studying me.

"Good Danu, Andi," Ursula exclaimed, swinging off her horse. "You've gotten enormous in the last few weeks."

"Thank you, Essla. What a delightful compliment," I replied drily. "Always lovely to see you, too."

"Don't you have a while to go?" she asked, eyeing my belly with a measuring gaze.

"Yes, though Tala gestate at a different pace. The mixed

blood makes it more difficult to predict." My actual delivery date depended on many factors. As did the outcome. I couldn't bear to follow those visions too closely. And I had more important futures to chart.

"Ami wasn't this big at this stage, and she had twins." Ursula frowned at me. "Is everything all right?"

"Why?" Rayfe inserted sharply. "Andromeda's *condition* is… Is it… unusual?"

I managed not to roll my eyes. Now he'd discuss my 'condition' with my sister, but he still minced words? *Give him a little room to be awful. It's taking everything in him just to hold himself together.* I took a steadying breath, nodding at Jepp and Kral. She lithely leapt from her horse, scanning the area with her sharp dark eyes, while he and Harlan dismounted more slowly. Harlan and Kral moved lightly for big men, and for mossbacks, gathering up the horses' reins and handing them off to our waiting Tala grooms.

"I only know how Ami looked," Ursula was saying to Rayfe, both of them frowning at me. "What do your healers say?"

"Standing right here," I reminded them. "Available to answer questions directly posed to me."

They both ignored me. Zynda, at least, flashed me a sympathetic grimace, before she drifted after Marskal to say hello to the others.

"Healer Vanka has grave reservations," Rayfe replied to Ursula. "It's not good for Andromeda to be under so much strain."

"No, it isn't." Ursula nodded, gray eyes clouding with worry as she considered. "I've been concerned that she's overextending herself."

"Very much so." Rayfe returned the nod and they exchanged looks of stern resolve, two commanders making battlefield decisions. Just my luck that the one thing my husband and older sister could agree on was bossing me around. I'd had about all of this day that I could take. "She was wounded battling the Deyrr creatures just this morning."

"Didn't your people heal her?"

"Yes, but look at her. She still looks tired."

"I agree," Ursula said. "Kelleah is with us, near the rear of the caravan. I'll ask her to examine Andi."

"Caravan?" Rayfe replied. "You brought *more* people?"

"And supplies," she replied, frost creeping into her tone. "Don't start with me, Rayfe."

He held up a hand. "We'll discuss later. What's important right this moment is Andi's *condition* and what we—"

*"Enough."* I amplified my physical voice on mental and sorcerous levels, focusing it on the pair of them, but loudly enough that everyone winced, even those with no Tala blood, like Harlan and Marskal. Rayfe and Ursula spun on me in shock. Marskal shook his head, silently laughing, and Harlan actually grinned.

Zynda's mental laugh rippled through my mind.

I drew myself up, letting magic from the Heart fill me. Rayfe and Ursula both topped my height by a fair amount, but when I crackled with sorcery, I more than made up for it. "I am the Sorceress Andromeda," I informed them, "and Queen of the Tala by birthright and by proof of might. I also have more important things to do than listen to you two try to run my life."

Fully fed up, I went for the dramatic exit, slightly delayed by my needing to pause before shifting. *Concentrate. Focus.* With a clap of wings, I leapt into the air, and soared as the heron over the calm blue waters.

~ 5 ~

THE GATE SCREAMED in my mind, trembling under the strain of attack as the forest creaked with a massive internal groan, trees shuddering out audible booms as they fell before the Deyrr monsters. The ocean teemed with ships, so thick I couldn't see the water, though it was no longer aqua blue, but swirling deep red with blood, gray with ash, and black with the oily stench of Deyrr. A dragon swooped down—the smoke too thick for me to make out which one—blazing with fire. People screamed, but theirs or ours, I couldn't tell.

Dasnarian boats, disgorged by the enormous troop carriers, bore down on the beach. I stood on by the old stone lionhead on the breakwater, hands outstretched, holding them back with sheer force of will. Though it hardly mattered. They'd outflanked us and, behind me, thousands more Dasnarian soldiers thundered through the Gate of Annfwn, trampling my wards as they passed, ripping the connections from me along with gobbets of magical flesh. I'd failed to stop them.

So many futures held this scenario. I'd seen it countless times and it varied little except in minor details. I also intimately knew the various cascades of events leading up to this scene. The closer we got to this point in time, the more the events settled into a consistent shape. One, two, three, the decisions clicked one into the next, all leading to this: Annfwn overrun, the forest falling, the threshold breached.

I'd looked at everything Moranu let me see in this vision, accumulating details without understanding anything more. With effort, I wrenched my mental eye beyond that moment. What about after? If nothing seemed to alter this future—in fact, it had only grown more consistent—maybe we could do something after it. I scanned the scenes of the further future. A tumult of conquest filled my mind, kaleidoscopic images of the twelve kingdoms falling one by one. Pitched battles at Ordnung and Windroven. More dragons in the sky and then dragons falling into the sea, sending tidal waves of reaction. Ami facing down Deyrr creatures in the dark. Ursula disappearing into the sea of charging beasts.

So many dead. Scattered like withered leaves to the wind. Moranu, with Her silver moon eyes and changeable face gazed at me with challenge. *What will you do, Sorceress? What are you willing to sacrifice to save them?*

My mother's face filled my mind, storm gray eyes glittering with the same challenge. *I made sacrifices—would you do less?*

"You're more like her every day," Ursula commented. Her voice scattered the visions, jerking me back to myself.

For once I didn't mind the interruption, gratefully seizing the opportunity to clear my mind for a moment. Ursula clambered over the last rock and paused by the old stone lionhead, looking it over with interest. She still wore her fighting leathers and sword, but had shed her boots and was incongruously barefoot. "Salena," she clarified, as if she needed to. She sat beside me and stretched out her long legs toward the gentle surf.

"By that, I really hope you don't mean crazy as a loon and wasting away," I replied.

She snorted out a laugh. "Well, at least *you* seem to be washing your hair."

Our mother hadn't, near the end. Some of my most vivid memories of her were when I'd spent hours brushing out the tangled mass of her long hair while she sat and stared unmoving out the window toward Annfwn, the home she'd never see again. She'd been pregnant with Ami, and wouldn't let anyone but Ursula and me touch her.

"Today I did it the regular way, which reminded me how much work it is. Usually I don't. It's a side-benefit of shapeshifting," I explained, suddenly understanding that aspect of my mother letting herself go. She hadn't been able to shapeshift at the end. "When I return to human form, I come out clean."

"Convenient."

When she said nothing more, I knew she waited on my next move. Ursula had always had been able to outwait me, so though I was tempted to match myself against her, I figured I'd better save the effort for a more important battle. "How did you find me?"

"Rayfe said you'd be here." When I glanced at her in surprise, she lifted a shoulder and let it fall, a very Dasnarian shrug she'd clearly picked up from Harlan. "He said you like to come here to be alone."

I digested that. Rayfe had never indicated he knew I came to this rock outcropping to sit with the silent stone lion and stare at the sea. It was a quiet place to follow the future paths and branchings of possibilities, and not far from the Heart, so I could easily draw on its magic for strength. Or just soak in its magic in the quiet, restoring my internal equilibrium. When I returned, Rayfe never asked where I'd been. Sometimes that had annoyed me, especially when he seemed so absorbed in other things that I wondered if he'd even noticed my absence.

That he had known where I went all along, and also knew why … I didn't know what to think of that.

"I apologize," she said, "for my behavior at the gate. It was wrong of me."

I raised a brow, though I didn't look at her, tempted to make a remark that an apology from her surely meant we'd reached the end times. But that would be petty of me and also too uncomfortably near the truth. The closer we got to the final conflagration, the more we all seemed to change, as if that ultimate fiery crucible melted us further out of shape.

She blew out a long breath, dipping her chin in acknowledgment, staring out at the sea. "I know this is no excuse," she continued, "but we both love you. Rayfe and I… well, we're alike enough that we both deal with the vulnerability of those we love by putting walls around them, so we'll be safe."

"You mean, so the people you love will be safe?"

She shook her head ruefully, running a hand through her fiery hair. Longer now than in recent years, the locks curled in the sea air, softening the hard lines of her profile. "We'd like that to be the case, because that motivation would be ever so much more noble, but no. As long as we love people, we're in danger of being hurt. Taking a wound ourselves is nothing compared to seeing the people we love in danger. So we protect ourselves from injury by trying to keep you wrapped up and safe."

I considered that, placing her explanation alongside how I felt watching her swallowed up by that army in the visions. Blowing out the emotion and tension, I rubbed my belly. "I know you've always tried to protect me, that you did keep me safe from terrible things. I understand, and appreciate, the lengths you went to for Ami and me when we were growing up—but I'm an adult woman, who's going to have a baby. I can protect myself, and my child." To the extent I could protect anyone in the coming days, but no use saying that aloud.

"I know you can," Ursula said softly. Then she straightened, sweeping her hands in a grand gesture. "*I am the Sorceress Andromeda,*" she intoned in a booming voice. "*Fear my wrath!*" She snickered.

I stared at her in outrage. "I did *not* sound like that."

"Oh, honey, you so did." She tried to swallow the snicker, choked on it. Swallowed, then burst out into a full belly laugh.

"I cannot believe you are laughing at me."

She tried to pull herself together, but took one look at my face and cracked up again. I just stared. Her Majesty High Queen Ursula folded over in a fit of helpless laughter. My lips twitched, and my cheeks felt the strain of wanting to break free, like ice giving way in spring. A giggle escaped me, despite everything. I laughed harder, and it felt so good.

To my shock, Ursula slung an arm around me, pulling me close as we laughed together, tears rolling down our faces with it. And in that laughing, I realized we also laughed in the face of doom. Far better than weeping.

At last we quieted, Ursula letting me go and wiping the tears from her face. She smiled, though, gazing out at the lovely sea, not at all ashamed of the emotional display, as she once would've been.

"Marriage has changed you," I teased.

She snorted. "Like magic? Ha to that."

"Was it only to circumvent the treaty terms?" I asked, terribly curious and for once feeling able to ask the question I normally wouldn't have dared pose to my prickly sister.

"Yes and no." She wiggled her toes, staring at her feet thoughtfully. They were as long as the rest of her, and white from being in boots for weeks of the colder weather on the other side of the mountains. "The Dasnarian offer made the timing critical, but it had been looking like I'd have to marry, one way or the other. I bet you knew that." She gave me an owlish look of inquiry, then smiled thinly when I didn't give her any hints. "Well, I didn't need a sorceress to explain that future. I've always known sitting on the high throne would require me to marry someday. With our current conflict, I'd come to the inevitable conclusion that I'd have to marry a Dasnarian prince. And, well, if I had to shackle myself to a Dasnarian, there was only one I could marry."

"Regardless of his political status with his family."

She side-eyed me. "Details that can be handled given suffi-cient motivation."

"Harlan agreed to that?"

"I can be persuasive."

"Besides that, he fell in love with you at first sight and swore a life oath to you."

"True. The man *is* daft in the head, but I love him anyway."

"The bond between you was clear from the beginning," I acknowledged, remembering how I'd seen it, like a ribbon of gold connecting them, even though she'd refused to acknowledge it. That ribbon wound through the future events, embedded in the causalities. "Still, I'd thought he was deter-mined to clear the way for you to have a marriage of state with a legitimate ruler. That's what he said every time we discussed it."

She slanted me a wry glance. "I manipulated him into marry-ing me."

"Of course you did."

She wrinkled her nose at me. "You could have the grace to act surprised."

"No, I couldn't." I grinned at her.

"Oh, right, I forget who I'm talking to. You know everything before it happens." She wiggled her fingers in the air, in a pantomime of branching paths, and possibly weird magic.

"Not even close," I said. "I'm not our mother. I don't have

half her abilities."

"How could you? You're not even half the age she was when she left Annfwn, and you've only been practicing, what, two years. Not even that long. At the rate you're progressing, though, you'll eclipse her powers."

Something about the matter-of-fact way she assessed my skills reassured me more than Rayfe's glib praise or Zynda's similar observations. Ursula had a gift for knowing people. Yes, she used that ability ruthlessly to get the most out of people, but she didn't dish out idle flattery. Besides, I'd probably never get over wanting my big sister to think well of me.

"*If* I live that long," I had to say, though.

"At least you're less crazy than she was."

"She wasn't crazy at my age. She got that way over time." Salena had been so present in my mind of late that I wondered if she'd sat on these rocks and communed with the Heart, traced the fearsome future. Maybe she'd glimpsed me in her visions, her ghost and shadow.

"Uorsin had a way of doing that to people," Ursula said in a hard voice.

I smoothed my hand over my belly. "It wasn't all him. Losing all those babies broke her bit by bit, long before she met our father."

"Could you be afraid of that happening to you?" She asked the question of the ocean, and managed to pose it almost philosophically.

So I answered honestly. "I would be a fool not to be afraid. But Kiraka showed Zynda how to stabilize the pregnancy, and the baby is doing well. I'm mostly tired of the constant hovering. Rayfe and I…" Ouch, that burn of shame that my marriage was failing. Or, rather, that the relationship inside the shell of our marriage was crumbling. Ursula had tried to stop me, and I hadn't listened to her. I couldn't possibly confide in her at this point. "We're all under pressure, and I apologize that I took it out on you."

She shrugged that off, unbothered. As usual, her expectant silence drew me to keep talking.

"Honestly, I'm more worried about everything else. A lot can happen between now and when this baby will be born." *Will happen.*

"You've seen?"

"Not everything." I shook my head. "Like you marrying Harlan, I didn't see."

"It happened fast. We started out that day with an enormous argument where I threatened to exile Harlan if he couldn't resolve his conflicting loyalties."

I had to close my sagging mouth, and she clicked her tongue in satisfaction as she smiled at my shock. "Harlan?" I said, trying to assimilate that information. "I don't believe it."

She went very serious, jaw tight and gaze flinty. "Believe it. He's kept some critical secrets."

I wondered if those secrets had to do with that strange Dasnarian-looking woman in the land of elephants—but Ursula had her mouth set in a way that I knew meant she wouldn't tell me more. I was tempted to take a peek at her thoughts, but it might not be necessary yet. "Well," I said, "that kind of turnabout explains a great deal."

"Does it?" She turned to face me fully. "Tell me, did this marriage shift the future?"

She rarely asked me questions like that, flat out, having been through this sort of conversation with me before. I contemplated how much to confide in her. Telling people the possible futures required a delicate balance. Often the best outcomes depended on them blundering rather than trying to create specific results. And often their efforts to change a future they didn't want only made it more certain. I sometimes wondered at the influence of the goddesses in that. They didn't seem to like mortals interfering with Their purview—and They imposed consequences for our arrogance.

Also, I knew that she'd take the guilt for her decision very seriously, and I wouldn't wish that on her. On the other hand, while we all had our parts to play, Ursula was High Queen and as such she led the top-level strategy. I wouldn't lie to her to spare her feelings—she wouldn't thank me for it.

"Yes," I told her honestly, "and no. But more yes than no."

"Now you sound like me."

I acknowledged that ruefully. "Let me put it this way: there were a set of futures where we allied with Dasnaria, and there are fewer of them at this point in time."

"But it's still possible?"

"Possible, yes, but unlikely."

She nodded grimly. "That was Harlan's primary argument, that I should marry one of his brothers because I could've stopped this war. It was a selfish choice, and I only hope I didn't doom us all."

"Well, I can set your mind somewhat at ease. With your usual good luck, the one selfish choice you ever made didn't change *that* much."

She eyed me, searching out evidence of a soothing lie. "An alliance with Dasnaria against Deyrr might've stopped the war cold."

I shook my head. "Nothing you did could've stopped the war entirely. Deyrr is too powerful, and while we speak of the Dasnarian Empire as a single unit, there are many factions at play there, too. Agreeing to the marriage and treaty would've tipped the balance of some things, but not everything."

"Hmm. That's something."

"Yes. I imagine Danu wouldn't have let you make such a misstep."

"I don't know about that. I wish I could be as sure of Her hand as you and Ami are of Moranu and Glorianna's guidance."

I laughed at that, though without humor. "Funny—I was just thinking the same thing about you and Ami. The goddesses can be… obscure, and the goddess of shadows and changeability more than most, I'd think. At least Danu, with Her clear, bright lines, makes Her will known without uncertainty."

Ursula tipped her head thoughtfully, then shook it. "No, I won't put this on Danu. I made the choice on my own. Because I couldn't be true to myself, couldn't look at myself in the mirror, and vow to marry one man when everything in me is devoted to another."

Her words took my breath away for a moment. When I could, I said, "You never were someone who could promise one thing and mean another. And isn't that Danu's way? She is the goddess of clear eyes and unflinching decisions."

"Heh." She half-smiled, a wistfulness in it. "It might be wishful thinking, but it did feel like Danu blessed the marriage. Kaedrin turned up for it, performed the ceremony."

"Did she?" I tried to sound surprised. Dafne had sleuthed out the location of Ursula's old teacher for the coronation, but then the peripatetic priestess of Danu had vanished again. However, I'd seen Kaedrin and her pivotal role in near future events, so that piece fell into place.

Ursula wasn't fooled. "What aren't you telling me?"

I laughed without humor. "I couldn't begin to answer that question, even if I wanted to. There is too much to see, I can't sort it all—certainly not how my revealing events will then affect things."

"What do you mean by 'too much to see'?"

She'd phrased that question carefully, so I'd try to answer. I stretched, contemplating how to explain the arcane subject to my very pragmatic sister. "Think of this moment. You chose to ask me that question. For simplicity's sake, let's say you had two choices: ask or not."

"Actually I was thinking of several questions I could ask, since there were multiple parts to what you said."

"Of course you were, so that immediately complicates things. Imagine a possible future for each potential question you considered asking. Then the possible futures divide again, depending on how I answered each one, and then how our conversation went from there, and how we each decided to act on the information we exchanged. And that's just two people in a single conversation. With something huge like this conflict, there are tremendous numbers of people involved—here, in Dasnaria, within the Temple of Deyrr, other parts of the world—and ramifications that ripple out to affect even more. With Deyrr using animals and dabbling in death magic, the balance of nature itself alters across the world. We half-joke about the goddesses becoming involved, but Deyrr is at least a demigod, so maybe they are. We're facing a truly all-encompassing conflict."

She was quiet, thinking. "That sounds nearly impossible to sort."

"If not absolutely impossible," I agreed.

"It's exhausting just hearing about it."

"It's not that bad. The pregnancy and reinforcing the barrier can be draining, as are some of the sorcerous techniques I've been using for combat. Looking into the future so much… it's a draining enterprise, yes, but mostly because…" *Because it was so depressing.* But I didn't want to say that.

Ursula turned, drawing up one knee and facing me, expression solemn. "Then stop doing it, Andi."

I opened my mouth and she cut me off by raising her hand in an imperious gesture. "It's not worth your sanity. Don't do what our mother did. The future will come as it will, regardless."

"We need good information, to make the right decisions."

"Then we'll get good information, the traditional way mossbacks do—with spies and subterfuge." A brief grin lit her face before she sobered again. "I'm serious. Don't force me to make it a command from your High Queen."

I rolled my eyes at her, absurdly touched. "As if you could enforce it."

She narrowed her eyes threateningly, not entirely being playful. "Try me."

"Essla." I sighed, a surprising surge of affection for her rolling through me. "Even you cannot command a goddess. Moranu sends me visions of the future whether I want them or not."

"So much for pretending you half-joke about the goddesses being involved." She studied me through those narrow gray eyes. "You're splitting hairs and I'm not fooled. Receiving visions from the goddess isn't the same as intensively tracking all those ripples."

"No, but some paths are like flooding rivers. They sweep me up and drag my attention along whether I will it or no. Whether I want to see or not."

Studying my face, she assessed the truth of that, then blew out her breath in a puff of resignation. "So, it's bad."

"Yes." I searched for something to add, but what more was there to say? Knowing the particulars wouldn't help her. That much I'd seen. I wished I could say something optimistic, promise that we'd triumph, but I couldn't lie.

"Do you remember?" she said slowly. "Back before you met Rayfe in the Wildlands, when you still lived at Ordnung. One day, after Ami married Hugh, we were talking, and you told me that my reign would be extraordinary."

"I remember talking about it, but not using that exact word."

"That's the word you used. 'Extraordinary.' I remember it like yesterday, because it's stuck in my mind ever since." She made a soft snorting sound. "Such a mixed blessing. Like 'may you live in interesting times,' which is more curse than anything else. I also remember that moment because it was the first time I clearly saw Salena in you. There was magic in your eyes as you said it, and I knew your words would come true."

A shiver ran over my skin, despite the warmth of the sun. "And they have," I said lightly. "Already you've been an extraordinary queen."

She gave me a look of cool disbelief. "Kissing up to me—you? Don't bother. We both know that nothing about my thus far brief reign has been all that noteworthy, aside from a little patricide to gain the throne and that's been done so often it's practically cliché."

"You did expand the twelve kingdoms our father brought together into an empire that includes Annfwn, most of the Nahanaun Archipelago and the goddesses know what else."

"In truth, *you* did that. It's the Tala magic fueling the barrier that defines those boundaries, not anything I did."

"You guided the extent of the barrier."

"You're still quibbling over fine lines. No, whatever will happen that made you call my reign extraordinary, it's still coming."

I couldn't reply to that because she was, of course, absolutely correct.

"When that bitch of a high priestess nearly killed me," she

continued in a reflective tone, "even as I lay there, bleeding out, feeling my life force ebb away, I wasn't concerned. I hadn't done anything extraordinary yet, so I knew it wasn't my time."

She hadn't told me that before. "Was it a comfort?"

"Good question. I don't know. It just... was." Her brows drew together. "No, I take that back. I was relieved, because Harlan was begging me to hold on, to stay with him, and I knew I would. I wanted to be able to tell him that, to reassure him, but I had no breath to talk, so that was frustrating." She huffed out a dry laugh at herself. "In some ways, I'm still convincing him I'm alive and kicking."

How would I feel if that happened to me—and what would Rayfe do? If only I didn't feel this deep uncertainty about his love for me. He'd mourn my death, I had no doubt of that. And he'd certainly fight to save me. His anguish, though, would be rooted in what my death would mean to Annfwn, his true love. Which should be enough for me, and somehow wasn't anymore.

With so much facing us, the degree and depth of my husband's love for me should feel incidental, far down on the list of things to worry about. Not so critically important. I needed to find a way to let it go.

"I'm convinced that Salena saw all of this coming," I told Ursula. "This conflict with Deyrr and Dasnaria. Everything she did: leaving Annfwn, marrying Uorsin, bearing him three daughters—you, Ami, me, with the different abilities we have, each with our connection to one of the three goddesses—I think she planned to have us in place to fight this war."

Ursula raised her brows. "Not to save Annfwn?"

"Annfwn is a small piece of a much greater world, and this conflict has been building for centuries, since before Annfwn existed."

"Between n'Andana and Deyrr."

"Yes. I suppose *that* is a comfort, in a way. I don't think we could have done anything differently—nothing major enough—that we wouldn't have all assembled more or less in this place, at this point in time."

"So, you believe fate controls our lives." She didn't frame it as a question.

"I suppose I do. Now. I never did before, but…" I shrugged in the face of overwhelming evidence.

She tilted her head thoughtfully. "Comforting, and… not."

"True. But you can at least enjoy your happy marriage with a clear conscience." I elbowed her with a little grin.

Ursula didn't smile back, though. "You know that I didn't want you to marry Rayfe."

That caught me by surprise, a painful prodding of the fresh wound. "The fact that you waged a war to stop it gave me a hint, yes."

"From what you say, nothing I tried could've stopped it."

"I think that's probably the case." I'd been fated to marry Rayfe, not just from the moment of my mother's bargain with Uorsin, or the betrothal at my birth, but by centuries of events aligning to force us together. Who could expect anything like a loving marriage under circumstances like that? My mistake clearly lay in my expectations.

"I'm going to offer you another memory," Ursula turned to look out at the sea, the water turning gold now as Glorianna took over the light. No longer Danu's bright day, sharp and clear, free of gray areas, but the gloaming. The time between the sharp lines of the goddess of unflinching justice and Moranu's night, filled with shadows and blurred lines. "The night before we attacked Ordnung, and I killed Uorsin, you—"

"*We* killed Uorsin," I corrected. "Your hand held the blade, but Ami and I share the blood on our hands."

She inclined her head, not arguing, but not agreeing either. "You told me that I look for everyone to betray me, to leave me, to fail to love me."

I winced. "That was harsh of me."

"No, it was honest." She glanced at me with a wry smile. "Another moment etched in my mind. And I feel I should point out to you that you come from the same place I did. That this is your burden, too."

I gaped at her, struggled to wrap my mind around that.

"You also said, 'nothing will stop any of us from being at your side tomorrow, no matter how you might attempt to shield us or push us away. Try to keep in mind that we're all on your side. There is an enemy and it's not any of the people here tonight.'" She dipped her chin at me meaningfully. "That's a direct quote. I've been waiting a long time to throw those words back in your face."

"Consider them thrown," I replied faintly.

"Good. Then we'd better go meet, so we can all be on the same page, as well as the same side." She uncoiled to her feet— her liquid grace something I now recognized as coming from her Tala heritage, though Ursula couldn't shapeshift—and held down a hand to me. I took it, her skin tough and sword-callused against mine. She didn't let go immediately, steadying me, giving me an intent look. "As for Rayfe, I'm the last person to be giving relationship advice—"

"Thank Moranu, because I can't take any more."

"But I will tell you what you told me."

"Please no."

She grimaced a little, half that wry smile. "Have a little pity on those of us who love you—it's not always easy."

"Ha ha." I should push her off the rocks and enjoy watching her thrash in the surf. "I happen to be eminently lovable. You're the hard ass."

Unexpectedly she grinned. "Fair enough. I assume you summoned Ami?"

"Are you the sorceress now, that you guessed that?"

Her smiled faded. "No. We just all have to be together, don't we? For the end."

I didn't say so, but she wasn't wrong.

~ 6 ~

U RSULA AND I entered the council chambers together, the conversation around the big table dropping to a mutter drowned by the scraping of chairs as everyone—most everyone—stood and bowed. Rayfe, in one of the three big chairs at the end, naturally wouldn't bow to Ursula and she fortunately had never pressed the issue. Zynda and Zyr, Tala to the bone and thus irreverent to the core, remained as they were, both nodding to me with twin expressions of amusement—though Zyr's turned to a wince when his consort, Karyn, pinched him, whispering at him to show respect.

"You can relax."

"At ease."

Ursula and I spoke at the same time, then exchanged wry smiles. "By all mean, Your Majesty, High Queen Ursula," I said, trying very hard to sound sincere. "The floor is yours."

"Oh no, Queen Andromeda and King Rayfe of the Tala," she replied in a coolly ironic tone, "the High Throne is happy to yield to local authority." To demonstrate, she went to the long side of the table to sit by Harlan. Marskal immediately yielded his chair, saluting her in the Hawks' style before bowing and moving to a seat on the other side of Zynda. Harlan held Ursula's chair for her, smiling briefly at something she said.

I managed not to roll my eyes at Ursula as I walked around

the large table to the far end, conscious of everyone's eyes on me. Rayfe rose then, rather pointedly, and pulled back the heavy chair for me. His blue eyes caught and held mine, reading my mood.

*"Everything good?"* he asked mentally, or rather, a question to that effect, face betraying nothing. Not all Tala could speak mind-to-mind, but he and I had worked diligently to develop the skill as far as we could. We found it particularly useful during meetings with the Tala High Council, so we could work as a team to pacify and outflank our more restive councilors. We had to keep the messages simple, and we did best in close proximity if we wanted to convey more than a feeling, but the trick gave us a decided advantage.

Now I wondered how much of my doubts and unhappiness he sensed when he touched my mind. The wariness in his gaze, the tentative brush of concern quickly withdrawn, made me think he wasn't as oblivious to my state of mind as I'd assumed. *Have a little pity on those of us who love you—it's not always easy.* I had no doubt Ursula had been right to throw those words back at me. I'd always been something of a solitary soul, happiest in my own company, or with my horse, Fiona, and Rayfe was far more of a pack animal by nature. Unfair of destiny, really, to saddle him with a moody wife who spent hours on the rocks staring at the sea.

I shouldn't feel so hurt and abandoned. I'd been the one to offer that we sleep separately, so it was my own cursed fault that he'd agreed. Let's be honest: he'd jumped at the suggestion with unseemly haste. *But,* he was only making choices as king, doing the best for his people, which—to be perfectly fair—he'd done from the very beginning. Our match was never supposed to be more than a fulfilling of old obligations. All of it a product of Salena's manipulations to produce a daughter with the Mark of the Tala and make her Queen of Annfwn.

Truly, once I produced our heir—and our son bore the mark, I could feel it—then Rayfe and I need never share a bed again. We'd bred true and could be done with each other. The thought filled me with a nearly unbearable grief.

I wanted to touch his hand on the back of my chair, but thought better of it. *"I'm good."*

He searched my face, that assessing look—perhaps looking for the initial signs of insanity, of the mad queen everyone seemed to fear I would become—then nodded, his expression as opaque as his thoughts. A hint of smoky anger and frustration wafted from him, but I couldn't get more nuance than that. Certainly nothing I could suss out in front of an audience, all watching our silent exchange.

"Thank you all for waiting," I said regally, sitting and giving Rayfe the most gracious smile of thanks I could muster when he helped me ease the heavy chair closer to the table. He'd always been unfailingly respectful of me, supportive, and protective. I needed to revise my expectations and accept all the kindnesses he showed me. Mutual respect and polite attention might be all we'd have. Better than tearing out each other's throats.

Focusing on far more important matters than my personal grievances, I took note of those present. Ursula and Harlan were needed, as they had the most recent intelligence to transmit, and our High Queen remained our ultimate authority even if she deferred to us for the moment. Zyr and Karyn had become our experts on n'Andana and the minions of Deyrr hiding out in the old palace there, as well as commanding the moss-back/shapeshifter fighting pairs. Zynda and Marskal would be leading the dragon battalion, such as it was. Hopefully we'd be strengthening that. And Marskal no doubt wanted to discuss the merging of human and Tala forces. Ursula had put Kral in charge of our navy, so he sat at the table beside Jepp, former scout and surprisingly proficient spy, given her utter lack of subtlety, who would be by his side on the *Hákyrling*.

"Most everyone is here, but not all," I said, since Rayfe hadn't spoken to begin the meeting.

"I suppose Dafne went back to Nahanau?" Rayfe asked, following along with my assessment.

"Yes, Kiraka flew her there right after you all went to chase the sleeper infestation downcoast. She's due any day now and King Nakoa KauPo wanted her there for the birth."

Rayfe huffed out a laugh. "An obedient wife. Hard to imagine."

He said it like it was a fine joke, though no one laughed, so I tried to take it that way. Though he should know I wouldn't find it funny; we'd had far too many arguments over my intended course of action, as opposed to his preference, on any number of topics. Rayfe never tried to enforce my obedience—as if he'd have any luck with that—but I wondered how much those disagreements had rankled him. Did that lie at the foundation of his unhappiness with me?

With a mental sigh, I set the thought aside—again—and continued. "The Nahanauns are particular about birthing their children on Nahanaun soil—you know how they are about that—so she returned for that reason. As soon as the baby is born, she and Nakoa will come here." I didn't say that their little girl would be born that very night, and they'd be here the following day. Everything looked like it would be fine, but I'd wait for the future to become the present on that. "I know she's been in her library as much as possible, researching everything Karyn and Zyr discovered, particularly the bits the high priestess divulged about Deyrr history. Karyn, anything new you can tell us?"

The lovely blond Dasnarian startled and flushed. "No, Your Highness. She said so many things, and I still don't really know truth from lie." A hint of bitterness crept into her voice at how the high priestess had clouded her mind. "I'm sorry, Your Majesty, Your Highnesses," Karyn said, face tight with guilt.

"Sorry for not sacrificing yourself to their god and falling into Deyrr's plans to bring all of the Dasnarian Imperial forces under the temple's command?" Ursula snorted. "You did well, both of you, to survive and return. Never forget it."

"Besides, we know plenty." Zyr shifted restlessly as he spoke, tapping his fingers on the arm of his chair in an agitated pattern. "We know what we saw. I doubt anything has changed. She's on n'Andana, inside the barrier, with her living god, macabre zoo, and cadre of junior priests and priestesses, building her ensorcelled army."

"But we don't know why she hasn't attacked yet," Karyn reminded him. "We don't know her plan."

"She's waiting for something," Kral put in, raising his brows significantly at Ursula.

I should've thought to probe the high priestess about that. But then, it had been a fast conversation and I hadn't been prepared. I would be next time.

Ursula's brows had drawn together in thought. "You think she was waiting to see what happened with Hestar's treaty offer? I don't know." She glanced at me, then at Harlan. "Tell them your theory."

He stirred from his habitual still watchfulness. "To call it a theory would be putting it strongly. It occurred to me that Hestar's offer of alliance may be a sign that he recognizes the need to tear Deyrr from his own throat."

Kral made a fist, rapping it on the table, face sharp as his shark namesake. "It's a possibility. We know he admitted the high priestess to the Imperial Palace, perhaps along with others of the sect—*not* something our father, the former emperor, would've approved of," he added for the rest of us. "No right-thinking Dasnarian would soil themselves with the likes of Deyrr."

Karyn nodded along and Harlan, arms folded, made a sound of agreement.

"But Hestar," Kral mused, exchanging a look with Jepp. "He always was slippery, pulling out surprise advantages, winning at any cost. I could see him trying something this unsavory—and our father *did* die under odd circumstances. It could be that Hestar allied with Deyrr and their foul magics some time ago, even before he became emperor, thinking he could use and control them."

Harlan dipped his chin. "If Hestar believes he has been used by Deyrr instead, he could be looking to the Tala for help."

"Annfwn would not be inclined to assist a rampaging empire," Rayfe cut in coldly.

Harlan gave him a respectful nod. "Begging your pardon, Your Highness, but Hestar wouldn't perceive that. He'd only see the surface—that Her Majesty is High Queen and appears to govern Annfwn as one small part of her own empire."

Zyr snorted in disgust, and Kral eyed him. "You laugh, shapeshifter," Kral said, "but in Dasnaria, our highest authority *is* exactly that. Hestar would expect your High Queen to have similar power to his, which is absolute."

Karyn nodded in agreement, and Ursula slid me a glance, eyes glittering with humor. I knew she'd like to make a joke about how helpful it would be to have that much power, but she restrained herself. I returned the look, which Rayfe intercepted, a line between his brows, his claws coming to the surface. "And supposing the Tala *were* ruled in such a way, what would this

Hestar want from *us?*"

"The Tala are the descendants of n'Andana, ancient enemy of Deyrr," Harlan explained. "The Temple of Deyrr clearly knows this. We know from Jepp's spying that the high priestess is friendly with Hestar, so he also has access to this information. We also know that n'Andana contained Deyrr the last time around when they made the deciding move in their long war by taking magic out of circulation and starving Deyrr of it. The high priestess confirmed that to Karyn. In Hestar's place, who else would you bet on to defeat Deyrr, other than the people who did it before?"

"That's why she's waiting!" Karyn flushed at her outburst. "I beg your pardon, Your Majesty, Your Highnesses, Consort, General, Lieutenant."

"Are you going to list everyone's titles, or will you eventually tell us what you realized?" Zyr asked curiously.

She threw him a narrow look. "The high priestess—yes, she complained about that. How n'Andana had starved them of magic and how long she'd gone without it, how good it felt to be inside the barrier and be able to soak in all the magic."

"Yes," I breathed, amazed I hadn't figured that out myself. "That has to be it. By Karyn's accounts, the high priestess—and Deyrr, Himself—went centuries without magic. She's replenishing her reserves, maybe storing it in reservoirs."

"Is that possible to do?" Ursula asked, her expression sharp.

"There are various methods—as many as there are magic practitioners, as wielding sorcery is an individual thing—but yes, most find ways to store and save magic, or static spells, for quick use in an emergency."

"Like your sparkly blue magic globes," Jepp said to Zynda. "I've wondered about those, because they do different things at different times, like a dagger you can use with various techniques. *It* is the weapon, but *you* guide it."

Zynda inclined her head. "That's my personal trick, yes, one I developed because I'm not a very potent sorceress." Marskal muttered something to Zynda I couldn't hear, and she looked amused. "I'm truly not. Nothing like Andi. I can store magic over time to make those sorceries more potent than what I could do on the spur of the moment. Considering what the high priestess accomplished before she was inside the barrier, she would have considerably more sophisticated techniques." She looked to me. "Potent ones—and probably unlike anything we've encountered before."

Yes, she and I understood each other. I weighed how to say the next part. "I have her focus stone, the one Zyr and Karyn managed to take from her. I'm certain she wants it back, though the Star is far more powerful and she'd no doubt prefer to steal that."

"Where is the Star?" Ursula asked.

"In the Heart of Annfwn," I told her, since she needed to know, though Rayfe twitched beside me at the casual discussion of Tala secrets.

"What and where is this 'heart'?" Kral asked with a puzzled frown.

"Secret," I replied sweetly.

Ursula was giving Zynda a considering look. "You say you're not that potent of a sorceress, but your magic was effective enough to wipe out the undead creatures attacking Ordnung on a pretty broad scale, on very short notice."

Ah. This was the story I hadn't heard yet. "Would someone summarize this attack for me?"

Rayfe shifted irritably beside me. "We've heard it, and it's not that important."

"Yes, I realize I'm the only person in the room who hasn't

heard it yet—which is my fault, and I apologize for losing my temper earlier—but I'd like to hear it now."

"We haven't heard it," Zyr put in, sliding down in his chair and leaning his dark head against Karyn's shoulder. "Storytime, Cousin," he prompted Ursula.

She gave him a reproving frown—which bothered him not at all—but I caught the gleam of affection in her eyes when she turned to me. "It's not a long one," she said to me, not addressing Rayfe. He glowered next to me, emanating impatience. Probably he'd rather be pacing. Otherwise, I didn't know what had him so annoyed. Perhaps our continued disregard for Tala secrets. "It took us a while to figure out, but it seems that the potent magic of midsummer day stirred the ashes of Illyria's undead creations."

"They coalesced—on their own?" I sat forward. Just as I'd dreaded might be possible. How under Moranu's bright gaze could Rayfe not see this as important?

"Apparently so," Ursula replied. "Last fall, after we executed Illyria and liberated Ordnung, we had to... dispatch, then burn all the people she'd made into her creatures. I'm afraid the Hawks and Harlan's Vervaldr bore the brunt of that unpleasant duty."

Marskal, expression grim, nodded. "There were so many— too many for individual funeral services—so we distributed them among multiple pyres, burning them as fast as we could. Those we could identify, we gathered their ashes and gave those to the families that came to collect them. But there were so many who couldn't be identified, for various reasons." The normally stoic soldier broke off, face ravaged by grief, and Zynda took his hand, lacing her fingers with his. He gripped her hand tightly.

"The Vervaldr dealt with the unidentified dead," Harlan took over smoothly, his deep voice neutral. "With so much ash to handle—and the Hawks occupied with the terrible task of disbursing ashes to grieving relatives—my men and I decided against a mass grave. Instead we went with the Dasnarian tradition of scattering ash over the fields."

Karyn gave him a smile. "We did that, Consort, back home on the Hardie estates."

He nodded to her. "An honorable return of ash to earth." Then he shook his head at himself. "Stupid and shortsighted of me."

"No one could have predicted," Ursula said to him softly. "Get over it."

Flicking her a wry smile, he tipped his fingers to his forehead, saluting her with the *Elskathorrl*. As always, the potent magic behind the vow rippled through the space between them, that golden ribbon of devotion.

"So, yes—the ashes coalesced," Zynda took up the tale. "A good word for it. They appeared to be shadow creatures, composed of ash, but not well-formed, more like distorted echoes of their previous bodies."

"And they attacked Ordnung?" I asked.

Ursula, watching me intently, nodded. "With the typical single-minded focus of the Deyrr creatures."

I had to think about this. So many implications to process. "Ordnung, or *you*?"

She paused, surprised by that question.

"I'd say they wanted her," Harlan put in.

"Why didn't you say so before?" she demanded.

"I don't know," he replied easily, but with granite determination beneath. "Maybe I was afraid you'd take it in your head to sacrifice yourself to save Ordnung."

Jepp and Marskal bowed their heads to hide their smiles, while Ursula glowered at Harlan. She would do exactly that, too.

"Clouds of ash," Rayfe broke in contemptuously. "What harm could they possibly cause?"

I couldn't help myself. It was so unlike Rayfe to be so unfeeling, even about problems at Ordnung, that I sent him a thought of astonishment and offense. *Rayfe!*

He showed no sign he heard me.

"They suffocated people, King Rayfe," Jepp answered, dark eyes solemn. "They moved fast, enveloped people and animals, and left them dead."

"I was inside one of the clouds," Harlan added. "It was unlike anything I've experienced before. I lost my strength, like it drew the life from me."

"Dragon fire didn't work on them, nor did my nullifying presence," Zynda said. Marskal nodded along with her. "We tried numerous times."

"*Yes,*" Zynda said in my mind. *"I'm thinking about your experience of the magic bouncing off the Deyrr warthog, too."*

*"Also the dead drawing life from the living."* I nodded at her, then said aloud, "So you used another sorcery."

"Yes. To answer your question, Cousin," she said to Ursula, "I had some stored magic with me—what Jepp calls the sparkly blue magic globes—but that's why I asked for time to prepare. I combined several of those, and also drew on ambient magic in the land. It took a while, and that delay nearly cost us Harlan's life," she added.

"But you executed the spell in time to free Harlan?" I asked.

"No," Ursula replied, giving me a long look. She held up her wrist, showing me the cuff she wore, embedded with our mother's rubies. "I think this did it."

Rayfe leaned in, narrowing his eyes at the jewels. "Those are the Queen's rubies."

I rolled my eyes, unable to restrain my irritation with him.

"Yes, darling. Queen Salena left them to her daughters. We all have some. You've seen mine."

He gave me an incredulous—and yes, most annoyed—look. "I have not. When have you worn them?"

Well, I *didn't* ever wear them. Life in Annfwn didn't lend itself to many formal occasions requiring jewelry. My gaze went to my hand on the arm of my chair, and the bloodred ruby ring I'd worn ever since Rayfe placed in on my finger on our wedding day. It was the only piece of jewelry I habitually wore, but perhaps that should change.

"You used the cuff?" I asked Ursula, ignoring Rayfe for the moment.

She scooted her chair back and drew her sword, Rayfe tensing beside me. I gave him a questioning glance—what was *up* with him?—but he had his suspicious gaze riveted on Ursula. With her agile, easy grace, she reversed the sword, showing me the cabochon ruby embedded in the pommel. "After I prized the Star of Annfwn out of its place, Dafne said it looked bad for me to go around seeming like an impoverished noble who'd sold off the family jewels. I used one of Salena's rubies here, had a few set in earrings, that kind of thing, then gave you and Ami the rest. Dafne, too."

"*Dafne* has some of the Queen's rubies?" Rayfe sounded dangerous.

Ursula regarded him evenly, not seeming to register the snarl. "She was practically Salena's adopted daughter. Dafne was a little girl, an orphan, her entire extended family dead at Uorsin's hands. Salena took Dafne under her protection and kept her safe. So, yes, I used my judgment as the one in possession of our mother's jewelry to distribute it as she would've wished."

Rayfe opened his mouth and I put a hand on his forearm.

He tensed under my touch, nearly flinching, and I sent another mental nudge, transmitting my wordless confusion and displeasure. "Besides," I said to him. "I am the Queen of the Tala now, so the rubies are mine, regardless. I officially approve of Ursula's disbursement of them."

A brief silence fell, Rayfe palpably fuming.

"I think that's enough," I declared, not willing to push his temper further. "I'd like to have everyone together before we discuss the rest of our strategy. There are only a few remaining details to take care of: first, I already sent a message to Ami a few days ago, asking her to come to Annfwn, and bring Ash and the twins. But since recent events have accelerated the timeline, it will take too long for them to travel overland—and that's not counting however long Ami might dawdle about leaving in the first place."

"I can go get them," Zynda volunteered, glancing at Marskal who nodded in agreement.

"Would it be possible for Zynda to take Jepp and Kral to the *Hákyrling*, so our reply to Emperor Hestar can be delivered?" Ursula asked me.

I gazed back at her, aware of the many levels of her question—and why she asked me, in particular. "Are you ready to do that?"

"Is there any benefit to waiting?" she countered.

I didn't have to check the futures. They'd already changed. "The marriage is sealed, and the effects already moving outward. Delaying your missive will only change when Hestar knows of your decision."

Ursula and Harlan exchanged a long look, then she tipped her head at me. "Timing like that can be a key strategy point."

True. "Give me a moment of silence please."

"Andromeda, you shouldn't—"

I held up a hand to quiet Rayfe's protest. "It's important." I turned my gaze to the future threads, letting the rush of familiar horrors flow past unheeded, focusing on Hestar. Once I found him at a key future point, I traced backward, the timelines consolidating into fewer, thicker rivers of probability. Until I reached a decision point in the near future. Then glimpsed a scene that might be present or near past. "Hmm."

"What?" Ursula demanded.

Better to tell her fast. "It seems he already knows."

# ~ 7 ~

EVERYONE, INCLUDING RAYFE, tried to say something at once. I kept my face smooth, not revealing how the hubbub made my head—already aching from effort of sorting the futures that fast—throb even more.

"Order!" Ursula's voice cracked across the table, carrying the weight of the high throne, and instilling instant obedience. Nearly a sorcerous ability right there, and a skill she rarely employed, especially when she wasn't actually sitting on her throne. For all that Uorsin had been an utter bastard, he had known a few things about power and leading people—and he'd taught his eldest daughter well.

Satisfied, Ursula looked to me. "Are you able to explain further?"

I smiled at her ruefully, grateful for the phrasing. "Only that I glimpsed a scene of the present or near past. A Dasnarian man in silver armor, mirror bright, inset with clear jewels. He wore a helm like Kral's, but with crown-like spires, also heavily jeweled."

Kral nodded. "Hestar. But how can you not know if it's present, past, or future?"

"It's not as if the visions come with convenient notations like Dafne's calendar dates. I have to extrapolate from adjacent events that I know have occurred or are occurring." When Kral frowned but asked nothing more, I continued. "He was angry, raging about Harlan." I glanced at him apologetically. "He called you by any number of unpleasant epithets, which I won't repeat."

He lifted a shoulder and let it fall, dipping his chin philosophically. "It has been many years since my eldest brother has had the power to harm me—by word or deed." He covered Ursula's hand with his. "I *am* sorry, though."

"I'm not," she replied crisply. "If we make false vows to gain advantage in war, then we're no better than the ones who wage it."

Kral laughed, a harsh, contemptuous sound. "The Dasnarian Empire has crushed many a virtuous kingdom who sought to stick to their ideals. Will you feel the same, I wonder, when you lose?"

Ursula opened her mouth, but to everyone's surprise, Karyn spoke up. "I used to think the same, General Kral, that strength, winning at any cost, was always preferable to the alternative. Now I understand it's possible to reign over every mind and body in sight and still be hollow inside, and it's equally possible to resign oneself to losing and still be full of the richness of love."

He snorted at her, but gently. "True enough. But it's good to test the resolve of our partners in this futile war." He winked at her, and Jepp rolled her expressive dark eyes, twirling one of her small daggers as if she longed to plant it in some enemy—or possibly in Kral, wherever it would smart the most.

"The important question is," Rayfe cut in, voice cold. "How did Hestar discover this information as soon as, or even before we did in Annfwn? I suspect you have spies in your midst, High Queen."

She regarded him a moment, the gray of her eyes going

flinty. "Of course we do. It's a foregone conclusion among warring realms that they'll spy on each other. I'd be a fool to imagine otherwise."

Her words hung in the air, inviting Rayfe to comment. She remained languid, but I knew she had a counterattack ready should he cross the line with her again.

He moved, opening his mouth to speak.

*"Don't,"* I told him mentally, and his annoyance flashed back at me.

"I mention this," he said coolly, his accusing gaze going from me to Ursula, then around the table, "because Annfwn is now teeming with foreigners, any number of whom could be spying on us."

"Oh, for Moranu's sake!" I burst out. "For that matter, the minions of Deyrr are perfectly able to spy on us from a distance using any number of sorcerous techniques. They've been inside the barrier for some time, and the high priestess at least is massively skilled with mind magic. She could walk among us and we'd never know."

Zynda gave me a thoughtful look but didn't disagree. Rayfe fumed, but said nothing more.

Ursula let the mood around the table settle. "Suggestions for next steps?"

Everyone looked at me. "Send the missive. We need to tie that up, make it official. Zynda, Marskal—are you willing to take Jepp and Kral to the *Hákyrling*, then head to Windroven?"

"I wouldn't mind stretching my wings," Zynda replied. "We can drop them off and bring Ami, Ash, and the kids back here."

"Can you carry that many people in dragon form?" Ursula asked, sounding more curious than challenging.

"Three adults and a couple of toddlers? Sure." She shrugged in the elaborate Tala style. "Kral in his armor weighs that much all by himself."

Kral scowled at her. "We're not all so lucky to be able to grow scales naturally, shapeshifter."

She grinned easily, then looked to me. "Do we need to leave tonight?"

I turned my thoughts inward, scanning the near future for Annfwn and Windroven. That took less effort as I'd studied these sequences the longest, so I practically had them memorized. Really I only needed to check that nothing had changed.

Things *had* shifted, though, a fair amount in the short time since I'd last looked, and not to our advantage. No matter what Ursula said, even if she did make it a command and even if Moranu stopped shoving the visions down my throat, *this* was why I couldn't stop looking. I lifted my gaze to find her studying me intently, reading it in my face. "Yes. Tonight is better," I said.

"Off we go then." Zynda flowed to her feet, Marskal right with her.

He looked to me. "Your Highness, past experience indicates that Queen Amelia will require considerable time to pack. If we return by morning, is that sufficient or—"

"If Ami won't cooperate," Ursula cut in, "tie her up and throw her on Zynda's back. Ash will no doubt assist."

"We'll have to strap Willy and Nilly down to keep them from wriggling off anyway, Captain," Marskal replied to her gravely, falling into the old familiar title from the Hawks. "Perhaps a wicker cage in case they shapeshift, that Zynda can carry in her talons. What?" he asked in the face of Zynda's glare. "It was a joke. You know I wouldn't cage the twins—not for long, anyway."

"Some things aren't funny, Marskal," she shot back, though her mouth twitched with a smile. "They'll obey me."

"I know, I know. You are the shapeshifter-baby whisperer."

He smiled at her, undaunted. "Shall we, Lady Dragon, General, Scout Jepp?"

Ursula lifted a hand to stop them from going, looking to me. "Marskal raises a good point, though. We need Ami, and I'm sure you all would like to have Ash back in Annfwn, but shouldn't the twins remain at Windroven, where it's safer?"

"It's not safe there at all," I answered.

A fine line etched itself between her brows. "I can send additional troops to Windroven if that's—"

"That's not the problem."

"With the attack on the training ground, there's a challenge to keeping even the Tala children safe here in Annfwn," Kral pointed out.

Ursula tipped her head at his point. "Children don't belong in a war zone, Andi."

"Everywhere will be a war zone," I replied, holding her gaze, letting her see my resolve on the subject.

She sat back, clearly annoyed at not having all the information, but this I absolutely wouldn't tell her. I shifted my attention back to Marskal and Zynda. "By morning is sufficient. We'll reconvene our strategy session then, over breakfast."

"Thank you, Your Highnesses." Marskal bowed to me and Rayfe, gave Ursula the Hawks' salute, and offered Zynda his hand.

She took it, giving him an intimate smile. "I have an idea. After we relay the royal command for my cousin to start packing, we can duck out of the line of fire and go stay at your house for the night. We can return to Windroven early in the morning, load them up, and be here in time for the breakfast strategy session."

He brightened, lifting her hand to kiss it. "You read my mind, quicksilver girl."

I wanted to look at Rayfe, who'd been oddly quiet since the argument about spies. I didn't, however, because I felt a little too nervous about what I might—or might not—see. "Please ask Ash to bring Djakos, too," I said.

Ursula sat up straight again, abruptly enough that Harlan set a calming hand on her arm. "Who in Danu's bright gaze is Djakos?"

"The dragon we woke and released under Windroven," Zynda explained for me.

"It has a name?"

"All living beings have names, Cousin," Zynda replied with exaggerated patience. "It's simply a matter of learning what they are."

"And you named this one Djakos."

"No, he told us his name, and Kiraka has visited him, too. He's very nearly sane now." She glanced at Marskal, their hands still interlaced. "We've been popping over to Windroven periodically to teach Ash how to work with Djakos. They're shaping up to be a good fighting pair. Could be Ash and Ami will ride Djakos and I'll carry the twins. *Not* in a cage." She mock glared at Marskal, who only shrugged.

Ursula transferred her bemused—and irritated—gaze from Zynda back to me. "How is it that I'm High Queen and yet I'm the last to know these things?"

"Because you *are* High Queen," I retorted. "You're supposed to delegate details, remember?"

She muttered something to herself. Harlan's lips twitched in amusement, and he patted her arm. Jepp and Kral stood, exchanging quiet words. "We'll send an update from the *Hákyrling*, Your Majesty," Jepp said. "Maybe we'll have word from your mysterious correspondent."

"We'll see you off," Zyr abruptly declared, flowing to his feet and pulling Karyn with him. "I've had my fill of meetings." He hissed the words, throwing a glare in our direction, and they all went out, Zynda and Karyn tossing me exasperated and apologetic looks, respectively, over their shoulders. I waved it off, warmed by my affection for all of them.

They departed, leaving the four of us alone in the council chambers.

"There's a 'mysterious correspondent'?" Rayfe asked, sounding confused. That had caught my attention, too.

Ursula let out a long breath and slouched back in her chair. "So, that's a story, too. Is it too early for wine? It feels like it's been a long day."

With a thought I sent a nearby staymach songbird to pass the message, and smiled at her. "I think wine is certainly called for."

"It may not be a good idea," Rayfe cautioned me, giving me that worried *look*.

"We're not having a drunken festival."

"I meant if there's an attack."

"I don't think there will be this evening."

"Even you are not infallible, Andromeda."

"You needn't remind me."

"I have many things to see to yet this evening," Rayfe said, still sounding befuddled. "Perhaps I should leave you all to your chatting."

"You asked the question," I reminded him.

"Oh. Yes, but—"

"Ah, thank you," I interrupted him. A Tala woman dropped off a pitcher of wine and three goblets. A second followed her with a platter of cheese, fruit, pastries, and meats. My stomach growled, and I realized how hungry I was. A third woman came in, setting a pot of tea and my favorite flower-painted cup beside it.

Rayfe looked from the tea to my face, chagrin wafting from him. "My apologies," he muttered. Then he tried a smile, filling a plate for me. "Allow me to see that you're fed."

I tried to smile back at our old joke, but the reminder only saddened me. He changed moods so fast I didn't know what to make of him. Harlan had poured wine for Ursula and himself.

"King Rayfe?" He inquired, holding the pitcher poised over the remaining goblet.

"Please," Rayfe said. "I'm afraid I've been a poor host."

"We're all under pressure," Ursula agreed easily, passing the full goblet to Rayfe. "It's an unfortunate fact of life that we often behave the worst to those who love us best, simply because we trust that they'll understand and forgive."

Harlan huffed out a laugh, shaking his head.

She took a sip of her wine, sighed in pleasure. "Nothing beats Annfwn wine. It truly is ambrosia."

It was the right thing to say, because Rayfe relaxed. "The best grapes in all the world."

"Indeed. So, the short answer is we believe that I've been receiving coded messages from Harlan's sister."

"His sister?" I repeated, searching my memory. "Did I know you have a sister?"

"Why should you know when I didn't?" Ursula raised her brows at me, and I realized this had been part of the argument that had led to her accusing Harlan of compromised loyalties.

Harlan put his hand over hers, enfolding it. "It's true. Kral and I have… sisters, who I've neglected to mention. Jepp met Inga and Helva at the Imperial Palace but kept certain information to herself at their behest."

I must have made a face because Ursula, relaxed back in her chair and holding her wine goblet, gave me a return look that spoke volumes. Truly, we were lucky she hadn't simply gutted Harlan before asking questions.

"Ursula has of late been receiving letters from someone claiming to be a friend of mine, giving warnings and information that seems to come from inside the Imperial Palace."

Rayfe and I glanced at each other, momentarily in solidarity in surprised interest over this information. "You think it's Inga and Helva?" I asked.

"Yes." Harlan nodded, setting his goblet on the table. "Certainly Inga. I've read the missives and they have her style to them."

"Not her handwriting, though," I pressed. "Because Karyn gave me to understand that she's quite unusual among Dasnarian women in being able to read and write."

"That's true, unfortunately." Harlan stroked a finger thoughtfully along the back of Ursula's hand, some deep sadness in him.

"The letters are written in Common Tongue, excellently so," Ursula explained. "We believe that she's using a translator, probably a young Nahanaun man, Akamai, that Dafne sent with Jepp and Kral on the *Hákyrling*—and who they smuggled through the barrier and haven't seen since."

"So, we do have spies inside the Imperial Palace," I mused. "Have you tried writing back to this correspondent?"

"How?" Ursula asked. "We're not sure of any of this, much less how to contact them."

"There might be ways. I've been working on sending messages via staymach songbird and this would be an excellent application. Dafne will be able to tell us if it's Akamai—you know how good she is at recognizing handwriting. If you brought some of those letters with you, she can look at them in the morning and verify that much," I said, thinking through the ramifications. "Then we can decide which steps we want to take from there."

"I did bring some, but 'in the morning'?" Ursula asked with a keen glance.

"The baby must be coming tonight then," Harlan agreed, holding up his wine goblet. "To the health of mother and child."

Oops. But, oh well, that slip shouldn't matter much. I raised my tea cup as Ursula clinked her goblet to Harlan's. Beside me, Rayfe had gone stony, white-knuckling his own goblet and holding it firmly against the table. Ursula and Harlan paused in their toast, uncertain.

"The Tala believe it's bad luck," I explained, and Rayfe threw me a betrayed look.

"As I said, I have things to do." His chair grated as he pushed it back and stood. "If we're done here?"

"Apparently we are," I agreed, also standing, though he didn't help with my chair this time. "I'll go with you."

"No need. Stay here and talk all night if you like," he returned coolly.

"In truth, we need to go see to some things, too," Ursula said, she and Harlan finishing their wine and standing as a unit. "These are your council chambers, and Andi—don't bite my head off—but you didn't eat anything. I know you're hungry, so take a moment for that. Please."

They left with enough alacrity that I didn't think of a protest in time. But she was right in that I was starving, and I had forgotten about my plate. I sat again, rather heavily, weariness taking over, and put some food in my mouth.

After a moment, Rayfe sat again, too. Also filled a plate. "I think we missed a couple of meals today," he finally said.

"Oh, are you still here?" I looked at him in mock surprise. "I thought you had important things to do."

He set his teeth, a muscle in his jaw flexing. "What are you angry about now?"

I nearly choked on my food in astonishment. "Me?" I turned in my chair to find him right in my face, blue eyes turbulent with feral emotion. "You're the beast who behaved like a total ass during that meeting. What in Moranu has gotten into *you?*"

"I did not behave like an ass or a beast," he snarled.

I grabbed his hand, catching him more from surprise than better speed, and showed him his fingertips, the thick, sharp nails. "Claws." I dropped his hand and swept mine at the table. "*We've heard this story and it's not important,*" I mimicked him.

"What should the Tala care for what happens at Ordnung?" He stabbed a paring knife into a slice of meat and tore into it. "For that matter, why should *you?* You're supposed to be Queen of Annfwn, not a toady to your sister. When are you going to prioritize your own people instead of making plans to sacrifice them to a mossback cause? You're Salena over again," he added with a nasty bite.

I regarded him in sputtering silence, unable to gather my tattered emotions into rational thought. That Rayfe, of all people, would accuse me of that…

"I thought you agreed," I spoke slowly in order to master the urge to howl at him, "that we all needed to work together to fight Dasnaria and Deyrr."

"I haven't had any choice, have I?" he replied. "No, I'm just along for the ride. You make decisions without me, act without my consent, gather foreigners in Annfwn like it's your personal garden, and you treat me like a pet dog."

I had no words, the sick feeling in my stomach crowding them out. Pushing my plate away, I propped my elbows on the table, putting my face in my hands, willing myself to think through this.

"I apologize," I said into my hands. "I thought we were in agreement, that you also—"

"You don't know, do you?" he said, cutting me off. "Because you don't ask me."

"I thought I did." I lifted my head, made myself look at him. "I'll do better."

He studied me, jaw rigid, eyes a cobalt blaze of emotions he had locked behind a shield of mental iron. "Do you remember, when you first came to Annfwn, and I confessed that you hadn't needed to marry me? That you could've simply deposed me as king, and ruled alone."

"I never wanted to rule." I still didn't. A part of me wanted to saddle Fiona and ride her into the wilderness of the northern mountains. I could find a cabin to live in, hunt as a mountain lion, and be alone with no one to witness how the mark melted my mind into nothing.

"Are you sure?" he asked quietly, the words hissing.

For a moment I thought he meant about my plan to flee.

"Because you seem to enjoy the power. I'm not sure I believe you," he added. "You're so like her, Salena, and more so every day. She lived for power like that. So did your father."

"Oh, so now all of this—" I dashed my hand against my plate, sending it flying to shatter on the floor. "*This* is all a result of my elaborate plan? Somehow *I* tricked *you* into tracking me in the Wild Lands, into chasing me in my dreams, into laying siege at Windroven so I had to come out and marry you. What an amazing strategist I've turned out to be."

His gaze came back from the shattered plate, his expression set. "I didn't say that."

"No, you only accused me of being like my mother, a sorceress driven insane by heartbreak, and my father, a brutal tyrant who had to be put down like a mad dog by his daughters." I shook with anger. "You can say Salena lived for power. I don't know. It's a great irony to me that you spent more years with my own mother than I did. I can tell you, though, she gave up *everything* to save Annfwn. She sacrificed shapeshifting, her wellbeing, her very life to make sure I'd be born and come to Annfwn to fight this horror descending on us. I'm going to do my utmost to do as she wanted, and I'm very sorry if your male pride gets bruised along the way."

Rayfe stared at me as if I'd become a stranger. Maybe I had. "Do you want me to abdicate as king, let you rule alone as queen?" he asked, his tone eerily calm. "I can get out of your way altogether."

"You already moved out of my bed," I replied bitterly, on the verge of tears again.

"Because you asked me to."

"No." My voice shuddered with emotion. "Don't put that on me. I offered you an out and you took it, with unseemly haste, I might add."

He raked a hand through his hair and sighed, frustration and exhaustion in it. He'd had a long day, too, flying all the way back from wherever they'd been, then dealing with me, our guests, and all the hundreds of decisions we both made every day.

"It's late," he said. "And we're getting nowhere with this argument. You may not believe me, but I really do have things to see to before I can sleep tonight."

"Of course I believe you," I replied wearily. "There's so much to do. Can I help with anything?"

"No. I did manage to govern Annfwn for years before you came along."

I stared at him, shocked and bewildered. He shook his head at himself, the wolf shedding water and rage from its fur. "I apologize," he said. "That was uncalled for. I'm angry and need some time. And you need food and rest. We can talk in the morning."

"Rayfe," I called, as he strode out of the room. My voice wasn't strong, but he heard me, pausing and then turning. "What's happening to us?" I asked, sounding plaintive and pitiful.

His stern expression softened, barely, but there. "It's just an argument, Andromeda. People disagree. Eat. Sleep. You'll feel better in the morning." With that he left.

Alone but for my staymach guard, songbirds perched around the room on their quiet roosts, I put my head down on my folded arms, and sobbed.

$$\sim 8 \sim$$

I WOKE IN the morning from a long, deep sleep, surprisingly refreshed and filled with a sense of well-being. Sleepily, I reached for Rayfe… His side of the bed was cold and empty. Memory flooded back, and that brief moment of peacefulness shattered under the deluge of emotion. My eyes prickled with tears, the sting reminding me of how swollen they already were from the previous evening's torrent of angry grief.

Enough of that. I'd shed tears enough to last a lifetime and my mountain of problems remained just as high.

Turning onto my back, I gazed up at the mosaic ceiling over the bed, the colors bright even in the dawn shadows. Tropical fish of many varieties swirled in clear aqua currents, exactly the shades of the sea on the journey to the Heart of Annfwn. Some ancient artisan's magic had infused the tiles with the illusion of motion. I'd lain here often in Rayfe's arms, gazing at the scene, noticing new elements every time.

Without his reassuring presence, I felt more than ever like an echo of my mother. I could picture her, as vividly as in a vision, lying in this bed, staring at this same ceiling in loneliness and despair, seeking a way out of the coiling maze of future doom. How could it be that, more than three decades later, we'd come no closer to finding a way out of that maze? Indeed, we'd only gotten lost deeper in the bowels of it.

I thrust that image away, clearing my mind. The day ahead would be grueling. *Moranu grant me at least the questionable peace of only the most relevant images.* As if summoned by my prayer, a vision flooded my mind of a regal blond woman with striking aqua eyes the same shade as the shallows of the mosaic sea. Surrounded by tropical greenery and a landscape painted on the walls, she wore a kingdom's wealth of jewels and a klút of vividly embroidered silk. The style of her traditional Dasnarian garb and the location indicated that she must be in the seraglio of the Imperial Palace.

She curtseyed deeply to another woman, much older, with elaborately styled hair so pale as to appear white. Though the bones of her face spoke of a once-extraordinary beauty, unhappiness and cruelty had carved itself into the older woman's face. Cruel lines bracketed her mouth as she sucked on an enameled pipe, smoke wafting out of her flaring nostrils, making her look more than a little like a dragon. The aqua-eyed woman straightened and spoke to her elder, calling her Dowager Empress Hulda, and promised to see her will done.

She rose and glided away with the same tutored grace Karyn displayed. Another blonde, who'd been standing back, face demurely lowered, raised her head. They were clearly sisters, though the second woman's hair was a much deeper bronze, and her large eyes were golden brown. "What does Hulda want now?" she asked.

The aqua-eyed woman glanced back, walked a bit farther, then inclined her head to the other. "It seems Hestar's bid to marry Harlan's queen has failed."

"Surprising no one. Jepp said they loved each other. No woman Harlan loves would betray him by marrying another."

"And yet, arguably unwise of her."

"You did warn her."

"Yes, and now I must send a new warning."

"I'll ask Akamai to meet us for tea. But you still haven't said why Hulda summoned you."

The aqua-eyed blonde glanced back once more, then around them where children splashed in a tiled lagoon and an elderly woman reclined on pillows, smoking another pipe as Hulda had. She lowered her voice further. In the way of visions, though, when I *could* hear anything, I heard every word. "She wanted me to tell Kral that his time has nearly come. I'm to summon him home."

The sister took a breath. "Will you?"

"What choice do I have? It's my place to obey." Her smooth voice revealed no emotion.

"But will Kral obey?" the darker blonde asked with a crafty smile that the other echoed.

"We shall see," the elder sister allowed. "And we shall be very careful of our phrasing."

The vision receded as gently as it had arrived, and I breathed a sigh of relief. At least no death and horror—only unsettling information. The sky had brightened and cries of sea birds echoed from the water, along with the calls of people in human and animal form. A null space crossed the southern border of Annfwn, followed by a second. Zynda and Djakos, on their way. Which meant I couldn't loll in bed any longer.

Getting up, I stretched, still feeling the effects of yesterday's fight, along with a faint twinge in my injured hip as I moved into the bathing chamber. I looked awful, my face puffy and eyes even more swollen than they'd felt from my prodigious weeping the night before. This morning that definitely called for the shapeshifting shortcut to personal grooming. *Concentrate. Focus.* I shifted into my First Form, the lion, taking a moment to settle into it. Then, with meticulous care, I shifted back to myself, holding firm in my mind how I should look in human form.

Tala children drilled in this—one of the skills they practiced in the once-safe training arena—until they were able to return to a groomed form out of habit. What they were able to do without a second thought, I had to carefully think through, as if shapeshifting would forever be a second language for me.

I supposed it was—and having a second language was better than only one, or none at all.

The woman who faced me in the mirror looked considerably better, hair flowing unsnarled, face smooth and eyes bright, showing no sign of the ravages of emotion. Since I'd be playing queen more than sorceress in the coming hours, I exchanged the simple shift I'd taken human form wearing for a more formal gown. Nothing like what my ladies used to garb me in when I was a princess, the dress was nevertheless fancier than most Tala clothing. In a deep red that looked black in the shadows, it fit closely enough in the bodice not to hamper my movements, then flowed into a long, full skirt.

Spurred by the conversation of the night before, I dug Salena's ruby necklace out of my jewel chest and donned it. If the gems truly contained helpful magic I could use against Deyrr, I'd be a fool not to take advantage of them. It struck me then, how exactly they matched the bloodred cabochon ruby in my wedding ring. I held up my hand, moving it so the stone gleamed in the early morning light. In an elegantly carved setting of Moranu's shining silver, the smooth, convex surface of the ruby looked nearly black—until it caught the light just right, and the intense scarlet depths flared to life.

It suited me—and reminded me of myself, someone who had always appeared to be unspectacular, but with hidden depths. That was no doubt vain of me to see the jewel and myself that way, but I'd kind of thought that Rayfe had seen the parallel and chosen the ring for that reason.

Now I realized that this ring, too, came from the Queen's jewelry collection. As king, Rayfe would've had access to it, and it made perfect sense for him to have given it to me, the woman he'd married to bring back and serve as Queen of the Tala.

What other ring would have been appropriate?

And yet...

Probably it was a reflection of my overall unhappiness with him, but the realization was salt in the emotional wounds. The ring hadn't been the gift from *him* as I'd always believed. No—as I'd always *assumed*. He'd never said as much, so the error was mine. He'd simply restored my legacy to me. I could hardly fault him for that.

I only wished my bruised heart could follow that simple logic.

After a moment of hesitation, I donned my crown— something else I also almost never wore. It would make a statement, however, and I felt I needed it. Bracing myself to face Rayfe, I opened the door to our sitting room and strode in serenely, head held high.

A wasted effort as he wasn't there. The door to the spare bedchamber stood open, and for a moment I thought maybe he'd never returned the night before. But, no—the bedclothes were in disarray. Savagely so, as if he'd tossed and turned all night. I didn't wish him ill, but it also made me feel somewhat better to see he'd been more bothered by our argument than he'd made out to be.

*It's just an argument. People disagree.* He'd said that as if the hateful, hurtful words meant nothing, as if our marriage couldn't change, decline, or die. Surely there would come a point at which we would injure our relationship so much that it couldn't recover, and what then?

Another blank spot crossed the Annfwn border, this time to

the west, and it shook me out of my gloomy self-involvement. That would be Kiraka bringing Dafne, Nakoa, and the new baby. There—at least meeting their little girl would bring some much-needed joy to the day.

I made my way out through the palace, such as it was. No one in the twelve would give that name to the tiers of interconnected rooms and balconies that formed our home. Servants and various workers greeted me, and I pasted on a gracious smile, pretending I wasn't looking for Rayfe. I didn't see him on the road to the council chambers either. Pausing at one overlook, I watched Zynda wing in for a landing on the beach, her sleek form as brilliant as a star sapphire in the rising sunlight. Another dragon settled beside her, this one silver. I'd only seen Djakos in visions and through other eyes, but I'd know him anywhere. And not only because there were but three dragons to know. So far.

Even from the distance, I could easily spot Ami riding behind Ash on Djakos. She was resplendent in a pink gown that flowed artfully over his sparkling silver scales, her hair somehow more radiant than the rose-gold sunrise. Ash climbed down the harness they'd strapped to Djakos—similar to the one Marskal had rigged up for riding Zynda's dragon form, improved with modifications from the fighting harness Karyn and Zyr had found in n'Andana for his gríobhth form—then held out his arms to Ami. She swung a leg over, stood a moment in the foot strap with her arms raised high, like a painting of Glorianna as harvest mother, then let herself fall. I could imagine her delighted peal of laughter as Ash caught her.

"Never less than dramatic, our Ami," Ursula commented, moving up beside me, her arm through Harlan's. He nodded a good morning to me, also watching the scene on the beach, a half smile on his face.

"But she does it so well," I replied.

"Indeed. Good thing we love her so much," Ursula said, and we shared a smile. She looked me over. "You look queenly today."

Ursula so rarely commented on anyone's appearance that her words struck me with a sick realization. I'd dressed entirely the wrong way if I wanted to soothe Rayfe's ire. I should've tried to look *less* queenly. Instead, I'd gone further. Well, too late now—and, besides, I'd followed my own inclinations. While I hated having him so angry with me, I wouldn't stop being who I needed to be in order to make him feel better. I returned Ursula's scrutiny, noting her fighting leathers—boots on her feet—sword and plenty of knives strapped on in various places. She also wore our mother's ruby jewelry, which oddly didn't look out of place with the warrior's gear.

"And you look ready for war," I noted. Harlan, too, in the sleeveless leather vest he liked to wear in Annfwn's heat, his broadsword sheathed on his back.

Ursula smiled thinly. "Yes. Yes, I am. We both are, in different ways, aren't we?"

An excellent point.

"Marskal has his hands full," Harlan commented, tipping his head at the scene below.

Zynda had snaked her long neck around, dropping her pointed jaw so her man-sized eye stared down a bear cub struggling to escape Marskal's grip as he tried to shimmy down the harness. A black kitten made an amazing leap to land on Zynda's snout, running lickety-split up between her eyes to perch between the curving blue-black horned ears. Zynda snorted a lick of flame, which made both children freeze long enough for Marskal to leap free. As soon as he hit sand, Zynda's massive form collapsed into her human one, the black kitten held firmly in her arms.

"Impressive that she can do that," Ursula said, "move Stella from her head to her hands as she shifts."

"Zynda is renowned as our most talented shapeshifter for a reason. She truly shares Salena's gifts in that way."

"But she doesn't carry the mark of the Tala," she replied, watching me keenly, "so she could never be queen of the Tala."

"Well, that's correct and not," I temporized. "Don't snort at me. These things aren't clear cut. Zynda has the right blood to be queen, but the wrong temperament—and she flat refused to consider it, even as a girl. Zyr has all the qualifications, too, but he can't be king, though for different reasons. Rayfe does not have the mark, and he was able to win his place as king anyway. The mark has more to do with ability to access the Heart and manipulate that magic than anything else."

"And Stella has it, but Astar doesn't—and yet they can both shift."

"Exactly." I smiled sunnily at her frown. "Lots of those with Tala blood can shapeshift. The mark is something extra. Here comes Kiraka with our Nahanaun friends."

The great bronze shape of the ancient dragon Kiraka winged in low over the sea. *"Greetings, Queen Andromeda,"* she said, her mind-voice rustling like dried leaves. *"Permission to land on your shores?"*

*"Always, Lady Kiraka. Annfwn is also your home."*

*"Hmpf. I prefer to be certain of my welcome when mighty sorceresses are involved."*

I laughed mentally, partly in affection for the cantankerous old dragon, and partly at the implication I could do much of anything against the n'Andanan shapeshifter who'd once been a substantial sorceress in her own right. I doubted that had changed just because she'd permanently settled into dragon form. Besides, not much stood up to dragon fire.

"Something amusing?" Ursula asked.

"Kiraka. Her humor is quite dry." Kiraka winged to a neat landing, barely stirring the sand, and practically melted into a boneless slide that put her passengers within easy reach of the ground. Still, Nakoa simply gathered Dafne's slighter body into his arms and leapt powerfully to the sand, the silver threading his dark hair glittering, the golden dragon torc and armbands a bright counterpoint.

"Showoff," Ursula muttered.

"I could do that," Harlan pointed out, "if you're feeling like you need to put on a display."

She gave him a withering look. "No, thank you. We're full up on manly muscular displays. Looks like they've got the kids corralled and are heading up. Let's walk on to the council chambers and eat something before the rest of the hoard arrives."

He smiled easily, saluting her with the *Elskathorrl.* "As my lady wife commands."

"Could I have a word with Harlan?" I figured this might be a conversation better had in private.

He and Ursula exchanged glances. "I'll meet you there," she said, moving to go.

"No." He caught her elbow, changing it to a caress that slid smoothly down her inner arm. "Stay. No more secrets."

She softened, then looked to me and shrugged. "Andi?"

"Yes, that's fine. My discretion was more out of consideration for you, Harlan. I had a vision this morning, and I'd like to get your insight." I described what I'd seen and heard, and he sobered as I spoke.

He scratched his fingers over his scalp. "Inga," he said. "She had eyes that color. And Helva's were brown, like our mother's. Hulda is Kral's mother. She's dowager empress now, since

Hestar's first wife is ostensibly the current empress."

"What is her name?" Ursula frowned as she searched her memory. "I don't recall hearing it."

He lifted a shoulder and let it fall. "I have no idea. If she even holds the title of empress, I doubt it does her much good. Hestar was never one to share power. Nor was Hulda, for that matter. She always ruled the other wives, so I imagine it's no different with her daughters-in-law."

"So, Hulda is the one to watch," Ursula nodded to herself, filing away that information.

"Do you have any idea why she'd try to summon Kral?" I asked.

Harlan sighed. "Hulda has spent the bulk of her life maneuvering to make Kral emperor. There's been nothing too cruel or too ruthless for her to attempt in pursuit of that goal." He and Ursula exchanged a long, speaking look, a potent secret humming through the golden bond between them. Interesting. "According to the conversation you saw," he continued, "Hulda sees Hestar's failure to wed Ban to Ursula as an opportunity."

"For my part, I'm most interested that Inga mentioned sending a message via Akamai," Ursula put in. "That verifies that she's our correspondent, that Akamai is with her and she's attempting to help you."

"Yes," he replied absently. "Dafne will want to know that. But I think we need to take Hulda's machinations very seriously. Whatever she's plotting against Hestar will absolutely affect us."

"From what you've said, women have no power in Dasnaria," Ursula countered.

"No official or overt power," he corrected. "Hulda may not have left the Imperial Palace since the day she entered it as a sixteen-year-old bride, but she's used a life of enforced idleness to consolidate her influence. She ever was clever and ruthless. If anyone could discover how to extend her reach from the prison that is the Imperial Seraglio, it would be Hulda."

"Arguably, Inga, at least, has done so also," Ursula mused. "An apparent coincidence we can't ignore."

"There's a reason Moranu showed me this vision," I agreed. "Following our speculation that Hestar offered the treaty in order to tear Deyrr from this throat, then Hulda seeing his failure as an opportunity could mean she's allied with the high priestess."

"We know that they've been in the same place at the same time," Harlan said. "I doubt Hulda would scruple at working with the practitioners if Deyrr if it furthered her ends."

As I suspected. "Then my next question is if Kral will answer the summons."

Harlan considered it seriously, in silent communication with Ursula. I knew full well that they couldn't speak mind to mind—neither had those capabilities—but for all that, they seemed to hold more extensive conversations that way than Rayfe and I could.

"I'm going to say no," Harlan finally replied. He shook his head minutely when Ursula shifted in disagreement, and spoke more to her than to me. "There was a time, certainly, when Kral wanted nothing else. And I'd be the first to condemn some of the things he's done in pursuit of that power. But he's a changed man."

"Because of love?" Ursula sneered in derision.

Harlan tapped her on the nose, something I'd have once sworn to all three goddesses Ursula would never allow anyone to do. "Don't pretend you don't understand the capacity for love to make us want to become better people. Kral loves our Jepp, yes, and wants to do whatever it takes to keep her with him—but beyond that, Jepp opened his eyes to the more sordid aspects of the empire and our family. When you grow up embedded in a culture, when a way of doing things is all you've known all your life, it can be hard to see its flaws. Having someone you love and admire point out those flaws can make all the difference."

"Many will argue that people don't change—that they can't change."

"Then they don't know us," Harlan replied with quiet meaning.

She huffed, making him smile. "Well, this will be a good test. I just hope that if he decides to chase after Hulda's offer that we won't lose Jepp, too. Any other questions, Andi?"

"Not at the moment. Let's head to the council chambers."

"Is Rayfe meeting us there?" she asked as we resumed walking. She spoke with an innocent air, but I sensed her keen attention on me.

"I believe so," I replied carefully. "Unless some emergency detains him."

"Hmm."

I knew that noncommittal hum of hers and Moranu take me if I would rise to that particular bait. We made it down another turn in the road before she spoke again. "He seemed out of sorts at the meeting yesterday."

"We're all out of sorts. It would be surprising if the pressure *didn't* make us irritable."

"Granted, but—"

"Auntie Andi! Auntie Andi!" A naked little girl with tumbling black curls ran at us full tilt. Ursula caught her neatly in her leap at me, snagging her around the middle with quick hands and holding her as she writhed.

"Easy, Nilly," she cautioned. "Auntie Andi is pregnant, and we don't leap on pregnant ladies."

"I won't break," I replied, amused that even Ursula had

adopted Ami and Ash's habit of calling the twins Willy and Nilly.

"No, but you can bruise. Do you know who I am?" Ursula asked.

Our niece stilled and contemplated Ursula. "You're Auntie Essla. Her Fucking Majesty."

Ursula's smile at Stella's recognition faded into a frown. Harlan snorted, manfully swallowing a laugh. "I'll be having words with your mother," she said, passing Stella to me as Astar, still in bear form, came galloping towards us, his parents nowhere in sight. Stella planted kisses on my face with glee, squirming as I tried to plant a few on her.

"And here's a fine bear cub," Ursula declared, canting her head at Astar, "but where's my nephew?"

Stella giggled. "That *is* him!"

Ursula got down on one knee, taking the bear cub tackle with a laugh, then wrestling him to the ground. Another sight I would've sworn could never be.

"Where are your clothes, missy?" I asked Stella.

She put her little hands on my cheeks, her lower lip thrusting out in a pout. "I don't like them. Cats don't wear clothes."

"But cats don't talk either," I reminded her. "Walking, talking, and looking like people comes with certain rules, and clothes are one of them."

"My mommy says I don't have to wear clothes," she insisted.

"Ah, but I am queen here, which means I outrank your mommy."

Stella considered that, taking in my crown, her gray eyes solemn. "I thought you're a sorceress."

"I'm both."

"Have you seen the other sorceress—the mean one with no eyes?"

Something in me stilled, frozen to the core. "Does she talk

to you in dreams?"

"They're not dreams." Stella stared at me, betrayal crumpling her face. "I thought *you* would understand."

I hugged her close, her little body so warm and thrumming with magic. "I do understand. And yes, I've seen her. I think you shouldn't talk to her, no matter what she says."

"All right. I don't like her."

"Me neither. I will teach you some tricks to make her go away."

She nodded. Frowned. "Why is your hip hurt?"

"I was fighting a giant warthog and I caught a tusk in my hip," I told her, not surprised she'd sensed my injury. Stella had the gift of empathy, a rare talent that I worried would bring her more grief than anything.

"There," she said with a bright smile and another kiss. "I fixed it. Can I feel the baby?"

"Yes, but later, all right?" Quite a few Tala had gathered to watch the scene, quite amused by the sight of the High Queen wrestling a bear cub. Astar appeared to be winning, too. Harlan stood by laughing, so Ursula must not be in too much trouble. Ash arrived at a jog and dove in to assist.

"Stella Andromeda!" Ami's stern voice rang out. "What have we discussed about being naked?"

"Uh oh." Stella rounded her mouth, giving me a beseeching look. "She only uses my real name when I'm in trouble."

"Just this once," I whispered. I rarely used the power of the Heart to manifest things, and never frivolously, but I did this time. I set her down and was more than rewarded by Stella's delighted smile as a simple Tala shift in a deep violet appeared above her head and settled over her in a loose swirl.

She grinned at Ami. "But Mommy, I'm *not* naked!"

Ami gave her a stern look, though her generous mouth

twitched with suppressed amusement. "Say thank you to Auntie Andi."

"Thank you to Auntie Andi!" Stella sang out.

Stella trotted over to watch as Ash and Marskal double-teamed the bear cub, pulling him off Ursula. She extracted herself, got to her feet, and punched the still laughing Harlan on the arm. "Traitor."

Ami turned a radiant smile on me, crossing the last short distance to embrace me. She smelled of sunshine and roses, her hair like silk, and she felt like pure love in my mind. Being Glorianna's avatar must be nice—no dark shadows or hard edges. "Andi, it is so good to see you!"

I returned the embrace. "Likewise. Sorry to roust you out of Windroven before you were ready."

"But we *were* ready." She released me, rearranging my hair around my face and shoulders for me, straightening the crown a little. "Nilly told us," she added, raising her rose-gold brows, violet eyes wide.

I groaned in sympathy, glancing over to where the barefoot girl danced from foot to foot, apparently offering advice on the men trying to calm Astar, who was still a bear cub. "It was too much to hope that she'd escape the curse of foresight."

"She says a mean woman with dead eyes has been talking to her. At first I thought it was a standard childhood nightmare, but…"

"Nothing so prosaic. Nilly just mentioned that to me, too. It has to be Deyrr's high priestess. She almost certainly senses the mark of the Tala in Nilly."

Ami's soft, sensual mouth went hard and those lovely violet eyes sparked fire. "That bitch has no business messing with my child."

Ah, there it was, the fierce face of love. Pretty, vain Ami

would stop at nothing to protect the ones she loved. She and Ursula had that in common. "That's one reason I wanted you all out of Windroven," I told her.

Ami nodded in glum agreement. "She infiltrated the castle Glorianna only knows how long ago. Since Zynda and Marskal freed Djakos, we've tried to keep those lower levels sealed, but it's fighting a losing battle. Sleeper spies keep creeping up from the depths."

"I can help our Nilly," I promised, hoping I wasn't wrong. "That bitch won't get to her again."

"Thank you." She took my hands and stepped back to survey my belly. "How are you feeling? I bet you're at the 'how in the Three can my body stretch any more?' and 'how can a bone be swollen?' stage."

I laughed. "That's about right—and I keep reminding myself I'll stretch more."

"You get kind of used to it," she confided. She ran a thoughtful finger over the ruby necklace lavishly sparkling beneath my collarbones. "Salena's?"

"Yes."

"Essla sent me a royal command to wear mine, but they don't go with pink." She made a face.

"Some things are more important than fashion accessorizing," Ursula noted, coming to join us.

Ami sniffed, casting a jaundiced eye at the white dust and crushed flower petals decorating Ursula's leathers. "Forgive me if I don't take beauty tips from you, Auntie Essla."

Ursula raised one auburn brow. "Don't you mean 'your fucking majesty'?"

Ami winced. "They're like little sponges, only they soak up all the worst things, and none of what they're supposed to."

To our surprise, Ursula laughed and opened her arms. "I

love you, too, Ami."

They embraced, Ami's sunrise hair a bright halo compared to Ursula's deep red. But for all that they differed in so many ways—Ursula all lean, sharp lines where Ami was lush as a blossom—the stamp of sisterhood showed clearly. Parting, they both looked to me, extending hands to include me in the circle. Me, the night darkness, the shadows, also like and unlike.

A vision stirred, this one clearly from the long ago past. Salena, as a much younger woman, standing in this same spot and seeing us three, her daughters in the far future. I looked across the years at her, those storm gray eyes exactly like my own, the same ruby necklace glittering around her throat. She gazed right back at me, dipping her chin in acknowledgment, and the years tightened like a string abruptly yanked, so that we almost stood in the same time as well as the same place.

She lifted a hand in greeting, smiled at us.

And the moment was gone.

# ~ 9 ~

"ANDI?" URSULA STUDIED me with a sharp gaze, the gray of her eyes lighter, steely, with a hint of blue, like the keen edge of a silver blade. Like and unlike the eyes I'd just stared into across the years. And Ami's limpid blue, just enough gray in them to lend that violet cast, like the sky moments before dawn.

I nearly didn't say, but… Salena belonged to them, too, her magic in their blood, the lines of her face in theirs. "I saw our mother just now. Standing right here, as clearly as either of you. She was having a vision of the future, seeing us in this moment."

Ursula looked briefly stricken before she mastered her expression. "Was there a message?"

I shook my head. "I think she simply glimpsed us in the future."

"Was she happy?" Ami asked, tentative, hopeful.

"I'm not sure she was ever happy, but she was pleased to see us. Proud," I added, and when they both smiled, I was glad I had.

"Is this a private conversation, or should I take my adorable daughter to be cooed over elsewhere?"

We all turned as one, exclaiming over Dafne, who'd arrived at a far more sedate pace. Petite, with gold-streaked bronze hair and caramel-brown eyes, Dafne beamed at us. She'd tanned to a copper warmth during her time in Nahanau, and grown sleek with happiness. Her husband, King Nakoa KauPo loomed possessively behind her, the lightning streaks sizzling in his dark curls, the dragon-scale tattoos dancing across his muscled arms and bare chest. A goofy smile spread across his otherwise stern visage. Dafne held a small bundle in her arms, wrapped in a sage-green silk blanket embroidered with looping dragons in copper thread.

"How are you even out of bed?" Ami exclaimed, deftly extracting the baby from Dafne, and holding her while Ursula and I peered over her shoulders. "It took me days and days just to stand on my own."

"Because you nearly bled to death," Ursula reminded her, and Ami wrinkled her nose at the memory.

Dafne leaned back against Nakoa, who put big hands on her shoulders, squeezing proudly. "Being Kiraka's human companion comes with decided benefits," she explained. "I feel like new again, which is good, since a woman my age shouldn't be cavalier about having babies."

"You even *look* ten years younger," Ami complained, "which is so not fair."

"No fear, Your Highness," Dafne said in a wry tone. "I won't ever be competing for your title of most beautiful woman in the known world."

"Only the known world?" Ami sniffed, then cooed at the baby. "*You* are the mostest beautiful, aren't you? So precious, my darling. Where's Ash? Ash, I need to have another baby."

Ash, still wrestling Astar the bear cub while Stella clung to his back, her arms wrapped around his neck, throttling him as she chattered merrily, called back. "Right this minute? Because I'll need to get undressed."

"Maybe you should wait for us to finish the war first." Ursula commented drily.

"Oh," Ami huffed in disgust. "You have no heart, Essla. Here." She slipped the baby into Ursula's arms, adjusting and supporting Ursula's hold until she was satisfied. "Now look at this precious face. Look—tiny fingers! Take a sniff. There's nothing sweeter smelling than a newborn. Can't you just feel your womb throbbing for one of your own?"

Ursula leveled a steely look on her. "No." But she did bend to sniff, then placed a kiss on the infant's forehead. "Danu's bright blessings on you, little one. May She guide your steps with a clear hand, wisdom, and fair justice. Have you named her yet, Dafne?"

"Well…" Dafne looked between the three of us, put her hands on Nakoa's where they rested on her shoulders still. "We've settled on a first choice, but wanted to ask for your permission. We'd like to name her Salena."

"Oh, how wonderful." Ami's voice came out hushed and weepy. "I say yes."

Ursula looked less convinced, tipping her head at my belly. "I thought Andi might want to use that name."

Dafne's face flushed with chagrined color. "Oh, Andi! How thoughtless of me. Of course you should—"

"No," I broke in, realizing I'd set my hands on my rounded belly, something I rarely did in public, given how uncomfortable the Tala were. Surrounded by my sisters—found and by blood— I let myself relax, smoothing my fingers over the taut mound. "Don't give it another thought. We'll be having a boy and I don't know that he'd like 'Salena' for a name."

"Well, pray Danu you won't name him 'Uorsin,'" Ursula muttered.

"No prayers needed there," I returned in the same tone.

"But for your next child," Dafne insisted. "You may yet have a daughter."

"My turn," I told Ursula, taking the baby from her. She looked a little abashed that she seemed to have grown comfortable holding her. I studied the little girl's face, her warm weight a comfort in my arms. Magic in her, yes. Not the mark of the Tala, but Nakoa's sort—of earth, ocean, and storm. "I like 'Salena' for her. Even if we should be blessed with a daughter, we wouldn't use that name. It's not a good name for a Tala child anymore— too much bitter history there—but for a daughter of Nahanau, child of Salena's adopted daughter, it's a fine name. An auspicious one."

"Thank you," Dafne whispered.

"If you agree?" I asked Ursula and she nodded, eyes soft with rare mist.

I kissed the baby's soft forehead, inhaling the sweetness of new life. "Moranu's blessings on you, young Salena. May you have the power of flexibility, the ability to embrace change, and may magic illuminate your darkest nights."

Ami took her from me, kissing little Salena in the same spot. "Glorianna's blessings on you, sweet Salena, namesake of the fiercest of queens, one who sacrificed her heart for us. May you always have what she did not: love."

Ami nestled the baby into Dafne's arms, then wiped the streaming tears from Dafne's cheeks with her thumbs. Nakoa nodded gravely.

"Many thanks to you all," he said in Common Tongue. "With such blessings, our daughter shall surely thrive."

"Your Common Tongue is excellent, Your Highness," I said, then wondered if I sounded too surprised.

He cracked a small smile, squeezing Dafne's shoulders. "I have a fierce taskmistress. And, please, call me Nakoa, heart-sister. This is the correct term, yes?"

"Yes," Dafne said, her voice still watery, and put her hand through the crook of his elbow as she smiled up at him. "And I add my thanks. With three magical and ferocious godmothers, our Salena shall surely lead a long and healthy life." A hopeful lilt lifted the end of her words into a question, her gaze sliding to me.

"You're banging your head against a wall," Zynda's voice rang loud with some impatience. "He'll shift back when he's comfortable and not before. You can't *make* him shift."

Grateful for the distraction, I seized on it. "Sounds like they need help."

Ami strode over, and we all followed, to where the men—Ash, Marskal, and Harlan—had bear-cub Astar corralled, Stella still clinging to Ash's back. Zynda flashed me an exasperated grimace. "Unless someone cares to force the matter."

"What do you mean?" Ami asked, a line between her brows.

"The King and Queen of the Tala can force shapeshifting," Zynda explained. "Usually it's a punishment, but occasionally the authority can be used to solve a problem. Every once in a while, a child needs the nudge. That is, *if* the child can shift at all." A ghost of grief crossed her face, quickly banished as she added, "Which is not Willy's issue."

"Go ahead then, Andi," Ami said, hands on her hips as she gazed at her obstinate son.

"I don't have that ability," I admitted, "as I came so late to shapeshifting in general. Rayfe handles those instances."

"Where *is* King Rayfe?" Ami asked. Though no one shushed her, the uncomfortable silence greeting her question had a quelling effect.

"I'm sure he'll be here soon," I replied, with easy confidence I didn't feel.

"And here I am." Rayfe prowled through our audience,

coming from higher up the road. "Andromeda." He lifted my hand and kissed it, lips cool, eyes inscrutable as the deepest ocean, mind tightly shuttered. "Greetings all. I apologize that I was not here to welcome you to Annfwn. Is this small bear the reason for so much consternation?"

"Hello, heart-brother." Ami swanned up to Rayfe, kissing him on each cheek, smiling merrily as if there had been no tension whatsoever. "My terrible son refuses to shift back."

Astar growled, wagging his ursine head. Rayfe growled back, and Astar froze, blinking at him.

"I can force him to shift, yes," he said to Ami, "but I agree with Zynda. Let him be. He likely feels more secure as a bear in a strange place, with strange people, and so much chaos."

I gave him a questioning look, wondering how long he'd been eavesdropping without announcing himself, but he avoided my gaze.

"But I'm given to understand that it's unhealthy for him to stay in animal form too long." Ami's brow wrinkled further in her concern.

"'Too long' is days," Zynda replied. "Not hours."

"Let him and Stella go play and have lessons with the other children," Rayfe said. "He'll shift back when he needs words. Or hands."

"He always does," Ash agreed in his hoarse voice, bowing his head to Rayfe. "But we understand the training arena was compromised?"

"Indeed it was," Rayfe replied. "Which is why I've been working on a new, more protected location, with dedicated guards." He swept a hand, and the crowd parted again to admit a cadre of Hawks and shapeshifter fighting pairs, Zyr and Karyn leading them. She, too, wore her fighting leathers—the ones she'd found in n'Andana—and she carried both a recurve and a crossbow, along with several quivers of arrows. Zyr looked as he always did, in the clothing he habitually returned to when he shifted to human form. Of course, his weapons manifested when he *wasn't* in that form. Why carry a weapon when you had formidable claws?

"These are our best teams, Tala and human," Rayfe continued. "They'll take Astar and Stella to the new, secure training ground, where the other children will gather to practice and play. The Tala take protection of our children very seriously." He glanced at me meaningfully as he said it, though I wasn't sure what response he looked for. I managed a regal nod and smile, proud of myself until his gaze drifted to the crown and rubies— and hardened at the sight.

Ami was kissing the twins goodbye, issuing motherly instructions while they both squirmed to get gone. Some of the guard shifted to animal form, cavorting as the human throats sang a Tala children's song, and they all danced away. Except for Zyr and Karyn, who remained for the meeting.

Zynda drifted over to me. "That meeting you requested?" she said in a low voice. "At your convenience following this session."

"What's this about?" Rayfe demanded of me, suspicion creasing his brow. I didn't know how to reply, trying to recall which meeting I'd requested of Zynda.

*"With Shaman,"* she reminded me in a discreet mental tone.

Ah, right. "With Healer Kelleah," I told Rayfe, offhandedly so he wouldn't detect the prevarication. I hated lying to him, but I knew well how he felt about Shaman and what he called the Cult of Moranu. This was something I needed to do, and I did not need to fight with him about it. Besides, it wasn't precisely a lie, since I intended to see Kelleah also. "You'd suggested that I have her examine me, yes?"

He nodded curtly, as always anxious to drop *that* topic of discussion. "Shall we convene? I believe we were promised breakfast." Rayfe indicated the entrance to the council chambers, gesturing at the doorway, formally offering me his arm. He didn't move immediately, however, instead hanging back as the others preceded us.

"Thank you for handling the safety of the children," I said, squeezing his arm, figuring this would be a safe topic of discussion. "That was well done. I didn't think to move the training arena elsewhere." It actually hadn't occurred to me that it *could* be moved.

"It wouldn't be the first time we've had to," he replied, in that coolly neutral tone. "There's a long history of it that you wouldn't know about."

Ah, so we weren't done slicing at each other. The thought made me weary. And after the warmth of talking with Dafne and my sisters, I felt the chill all the more. I clung to my resolve not to fight with him, as it seemed to only make things worse. "Still," I said, trying to keep my voice and thoughts light, "you reassured Ami on several levels and that was kind of you."

"Mossbacks have no business raising shapeshifter children," he said, a growl rolling in his voice. "I regret agreeing to this arrangement. Stella and Astar should have stayed in Annfwn, with their own kind."

That fast, my resolve crumbled—and rage billowed up in me at his cruel attitude and careless assumptions. At least it burned away the chill. I removed my hand from his arm, letting him feel my anger. "You don't get to decide to take a mother's children from her," I hissed, feeling as if steam came out of my ears at the same time. Nor did he have any business criticizing my baby sister. "How—or where—my sister raises her babies isn't something *you* get to agree to or not."

He assessed me with hard eyes, his gaze flicking over the still dispersing gathering. "Have a care, Andromeda," he said quietly. "You will be overheard. You don't want to embarrass yourself. Any more than you already have."

I wanted to scream at him that I didn't care, but I knew I'd regret losing my temper. "What is *wrong* with you?" I demanded through gritted teeth. "The last few days it's as if I don't even know you anymore."

His face chilled further, into icy lines of disdain. "I haven't changed. You're the one acting unhinged lately."

"Call me crazy one more time," I warned, fury boiling through me to crackle in the air. My hair lifted with the static magic.

Rayfe leaned in, nose nearly touching mine. "Control yourself, Andromeda."

I growled, inarticulate with the need to blast that supercilious look clean off his face.

"What are you going to do?" he asked, a taunting note in the question. "Perhaps you should storm off to your rocks to sulk while the grownups keep their tempers and plan this war."

Perversely, rather than enraging me further, the painful shock of those words acted like a cold ocean wave, bitter anguish dousing all anger. I stared at him, struggling to grasp how things had gone so foul between us. I straightened, letting the magic settle back into my blood, my hair falling around my bare arms, silky again, not stinging like lashes of fire.

This was about more than giving him room to master the fears my pregnancy aroused in him. This was more than the pressures of war.

"How can you say that to me?" I asked him, raw and honest emotion in my voice. "I understand if you don't love me anymore. Or if you can't, or never did. But I don't understand how you can speak to me with such contempt. You sound like you despise me."

"I don't…" He shook his head, shedding the thought. "I'm only asking you to be mature in these conversations."

"Mature?" My voice cracked on the word. "Even in the beginning, when I was admittedly young and inexperienced in the world, you never talked down to me. You always treated me with respect, as someone…" Ah, how it hurt my heart to think he'd changed his mind in this. "Admirable. And now you speak to my toddler nephew with more respect than you give me."

He gazed back at me, something of his old self stirring deep in his eyes. "Andromeda—I didn't mean… That is…" Again, he didn't finish. I waited, hoping he'd say something to allay my worst fears, but he seemed to be floundering. Finally he said, "This isn't the time or place for this conversation."

I nodded, because that was true. And because I needed time and space to think, to harden my heart against him and his careless slights, before we went another round in this fight. "Dafne and Nakoa are naming their daughter Salena," I informed him, taking refuge in cool formality. "She's a lovely, healthy baby girl. If you intend to join us in the council chambers, she's with Dafne. You might offer them congratulations. That's a tradition of my people it would behoove you to honor." I turned to go inside and he caught my arm.

"Andromeda…"

I raised an eyebrow, glad I could maintain that much remove. Waited. Hoped for… I didn't know anymore. Still he seemed unable to find words.

"We'd best go in," I finally said.

"I suppose so," he replied on a sigh.

I nodded and walked away, not bothering to see if he followed.

EVERYONE WAS SEATED around the table, plates filled, conversation burbling. The discussion fell off noticeably as I entered the room, then several people valiantly picked it up again with renewed vigor. I pretended not to notice, just as I planned to make sure no one noticed the bleeding hole in my heart.

I slipped into my chair, noting that some thoughtful soul had filled a plate for me, and that a pot of tea sat ready, with my favorite teacup clean and waiting. I poured some tea and sipped, cupping the warm, gaily painted cup in hands gone icy with despair, willing myself to thaw, to steady. A moment later Rayfe strode in. He paused by Nakoa and Dafne, offering him a handshake and Dafne a pat on the shoulder. He even bent over to peer at little Salena's face, saying something I couldn't hear, but that made the proud parents smile widely.

The charming smile he'd put on for them faded as he sat beside me. "Happy now?" he inquired in a silky tone that didn't fool me for a moment.

Since I had no good answer—and no energy to fight with him anymore, maybe ever—I simply thanked him, set my teacup down, and began eating. He paused a moment, as if expecting more from me, then reached for a platter and filled his own plate. He ate with efficient speed, chewing with more vigor than required, making me wonder if he imagined biting more chunks out of me instead.

"Ursula," I said, when Rayfe appeared to be making no move to lead the discussion, "would you summarize our status for the new arrivals? And to help us all sort priorities and next steps?"

"Certainly. Including your most recent vision?"

"If Harlan agrees."

He nodded to her inquiring look, so she shoved her plate aside and began speaking. Dafne had handed little Salena to Nakoa, deftly extracting a book bursting with bits of loose paper, parchment, even strips of leather. She arranged pieces as Ursula spoke, situating them in groups, and also making notes on a fresh sheet of paper. Moranu bless her.

I'd always admired Ursula's ability to memorize facts and keep them in order, particularly as they pertained to her role as High Queen. With succinct ease, she laid out the major players, current status, and possible courses of action. Dafne, long accustomed to working with Ursula, seemed to keep up fine.

"Dafne," Ursula said on finishing, "would you recap from your notes?"

"Yes, Your Majesty. I should—"

"Let's keep to first names in these sessions," Ursula interrupted. "There are enough titles and honorifics in this room to stymie even the most diligent courtier."

"Uh oh, gréine." Zyr tugged on Karyn's hair. "Whatever will you do?"

"Hush," she hissed at him.

Dafne cleared her throat. "As I was about to say, I should mention that Kiraka is listening in, and Djakos through her. They may ask me to pass along various insights and questions."

"Fine by me." Ursula waved a hand for Dafne to continue.

I stopped Dafne. "Rayfe?" I asked pointedly.

He gave me a glittering glance for forcing his hand, but I wasn't going to have him claim his authority had been circumvented again. "Fine by me, also," he said diffidently, lounging back in his chair with deliberately assumed indolence.

"My apologies, Rayfe," Ursula said. "Perhaps you should lead this session, as we are in your territory."

Dafne and Ami looked between us, clearly wondering at the undercurrents, while the others maintained a level of watchfulness.

"Not at all, heart-sister," Rayfe replied, startling me by taking my hand. His felt hot, so I knew mine still retained the chill of the hurts he'd delivered. "Lead away. You're so good at it."

Dafne cast a doubtful glance at Ursula, then consulted her list. Rayfe continued to hold my hand, his fingers gliding over my skin in a way that felt not at all reassuring, and even vaguely threatening. All wrong. Even in the beginning, when Rayfe had frightened me with his ruthless declarations that he'd drag me to Annfwn kicking and screaming if necessary, I hadn't felt this kind of threat from him.

I pulled away with the excuse of pouring more tea, and glimpsed a small, satisfied smile curve his lips, as if he'd won a point in whatever game he played. So wrong. He'd never been anything less than direct with me. I would've said he didn't have it in him to be evasive and mean-spirited. *The last few days it's as if I don't know you anymore.* Was there more truth in those words I'd flung out in anger than I'd realized?

"I've listed people into columns," Dafne was saying, and I made myself pay attention. "They're categorized as enemy leaders, their allies, neutral parties, our leaders, and our allies. Leaders of our enemies are: Emperor Hestar, Dowager Empress Hulda, the high priestess of Deyrr, and likely the demigod Deyrr Himself. Hestar controls the Dasnarian military forces, acting as commander in chief, with his brother Mykal most likely in charge of the navy. Also under Hestar, we assume that the brothers remaining in Dasnaria—Leo and Loke—also support Hestar, possibly in charge of other military branches."

"Though we don't know that for sure," Harlan temporized.

"Lacking intelligence to the contrary, however," Ursula said, "it's a good assumption." He conceded with a reluctant nod.

"Hulda is an enemy who may be working against Hestar," Dafne continued, "possibly allied with the high priestess, who I've listed as a third enemy leader. She's aided by an incarnation of Deyrr. It's not clear if she controls Him or vice-versa. Allied with her are at least ten less-senior priests and priestesses of Deyrr," she looked for confirmation to Karyn, who nodded, "all of whom we must presume to have at least equivalent power to Illyria's. We must also consider all of n'Andana's population as belonging to the high priestess."

A thick silence fell as everyone contemplated those numbers.

"Also Kir," Ami said, exchanging a look with Ash. "Former priest of Glorianna. Jepp saw him in the Imperial Palace with Hestar and the high priestess. He should be on the list of enemy leaders, and traitors."

## ~ 10 ~

D AFNE HELD HER quill poised. "Keeping in mind that we're aren't certain of the alliances between the three major enemy factions, would you put Kir as allied with Hestar, Hulda, or the high priestess?"

Ami looked to me and Ursula.

"He is allied with the high priestess," Ash spoke, bitterness edging his already rough voice, his scarred face grim. "If she is locating people with latent shapeshifter blood and forcing them into animal form to make sleeper spies and other mind-controlled members of her army, as we're fairly sure she's been doing, then Kir is in the thick of it. I'm certain he and his people are behind the disappearances of the ex-patriot Tala and others with Tala ancestry, whether they're aware of that fact or not."

"But how?" Ami asked. "He no longer has the doll that Mother left me. Without its magic, how can he locate those with shapeshifter bloodlines?"

"Maybe that's why he needed Deyrr," Ash replied darkly. "Salena made those dolls with blood magic, not dissimilar to what Deyrr uses. Could be Illyria taught or gave him the means. I just know that someone is always there ahead of us, and those people are going somewhere we can't find. He knows our ways, and he has the motivation. Could be he has the blood magic spell to do what the doll did—only with more power and precision."

"And in exchange, he betrayed us to Deyrr," Ursula inserted in a hard voice. "It makes sense. Let's go with that assumption unless we learn otherwise."

"How did Salena learn blood magic?" Dafne asked. "I don't want to go off on a tangent if it's not important, but I thought blood magic was part of Deyrr's worship, not Moranu's."

Because they seemed to expect me to reply—and I only knew bits and pieces I'd heard—I looked to Rayfe. He seemed consumed in sullen thought, not even glancing up.

Fortunately, Zynda spoke. "It's important to remember that the Tala are descendants of n'Andana, and that the practitioners of Deyrr are likely a remnant of a civilization that included both Dasnaria and n'Andana. There are those in Annfwn—shamans and some wizards—who practice degrees of blood magic."

"It's frowned upon," Rayfe said, giving her a dark look from under his brows.

"Though not against Tala law," she answered coolly. "And not without its place. It could be important, Dafne," she added. "I'll ask Shaman what he knows about Salena's training."

"I don't like that guy," Zyr muttered.

"For good reason," Marskal said, nodding in curt agreement.

Zynda rolled her eyes at both of them. "You two don't need to talk to him then." She smiled thinly. *"You, of course, will be part of this conversation,"* she added to me privately.

"The other thing I'm wondering," Dafne said slowly, tapping her quill and sliding a cautious look to me, "is if the practitioners of Deyrr can learn this blood magic—and are using it against us—and if Salena learned this same magic, and if Andi's sorcery is inherited from the same bloodline—Andi, can you do these same things?" Her wise eyes held regret for the question, but also challenge.

It seemed so long ago that she'd first given me that look, back in the converted cellar rooms of the library at Ordnung, when Dafne had been the one to put the books in my hands—after making me don gloves so I wouldn't mar the pages—that explained my mother's strange nature and my own heritage. As I gazed back at her, I realized she knew the answer to her question—and that she'd posed it here, before everyone, to force me into the open.

I sighed out a breath. "Well, what I have—"

"No," Rayfe interrupted. "And there are good reasons for it."

Dafne tilted her head in curiosity. "Thank you, King Rayfe." She returned her gaze to me. "Andi?"

I nearly winced at her deliberate dismissal of Rayfe's terse reply, but I schooled my expression. "I have been careful to stay away from blood magic, it's true."

"But if we need to fight fire with fire?" Ursula asked, keen gaze going between Dafne and me.

"That would be a good reason for me to try," I conceded.

"Except that you don't know what you're doing," Rayfe slammed a hand on the table. "And these are potent, ancient magics that have destroyed better magic wielders than you."

I swallowed hard, clinging to my composure. I would not engage with him in front of everyone. "And those are good reasons for me not to try," I agreed evenly.

Rayfe turned on me with a snarl. "You cannot jeopardize yourself, Andromeda. In your *condition*, you—"

"Are not having this conversation now," I interrupted firmly. I held his furious blue gaze until he jerked it away, then nodded to Dafne. "Point taken, Dafne. I think you can continue."

"All right, then. Moving to allies within the Dasnarian Imperial Palace," Dafne said without missing a beat, and sliding a second document to the top, "we have Inga, Helva, and Akamai. We consider them primarily spies and friends, however, with no forces to command. I'd like to send a message to Akamai as a test, however, to verify that he hasn't been compromised."

"How will you do that?" Ursula wanted to know.

"I'll write to him in a code we established," Dafne replied mildly, then continued when Ursula nodded. "Moving outward, for allied leaders we have Nakoa and myself in Nahanau, Rayfe and Andi in Annfwn, Ash and Ami in Windroven—"

"Ash and Ami, and the kids, will remain in Annfwn for the foreseeable future," I corrected. No one argued, and Dafne made a note.

"Ursula is commander in chief, aided by Harlan, who captains the Hawks and remaining Vervaldr," she continued. "Kiraka wishes to be listed as leader of dragons, with Zynda and Djakos as her lieutenants."

She looked to Zynda for approval, who rolled her eyes, but nodded.

"With your permission, Captain," Marskal inclined his head to Harlan, "I'm with Zynda."

"We'll miss you, but I understand. You two make a good team," Harlan said.

"All right," Ursula said. "Marskal goes with Zynda under Kiraka."

"Which means I should be with Djakos," Ash put in. "I need to be useful," he said when Ami opened her mouth to protest. "I owe it to all the part-bloods I've failed. And Djakos and I have been training together."

Ursula waited, but Ami pressed her lips together, sitting back in her chair. Dafne made a note, then scanned the document. "Rayfe is, of course, commander of the Tala fighting forces, and Karyn and Zyr will lead the non-dragon shapeshifter fighting pairs under Rayfe's direction. Andi will handle the barrier, all prognostication, and battle Deyrr's sorcery." She gave me a rueful look and I smiled reassuringly. It wasn't as if anyone else could do those things. "Nakoa will command the Nahanaun fighting forces, and also contribute storm-brewing to aid in naval battles. I will continue to serve as the compiler of notes and communications."

"All that remains," she finished, ticking a point on her list, "is Kral. Jepp is obviously grouped with him on the *Hákyrling*, rather than with the Hawks. I have him on the list of leaders on our side, as Ursula appointed him general of our forces in the field, but it's possible that he'll change allegiance to Hulda in order to unseat Hestar."

"Excuse me," Karyn said. "I stayed quiet before, when you described the vision of Inga and Helva, who I should mention I know quite well. I feel I must speak on General—on Kral's behalf. I truly believe he will not answer Hulda's summons. I can also say that Hulda was my mother-in-law for many years. She is… not a kind woman. Now that he's free of her influence, Kral will not be eager to return to it."

Harlan nodded. "I agree. Kral won't go back. He made his choice, and he's made vows."

"He's gone back on vows before," Ursula reminded him, then gave Karyn a steely look. "As you should know better than most, having been wed to him and then forsaken. I'm surprised you defend him."

Zyr shifted as if to protect Karyn, invisible plumage lifting, but she put a steadying hand on his arm, standing up to Ursula with calm courage. "I *do* know better than most, Your Majesty, and thus I know this: when Kral made the choice to rescue Jepp, he knowingly cut all ties with the Empire. He could have left her—and me—to face our fates, but he didn't. He did not forsake me, but instead gave me a choice that most Dasnarian men would never have the open-mindedness to consider, much less offer. I have no doubt that Hulda's message will come as a shock to him, and that he'll pitch it into the sea."

"Hmm." Ursula looked unconvinced and Harlan tapped her arm to get her attention.

"I know that what I told you of the past is coloring your judgment in this," he said gravely. "I'm asking you to set that aside."

"He's at our front line. If the Dasnarian navy crosses the barrier and he betrays us, that could be our destruction." Ursula's words dropped heavy among us.

"He won't," Harlan said, and Karyn nodded.

"All right, I'll trust in you two." Ursula clearly didn't like it, but she conceded—something else she'd have been far too hardheaded to do even a year before. "If we're done with the list of allies, then—"

"I have something to add," Ami declared. "We need to list Glorianna, Danu, and Moranu on our side."

Ursula made a face. "We are not counting on the goddesses as our allies."

"We put the demigod Deyrr on *their* list," she pointed out.

"Because Karyn saw a statue come to life as an incarnation of it," Ursula argued. "It might not even be a deity, but it definitely exists. Who knows—it might be some kind of ancient magical creature."

"The high priestess implied that the palace she occupies in n'Andana belonged to Moranu," Karyn put in. "She also claimed that Moranu was a Dasnarian woman, and an acolyte of Deyrr. That She created shapeshifters by forcing enslaved humans to mate with animals, and that's why shapeshifters have a First Form—from that initial mating."

"If that's true," Zyr said with a lightness that didn't match the set of his face, "I pity my ancestor who mated with a gríobhth. Ouch."

"It's *not* true," Rayfe grated out. "That's just one more of her stinking lies."

Dafne met my eyes and I subtly shook my head. She'd found documents that partially bore out the high priestess's claim, but it didn't matter for this conversation.

"Regardless," I said, "the goddesses as we understand Them are ineffable. We can't count on deities as allies."

"You always say that Moranu is behind your visions," Ami said, and Ursula tipped her head at the point.

"When I say that, it doesn't mean I think—" I began.

"Moranu spoke to me when I died," Zynda interrupted in a firm tone, uncharacteristically serious. "I don't care if She started out life as a Dasnarian sorceress, She absolutely intervened, and She gave me my life and body back—entirely because I had a role in this conflict. I agree with Cousin Ami."

"Besides," Ami said, smiling sweetly, "I don't know if anyone noticed, but I wasn't assigned a responsibility on Dafne's very thorough list. As I'd like to be something more than decorative, I'll be the divine liaison."

"Liaison to deities," Ash corrected. "Not a liaison who is, herself, divine."

"That's a matter of opinion," Ami retorted loftily.

"What, exactly, would this job entail?" Ursula asked with some bemusement.

"I'll watch for signs from the Three, interpret them, and pass that information along to the compiler of notes and communications," Ami replied in a defiant tone. When Ursula opened her mouth, Ami pounced. "Tell you what, Essla—if you find that my doing this is taking away from my crucial being-decorative duties, I'll immediately switch tasks."

I could see Ursula badly wanted to say something, but after a moment longer, she shrugged fatalistically.

"Glorianna, Moranu, and Danu go on the list of allies. I can only hope Danu will guide me truly. Anything else? Please say no." She looked around the table, giving it a moment longer. "All right, given this list, what actions do we want to take?"

Everyone looked at me expectantly.

Rayfe made an irritated sound and, for the first time in several days, I felt in absolute agreement with him. "I can't tell you what to do," I said, my voice rising defensively. "Even I can't—"

"I know. We know," Ursula said, holding up a hand as if to pacify the group, though no one had disagreed. "Let me start over. The last time we gathered to discuss our strategy in this war, Kral suggested that we consider attacking, rather than waiting to be attacked."

"And yet that hasn't happened," Rayfe said. "Why not?"

Ursula grimaced. "This is on me, I know. One answer is that it's taken time to gather and move our forces into position, shore up physical defenses as best we can, stockpile food and weapons, and plan for supply chains—and we've done all that. We're as ready as we can be." Still…" She stroked a finger over the talon scar high on her cheek, looked around the table.

"Still you hesitate," Rayfe filled in. "Could it be that you're afraid?"

I tensed, not at all sure what I'd do if the pair of them came to blows, but Ursula kept eerily calm. She even dipped her chin at Rayfe.

"To be perfectly candid? Yes. I agreed to that plan, I know, but I'm still not convinced. I've been over and over it in my mind and I can't see how attacking n'Andana would be anything but suicide. I'm open to counterarguments."

Everyone assimilated that. I kept my expression neutral, making sure I didn't nod. I needed to be very careful not to push this decision one way or the other.

"We are strongest on our own territory," Rayfe declared.

Ursula regarded him thoughtfully. "Maybe yes, maybe no. If we wait for the war to come to us, it's our lands that will be devastated, our people who will suffer, warriors or not. Annfwn has a history of insularity, of hunkering down behind the barrier and depending on being forgotten for protection. That's a luxury you no longer have."

"Which side are you arguing for?" he bit out, losing his indolent posture and coiling like a snake.

"The side where we win," she snapped back.

"We should consider," Zyr said, "that regardless of strategy, attacking at least the high priestess's fortification in n'Andana would be the right thing to do. To free the people she's enslaved," he added, seeming to think the reason we all stared at him was because we didn't understand. "They are our kin, however far removed, and we owe them that. Some of them"— he nodded to Ash—"might be the people you sought and lost. Is this such a bizarre reason to act?"

Karyn patted his arm. "They're just surprised by your sudden altruism."

He made a face at her, but his eyes glittered with the gríobhth's ferocity when he looked at us. "They are our children. They kept me in a cage. There are others—human minds trapped in enslaved animal bodies—still in cages and chains. Yes, I absolutely volunteer to go on this mission, King Rayfe, Queen Andromeda." His rare use of our titles sealed his sincerity, and even Rayfe gave him a solemn nod.

"There's a second potential front for attack," Dafne put in after a beat of silence, "which would of course be the Dasnarian navy amassing at the barrier."

"Three," Ursula corrected. "There is also Dasnaria itself. The capital is Jofarrstyr, or there's the Imperial Palace inland."

An uneasy silence fell as everyone digested that startling suggestion, the only sound the scratch of Dafne's quill as she wrote that down.

"The Imperial Palace is an impregnable fortress, according to Jepp's reconnaissance," Marskal said in his quiet, unhurried way. "It's some distance from the city, set in a deep lake, which is in turn surrounded by a cleared area inside a dense forest. There are multiple lines of defense and it's impossible to approach undetected. The palace itself can be entered only via a long bridge with multiple guard stations and checks."

"There's the air," Zynda replied, with an unsettling edge to her smile. "Dragons don't require stealth. And dragon fire can repel many guards at once."

Marskal tipped his head at her point.

"The lake is cold and deep," Karyn observed, "but shapeshifters in aquatic form could swim in."

"I'm not sending my people to Dasnaria," Rayfe cut in decisively. "No discussion."

"Would you forbid us?" Zynda asked softly, a light of restless rebellion in her eyes.

I stepped in before Rayfe could reply. "We haven't settled on a course of action. Let's not debate disposition of personnel for something we may not do."

Rayfe flashed me a hot, unsettling glance, but subsided.

"Jofarrstyr would be the more logical target," Marskal continued, as if no one had interrupted his report. "It is a harbor city, heavily populated, expansive, and much less defensible. It is also where the Temple of Deyrr itself resides."

"A large city like that would be full of innocent people," Ami said.

"N'Andana was also full of innocent people," Zyr answered. "Now they're all converts to Deyrr's mind control."

"The Nahanaun Archipelago is home to hundreds of thousands of innocents," Nakoa said in his deep, smooth voice, surprising several people who'd grown used to his taciturn silences. He cradled the sleeping Salena in the crook of one muscular bare arm, managing to look all the more masculine for it. "I would sacrifice the Dasnarian innocents before my own."

"Annfwn, the Twelve Kingdoms, and our allies are all home to innocents," Ursula agreed, still thoughtfully stroking the scar on her cheek. "I'm not an advocate of killing civilians, but I'm also not willing to knuckle under because we're not able to make the hard choices. It makes strategic sense to strike the leadership of all three targets: the high priestess's residence in n'Andana, the Imperial Palace, and the Temple of Deyrr in Jofarrstyr. Cut off the heads and the monsters will die."

"Except the Deyrr creatures *don't* die," Marskal reminded us.

"Maybe they'll die when the high priestess does," Ash offered.

"No." Karyn spoke with firm conviction. "I've been there, and I've felt her control." She rubbed light fingers over the ink-black tattoo ringing her upper arm. I'd cleansed her of Deyrr's taint, but the mark remained as a permanent reminder in her skin. Then she met my gaze. "Andi knows. The creatures are connected to the god, not *her.*"

"I'm afraid Karyn is correct," I said. "Even if we find a way to kill the high priestess and her minions, we risk having their undead creatures plaguing us until we eliminate them, one by one." *And even then their souls would still belong to Deyrr.* "While I understand Zyr's desire to liberate those enslaved beings, it's entirely likely that—no matter the outcome—those people are lost forever."

"Unless there's a way to undo the blood magic," Dafne pointed out remorselessly, no apology in the gaze she rested on me.

"Again with that?" Rayfe snarled. "That's a dead end. We all know Andromeda can't come close to the high priestess's level of power and expertise."

The words echoed in my mind. I'd heard them before, in almost that exact phrasing. Under the guise of soothing Rayfe, I put a hand on his arm.

"Something to consider," I agreed, "for after the war, not as a point of strategy. We can't make decisions based on that possibility." As I spoke, working subtly, I did to him what I'd never done before, not without permission, not outside the intimacy of sex. I began working silver threads of thought into his mind, so slim he shouldn't feel it.

Ursula watched me a beat longer, as if she expected me to say something else, but I was concentrating. "Let's take this in steps," she finally said. "Before we decide the implications of killing the high priestess, before we determine *how* we can destroy her, let's examine if we can get our people to n'Andana in the first place."

"I can find my way back there, and I volunteer to go," Zynda said with grim determination. Marskal made a sound of protest, and she glanced at him. "Any risk would be worth it, if we could kill her and that anathema of an incarnation now."

"We volunteer, too," Karyn said quietly, taking Zyr's hand. "Obviously."

Zynda nodded "I could carry Karyn and Marskal, so Zyr wouldn't be too overburdened."

"Four people against the might of Deyrr?" Rayfe sneered. "No, I forbid it. Zyr nearly died just making the trip itself—he would have without the high priestess healing him—and we're too few as it is to spend our people on an imbecilic errand of this type. This is a circular discussion." He fixed Ursula with a hard stare. "And I disagree, Your Majesty. The *how* you'd kill the high priestess is the critical place to start—and finish. She is immortal and cannot be destroyed. Deyrr is a god with power beyond measure. We cannot hope to even scratch them."

Zyr raised his head, cocked it, then sniffed the air. "I believe I *do* smell cowardice. But not in my cousin Ursula."

Rayfe growled and I narrowed my eyes at Zyr. Zynda looked between us warily. "But Rayfe, you know that we discussed our plan to—"

*"Don't say it,"* I sent to her, praying Rayfe wouldn't overhear it. *"And tell Zyr to shut up."* She widened her eyes fractionally, shrugging a negative. I'd hoped the siblings could talk mind to mind, but apparently not. Oh well, I couldn't have kept this subterfuge going much longer anyway. I knew what I needed to know.

Turning to more fully face Rayfe beside me, I met his shuttered gaze. "What makes you think the high priestess cannot be destroyed? She doesn't seem like all that much to me."

Anger flared in his face, contorting it to someone not him at all. "You said you cannot prevail against Deyrr's superior sorcery. You know that's true."

"I never said that." I spoke loudly and clearly, silencing the several people who began to protest. Not daring to draw on the Heart, I used my own reserves to reinforce the connection, part mental, part magical. "I know no such thing."

"You told me that the high priestess of Deyrr is more powerful than you are," he replied. "Just yesterday—remember? And you said that you're not the sorceress your mother was."

"Oh, I remember. And both of those things are true," I

continued, holding up a hand when the others started to protest. I focused on Rayfe—and whoever else listened through him. Deftly, I slipped my silver threads of control through Rayfe's mind, easing him toward a trance I desperately hoped he wouldn't remember. "Listen to me very closely. Neither of those things means I cannot prevail. I don't need to be my mother, and I don't need to be a more powerful sorceress. Because I have more than myself. I am more than myself."

With ruthlessness and regret in equal parts—crossing a line I'd never wanted to even consider—I snapped my careful net into place, holding Rayfe's mind and will in my grip. It was terrifyingly easy to do. I stared deep into the darkest ocean blue of his eyes—so familiar to me, and grown so foreign. Unreasoning rage glittered there. And fear. Pride, ferocity, the primal feral nature of the wolf, his First Form.

*Don't ever forget that it's a talking animal, and the beast is never far beneath that handsome face.*

The high priestess had said that to Karyn. I'd pulled that scene from Karyn's memory, with her permission, and reviewed it many times. And I'd learned from it.

Like Moranu, the many-faced goddess, I was many in one. I was the descendant of shapeshifters and I also carried the bloodline of the sorcerers who'd created them. My mother had married Uorsin to create this mix, to create me. And now my nemesis had taught me how to use this power of my legacy.

"Andi," Ursula said with insistence, making me realize it wasn't the first time she'd called my name. "What's going on?"

I shook my head minutely. We had to stop talking in front of Rayfe.

Holding his mind in my snare, his thoughts suspended in my grip, I gently extracted the memory of my being there, along with the recent minutes of his life. I asked a staymach bird to fetch one of our attendants, then I sent a mental tendril to

Salena, poking her awake and suggesting that she must be hungry. The formerly peaceful baby awoke with a furious wail, startling everyone. At the same moment, I slipped the threads of control from Rayfe, releasing his will again, counting on the noise and confusion to cover my tracks.

"That's the end of this session for me," Dafne declared, taking her daughter from Nakoa. The Tala girl I'd asked for appeared at Dafne's elbow.

"Nisia will take you to some nearby guest rooms," I told them. "Little Salena can nurse and you both can take a rest." Despite Dafne's cavalier reassurances of Kiraka's healing abilities, both she and Nakoa had begun to look pale and shadowed, the result of a long and tiring labor. That assuaged my guilt a bit.

In the corner of my eye Rayfe blinked in confusion—and consternation. "We're done?"

"Yes," I replied, watching Nakoa and Dafne hasten out, the baby's wails dimming, then abruptly silenced as a door closed between us. "I know you have things to see to."

"I do." He rose, paused when I remained seated. "Which things?"

I nearly crumbled in the face of his confusion, the guilt and shame of what I'd done eroding my resolve. "You, Karyn, and Zyr are going to show Harlan, Ash, and Marskal the recent changes we've made to Annfwn's defenses." That would be nothing Rayfe didn't already know. At least the time would be spent detailing in their minds everything we'd have to change now.

Karyn looked confused and Ash frowned, but Harlan and Marskal immediately rose. They were well-trained soldiers, quick to accept a change in orders.

"Yes, we'll go do that," Harlan said, laying a hand on Ursula's shoulder, but giving me a concerned smile. She nodded absently, her penetrating gaze still on me.

Rayfe still looked puzzled, but he picked up my hand, his thumb stroking over my palm as he used to do, a hint of his old self in the sensual gesture. "I'll see you later, my queen?" He bent and kissed my hand, his lips warm.

A sob rose in me and I quelled it with cold determination. "Yes," I managed to say.

"We planned to discuss… something?" His winged brows drew together.

"Later," I agreed, then said more loudly, for all of them. "We'll reconvene later."

Zyr smiled without humor, tossed an ironic salute in my direction, and they all strode out, striking up a lively argument about defense tactics.

Zynda gave me a thoughtful look. "Do you suppose they'll figure out they should feed him bad information?"

"I hope so," I replied, weariness washing through me as my energies had been depleted. Drawing on the Heart, I refilled my reserves.

"You're pale," Ami informed me. She got up and filled a plate, then slid it in front of me as she sat in Rayfe's chair. "You have to keep eating to sustain your body."

"I know," I agreed, digging in. The food would help—at least to help me feel physically stronger. Nothing could ease the pain of what I'd done.

"Any time you want to explain what just happened would be good with me," Ursula said drily. My mouth was full so I rolled my eyes at her. She snorted, shaking her head.

A blue glow shimmered, settling over the room. "I just shielded this space so we can't be overheard," Zynda explained. "I'm guessing Andi believes Rayfe is being mind-controlled by the high priestess."

# ~ 11 ~

"**I** DON'T BELIEVE it." Ursula sounded outraged.

I wasn't sure if her indignation was on Rayfe's behalf or mine. "Put away your sword." My words came out beyond weary. "This isn't a monster you can slay for me."

She looked taken aback that she had indeed risen and half-drawn her sword. Sliding it back into its sheath, she impatiently pushed back her chair and began pacing. "But we *are* talking about monsters. Mind control, Zynda said. Like the creatures of Deyrr. Rayfe is... *that?*"

"Not exactly the same." I blew out a long breath, finding it ragged, my heart beating erratically. I'd looked into my husband's mind, held him captive to my will, and then taken his memories so he wouldn't know what I'd done. The food sat cold in my stomach, and the baby twisted, sensing my anxiety. I rubbed a hand over my belly, sending him loving and soothing thoughts, but my hand shook.

Even if I could wrest Rayfe's will back from the high priestess—and that wouldn't be as easy as when I'd done it with Karyn, given what I'd sensed just now—I'd have to eventually confess what I'd done. And Rayfe would never forgive me for that profound violation. Even if he and I could find a way to survive this, if we could resolve the differences that had created the chasm between us in the first place, I'd betrayed a fundamental trust. Worse, I'd done to him what the practitioners of Deyrr did to all shapeshifters: harnessed his will and treated him like a lesser being.

Ami poured tea for me and pressed the cup into my shaking hands. "Small sips," she advised, rubbing my back.

"When Karyn and Zyr were taken captive in n'Andana, the high priestess was able to enslave Zyr, and take over Karyn's will." I said, forcing myself to address Ursula's question before she wore a rut in the floor. "She forced Zyr into gríobhth form and had Karyn as a docile, even enthusiastic acolyte."

"I know you all said you have ways of locking a shapeshifter into animal form, but I would've thought Karyn is too stubborn and strong-willed for that," Ursula said.

I shook my head. "That's false thinking. Will has nothing to do with it. It's a fallacy to believe anyone can keep the practitioners of Deyrr out of their minds. Remember what Illyria did at Ordnung—the people and events she made you forget?"

Ursula glowered, hating that reminder of her mistakes, how easily Illyria had clouded her mind, and our father's, with disastrous results.

"Exactly," I said. "And Illyria was a lackey. Expendable. She was nowhere near the age and skill level of the high priestess, who can control shapeshifters and who used Karyn's own wantings against her. She found the cracks where Karyn had emotional wounds and wormed her way through them into Karyn's mind." Just as I'd done to Rayfe. I swallowed more tea against the urge to vomit. "She used Karyn's desire for friends, community, to not feel so alone, to have a purpose, to be loved—and she twisted that very human longing into bonds that chained Karyn's will to hers. Karyn didn't even know that she'd lost herself. She was... happy." My voice broke and I had to set down the teacup lest my shaking sloshed tea over the fluted edge. Rayfe's mother, Garland, had given me that cup, a special nod to my early days as a new bride assimilating to vastly changed circumstances. She'd been only kind and welcoming to me, and I'd done *this* to her son.

"How did Karyn free herself from that?" Ami sounded aghast, and I covered her elegant hand with mine. Love was both Ami's strength and the chink in her armor. She embodied Glorianna's love, but also craved it. She no doubt deeply felt how this would work on her, too.

"She didn't. I did it for her." I held up a hand as Ursula wheeled around at that. "And before you ask, I won't explain how I did it. Suffice to say that it wasn't easy."

"Is Karyn still bound to the high priestess?" Ursula demanded.

"No." I gave her a sour look. "I'm not an idiot, Essla."

"Apologies." She resumed pacing. "So you can eventually free Rayfe with the same method."

*Eventually?* "Yes, I can and will. But it's more complicated than with Karyn."

"I can't wait to hear this," Ursula muttered in such dire tones that Zynda looked wryly amused, still lounging back in her chair.

"She has Rayfe doubly harnessed—via his needs as a person, and also through her control of shapeshifters. It gives her even greater control. She can listen through him, have him speak her words, and she knows what he knows."

"The perfect spy and saboteur in one," Ursula murmured.

"Very true. The high priestess has invested a great deal of herself in controlling Rayfe. She's quite close and actively paying attention. She knows that I'm the reason Karyn broke free of her—she'll fight me to keep Rayfe on her leash."

Zynda gave me a sharp look. "Andi, how do you know that?"

I supposed I'd better tell them this, too. "I want to tell you three—and *only* you three—that I had a conversation with the high priestess yesterday, just before the attack on the training ground."

"*What!*" Ursula nearly shouted. "Danu's freezing tits, Andi. You can't—"

"I'm not your kid sister anymore," I said, cutting off her tirade. "I'm the sorceress standing between your kingdoms—and mine—and their utter annihilation." When she subsided, I withdrew the high priestess's focus stone from my pocket. "This is hers. I… connected to it, and she answered. We met in a non-physical realm and spoke briefly."

Ursula swore under her breath but stayed otherwise silent.

"What did she say?" Zynda asked, gaze deep and somber.

"Mostly taunting and bragging—not unlike some of what you heard coming out of Rayfe's mouth, which is partly what gave her game away. Nothing useful, except that she realized I'd been behind Karyn's defection. The attack came immediately after, so I assumed…"

"That she'd used the taunts to distract you," Ursula finished. "Did she?"

"I'm not sure. I still intercepted the attack before the sleeper spies got very far. What I'm considering now is that she may have distracted me from immediately noticing her taint in Rayfe when he returned. I think she interfered with him when he went downcoast chasing a sleeper spy infestation. One that turned out to be nothing much."

"But he returned changed?" Zynda asked.

"Now that I've taken a step back and am thinking more logically, yes, I can see that he did. I was… too caught up in the trouble between us to notice what I should have."

Ami squeezed my hand, her pansy-blue eyes soft with compassion. "Fights like that, with the one you love, who loves you above all else, can be shattering. I've been there. It's almost impossible to get past the disruption to handle anything else."

I nodded, unable to speak for a moment. I couldn't give voice to the eroding fear that I'd killed whatever love we might've had, by using it against him.

"What emotions of Rayfe's did the high priestess exploit?" Ursula asked. "You and I talked about him being afraid for you, but you didn't say things were this bad."

Needing to pull myself together, I took a deep breath, squeezed Ami's hand in return, and made myself let go. "I didn't think my unhappy marriage was all that relevant. Yes, we've been fighting lately. For weeks now, really. You saw some edges of that. We've both been tense, the pregnancy is an issue, along with his fears for my safety, yes. But when he returned yesterday, he'd escalated. Everything he was unhappy with me about was that much worse. He moved out of my bed into the spare sleeping chambers, and I—" I caught my breath on the sob, surprised and appalled at the loss of control. What a wreck I was. How badly I'd fucked up every challenge the high priestess had thrown at me. I'd played right into her manipulative hands. "That part doesn't matter."

"Oh, honey, it matters." Ami said, still rubbing my back. "I'm sorry. How distressing."

"Yeah," Ursula chimed in. "The hell it doesn't matter."

Zynda listened with interest, raising her brows at me. Ami and Ursula definitely expressed a different perspective than the Tala would have. How Tala I had become in my thinking after all?

"Even before this, he's been so... *distant*," I said, setting down the cup to scrub away the tears that fell of their own accord.

"Does that mean no sex?" Ami asked. "Because sexual release and intimacy are very important—for your physical health, mental wellbeing, and to maintain closeness."

"I really don't need to know about my sister's sex life," Ursula muttered.

Ami rolled her lovely eyes. "Then plug your ears, honey. This matters, too."

"No sex for months," I confirmed, gratified by Ami's horrified expression. Zynda grimaced and even Ursula looked shocked, though that could be for the uncomfortable topic still. "He's afraid it will hurt the baby."

"Has anyone explained to him that sex is actually good for you that way?" Ami demanded, all Glorianna-as-mother in that moment.

"Yes and no." I met Zynda's rueful gaze. "Healer Kelleah is in favor of it, but the more traditional healers—including the one that Rayfe favors—is adamantly against it."

Zynda sighed. "Some traditions among the Tala become so set, so fraught with superstition, that they're practically sacred law."

"I didn't mean to get into these details," I said firmly. "My point is that I can't be sure of anything with Rayfe at the moment because I looked into his head and I can see the high priestess's strings everywhere. It's similar to what she did with Karyn. The high priestess hooked into Rayfe's existing doubts, his anger…"

"Pride," Ursula added.

"Fear," Ami agreed sadly.

"Love," Zynda put in softly, then nodded at my dubious glance. "That's a powerful emotion for her to twist to her purposes."

"But to *what* purposes?" I demanded, knowing full well they didn't have ready answers.

Ursula, however, did answer. "Exactly that—to twist you up. You said it yourself: you are what stands between us and her. You're the one our mother put in place to battle the high priestess and Deyrr. As Ami pointed out, fighting with Rayfe has undermined your foundation. You're kind of a mess."

"Wow, thanks." I wiped my face again, making sure my cheeks were dry, determined to be done with sniveling over my sorry self.

"Understandably a mess," Ami put in with a fierce look at Ursula.

"Also, obviously, Rayfe is King of the Tala," Zynda added. "We've been working on the assumption that Hestar wanted Tala help to tear Deyrr from his throat, and we confirmed that Rayfe will lead the Tala forces, except for Kiraka's select division. What if the Tala *can* be effective in destroying Deyrr? With this move, the high priestess has attempted to nullify or subvert our two most effective leaders for that effort: Andi and Rayfe."

"Hmm." Ursula paused in her pacing. "Thinking over the discussion just now, Rayfe very much wanted to dissuade us from finding n'Andana. He went so far as to forbid his own subjects from looking for it."

Zynda smiled easily. "Fortunately for us, his subjects aren't terribly biddable."

Ursula blew out a breath, rolled her head on her shoulders, and finally returned to sit at the table. "I don't like overruling Rayfe's commands."

"I'm sure he'd be shocked to hear it," I replied drily. "Still, you are Her Fucking Majesty the High—"

"I was mad when I said that," Ami protested. "There's no reason to keep bringing it up."

"Andi is right," Zynda put in gravely. "As Her Fucking Majesty, High Queen Ursula can overrule Rayfe's commands." Ami glared at her.

"He won't like it," Ursula warned us, unnecessarily.

"We already had a terrible fight last night about me not respecting his authority and making decisions without him," I agreed glumly, remembering how I'd cried my eyes out over it the evening before. So many tears—and how it grated that the high priestess had been the one to reduce me to it. That she'd witnessed my flailing and no doubt gloried in it.

"Is that something you and Rayfe fight about regularly?" Ami asked sympathetically.

"Actually no. That's part of why the argument floored me. Rayfe has always respected my opinions and autonomy as queen. It wasn't like him to—" I sat up straighter. "Oh."

"See?" Ursula nodded at me. "Another way for the high priestess to undermine your decision making—and to get you to defer to what she has Rayfe pushing us to do."

Still, it worried me, because there had to have been a kernel of disrespect in his heart for her to make it grow into that ugly monster. How could I know what was real? *I don't know what's real anymore*, Karyn had complained piteously when I freed her of the high priestess's control. I'd have to apologize to her that I hadn't been more sympathetic at the time.

"So," Zynda announced, "since the high priestess clearly doesn't want us to, we should attack n'Andana. Marskal, Zyr, Karyn and I can go as a small strike team."

"It's still a good point that you won't have allies when you get there," Ursula said. "Four of you can't fight all of Deyrr and their minions."

"We don't have to fight *all* of them," Zynda insisted. "Cutting off the head is a valid strategy."

"It won't free all those mind-controlled people and animals, according to Andi," Ursula replied, glancing to me for confirmation.

"Nothing will," I said, "except maybe divine intervention. That magic derives from Deyrr, so either it or a more powerful deity would have to cut that connection."

"But we *can* destroy the incarnation of Deyrr," Zynda said with relish. "I bet dragon fire will melt that thing."

"That might work," I conceded, "but remember it's only an incarnation. Destroying it no more affects Deyrr than killing me would affect Moranu."

"Then you're against this plan," Ursula said, watching me keenly.

"I'm neither for nor against any plan," I explained patiently. "I can't be. Stop trying to get predictions out of me."

"Never," she replied with a wolfish smile. "I figure you can't commit to particular advice, but there's a long history of rulers and military leaders tricking information out of their oracles."

"What I can say," I continued, ignoring her, "is that removing the high priestess won't free her minions—and there's still the cadre of lesser, but still powerful, junior priests and priestesses—but they will be without her direction and ambition. That void would create room for us to act."

"That sounds promising." Ursula considered. "Though melting her with dragon fire can't be all that easy or the n'Andanans would've done it in the first war."

"No—she almost certainly can defend against that. And she'll know we're coming, so we have to factor that into any plan," I said. When Zynda opened her mouth to protest, I cocked my head at her meaningfully. "Even if we keep Rayfe from knowing, if I can sense you, she can, too."

Zynda subsided, unconvinced, but she waved a hand at me

to continue.

Time for me to take the gamble that my suggesting this possibility wouldn't damage the timeline. "I do have an idea. If our people can get to the high priestess, they could 'accidentally' lose the focus stone to her." I waved a hand at the gleaming jewel still lying on the table. "Through it I can get to her, and likely the physical incarnation of Deyrr, also."

"You can do that?" Ursula brightened. "That would be an ideal scenario."

"I'm pretty sure I can, but keep in mind I've never tried this sort of thing before."

"The Star of Annfwn would be even more effective," Zynda said with quiet meaning.

"Yes." I nodded. "Yes, it would."

"But would losing the Star to her be wise?" Ursula asked, frowning.

I laughed. I couldn't help it, though she only frowned more darkly. "No. It isn't *wise* at all. But Zynda is correct. I've worked with it enough that I'm well practiced at channeling magic through it. The Star is attuned to us, to Salena, to you, to those queens in Annfwn who held the Heart over all these years, and to the Heart itself. The Heart is the wellspring, the ultimate reservoir of the power the high priestess believes was stolen from her, and she wants it badly enough that she might ignore the coincidence of it being thrust into her hands."

"The perfect bait and the perfect weapon to turn against her," Zynda confirmed. "I like this plan."

"But she wants the Star because she can use it, right?" Ami asked. "Once it's in her possession, she'll be that much more powerful."

"Very true. But there will be a tipping point, a brief moment when she connects to it—and to me—when I can strike before she's able to use it."

"You slipped into future tense," Ursula noted. "Does that mean you've seen this and it will work?"

I sighed mentally for the slip. "I have seen it, yes." And hadn't been at all sure how such a thing would come to pass, so it was interesting to see those pieces fall into place.

"But there are no guarantees it will work." Ursula nodded to herself. "With those odds, I'm against—"

"Ursula." I interrupted, cutting off that line of thinking. "There are no guarantees. *Nothing* we do is certain to work. I told you before—the odds are crushingly against us. There are simply a few possible actions that have a chance of working. Maybe."

She stared at me, obviously searching for a reply.

"I know," I said. "I wish I could say differently, but that's where we stand. We are at the end of the maze, the final sticking point."

"The one Mother saw coming long ago," Ami said, sounding wistful.

"Maybe our ancestors saw it even longer ago than that," Zynda put in. "The ancient n'Andanans knew this when they took all the magic and put it in the Heart to starve Deyrr of it. And the Tala forebears knew when they fled n'Andana and expanded the barrier from the core of the Heart to encompass enough land to live on. They saw this final conflict coming and planned for it."

"We noticed," Ursula mused, "Harlan and I, when we sailed into Annfwn with you. We always thought the cliff city here seemed so poorly secured, with so many open windows and balconies, so few doors—or even doorways that can be barricaded. But from the sea, from the beach, the cliff face looks like it can be locked down tight, unassailable below a certain level." She glanced at me.

"Yes," I told her. "There are stone wheels our wizards can shift into place, sealing off tunnels below and preventing access to the cliff city above."

"But how long can you withstand a siege?" Ursula asked with quiet meaning.

"That's always the question. Not long. We've been laying in stores, but nothing like, say, Ordnung or Windroven would have. A drawback of living in a fruitful paradise is that food storage isn't a concern."

We were all silent a moment, contemplating that.

"So," Zynda said, coiling up her long, dark hair and sliding a jeweled pin into it to hold it in place, "this is the best plan. Avoid a siege to begin with. The four of us go to n'Andana, 'lose' the Star to the high priestess, and Andi takes her out."

"It sounds so easy, put that way," I murmured.

"We'll need a distraction, so the high priestess doesn't realize our true plan," Ursula said, tapping the ruby in the pommel of her sword. "We'll need to appear to be truly attacking. We need to send aerial troops at least, to appear to be launching an offensive. That will also give us something to discuss in strategy sessions that Rayfe attends, so we can feed her misinformation."

"Misinformation?" I sat up straighter.

"Information we choose," Ursula clarified, then paused. "The high priestess doesn't know, does she, that you're onto her trick?"

A trick. Just a light deception where my nemesis turned my husband against me and broke my heart in the process. "No, she doesn't. She knows I freed Karyn, but with Rayfe, I…" I couldn't confess to them how badly I'd violated Rayfe's mind and trust. "I made sure to cover my tracks."

"Excellent." Ursula's face sharpened with a predatory edge, fully in her element now. Zynda, however, looked at me with a line between her brows, knowing more about what I should and should not be able—and willing—to do. Hopefully she wouldn't guess how violently I'd broken Tala code, and the trust between lovers.

"But I can free him of her influence," I insisted. "It will take more effort than with Karyn, but with some concentration I can…"

Ursula was shaking her head. "Andi, I know that's what you *want* to do—and I don't blame you—but that's your heart talking. We can *use* this. It's the opening we've needed. Through Rayfe we can discern what she wants us to do. Through him, we can feed her misleading information that will give us a fighting chance to win this thing."

"I'm not leaving Rayfe in her control. I'm going to—"

"You're going to tip her off that we're onto her and lose this one edge over an enemy you've freely admitted has all the advantages?" Ursula asked, her voice sharp as a steel blade.

I sagged back in my chair, staring at her, horrified. "You don't know what you're asking of me."

She didn't bend, just gazed at me with resolute command, every inch the High Queen. "I know exactly what I'm asking, and I'm asking it anyway. Please don't make me command it."

"Could *you* do it?" I demanded, but my voice came out ragged. "If it were Harlan?"

"I don't know," she replied evenly. "I would hope that I'd still make the best choice to save my people, maybe even all the world. And if I couldn't, I'd hope that you'd step in and hold my feet to the fire."

I hated that she was right.

"It's only for a few days, at most," she urged me.

Needing the warmth, I poured some tea, and nodded in concession, not trusting myself to speak.

"Thank you. Truly," she said. "I *do* know what I'm asking." When I didn't reply, she bit out a sigh. "All right. Let's make the most of this gambit. The high priestess pressed us not to find n'Andana, to hunker down on our territory, so we'll pretend to do that in front of Rayfe, then appear to accidentally leak information that we're launching an offensive against n'Andana after all," Ursula continued, thinking aloud.

"And we still have the Dasnarians to deal with," Ami reminded her.

"As if we could forget. But I don't see attacking the Imperial Palace or Jofarrstyr as viable options, not with our comparative numbers."

"I don't know why we're not discussing infiltrating the Imperial Palace with stealth," Ami pointed out. "Why not do that, too?"

"Because it's a terrible idea," Ursula replied in a repressive tone. "We tried it once and Jepp barely got out alive. Danu knows, *Kral* barely got out alive."

"But we have friends on the inside now," Ami said sweetly. "And if this Hulda never leaves the palace, then we have to go after her there. If she's truly pulling the strings, we can destroy the entire Dasnarian navy and she'll still be coming for us. If we're cutting off heads, we need hers, Hestar's, and Kir's, too."

"Ami," Ursula answered with some impatience. "To infiltrate the Imperial Palace, we'd need a guide. Jepp had Kral as an escort and a plausible cover. We don't have that anymore. I may have agreed—with serious reservations—to trust Kral for the time being, but I'm not sending the pair of them into Hulda's clutches. From the sound of this woman, she'd happily torture Jepp to make Kral dance to her tune. Believe me, I know things that you don't. Besides, if we have a ghost of a chance against the Dasnarian navy, we need Kral's experience and expertise."

"I wasn't suggesting we send Jepp and Kral," Ami said, all sweetness gone, leaving stern resolve behind. "I could go."

"You… what?" Ursula looked torn between laughter and horror. "No."

"I'm not otherwise useful and I'd make an exceptional spy because nobody expects me to be anything but decorative." She fluttered her lavish rose-gold lashes.

"What about the fact that you don't speak a word of Dasnarian?" Ursula shot back.

"I don't have to. I could go as Queen of Avonlidgh and pretend to be seeking an alliance against my mean, murderous older sister. The world knows I'm officially a widow. I could go under the guise of pursuing this marriage of alliance, if only those big, strong Dasnarian men will protect my delicate self— and my wealthy kingdom with its fertile farmlands and mineral-rich mines. Believe me, they'll find a way to translate that."

Ami had actually managed to strike Ursula speechless. She eyed me, looking for clues, and I shook my head, still raw from her pushing me to essentially betray Rayfe.

"The idea has merit," Zynda stepped in. "Ami could possibly pull it off."

"Or they could figure out that Andi and I would do anything to save our baby sister and use her as a hostage against us," Ursula replied sourly. "No. This is a bad idea."

"It's a good idea," Ami insisted. "You just don't like it."

"You're absolutely right I don't like it. Also, I know you're suggesting this in part because you want revenge against Kir. I'll think about it, but right now I'm saying no."

Ami opened her mouth to argue, but Ursula pointed a finger at her. "No. First steps first. You are right that we have to deal with Dasnaria, but it will have to start with the navy. After all, they're the ones on our doorstep. Battling them can be a plausible distraction for us. If we're engaged in a war on two fronts, the high priestess will be more easily lured into Andi's trap, thinking we're exhausted and getting sloppy."

I nodded judiciously. It could work. "We could also exhaust our resources and actually make sloppy mistakes," I pointed out.

"Yes, but we'll battle their ships, no matter what. We have to fight them, so we might as well pick the time and place to best enhance our overall strategy. Unless you think the barrier will hold?"

"The barrier will be breached, sooner or later," I replied. I'd thought I'd made that clear, but perhaps I hadn't put it baldly enough. At least I could speak freely about that inevitability without Rayfe here to get riled up.

"Because you can't sustain it under concerted attack?" Ursula pressed.

I actually didn't mind the question coming from her, phrased that way, since she didn't assume I was stretched too thin. She truly wanted to assess the underlying problems. "I can sustain the barrier under concerted attack and have done so many times. I say that the barrier will fall because every future shows that happening. I don't know why it falls, but it does. I should be able to hold it, and if I didn't see otherwise in the future, I'd say that I could sustain it indefinitely, with the aid of the Heart. That's what it was designed to do, and it does the job well."

"Hmm." Ursula nodded thoughtfully. None of them seemed interested in voicing the possibilities there—either that the Heart might be compromised in some way or that *I* would. "So, unless something changes, the barrier will hold."

"With one exception. Deyrr has been using that peninsula of Dasnaria to eat away at the barrier like acid. It's thin and brittle enough there that they could potentially punch through, at least long enough for a ship to sail through. But I can and have been holding the barrier intact even there so far, so to my mind that's not the same as the barrier collapsing entirely. Still, if they can punch through, why haven't they? Why not take advantage of a doorway they worked so hard to create?"

Ursula's face got that sharp look, so like the Hawk she used for her symbol. She tapped a long finger against her temple, as if coaxing out the ideas. "Because they weren't yet ready to attack. Because Hestar awaited my reply. But he won't wait any longer. He'll move soon and to his best advantage. Our window of opportunity is narrow indeed, but we can use this. I know we can. We need time to put both strategies into action, to make them dance to our tune. How do we create a delay?" She held up a hand as if we might interrupt her. Ami, Zynda, and I exchanged bemused looks.

"Andi," Ursula said abruptly, startling me, "some time ago you demonstrated the barrier's properties to me by having me walk through it then locking me out. Can you do that on a larger scale—make a hole in the barrier and control its size?"

"I could, yes. It's usually the opposite of what I'm supposed to do, but I can make the barrier permeable selectively."

"Can you make it seem like *they* did it, not us? But at a time of our choosing—a few days from now to coincide with the attack on n'Andana—so their ships enter our waters, say, one by one, as we're ready for them. If we can keep them from overwhelming us with numbers, and employ Nakoa's storm-brewing abilities to hamper them, we might have a chance. We can make it seem they got the jump on us, and manage it so we look pressed to fight them off, but keep the upper hand in truth."

Understanding dawned, along with renewed respect for Ursula's canny mind. "I can. The only factor I can't control is if they punch a hole through it first."

"Aha! Why not retract the barrier past the point where the peninsula intrudes?" she asked.

"Retract it?" I echoed like an idiot.

"Yes." Ursula leaned in. "Pull the barrier back just enough that they no longer have a toehold in it, but keep it close enough that they'll think they do."

"I can't retract the barrier in just one spot. You remember what happened when we expanded it—it's like a globe with the Heart at its center. If I pull it back half a league at the peninsula, I have to pull it back that much everywhere."

Ursula nodded. "I know the implications. All those lands I inadvertently annexed, that were raked with magical havoc when we extended the barrier, that half a league all along the barrier will be affected again, and then exposed. Populations will be divided again. But if we have a hope of standing up any length of time to the Dasnarian navy, we have to be able to control their passage through the barrier."

"Maybe we send out a warning to all those places," Ami suggested. "So people aren't caught unawares this time."

"To the Nahanaun Archipelago, sure," Ursula agreed. "To the places within my rule or those we have diplomatic relations with, yes. But many of the places the barrier passes through are unknown to us. I sent delegations out to follow the barrier's circumference, to explain and open a conversation, but many haven't returned. Not surprising, but still concerning." She raked a hand through her hair, curlier now in the sea air of Annfwn, and the gesture made some bits stand out wildly. "I'll see to it that we map every bit of the barrier—and talk to the people in those regions—but we're talking about an effort that will take years if not decades, and we have to survive this war first."

I sighed and nodded. "We'll need to warn the *Hákyrling*, and the rest of our ships at the barrier, too."

"We'll need more than that," Ursula said slowly, eyeing me in a way I definitely didn't like. "We need to have instantaneous contact—or at least as close as we can manage—with at least Jepp and Kral. If you can talk to the high priestess mind-to-mind, can't you talk to our own people?"

My stomach clenched. "It's a violation. I'd have to do what she does, and it's a line I said before that I won't cross."

"I have to point out," Ursula replied, cool and remorseless, "that because you said that in front of Rayfe, the high priestess believes that you won't, which means you must. We need every advantage, Andi."

I nearly asked her what she wouldn't have me do, but I didn't want to know the answer to that. "I'll send a message to Jepp asking permission for me to go into her head. We can test out the communication by telling them about the barrier move."

"And you can retract the barrier soon?" Ursula pressed.

"It won't be easy, but I can do it." I sighed. "Tonight, at midnight. That gives us time to provide warning, and Moranu is at Her strongest then. I'll need that advantage. It will be good practice, anyway, in case I need to move the barrier again, as a final solution."

"What do you mean?" Zynda asked, looking worried, which she so rarely did.

"If we fail to defeat Deyrr, we cannot in good conscience allow them to be unleashed upon the world," I answered, as I watched Zynda for her reaction. I was saying out loud something I'd only thought about in the solid confines of my own skull, shielded so no Tala could overhear and name me as the ultimate traitor to Annfwn. Their hatred of Salena and bitterness over her betrayal would be nothing compared to what they'd say of her daughter. "Our last resort would be to do what the n'Andanans did: remove magic from the world so Deyrr will starve."

"Well that's not so horrible," Ami said. "Up until a year ago, the barrier only covered Annfwn and the rest of us lived just fine without magic."

"Except we can't allow Annfwn to have magic either," I explained, "or we risk all of this happening yet again. The n'Andanans sacrificed almost everything to confine magic to the Heart, and that was expanded by the Tala ancestors to just enough to live inside—with a sorceress shapeshifter able to access the Heart. If we don't want this to happen again, then I'll have to retract the barrier all the way to the inside of the Heart, and seal it so that no one can ever access it again."

Zynda had closed her eyes, bowing her head. *I won't tell anyone,*" she whispered in my mind.

"Can you do that?" Ami asked, hushed.

"I believe so." I knew I could. I'd seen it. "It could be that this is what I was born to do."

"As a last resort though," Ursula questioned. "Only if all is lost."

"Only if all is lost," I agreed. And it would be only if I had no other choice, because to seal off the Heart that way, I'd have to be inside it—and I'd trap myself there forever.

$$\sim 12 \sim$$

B Y THE TIME I finally left the council chambers, my queen's guard in songbird form swirling around me in bright colors as they tweeted happily of freedom, the sun had climbed to midday. It was Danu's sun now, high, bright and unflinching, the shadows as banished as they could ever be. A few messengers awaited my emergence, along with a smattering of other Tala requiring answers to questions or decisions on pressing issues.

Ursula had said she'd speak to Harlan, Ash, and Marskal about keeping a rotating guard on Rayfe. We'd keep the fact that Rayfe had been compromised to our circle—and her loyal Hawks—for as long as possible. Ami went with her to see about relocating the children to a location Rayfe didn't know about—a severe vulnerability there—and I greatly appreciated my sisters handling all of that.

I couldn't yet face Rayfe—or what I might find in his mind.

Once I dispensed with the immediate issues and deferred the less urgent ones for later—or delegated them to others to handle—I went to the small balcony terrace at the other side of the main cliff walk, overhanging the ocean. Zynda was to meet me there to escort me to meet Shaman, and if she could find Kelleah, Zynda would send her to me.

The balcony terrace was a good location, central and pleasant. On my first full day in Annfwn, after my first intimidating council meeting, where they'd criticized whether I'd ever be good enough to be queen, Rayfe had escorted me to the little table there. We'd lunched surrounded by blooming vines, with the lovely vista of Annfwn all around. He'd been charming, and I'd been dazzled by his powerfully sensual spell—and overwhelmed by my vastly changed circumstances. I'd been so afraid I'd never measure up to the crushing expectations, my mother's ghost haunting me at every turn. I'd felt very much on display, as we drank ambrosial wine and dined on succulent fish.

*They need to see us enjoying the treasures of Annfwn. Seeing their king happy will set them at ease. Seeing their queen will give them hope.* Rayfe said those words when I chafed at the seeming indolence, anxious and uncomfortable. Though Ordnung had been luxurious in its way, crammed with Uorsin's ruthlessly acquired wealth, we hadn't lived softly. Castle Ordnung had been a fortress first and foremost, and we'd lived as soldiers in a war he'd never stopped waging.

I could see that now. And I could see that, even when I hadn't known it, I'd also been at war all my life, with the pitch of it gradually increasing daily. How long ago it seemed that I'd first sat at that table with my new, foreign, and intimidating husband. When my worries had been about Uorsin and Ursula coming after me. About learning to shapeshift and manipulate the magic barrier in even the smallest way. Baby steps that seemed so small in retrospect, so minor.

When had Rayfe and I last sat here to savor the treasures of Annfwn? When had they last seen us happy? Far too long ago. I couldn't be sure when and why that had changed, when I'd begun to lose hope and so had none to give, even in pretense.

The table sat empty. By some tacit agreement—at least, to my knowledge, Rayfe had never made it a royal command— everyone left that little table on its private terrace for our exclusive use. I sat down in the bright sun, almost too hot, so I used a brush of magic to draw a silk awning overhead, suspended from the terrace posts. The staymach birds settled happily all around, singing a sweet song.

"Would you like wine, My Queen?" Nisia asked softly, having slipped up on quiet feet. "Or food?"

How I would love some wine. A lot of it. But I needed to keep my senses sharp. "Tea, please," I said instead. "And food, yes. Whatever is ready—don't go to any trouble." Maybe if I ate even small amounts at every opportunity, the nutrition would gradually accumulate without overloading my stomach. "Are Queen Dafne and King Nakoa KauPo settled?"

"Yes, Queen Andromeda. And the little princess, too. All three ate heartily and are now sleeping."

"Thank you. When they awake, would you send them to me here? And ask Dafne to bring her map of the barrier. I'm also expecting Zynda and Healer Kelleah. Otherwise, please see that I'm not disturbed."

"Of course, Your Highness."

She scampered off, and I took the moment of peace and privacy to cast my mind over the cliff city and the nearby countryside, the sea, and farther out around larger Annfwn. All seemed peaceful—but then, I'd learned that apparent peace could be an illusion, one easy to abruptly and violently shatter. I toyed with the high priestess's jewel in my pocket, the smooth topaz warm to the touch, half-tempted to contact her. I wasn't even sure where the impulse came from, except that I'd love to strike at her immediately. Hatred welled black and bitter in my heart, and I longed to smash her coy face against the stones at my feet. She'd fucked with me and my life, my husband, in the worst perversion imaginable.

I wanted to destroy her for what she'd done. And I would.

But with a clear, cool head.

Making myself let go of the jewel, I continued my mental patrol with a routine check of the barrier, running my mental hands over it, smoothing, strengthening, reinvigorating. As a last step, I visited the festering hole where the peninsula of the Dasnarian Empire invaded the circle under the barrier's protection. It had corroded the barrier a bit more since the day before. This time, however, I didn't spend effort fixing it. I itched to, the wrongness making an almost audible appeal to be rectified, like a sick child crying for help.

But Ursula's strategy was a good one. There were multiple futures where it could work. Not many, and not the majority of them—but strong possibilities. In at least that arena, in the inevitable naval conflict on the far side of the Nahanaun archipelago, our ships had a chance of not being utterly defeated.

Such were my best expectations.

I spent a bit more time reviewing those particular future threads, checking for changes resulting from our decisions today. Those battles had shifted now, mostly in our favor, and—oddly enough—included boats I didn't recognize. Most of the ships in our navy were of Tala design, which is why the harbor and outlying waters at the cliff city in Annfwn were so crowded lately. When Rayfe called the Gathering, he'd also called in every ship we could lay claim to, along with their sailing crews.

The Tala had preserved a long tradition of boat racing and other sorts of sailing tournaments. Another way the Tala ancestors had embedded military-style training in an otherwise decidedly nonmartial culture—again, with an emphasis on defense from an attack coming from the sea.

Out at sea we had the *Hákyrling*, along with a few other ships of Dasnarian design that Jepp and Kral had "appropriated"— mostly merchant ships that had been plying the Nahanaun

Archipelago when the barrier shifted. Fortunately for us, even supposedly peaceful Dasnarian traders prowled the seas heavily armed, so those ships would come in handy, too.

We also had a few—a handful, really—of sailing ships from the other twelve kingdoms. In general, those ships preferred the gentler seas—and plentiful trade—of the eastern and southeastern coasts of the realm. The few we had in Annfwn had been required to sail the long, turbulent, and difficult journey around the Crane Isthmus. Ursula had called in favors for those, and had considered conscripting more, but our merchant ships were not accustomed to battle. They'd be ripe targets and of little help.

My previous visions of the naval battles had included those ships, along with thousands of smaller Nahanaun boats—some sailing ships, but mostly canoes and coracles.

The current vision intensified, gripping me as Moranu's silvery presence took control, showing me what She willed. I saw a battle raging under stormy skies. Heavy rain obscured details, but brilliant flashes of lightning revealed vivid moments.

The composition of the navies had altered. There were the many Tala ships—distinguishable by the sleek, low-in-the-water profiles and airy rigging—and overwhelming numbers of the heavier Dasnarian ships, along with the innumerable smaller Nahanaun craft, but now mixed in with them were many more tall sailing ships like those plying the seas off Elcinea. Most of those, while familiar in design, flew banners I didn't recognize. Others, galleons and smaller ships that belched woodsmoke, weren't like any I'd seen before. I couldn't tell whose side they fought for.

I tried to look more closely at some of the banners. Unfortunately, the visions didn't always yield to changes in perspective—especially when Moranu wanted me to see something and I went in a different direction. Indeed, as I pushed for detail, the stormy battle scene darkened, then dissolved into wisps of smoke. Instead I looked out on the calm sea of Annfwn, all the ships in these waters well known to me, the bright sunshine making me wince.

"Your tea has grown cold," Dafne said, nodding at the pot and plate of food resting on the table. "Nisia said not to disturb you."

"I didn't mean for her to keep you two waiting. My apologies." I nodded to Nakoa, who'd been standing at the rail observing the scene below, a sleeping Salena securely tucked in the crook of his elbow. He nodded back, unconcerned.

"No need to apologize," Dafne assured me. "More visions?"

"Yes. And the tea is easily reheated." I caressed the smooth ceramic side of the pot with my fingers, warming it judiciously with a bit of fire magic. When I poured it into my cup, it steamed invitingly.

"Handy," Dafne noted. "Why can't you do that, Dragon King?"

Nakoa gave her a stern look, but his lips twitched as he came over to brush affectionate fingers through the rich copper and bronze strands of her hair. "Because you would be unpleasantly surprised if my lightning shattered your favorite teapot, little dragon."

"You have a point," she replied drily. "I brought maps, as requested." She indicated the maps and books of notes on the table. "What do you need to know?"

I explained the plan to retract the boundary. Nakoa frowned thunderously, but grudgingly agreed that it was a good strategic move. Dafne extracted metal tools from a lavishly decorated bag, and I watched with interest as she meticulously measured the length of the Dasnarian peninsula intruding through the barrier.

"How far back from the peninsula do you want to retract the barrier?" she asked.

A good question. "Far enough to get clear of Deyrr's influence, but not so far that the Dasnarians will immediately notice."

"Hmm." She studied the map. "Her Majesty will have to send word to pull our ships back, or the Dasnarians will certainly notice when the barrier runs over them. We'll have to count on them staying well back from their side of the barrier—which they're likely to do as they can't otherwise detect it unless they run into it—and create a plausible reason for our ships to move back without alerting them."

"We have a plan to contact them, yes."

"Excellent. Do you think there will be magical storms like the last time the barrier moved?"

Another good question. "I don't know, but probably."

"We'll need a storm at sea then," she said to Nakoa, who nodded. "Lots of that lightning you love so much. So," she returned to studying the map, "just far enough to clear the ooze slick in the water, but the least amount past that, to keep it as subtle as possible."

"If only we knew how far that Deyrr slick spreads out from the rocks. I can sense it via the barrier. Maybe I could try to estimate how big it is," I added, though I wasn't sure how to measure it and convey that to Dafne.

"No need. I have a recent report." She riffled through another notebook, opened it to a page, then made markings around the peninsula, looking back and forth between the notes and her map. "There."

"A report from whom?" I demanded, and she smiled innocently.

"That's on our side of the barrier, remember, and I have spies everywhere." She measured a distance from the ooze border she'd drawn. "You're moving the barrier soon?"

"Tonight at midnight."

She paused in her measuring and notetaking, looking up curiously. "Why midnight?"

"The peak of Moranu's power. I'll need all the help I can get."

Tapping the feathered end of the quill against her cheek, she gazed at me soberly. "How hard on you will this be?"

"Difficult, but mostly I want plenty of power—and any divine assistance I can get—because I've never done anything like this before."

"Except when you expanded the barrier the first time."

I shook my head. "I didn't do that. My magic assisted—and I provided the pathway to the barrier—but Ami's magic amplified the spell, and Ursula's mind guided the position of the barrier. Most importantly, we had the potency of the blood sacrifice of a king as a catalyst."

She frowned a little, intrigued and puzzled. "I don't quite understand."

"They set a match to the bonfire that was the king's death," Nakoa said in his deep voice. "Once the blood of a king—or queen—is spilled into the soil of their realm, it creates powerful earth magic. It only needed a little push from them to take shape."

I nodded at him. "I understand much more about it now than I did then."

"How did you learn?" Dafne's face lit up with curiosity.

"By doing, mostly. Not everything is in books," I teased.

"Hmm." She looked between us, then shrugged. "One day I'd love to interview you in depth, record some of this arcane information."

"There are good reasons not to write some things down."

"I disagree. Not writing things down is how critical information is lost."

"How about we debate that if we survive the war?"

"There is that." Returning her focus to the map, she checked her measurements once more, then marked the equivalent distance all along the circumference of a circle drawn in dashed lines that must represent the barrier. Withdrawing another instrument, she checked a setting, then drew a new arc of circle inside the old one.

"I'll have to reconfigure the big map, too," she mused as she drew, "but this handles at least Nakoa's kingdom. It looks like the barrier retraction will affect only the tail end of the archipelago—this chain of islands here. Particularly these three. Those should be the only ones that the new barrier position will intersect."

Nakoa peered over her shoulder, nodded. "I shall inform their neighbors, too, as a happy precaution, and give orders that all boats along the path find safe harbor from fearfully stormy seas." He sat, carefully transferring the bundle of sleeping baby to the crook of his other arm, and began writing a letter.

"How accurate is this map?" I asked Dafne.

"Very," she replied giving me an owlish—and perhaps slightly offended—look. "My data are excellent."

"I don't doubt you, but how do we know so precisely how far into our side of the barrier that peninsula and the surrounding ooze extends?"

"Because we've charted it. Look," she angled the map to show me the fine grid lines and numbers at each juncture. "I learned some of this from Shipmaster Jens and added to it with information in the library. Once you have a system in place, it's quite simple to measure the size and position of landmasses and their relative position to each other. From that you can know locations on the surface of the water, too."

It didn't seem simple. "It looks to me like your figures are within a ship's length."

"A bit less," she agreed with cool confidence. "I actually know with even greater accuracy than that. I allowed room for error."

"Room for error," I echoed.

"While I know my figures precisely, I don't how accurate your sorcery is—or what landmarks you plan to use—so I allowed for some distance on either side of this projected location." She tapped the new barrier circumference with her quill.

Landmarks. How would I know how far to pull the barrier? I suppose I'd thought I would simply pull until I didn't feel the Deyrr taint anymore. But obviously that wouldn't work as I knew full well the barrier retained the taint for some time. "I don't know either," I admitted.

"May I make a suggestion?"

"Please."

"How well do you know the Annfwn coastline to the north—even into the Northern Wastes?"

"Quite well." Not many Tala lived in that frigid realm, but those few with First Forms that preferred cold temperatures and icy landscapes thrived there best. What I hadn't traveled in person, I'd traversed in my mind.

"Perfect." She pulled out another map, this one showing much more of the world on a single sheet, everything shown on a much smaller scale. "Give me a moment," she muttered. She extracted a new tool, this one with two arms attached by a spring. Consulting her first map, she marked the distance off the Dasnarian peninsula we'd decided should be the location of the smaller barrier, then noted it on the bigger map. Setting one point of her instrument on that mark, she opened the hinge to put the other point down.

Right on the Heart of Annfwn.

I nearly jerked in surprise, and must've made some sound because she glanced up at me, then at Nakoa. "Nakoa, would you mind fetching my other book bag?"

He grunted, finished the line he wrote, and His Highness King Nakoa Kau Po strode off to fetch her bag. I would've been amused, if I weren't so alarmed that Dafne knew exactly where the Heart lay hidden, deep under the sea. Exactly under the center point of her circle.

"Sorry," she said, quickly and quietly, "but it's simple geometry. The barrier is a globe projected by the Heart—that much has been abundantly clear—and thus the Heart is at the center of its circumference. I figured out where it must be a long time ago. And I've told no one, I promise."

At least she'd marked it with a simple dot, no label. And I trusted Dafne. Her quest for knowledge would get her in trouble some day, however. "Just remember there are good reasons the Heart's location has been secret all this time." I raised my brows at her and she realized the import of my warning, nodding somberly. I studied the map, her perfect circle encompassing so much more than I'd realized. "So, tell me, do you know all the lands the barrier passes through?"

She smoothed a hand over the far south and east where some landmasses had been lightly sketched in. A few had labels, fewer still details of coastlines, cities, and other geographical features—more were mostly suggestions of lines. "I don't need to be familiar with those lands to know where the barrier goes, or where it will be when you move it. See?" She affixed her quill to one end of her instrument—the end not on the Heart—by way of a spring clasp. Holding the pin firmly on Heart, she spun the instrument so the quill drew the new circle all across the map of the world, just inside the previous circle. "See? Simple geometry."

I stared at it, more dumfounded than I should've been. "And this is a guess of where the barrier traverses?"

"It's an accurate depiction," she corrected. "Everywhere my people have been able to corroborate, the barrier exists in actuality within a forearm's length of my predicted location. And that error, frankly," she confided, "is most likely human failure to measure precisely. Not from my calculations."

"Well, yes. It doesn't bear thinking that your calculations could be imprecise," I said, deadpan, and she wrinkled her nose at me.

"At any rate, this is what I suggest," she said, tapping the map where the paired circles crossed the northern Annfwn coastline. "Instead of retracting the barrier out at sea, do it here: This landmark would be perfect. Then you can better 'see' what you're doing."

"That's rather brilliant," I said, bemused that it hadn't occurred to me.

"Thank you. High praise."

My eyes strayed back to those shadow lands, the ones barely sketched in, inside the barrier with us. "Has Ursula seen this?"

"No. I told her she could see it *after* she deals with Deyrr and Dasnaria. The last thing we need is for her to be fretting about being responsible for these other lands and sending diplomatic delegations to them. Time enough to save the rest of the world after we've saved ourselves."

"Most pragmatic."

"Thank you. And thank you, Nakoa," she said as he returned with the bag. He dropped a kiss on the top of her head and sat to review his letter.

I still couldn't stop looking at the map, at those distant lands in the southeast. Some intuition about them tickled the back of my mind. "May I see something?"

"Of course." She rotated the map for me.

I traced the coastline of one large continent, one with outlines only and very few details of the interior, then smoothed my fingers inland. That intuition warmed, as if the map itself emanated heat here, a sense of Danu's bright light. I peered at the neat lettering uncertain how to string the unfamiliar sequence of letters into a sound. "What is this place?"

"Chiyajua," she replied immediately, having been watching with intent interest. "Where you have your fingers is a region called Nyambura."

A great river had been marked as running through Nyambura, ending at a delta on a far ocean, with a city marked there.

"Chimto is the delta city," Dafne told me. "If the river has a name, we don't know it. Actually, we don't know much about Chimto except the name. This place—" She tapped a smaller town on the coast closest to the Port of Ehas. "This is the harbor city of Bandari. Ships from Ehas put in there from time to time, which is why we know anything about this place at all. Why are you interested?"

"I don't know," I replied absently, still trying to absorb what the buzz of intuition might mean. "Are there elephants here?"

"Elephants?"

From the surprise in her voice, I might as well have asked if Moranu's moon swam in that river. Dafne recovered quickly though, with her agile mind and lively curiosity.

"I'd want to double-check my sources—the relevant natural histories in the library at Nahanau—but there are elephants here, in Halabahna." She indicated another barely sketched continent well south of Dasnaria, then laid a straight edged instrument across it and over to Chiyajua. "The latitude is approximately the same, so it's possible. Because elephants require a particular climate," she explained when I blinked at her, "so there's a greater likelihood of a similar climate occurring on another continent at the same latitude, though there's no guarantee."

"This is what comes of having a wife who lives in the library," Nakoa rumbled, ruffling Dafne's hair with affection, showing a rare smile. "Little Fierce Lena is waking and will demand your loving attention soon."

Dafne began packing away her instruments. "Do you need the map still, Andi?"

"No, I have what I need. Thank you." At least as far as the map was concerned.

Dafne rolled it up with the other maps, assembling everything into neat packages. They both rose, Nakao giving the indeed fussing baby a thick finger to mouth. She gazed up at him with wide, deep blue eyes, and I realized I hadn't seen their color before. Tala eyes in a brown Nahanaun face. An image came to me of her as a young woman, rich caramel brown hair tumbling around a face with Nakoa's broad cheekbones, dominated by those deep blue eyes. Rain and lightning lashed around her and she laughed, arms upraised as if conducting the music of the storm.

"Is everything all right?" Dafne asked me, concern etched between her brows. She looked at her daughter, though, and I knew she meant with young Salena, not me.

"Yes," I reassured Dafne and Nakoa, who'd begun to frown also. The wages of being a sorceress: people always watched you for the least hint of how events would turn out. "I saw your daughter in the distant future as a young woman. Fierce, proud—and apparently she has your gift for storm-bringing," I told Nakoa.

His face broke into a wide smile, like the sun breaking through clouds, and he pressed a kiss to his daughter's forehead. "Of course she does."

"A certain future?" Dafne persisted, however. "Not just a possible one?"

I mentally sighed. "There are no certain futures, but yes—according to my data, which are very accurate—this seems most likely."

She made a face at me. "Funny. But I ask because… well, some of the ways you talk about us losing this war, of Deyrr taking over the world, makes it sound like there'd be nothing left. After."

I understood what she asked and debated how—or if—to answer. "If we lose the war itself, there are ways to defeat Deyrr. I have a contingency plan."

She glanced around, making sure no one listened. "As the n'Andanans did before us."

I nodded, appreciating her quick mind more than ever.

"I'm glad you've said so," she added. "That solution—extreme and last resort though it may be—had occurred to me also, and I'd considered mentioning it to you. I wasn't sure how the idea would be received, so you've laid at least those concerns to rest."

Salena finally decided Nakoa's finger wouldn't produce anything to sate her hunger, and she let out a frustrated wail of demand.

"Here now, little Lena." Dafne traded her things for the baby, cuddling her daughter. "Let's go feed you."

"You could nurse out here," I said. "The Tala aren't much concerned for modesty in general, you know, and especially not nursing." Once babies were born and healthy, the Tala loved them. They reserved all their superstition for before that point.

She grimaced. "I know. Maybe I'll get there, but for the time being I'll stick to privacy." She yawned massively. "Besides, it's a good opportunity to nap since she falls asleep once her tummy is full."

I smiled at the tenderness in her face, the child in my womb turning and stretching. I could wish that my visions of his future were as clear—and as promising—but even for a sorceress, such wishes are mostly wasted effort. Perhaps because we know better than anyone how rarely things turn out as we wish.

# ~ 13 ~

K ELLEAH FOUND ME next. She arrived so hard on the heels of Dafne and Nakoa's departure that I suspected she'd been discreetly lurking nearby.

"Your Highness," she called by way of greeting, striding up purposefully. She moved with the vitality of a woman with many things to do, but in a soft, almost dancing way. Her colorful dress swirled around her earth-mother's body, all of her bouncing with each step—and it made me smile just to see her.

She opened her arms to embrace me, so I stood, letting her enfold me. Kelleah's hugs aren't perfunctory—she holds onto you for a while, her abundant affection suffused with healing energy, even when she's not actively healing you—so I relaxed against her ample bosom, enjoying being held. It felt like being mothered, except I didn't much remember what that felt like. "You're tired," she murmured, stroking my hair.

I huffed out a sigh. "I'm beginning to think that's my name, everyone keeps saying that to me."

She laughed, finally releasing me and sitting, but keeping my hand in hers, a steady trickle of vitality flowing from her and filling all my empty places. "I won't tell you not to do all that you're doing—I'm sure you have plenty of people to tell you that, and we all know we're depending on you to do those things—but do keep in mind that you're only mortal. I can also tell you that the pregnancy is going well, but I know that you're sorceress enough to monitor that yourself. So why did you want to see me?"

Abruptly I realized I had no idea what to say. My original plan of getting Kelleah to intervene with Rayfe no longer applied. Knowing that Rayfe was compromised by the enemy—and not just being difficult, or moody, or overprotective—changed everything. "I promised Rayfe I'd have you check on me is all."

She gave me a knowing look. "Old crusty Vanka has been bending his ear with her caterwauling about sequestration?"

Despite everything, I laughed, some of the tightness around my heart loosening. "Of course. I think Rayfe would've packed me off up the coast by now if I weren't needed here." Or would he—how much of that was him and how much of it the high priestess trying to get me away from the cliff city?

"Vile custom." She snorted disdainfully. "I look to you to set a new fashion among the Tala women. Sending them off to live in caves where they have nothing better to do than brood and worry serves no one. Except maybe letting the fathers off the anxiety hook. I hope you and Rayfe will set a new example there, too."

"I'll do my best," I replied, thinking it doubtful any of the Tala would follow *my* lead, presuming that I—and Annfwn itself—survived the war.

She didn't miss that I didn't include Rayfe in my reply. "Is our king being difficult?" she asked in a gentle voice, peering at me knowingly.

I nodded, not trusting myself to reply. She'd know if I lied to her.

Kelleah narrowed her gaze. "Specifics, please. I can't help you if you don't trust me."

Oh, wonderful. As if I hadn't confessed this painful information enough. "He moved out of our bed," I said, hoping that would be enough for her to chew on.

"Ah." Kelleah squeezed my hand, comforting and earnest, then shook her head. "Men. I'll talk to him, all right?"

"Thank you," I said, suffusing the connection between us with my gratitude. I doubted Kelleah could do much against the high priestess's grip on Rayfe, but I appreciated her willingness to try. "I love him so much," I added, impulsively, and quite before I'd formed the thought to say so.

She put her other hand on top of mine, holding my hand in both of hers, warm green gaze steady on mine. "Of course you do. And he loves you. The love between you two will be the stuff of legends. I believe in that."

Though I was too choked up to say so, I could only hope that would be true. And that the legend wouldn't be a tragic one.

I SAT THERE only a few moments after Kelleah left before Zynda arrived, Shaman with her. Belatedly hopping to my feet, surprised enough to be awkward, I inclined my head in formal welcome. "Shaman. How blessed am I that you came to me."

He grunted in agreement, eyeing me askance, his Tala blue eyes almost black from performing the rites of Moranu. Without access to the Heart, Shaman and his fellows used other ways to amplify and focus magic—methods that also bleached their hair white. Among a wild people, Shaman and his fellows were the wildest. They scorned human vanity, excising the habits of childhood, so they never bothered with niceties like unsnarling hair or manifesting with clean garments when returning to human form.

I'd met him first on the blood-soaked battlefield below Windroven when he married me to Rayfe. Now, as then, the full moon silver disc of his office rested at his collarbone, and the Sword of Moranu rode at his side. He wore loosely connected strips of fur for clothing and his white hair fell in knotted ropes around his shoulders, braided with carved stones significant to Moranu, along with teeth, claws, scales, and feathers. All of it was emblematic of the rites of Moranu where Shaman and the others cut off parts of their animal selves, wearing them as totems on their human forms.

The first time Rayfe had explained this particular Tala cult, I'd been horrified. I'd always been drawn to Moranu's quiet darkness—never fond of the pink sweetness of Glorianna or the harsh taskmistress that was Danu—but this savage aspect of the moon goddess had repelled me.

Somewhere, deep in my mind, Moranu growled in quiet disappointment. Naturally the many-faced goddess wouldn't care for me embracing only the aspects of Her that I found comfortable.

"So, Salena's daughter comes crawling for advice," Shaman muttered, almost to himself. "The end times must indeed be nigh."

I looked down at my feet solidly on the stones of the terrace, making a show of it, then folded my hands and lifted my chin regally, very glad that I wore my crown and my mother's rubies. "You have been long out of polite society, Shaman," I replied coolly, "if you've forgotten what crawling looks like."

He grunted again, which could've been a laugh, then eyed Zynda. "Go away."

Unoffended, Zynda smiled broadly, then gave me an elaborate curtsey, clearly just to annoy Shaman. "I'm off to deliver a message," she told me, and I knew she meant to the *Hákyrling*. "You know how to reach me."

She became a hummingbird, flew up into the sky, then exploded into dragon shape. Magic oscillated as she changed mass so hugely and so rapidly, ripples flowing outward. Landing on the beach below, she waited briefly as Marskal climbed on to her back, then took off again.

Shaman was eyeing the scene with a mixture of pride and sourness. "Never enough humility, that one."

I raised one eyebrow. "I suppose the teacher must possess the quality to pass it along."

"Not true," he countered, "but well played. So, Salena's clever daughter, you want me to interpret Moranu's will for you?"

Covering my surprise, I sat and poured myself tea. "Did Zynda say so?"

He sat and helped himself to my cup of tea, draining it. "She didn't have to. I already know that you're not listening to Moranu."

"I listen," I replied, a bit stung. Nisia approached, ready to fetch more tea, but I waved her off.

"You don't know *how* to listen," he retorted. "Not your fault, raised among mossbacks like that."

"I'm so relieved to hear that."

"You have your mother's spine, that's certain. Don't make her mistakes. Salena tried to handle everything on her own."

Seemed like I'd been hearing that a lot. "All right." When he didn't say more, I asked.

"What does the voice of a goddess in my mind sound like?"

"Like your own conscience."

"That's hardly helpful."

Shrugging elaborately, he grinned with feral teeth. "You want helpful, go be an acolyte of Glorianna."

I reined in my temper and tried another tack. "What is Moranu saying that I'm not hearing?"

He grunted, this time a sound of approval perhaps, as he toyed with a desiccated fox paw dangling from his shoulder. "All deities require sacrifice."

"Moranu wants me to shift into fox form and cut off a paw?"

Shaman didn't appreciate my sarcasm. "Moranu *wants* nothing, you stupid girl. The goddesses don't have desires the way mortals do. *We* must make sacrifices to communicate with the goddess. It's our failing, not Hers. We must create a wound in order to open a portal, to reach through to Them."

A chill crawled up the back of my neck. That sounded very like how I'd described the way Deyrr's magic accessed our minds.

Shaman nodded, as if reading the thought. "You're going to need Moranu's help, and she can't do that if you lock Her out. Offer the sacrifice and She can come into you, show you the way."

"How do I know what sacrifice to offer?" I was proud of myself that I asked the question evenly, without quaver.

"Your firstborn child is the traditional choice," he answered, not entirely without compassion. "Fortunately, you seem to have one to offer."

I froze, simultaneously on fire and frozen. "I'm not killing my son for Moranu." I hissed the words, feeling the lion's claws rise to the surface.

He laughed, stoking my outrage and fury. Magic gathered around me, stirring my hair, and he met it with a dark, blood magic of his own. Leaning forward, completely unafraid, a fetid, animal odor wafting from him, he bared his teeth at me. Fangs, all of them. "Moranu doesn't want your son's death. There are plenty of dead. She wants his life."

"I don't understand what—"

"Figure it out, Salena's daughter, but do it fast. And stop prancing around the sunlit edges of who you are. Moranu is the many-faced goddess."

"I know that."

"Do you? Seems to me you're trying to pick and choose. If you want the power that is your birthright as avatar of Moranu, you must embrace all of Her, every face—not just the pretty bits." He stood. "Good tea."

And he vanished. Apparently.

Able to track the magic of his movements, I followed the tiny gnat he'd become as he zipped away. A nicely dramatic trick, though not one I cared to emulate, even if I could shift into something that tiny.

Needing to sort my thoughts, I went to the railing, leaning over it to survey the sights as I also cast my mind over the cliff city and beyond, letting habit guide my mental patrol. All seemed peaceful, with no intruders tripping the various snares I'd laid to alert me.

The harbor teemed with busy action, supplies going out to ships, people and animals climbing the rigging to perform various checks. The level of activity had increased, a sure sign that Ursula was implementing her initial steps to escalate our preparedness.

Farther out, several ships engaged in a mock battle, charging at each other and wheeling away. Tala wizards must be working with them, judging by the puffs of magical colors sparkling into the sky. I leaned farther over the balustrade, observing the guards at the base of the cliff face, ready to barricade the entry to the tunnels below and access to the city above, should we be attacked.

How were they keeping Rayfe occupied? I desperately wished I could discuss Shaman's advice with him, but even if that wouldn't be feeding critical information to Deyrr, I wouldn't have been able to talk to Rayfe about our unborn child, and certainly not in terms of sacrificing him to Moranu.

*There are plenty of dead. She wants his life.* What did that mean? I'd always known that any child of mine and Rayfe's would be born to a life of duty, as heir to Annfwn. It wasn't something I wished for them—and nothing I could save them from, not unless I walked away from my own duties and obligations. Would a life of allegiance to Moranu be that much worse?

Maybe.

Most of all, it didn't feel like my choice to make—and yet, I might have to. I seemed backed into a corner at every turn, forced to stack up the value of the people I loved against the fate of an entire world. Perhaps Uorsin and Salena had been the smart ones, to isolate themselves from everyone. A sobering thought.

No matter what, however, I was determined to avoid Rayfe until I departed for the Heart in a few hours. I certainly couldn't tell him where I'd be, lest the high priestess discover our plan or track me to the Heart's location. I also didn't want to outright lie to him or deceive him in any way—more than I already had.

I wouldn't be able to keep Rayfe in the dark forever, and there would be no getting around how angry he'd be with me, but if I could at least plead lack of opportunity to tell him, that would be a mitigating factor for my side of the inevitable argument.

The irony wasn't lost on me that I seemed to be forever thrown between longing for Rayfe and violently avoiding him.

Brooding was getting me nowhere, so I went to find Ursula.

She was busy with Harlan, devising a strategy for engaging the Dasnarian navy and planning defenses against any attacks. Harlan confirmed that they'd arranged with Meg, along with Zyr and Karyn's squadron of guards, to relocate the children yet again. It was a risky move—if Rayfe found out, the high priestess might know we were onto her. But it was a much greater risk to leave the children vulnerable to her.

Rayfe was training with Tala warrior groups, in the company of several of Ursula's most trusted Hawks. They knew to keep him focused on that, and to notify Harlan of any trouble. Theoretically, the high priestess couldn't learn much there that she didn't already know.

Zynda and Marskal had indeed flown to take a missive to the *Hákyrling*, telling them to start pulling our ships back from the barrier once Nakoa's storm began. He'd start the covering rainfall at sunset, gradually intensifying the storm as midnight approached. By the time I moved the barrier and incited the magical aftereffects, they should be largely disguised by the tempest.

"I told Jepp to be prepared for your mental contact," Ursula added, frowning at a map Harlan handed her.

"Excuse me?" I replied, a bit sharply, because she looked up.

"As we discussed," she said, setting the map down. "You said you could go into someone else's mind and speak to them."

"Yes, but we *discussed* asking permission."

She waved that off and picked up the map again. "Jepp is an excellent scout and a disciplined warrior. This is a critical link in our communication. She may not be officially a Hawk any longer, but she'll do as I ask."

"As you command, you mean."

She made a note on the map, then handed it back to Harlan, who studiously examined it, pretending he didn't hear us. Ursula steepled her fingers and leaned her chin on them. "What's the problem, Andi?"

"You don't order someone to allow their mind to be invaded by another person, Essla," I ground out. "That's an invasion of the most intimate privacy there is."

"You've done it before," she pointed out.

"With my husband, and with permission." As I said it, I felt my moral high ground crumbling.

"Even this morning?" She showed no remorse, sliding her argument through the chinks in my armor, neatly skewering me.

"You know that was different."

She nodded. "I do know that, because this is war and we're fighting an enemy with no such scruples. If we want to win—or escape this scenario with something less than utter defeat—then we must abandon some of the niceties."

Ursula's words uncannily echoed Shaman's. *You must embrace all of Her, all the faces—not just the pretty bits.* "I like Jepp," I said, realizing that the comment would sound random.

But Ursula seemed to understand. "I like Jepp, too. She has a clear head and good boundaries. She can handle this, Andi. That's one reason I chose her. Let her be good at her job."

I nodded, too, but vaguely. "This is a line I thought I'd never cross."

"I know. Blame me, if you need to. That's my job—to push you all to your limits, and beyond. It's necessary, Andi."

"I know." But did I? "I'm going to the breakwater for a while. Let me know what Jepp says."

"She'll say yes," Ursula replied crisply, giving me a level look. "Make contact with her when you're ready."

I SPENT THE next few hours on the breakwater, tracking futures until my head ached. Then I switched to looking through the eyes of northern Tala, verifying my landmark for the new barrier position. Then I returned to my lonely bedroom, changed out of my fancy dress, jewelry and crown, and napped for a few hours to build up my strength.

When I emerged—after first checking to make sure Rayfe hadn't returned to our rooms—I went to the window to do my habitual scan that all remained well. I still had time to spare. Traveling to the Heart of Annfwn requires very little preparation. Part of why this last remaining font of magic has remained so well hidden all these centuries—except, perhaps, from clever but discreet librarians who understand geometry—is because it's deceptively simple to access.

As long as you're a shapeshifter capable of taking multiple different forms over a short space of time.

Also, I didn't have to be there precisely at midnight. There's no particular magic to the stroke of midnight, no matter what the stories say. It's just that Moranu's power waxes greatest at the farthest point from her sister goddesses. Just as Danu is strongest at the bright light of high noon, and as Glorianna holds sway at the twin cusps of day and night, Moranu belongs to the darkness and shadows.

If I had time for it, the ultimate time for any sorcery would be in the middle of the night during the fullest of the new moon. But a new moon, like the full moon, occurred once a month— and that wasn't now. Also, though the new moon, again like the full moon, truly lasts about seventy-two hours, having the exact peak occur in the middle of the night is even more rare. The Tala shamans and wizards chart that assiduously for their rites.

One advantage, at least, of inheriting my mother's sorcery and having access to the Heart, was that I didn't *need* the magical boost the others did. It would be nice, but it would also be nice if the high priestess drowned herself in the sea.

So, I figured on getting to the Heart a couple of hours before midnight, which meant leaving an hour before that. I considered leaving even earlier, but the Heart could feel like a prison, a sealed bubble that trapped me away from the world.

Which is why I tried not to contemplate the last resort solution too long. An eternity in that... I shuddered and pushed the thought away.

"Andromeda." Rayfe's voice behind me almost made me jump out of my skin. I whirled, heart pounding furiously. "You're still awake. You waited up for me. Thank you."

He smiled at me, eyes lighting with affection and sensual promise, with that hint of a wicked edge to it that I'd always found so appealing. I risked a quick brush of his thoughts and detected nothing of Deyrr. That told me nothing, however, as I hadn't sensed anything like that from him before either. The high priestess had been terribly clever in leaving little trace of her work.

Rayfe prowled toward me, the natural predator, sexual and gorgeous. I still wanted him, craved his touch—and I couldn't let myself lower my guard. He might be himself for the moment, but for how long?

"Ah, no," I made myself say. "I was just going out."

Stopping a formal distance from me, his smile faded to something more tentative. "I thought we were going to talk."

Oh, Moranu curse it, I'd forgotten where he'd mentally left our argument this morning. Because, of course, I'd wiped his memory of what came after. "I don't have time right now. I have to go do some things," I said, not quite able to meet his eye. "I only stopped by for a bit."

"You have things that must be done in the middle of the

night? You know you need adequate sleep, Andromeda. Now more than ever."

"I also have tasks to take care of, now more than ever. I can sleep later."

I started to slip past him, but he caught my arm. We stood there a moment, facing opposite directions, looking past each other, my arm caught in his gentle grip. All I had to do was turn and I could be in his arms, something I wanted—no, needed—with a physical ache.

And couldn't afford.

"Are you avoiding me, Andromeda?" he asked quietly.

*Yes.* "No. I've been busy."

"Too busy to talk to me?"

I should say yes. I should cut him off and say I didn't want to talk to him. I took a deep breath to say so... but I couldn't hurt him. "Now's not the time."

"Then when?"

Moranu, I wished I knew the answer to that. This situation was simply unsustainable.

When I didn't reply, he took a quiet, determined breath. "I know you're angry with me, and I deserve that. This morning... I can't account for my behavior." A wealth of emotion made his voice uneven, ragged regret coming from him that I found it nearly impossible to resist. This was all him. I didn't know how it worked, the high priestess's influence and control, but surely she couldn't guide every word and gesture. Her attention had gone elsewhere. But I still couldn't speak to him honestly, because she almost certainly could read his memories when she returned to his mind.

"We both said angry things," I replied. "No need to resurrect them. Let's put it behind us."

"I don't want you thinking that I despise you." He turned to face me, turning me with hands on my bare arms, stroking. The deep blue of his eyes caught the gold of the lamplight, like a harvest moon glinting off a tranquil sea. "I love you, but more than that—I admire you. You know that. How many times have I told you so? And I've always, always believed in you, even when you, yourself did not. Remember?"

"I remember." My voice came out in a whisper.

"I told you in the very beginning that you could speak to me of your thoughts—and you've never shied from doing so. Even when I didn't like what you said." He tried a smile, but I couldn't make myself return it. "Won't you talk to me now? We've never not been able to talk things out."

He sounded so humble, so hurt and bewildered, that I nearly caved. I'd have to give him something. Karyn had said she'd felt like she was losing her mind. What if Rayfe tore his own sanity apart, trying to reconcile the disparities between his own thoughts and what the high priestess put there? I'd have to forge some kind of truce between us until I could rid him of her taint. Ursula truly did not know what she asked of me in letting this horrible situation continue.

"I hate what's happened to us," I said, a tremble in my voice. "The distance… You hurt me." That cursed distance that created an opening for the high priestess's opportunism. Maybe if our marriage hadn't been already broken and bleeding, she wouldn't have been able to scavenge the bones to make her puppet.

Rayfe nodded. "It's my fault. I know that. I've been…" He took a breath and set his jaw. "I'm so sorry, Andromeda," he breathed, "that I said you were acting unhinged. You're not, but I have been."

"No…" I protested, but without vigor.

"I have no excuse. All I can say is that I love you so much."

He swallowed hard, eyes shimmering with unshed tears. "I know I haven't been reasonable, but if I lost you, the world would turn to ash."

"And our child…" He slid his hands down to my wrists, holding them out and dropping his gaze to my pregnant belly. Making himself look, but then his steely expression softened. "How can I love him so much already? All these feelings—I wasn't prepared for this. I didn't know I'd be so torn."

I almost couldn't speak through the tears rising to clog my own throat. "I understand," I managed to say. "Zynda explained. I know it's hard."

He met my eyes again, a rueful half smile on his beautifully carved lips. "She explained that I'm an idiot?"

Now I did laugh a little. How I loved him. How I'd missed this. "Basically, yes."

He sobered. "That excuses nothing, though. I let you down. I let you believe that I don't want you, that I don't want this."

"No, I always knew that you want this," I said, but the tears had spilled over and my heart ached like it might break in half. "It's all right," I managed to add.

Rayfe lifted his hands to my cheek, wiping the tears away. "It's not all right. Not even close. But I want to make it up to you. Never, ever doubt how much I want *you*, my queen."

He slowly closed the distance between us, brushing my lips with his. So sweet. So full of love, rich and full. I gasped a little at the sheer humming pleasure of his touch, of the returned flow of love I thought I might never feel from him again. He gathered me close, deepening the kiss, running his hands over me in exactly the way he knew I loved. And I arched against him, purring like a well-fed cat. He trailed kisses along my cheekbone, taking my earlobe in a light, teasing bite that sent a bolt of arousal straight down my spine, fountaining in my sex. My body knew his so well that I opened like a flower to him.

"Kelleah talked to me," he murmured in my ear.

I made some inquiring humming noise, my mind whirling with desire that crowded out thought.

"She wasn't afraid to tell me I'm an idiot. She said what you did—that it's good for us to be together, that it won't hurt the child."

"What?" I opened my eyes, heavy lidded as his wickedly clever mouth worked its magic on my throat.

"It was wrong of me to move out of our bed, to abandon you like that," he said huskily. "I was a coward. I can't even explain what I was thinking. Tell me it's not too late, that you can forgive me. That I can mend what I carelessly broke. Come to bed with me. Let me love you."

"Oh, my wolf." The sob caught in my throat, fortunately sounding like a groan of desire, not despair. A day ago, even this morning, I would've given most anything to hear those words from him. And now…

Now I had to say no. Wildly I sorted options. I could go to bed with him and sneak out later. I could move the barrier tomorrow night, or even in the morning. But no—too many messages had gone out, too many people awaiting the moment. Nakoa had been brewing his storm for hours. People could die if I didn't come through on schedule. I could tell Rayfe the truth and hope that the high priestess… no. Too dangerous.

Especially for solely personal reasons. My duty to my people, to everyone, was far more important than my love life. I had to do this, but what could I tell him? I needed to make some excuse. Go and come back.

But he'd know the moment I moved the barrier—and that I'd deliberately withheld my plan from him—and I'd lose him forever. Any softening of his heart now would only make my apparent betrayal wound more deeply.

Rayfe slid the narrow shoulder of my shift down my arm, following with his mouth until he reached the upper curve of my breast. I shivered at the hot caress of his lips and tongue, my nipple peaked with anticipation. I threaded my fingers through his long, silky hair, holding on, savoring the scent and feel of him. I could... I could lose myself to this. Sate our mutual desire and reforge the connection between us. It wouldn't necessarily take long. And then I could use mind magic to put him to sleep while I—

While I violated his trust yet again. He wouldn't know it yet, but I'd have to confess someday. And he'd still know that I'd moved the barrier and kept the plan from him.

"Andromeda?" He lifted his head, looking at my face. I'd hesitated too long. "What's wrong? Come to bed."

"I can't." The words wrenched out of me, staggering in their regret. Silently I begged him to understand. To give me one more chance. Moranu, please, don't make this be my last chance.

His winged brows drew together. "Surely whatever you need to do can wait until morning. We've been slaves to this war. Let's take an hour for ourselves. To enjoy each other, to remind ourselves what we're even fighting for."

"I wish I could," I said fervently, meaning those words more than I'd ever meant them in my life. I took his hands in mine, extracting myself from his embrace. "Rayfe—I want nothing more than to be with you right now. And forever. I love you with everything in me. But, I swear to Moranu, there is something I must do."

He didn't pull his hands away, but suspicion flickered in his gaze. "You're being very careful not to say what it is, my queen."

I caught my breath, trying to quell the panic. Cool and calm. "I don't want you to be angry is all," I temporized, willing the wheeling birds of my scattered thoughts to align into some plan.

"Try me," he said tightly.

"I… promised to consult with Ursula. She won't sleep until I do."

He relaxed. Smiled. Ran a hand over my tumbling hair. "Is that all? I'll come with you. I should probably apologize to her, too, for my behavior earlier today." A faint, puzzled frown bent his brows again. "Though I can't quite recall why I have that feeling."

*Moranu save me from this.* I felt so ill that bile rose in my throat. And guilt clearly writ itself across my face, because Rayfe took a sharp breath, dropped my hands, and stepped back.

"You're lying to me." He sounded incredulous. "Why would you lie to me?"

"Rayfe," I said helplessly, reaching my hands for him. Dropping them when he looked at me with clear disgust.

"Never mind," he bit out. "It doesn't matter. Here I'd been thinking all last night, all day today, of how I could mend things with you—and you don't even care."

"I do care!" I nearly shouted at him. "I care so much that this estrangement has nearly broken me, and I—" I cut myself off, belatedly remembering the power I handed to my enemy with those words. "I can't do this right now. I have to go."

His expression had gone cold, the fine bones sharp as glass, his blue eyes arctic. "Is there someone else?"

"What? No!" I ran my hands over my pregnant belly without thinking. "When would I even—"

"I imagine that's my fault, too," he interrupted bitterly. "You made your demands clear and I refused to bend. Because I cared about you and our child! Can't you get that through your head, Andromeda?"

"No. I mean, yes. I understand, but I never—"

"Who is he? Or she? Some old mossback lover come to slide into your cold bed, eager to take advantage of what I treasured too much to risk injuring?"

"No! Rayfe, I don't understand how you could—"

*Oh.* I mentally sighed for my stupidity, for how easily I'd been baited into a fight yet again. "If this is how you're going to be," I said, chilling myself and pulling poise around me like a tattered cloak, bit by bit, and still not enough to cut the bitter wind, "then… I…" I stuttered to a halt, physically unable to deliver the appropriate ultimatum.

"Don't fret yourself, Andromeda," Rayfe replied icily. "I won't importune you again." He took a breath, considering, then pierced me with his gaze. "There could be other women, you know. They offer. I'm a proven breeder after all." He gestured at my belly, laughing harshly. "I'd said no to all of them, because I didn't want them. I only wanted you. What a fool I've been."

With a clap of dark wings, he became his favored raptor form, arcing out the open window and dissolving into the night.

A lone black feather lazily spun to the stone floor in the wake of his passage. Stunned, shattered, I picked it up, remembering that first time when he flew through Glorianna's rose window at Ordnung, coming after me, and left a feather in his wake. Even then, knowing nothing, I'd taken it for a message, a promise. I'd pocketed it, fingering its glass-edged, obsidian lines, wondering at this man who so compelled me.

Until Ursula had made me burn it to prove a loyalty that had already begun to shift away from her and our father, and to the land I'd been promised to before birth. I took one more precious moment to carry the feather back into my bedroom. I couldn't look at the bed, where—but for excruciatingly bad timing—I might even now have been entwined in the arms of the only man I'd ever loved. Going to my jewelry box, I laid the feather inside, then carefully shut the lid.

After a moment, I also put the high priestess's topaz in there. I didn't like to leave it where it could be reclaimed by one of her creatures, but I worried more about taking it inside the Heart where she could potentially track it. I'd underestimated her too many times.

Taking a few deep and calming breaths, I cleared my mind. *Concentrate. Focus.*

Becoming an owl, in deference to the night, I flew out the window also, and out over the dark sea. Though the waxing moon picked out glimmers on the waves, all the water was black, no hint of blue anywhere.

# ~ **14** ~

THE FIRST TIME I'd gone to the Heart, I'd been brand new to shapeshifting, had no idea where I was going, and executed all of it quite clumsily. After all this time, I'd gotten more efficient—and cannier—about the journey.

I never went directly there, as I had—more or less—that first time. I circled, flew or ran to various locations, before I changed to fish form and dove into the sea. On this dark night, it seemed unnecessarily exhausting to go too far out of my way, except that I was leery of being tracked by any of the sleeper spies. Not that they could enter the Heart even if they found it, but if the high priestess knew its location…

Well, since it seemed increasingly clear that our magic shared many qualities, it could be that Salena's line and the high priestess's line sprang from the same source. If I could get into the Heart, she might be able to also.

So, I expended energy appearing to hunt—though I released the bat I caught, unwilling to risk eating in animal form— gradually working my way lower, closer to the waves. I changed to heron form, keeping to the shadows, then slipped into the water in that form, diving deep before becoming a fish. After that, it was a matter of changing from one aquatic form to another as the water deepened, requiring a form best suited to each environment.

The Heart sits in an abyssal crevice some distance from the Annfwn shoreline. While much of the Onyx Ocean is relatively shallow until well past the Nahanaun Archipelago, there are these chasms, deep valleys in the ocean floor, that plunge to dizzying depths. Some Tala shapeshifters—those who loved to test the limits and extremes—had attempted forms that withstood those crushingly intense deep waters.

I was not one of those.

But I had found on that first journey, through sheer good luck or the guiding hand of Moranu, that I could reasonably easily take the form of a denizen of each level. I never took those forms at any other time. Most of them I had no name for. They were creatures of the cold and lightless depths, where sight became worthless. Everything became about sound, smell, and feel.

Until the Heart of Annfwn itself.

The emerald glow of it lightened the waters long before the dome came into view. Few creatures lived nearby. Those that loved the crushing depths did not love light, so they avoided the area. Only the blue crabs, their gleaming shells like polished lapis lazuli, greeted me as I swam up to the golden walled dome.

The Heart of Annfwn is essentially contained within another version of the magic barrier. Smaller by several orders of magnitude, the shield itself is correspondingly thicker, nearly opaque from the outside. The crabs crawling over its surface aren't living creatures at all, but constructs of a sort. Not unlike, it suddenly occurred to me, the creatures of Deyrr.

The crabs, whatever their origin, maintain and defend the dome. Knowing me well, they formed a shifting pattern like a salute, parting to allow me to flatten against the dome and ooze through. I didn't shift back into human form until the sudden lack of pressure and gasping of my gills made it painfully necessary. Far better that way, however, than to shift back too soon. My deep-water creature form could withstand a bit of low pressure and dry air for a few moments far better than my human form could bear the freezing, crushing depths of the abyss.

I'd learned *that* the hard way. And barely survived. I also hadn't mentioned that near fatal mistake to Rayfe.

The first time I'd entered the dome, I'd been naked in human form. In the beginning, it hadn't mattered, as no one could see me this deep in the ocean, in a place no one else could ever go. But then I'd learned to project my consciousness to other places. When I appeared to people, even in illusory form, they seemed to see me as I was in the place. Not naked was preferable, so I wore my usual loose silken shift.

On the smooth, curving chair formed of a giant abalone shell, probably created back when the first Tala expanded a second version of the Heart's shielding to create the barrier, sat the Star of Annfwn. I breathed a sigh of relief to see it there, where I'd left it. I'd considered hiding it, but other than the elaborate chair, the small dome was a barren space. Finally I'd decided the Heart itself would have to serve as hiding place enough.

Taking up the smooth topaz globe, I rolled it in my palm, heavy, radiating heat and light. Our mother had given it to Ursula, her eldest daughter, to keep and guard all those years. For a long time it had sat inset in the pommel of her sword, only the upper curve showing, appearing to be a cabochon jewel. Larger than the high priestess's stone, possessing perfect clarity, the Star focused magic. When it had finally come to me—a process I hadn't rushed, as I'd had a great deal to practice before I could begin to wield it—my abilities had grown by leaps.

I sat in the chair, soaking in the revitalizing energy streaming from below. The Heart of Annfwn, the great condensed sun of all the magic in the world—well, most of it—lay beneath this chair, sunk into the bedrock itself. It sat at the center of the golden barrier that surrounded me and kept the ocean at bay, only the upper side apparent as a dome. Much like a cabochon jewel set in the ocean floor.

Though I could follow all the surface of the Heart's globe, just as I could with the larger barrier, it had never occurred to me to trace it into the earth. Sitting in this place, boosted to supernatural levels by the furnace of magic beneath me, I became both globes, in all parts of each at once. I didn't really have time to dally, but I took a bare moment to sample the barrier where it traveled deep in the rock below, through fiery lakes of molten ore, frozen soil, and dense stone.

My first time in this place, I'd been so new to sorcery, to any sort of magic, that my human senses had been unable to fully process the sensations. I'd heard colors and smelled sounds. Over time, I'd come to understand the vicissitudes of magic and no longer experienced it as strange sensory contradictions. Now the magic spoke to me directly, with no need for sloppy translation.

Flowing into and through the barrier, I followed its curve north. There, where barrier met the ground and dove beneath it, the soil had been frozen solid for centuries, perhaps forever. Huge, immensely thick sheets of ice lay on top of that, some-times with deep covers of snow, new piled on top of old. In places along the coastline, the ice-covered land merged seamless-ly into the frozen sea. But, fortuitously, where the barrier crossed the coastline, a high line of rearing cliffs broke that surface.

I settled myself there, feeling as if I stood on those towering rocks. Though it was the middle of the night, it was also midsummer, and this far north the sun never set. Instead it hovered on the horizon, its light muted, but also clear and white.

To my right, the barrier shimmered with purity, clean and unchallenged. With a rush of gratitude, I savored its pristine power, beyond relieved that Dafne had steered me away from my initial impulse to deal with the barrier at the point that Deyrr had fouled it.

Below me, the sea foamed, hurling itself against the cliffs with a roar, determined to chew its way through the stubborn rocks. To my left, about a league south, I spotted the landmark I'd identified with Dafne: a rounded notch in the cliff face, where the water boiled into a glassy, deceptive calm. I only had to pull the barrier to just past that circle.

That location confirmed and set in my mind, I turned to my next task: speaking mind-to-mind with Jepp. I contacted the staymach Zynda had left with Jepp and Kral. In nightjar form, it responded to my mental touch with eager affection, then flapped its wings to alert Jepp. She jumped, a dagger leaping to her hand before she relaxed—thankfully without skewering my bird.

"Andi?" She asked tentatively. I had the bird duck its head in an approximation of a nod.

"I thought you were going to talk in my head."

All right then. Steeling myself against the revulsion, I pushed past her natural resistance, finding the cracks in her psyche to slip through. Where Zynda's mind had open windows she spoke through, Jepp's was closed. Feeling sordid as a rapist, I wedged a crack open and spoke into her mind.

*"This is Andi."*

She jumped about a foot, cursing in a language I didn't know—a dialect of the hill people she sprang from—but that translated in her thoughts just fine. "Fuck me sideways," she added in Common Tongue.

*"Sorry."*

"No, no. I'll be prepared next time."

"Who are you talking to?" Kral asked, entering the cabin in full armor, dripping with rain.

"Queen Andromeda is talking in my head and it's freaky."

"Tell her we're pulled back and in position," Kral replied without missing a beat.

"She can hear you, idiot," Jepp retorted.

"Good, then you don't have to repeat it."

She made a rude sound. "Got that, Andi?"

*"Confirmed. Good luck."*

I let go of her mind, a bit shaken at how easy that had been. Lines like that shouldn't be so easy to cross.

I focused back on the barrier, on that frozen cliff, taking a moment to clear my mind. Though I naturally wasn't physically present, I imagined the stark, pristine air flowing through me, cleansing me. *Concentrate. Do the job.*

Though I didn't need to, I extended my right hand to the barrier, sinking my metaphysical fingers into it, feeling the taut elasticity of its magic. It helped, sometimes, to imagine nonphysical things as material. I'd been grounded in one body for most of my life, so irretrievably mossback in much of my thinking that working with the image of that body helped me focus. Some of the shamans and wizards who'd attempted to teach me to wield my native sorcery had shaken their heads at me for this, muttering darkly about dilettantes, but I'd learned to ignore them.

This was mine, more than anything else, a legacy of my mother's and her mother's before her, all the way back to the n'Andanan sorceresses who'd started all of this, perhaps to Moranu Herself. No one could teach me how to be me.

I opened to that confidence, letting my own magic flow. A reflection and daughter of the Heart's magic, the barrier reached instinctively for it through me, intertwining. My small stream flowed into the great river of magic and, in turn, it flowed back through me. Sending a prayer to Moranu for whatever assistance She might give, I took a step toward the cove, dragging the barrier with me.

Of course, I wasn't truly walking—simply using that metaphor to focus the magic—but my muscles strained as I pulled. I dug my heels into the ground for purchase, using all my might. It felt like trying to pull the moon with a short rope, the bit under my grip yielding, coming with me, but the rest resisting.

I pulled harder, sinking into the Heart and the earth. Using all the stubbornness in me, I demanded that it move, that it obey me. Just beyond the body I'd left in the dome, far away from my consciousness, the crabs raced over the surface, digging with their claws, frantically attempting to follow my command.

*I am the Sorceress of the Heart. You will yield to my will.*

The entire barrier groaned inaudibly, a shudder running through it. It came unmoored, flexing, pulsating, tethered only to my will. I struggled to hold on, and for a panicked moment I thought it might collapse entirely. I supposed we should've planned for that possibility.

Too late now.

And too late to abandon the effort, for the barrier had budged—not much, but just enough to lose its anchored size and position. It billowed, in flux, an unwieldly balloon of immense magic tied to me by a thin thread of will.

I began walking, pulling the piece under my hand, the entire globe shuddering and contracting—thickening in some places and thinning in others, flowing like lightning and honey to compensate—and as it did, the magic residue it dragged in its wake sparked against the physical realm, stirring up storms.

"Oh my, Andromeda. What can you be doing?"

The high priestess appeared before me, blond hair whipping in the arctic wind. Her cloth of gold gown remained still, however, a piece of the illusion she'd neglected in her haste. She tried to look bored, but I'd surprised her. Good.

I should've predicted, also, that she'd feel this enormous of a sorcerous effort. That is, I'd suspected she would, but not that she'd pinpoint the location of my metaphysical attention so easily. I'd been worried about her finding my physical body in the Heart when I should have worried about her finding my consciousness, balanced out at the extenuated arm of my will, precariously unprotected.

I did the only thing I could do: I ignored her and kept walking. The barrier responded more easily now, as if it had gone from a solid to a liquid, lighter and flowing with resilience. My metaphorical walking turned to leaps, as if I wore magic boots from the old tales, allowing me to travel leagues for each step.

Forced to move by the encroaching barrier, the image of the high priestess flew beside me. She'd abandoned the effort to make her hair move, her expression angry—and satisfyingly anxious. "What are you *doing*, Andromeda!"

"Grownup things," I replied tersely. "Mommy is busy. Go play somewhere else."

The barrier billowed and furled, momentarily destabilizing with my lapse of attention. I moved faster, blocking out the high priestess. She couldn't stop me. If she could have, she would have attempted it by now.

"Almost lost control there, didn't you?" she simpered, adding a giggle, but it didn't work to disguise her panic. "You're an amateur. This is way beyond your abilities."

I didn't bother to reply, accelerating toward the cove, the magic globe once again reasonably docile. As long as I kept moving, it seemed to do all right.

"You can't do this!" the high priestess screeched in my ear, startling me. Amazing how painful that kind of manufactured input can be on an eardrum that doesn't physically exist. No longer needing to dig into the earth I also flew, the barrier flowing into an obediently tighter circle. "It won't work, baby sorceress," the high priestess informed me. "You think you can bring the barrier back to shelter only Annfwn again, that you can starve me of magic like before. But I have reserves you don't know about. I can penetrate your barrier like that." She snapped her fingers, the click reverberating through several realities.

"I seriously doubt you can," I replied. I knew bluster when I heard it. The louder Uorsin had roared, the more impotent he'd felt. "All you do is talk, talk, talk."

"You think the barrier will be stronger if it's smaller, but it won't be," the high priestess insisted. "You can't keep me out because I'm already inside. I've won; I've murdered you and you're too stupid to know you're dead."

"Or smart enough to know I'm not."

"I have hooks in your very heart. You have no idea."

Rayfe. I determinedly didn't think about him. I bit my tongue against retorting that I knew very well what she'd done and that I would undo it. What I knew and she didn't was my weapon to wield.

"You've lost this war, half-breed," the high priestess sneered. "This is a desperation move. You've revealed your panic and terror. You've exposed yourself."

I'd reached the cove, sailing over the deceptively calm water that became a cauldron beneath. As I drew the barrier through the water like a curtain, the sea tumbled with uncanny colors that didn't exist in the physical universe. A sea monster exploded out of the water, hurling itself in a leap farther inward, like deer running from a forest fire. All over the world this would be occurring. People who couldn't cross the barrier without my help would be scraped out of their beds, flung against walls by its inexorable travel.

I should've thought to make it permeable before I moved it. Too late now. And, knowing what I knew now about my tenuous control of the untethered globe, I might have lost control if I'd thinned its nature that way.

Nearly there. The far side of the cove drew close. Even if the barrier slipped my hold, I'd probably brought it within Dafne's margin of error.

The high priestess wrapped her hands around my throat. Her icy fingers, shards of bone encased in death magic, clamped down on my windpipe. I choked before I remembered I didn't physically exist in this place. No more than she did.

But so interesting that her magic could grapple mine this way. Her matte black eyes from this close were pits into the eternity of soulless death. They held nothing, no expression, no glimmer of anything but the void. Around them, her lovely face contorted with rage and terror, the rest of her body shredding away like a wraith's.

I screamed, to make her smile, to make her overconfident. Allowed myself to falter. Pretended to fumble, the barrier slipping out of my metaphysical hands… And I parked it at the far side of the cove, exactly on the planned landmark. Dafne would be proud of my precision.

Letting my personal albatross hang from my neck, I ignored the stream of curses and promises she hurled at me. I settled the barrier into its new place, calming it like a living creature. Which, in a way, it was. A short distance from my body and far away, in an abyssal crevice, the crabs worked furiously to secure the new shape and position.

Like hot glass congealing in the cool water of a glassblower's bath, the barrier ceased its liquid shifting, smoothing into position. Outside the shimmer of the barrier, in the eternal noon of the arctic night, the sky churned with magic waves.

I sagged, seeming to succumb to the high priestess's grip. She screeched in triumph, letting me go when I dropped dramatically to the snow beneath me on the far cliff face of the cove.

"See?" she sneered, her body reforming, all golden perfection. "All that effort, wasted. You moved the barrier, what? Barely a few leagues? You failed, Andromeda."

I sat up, careful to look defeated, utterly dejected. It worked perfectly with our plans for her to believe our focus lay with moving the barrier all the way back to shelter only Annfwn.

"I'll just try again," I said, wary of being in this metaphysical state where lying simply did not work. We were projections of our thoughts and while I could physically speak words counter to my thoughts, I couldn't think anything other than what I knew to be true. This, however, was no lie. I would try again—the last resort solution—if it became necessary.

"And I'll just stop you again," she replied carelessly. "Look, Andromeda. You're a decent sorceress—especially for such an amateur, but you truly are a green and naked child trying to fight armored warriors. You cannot win against us. We've been preparing for centuries. I hate to see you destroyed for no reason at all. Join me. I'll teach you."

"I'd rather die," I informed her, letting her see all my hate for her and everything she represented.

"You will die," she replied with frankness, even compassion. "Even if you somehow survive this war, which I don't see happening—and if you can see the future, you know I'm right—then you'll eventually die anyway. Like all mortals, you carry your death in every cell of your decaying flesh. You'll be an old crone, withering to dust while I'm still young, vibrant. Beautiful."

I snorted my disdain. "Young? You're not even alive. You're a twisted ghost of a woman who once lived."

"I'm immortal!" she screeched at me.

"You're an echo," I informed her. "A pitiful whine of someone long dead, a whimper that will be silenced when I destroy you."

She laughed, the sound false and metallic, then pursed her lush mouth in sympathy. "Oh, honey. You understand nothing. Deyrr has made me His. I'm practically a deity myself. The gods cannot die."

"But their servants can be extinguished," I replied sweetly. "And even the gods can be imprisoned and neutralized by powerful magic practitioners."

"You?" She snorted. "You might have the power in time, but not yet. You certainly lack the knowledge, the skill to use the tools you have. Look at you, all the power of the Star and the Heart at your command—don't think I can't see it, oozing out of your illusory pores—and you lost control of the barrier, managing to move it a pitifully small distance. You're like a toddler trying to lift his daddy's broadsword and failing."

Ha. An apt analogy. I often felt that way. "And yet, the Heart and the Star are mine, not yours."

"A waste," she spat. "Think about it, Andromeda. You know I must speak the truth here. This isn't something you can do on your own. Your mother died when you were a child. She taught you less than nothing. A shame and a pity, but there's nothing to be done about that. You know just enough to be dangerous."

"Dangerous to you," I pointed out.

She laughed, light and tinkling, managing to sound genuinely amused this time. "Oh, sweetling, no. You are no danger to me. You think you understand the Heart and the Star. You believe you have power. But you've only scratched the surface of a world of magic so immense and rich that you can't even comprehend it as you are now. Like that silly child, you are a danger only to yourself—and to the people too stupid to get out of the way."

I made a sympathetic face, wincing on her behalf. "I know you're too stupid to duck, but how sad for you that you know it and still can't help yourself."

She opened her mouth and hissed in fury. "You think you're so clever. But there is only one answer for you, if you are smart enough—and humble enough—to embrace it. There is one person in all the world who can teach you. Me. There is no one else who can teach you what I can."

"I could learn from you, it's true," I said, feeling the weight of those words. I didn't even have to try to find a way to disguise my meaning. It was true, and the thought had occurred to me more than once. If I managed to destroy the high priestess, the world would lose centuries, perhaps even eons of sorcerous knowledge. I might as well set fire to Dafne's library.

But then, Dafne's books weren't trying to eat the world.

Her expression lit with triumph. She believed she'd gotten me to agree with her, but I knew to be wary of that. Affirming what I already knew to be true didn't give her power over me.

"Then you agree," she prompted. It had begun to snow, and the blizzard whipped through her lovely form. What had she looked like when she wore a real, mortal form? Not like that, I bet.

I said nothing.

"Leave those animals," she coaxed. "It's beneath you to be wed to a dog. What do you owe them besides duty to a mother you barely remember? You could live a life that *you* choose. Come to me and you could have everything."

I pretended to consider her offer—easy enough as my mind raced to weigh the various options. This could be my opportunity to find a path into her mind, so when I was able to strike, I'd know the way. But I didn't delude myself that I could remain immune to her mind control. Only a fool would underestimate her ability to erode thoughts and manipulate emotion.

"It would be wrong," I finally said, making a show of reluctance. "I have a duty to my people."

"What is wrong?" she cooed. "What is duty? A construct, taught by our parents to control us as children. Then laws, imposed by others—mostly men—to govern our lives. Those laws serve society, not the individual. When have you ever done something only for yourself, Andromeda?"

"I was born to rank, to duty," I replied. "I've had luxury and power. In return, I serve my people."

"And why must there be an exchange?" she demanded, as if indignant on my behalf. "Did you agree to this bargain before you were born? Did you agree to *any* of it? Your mother *sold* you to a man in marriage before you were even conceived. What about *your* fundamental right to happiness? I don't understand how a woman as intelligent and powerful as you are can submit to being enslaved like this."

Oh, she was good. And I must tread carefully, because she'd gone straight to the core of my unhappiness. What had she said to Rayfe? I never wanted to know. "I'll think about it," I said.

"Don't think too long," she warned with a conspiratorial smile. "I don't want to ruin the surprise, so…" She pressed her lips together and pantomimed locking them with an invisible key that she threw away. Glancing around at the barrier, the snowy waste, she lifted a shoulder and let it fall, a Dasnarian shrug in every way. "So much wasted effort, trying to move this barrier. You'll see. And you know how to reach me. See you soon.

Sooner than you think!"

She smiled brightly, waggled her fingers in a goodbye, then vanished, her toothy smile the last to fade.

## ~ 15 ~

OURS BEFORE DAWN, when I returned to the cliff city, it was still fully shrouded in Moranu's night—and glowing with lanterns, bustling with even more activity than when I'd left. Ships in the harbor creaked with the sounds of ropes, sails, and wood. People moved supplies along the beach and out to the waiting ships. Others moved stores into the tunnels below and the cliff city above. Ursula was planning for siege, too.

Annfwn was never fully asleep, as our more nocturnal denizens carried on their business at night, but this was another level. Such are the effects of looming war.

I was too keyed up to sleep, so I went to find Ursula, who I felt sure would be awake, monitoring the effects of the barrier shift, and directing all this preparation. If I encountered Rayfe there, well... I could hardly avoid him forever.

Sure enough, I found her in the first place I looked, sitting in her now favorite chair along the side of the big conference table in the council chambers. The room blazed with light, and her auburn hair stood out in wild tufts where she'd raked her hands through it, but she looked alert, vividly in her element with an array of notes and missives spread around her. Marskal stood at her shoulder and nodded to me as I entered.

To my surprise, Dafne was awake also, little Salena asleep in a Tala-made wooden cradle at her feet. She rocked the cradle absently with one foot, her attention on some message a staymach nightjar had just delivered to her, checking the missive against a detailed list as long as my arm.

To my utter lack of surprise, Harlan sat nearby, shifting markers around a new map—possibly a schematic of a naval battle—and making running calculations down the side.

Ursula glanced up from what she was writing, Marskal clearly waiting to take it. She gave me an apologetic grimace. "Hope you don't mind that I took over this space. It seemed like the logical choice—central, and where we'd be unlikely to bother anyone actually trying to sleep."

I waved that away and sat nearby, not in the queen's chair. "It's fine. It is the logical choice."

She sat back and studied me. "How did it go? Successfully, according to early reports, but you look tired."

"One day people will stop telling me I look tired," I replied wryly.

"Better than people saying you look dead," Dafne commented, not looking up from what she was reading.

"Thanks for that." I turned my attention back to Ursula. "It went according to plan, so far as I can tell." I'd spent a bit of time in the Heart once I returned to my body. First I'd made contact with Jepp, both of us keeping it brief, to verify that all was well with the fleet. Then I'd checked the barrier, confirming that it had anchored into its new position—we did not need it to start drifting—and purging the former hole of the Deyrr taint. It came clean fairly easily. It would take some work yet, but already I felt the relief of not having that infected wound plaguing my mind.

I'd also taken the time to cool my rage. Oh, I still wanted to rend that perversion of a priestess limb from limb, but I finally felt I could plot her demise with cool resolve—rather than feeling like I wanted to drink her blood.

"It went to plan according to our data too," Dafne replied. "Reports from our affected islands indicate that the barrier moved, then fixed at precisely the predicted location." She finally looked up at me with raised brows. "Well done, Sorceress Andromeda."

"I echo that," Ursula said. "Anything more you can tell us?"

"Jepp says that the pull back went well—they were still accounting for everyone, but they think none collided with the barrier—and Nakoa's storm was beginning to calm."

"Yes, Nakoa says it should blow itself out before dawn." Ursula finished her missive as she spoke, sealed it, and handed it to Marskal.

He gave her the Hawks' salute, then glanced at me. "We'll be ready later today to head out on our mission, Your Highness," he said.

"Won't Zynda need to rest after all of this flying back and forth?"

His mouth quirked in a rueful smile. "She says dragons are tireless. They also breathe flame, so I'm not arguing with her."

I smiled back. "An excellent point. I should be ready with my end of the plan." He bowed to me and left, and I turned back to Ursula. "Is that where Nakoa is—still managing the storm?"

"Yes," Dafne answered. "He's out on your favored breakwater. Another invasion of your space we hope you don't mind."

"I told him where it was," Ursula put in, "as he'd asked for a quiet place where he could concentrate without being bothered."

I did feel a little invaded, but that had also been a logical choice, so I nodded. "Any reports on damages from the barrier moving or the resulting magic storms?"

They exchanged glances. "Nothing of grave import," Ursula

said, shifting her gaze as another staymach nightjar flew in with a missive, dropping it in front of her.

The bird came to me then, clucking with pleasure and conveying images of storm-tossed seas and magic-streaked skies. I stroked it, thanking it for its hard work. Clearly there had been damage and casualties, but I wouldn't press for details. We'd known that would be the price—and we'd be paying heavier prices in the days to come. Still, I felt like I had years ago, trapped inside the fortress of Windroven castle while people died outside the walls.

"Don't look like that," Ursula ordered. "You did what you had to do, and you executed it perfectly."

"I know that. And don't pretend you wouldn't feel the same."

She raked a hand through her hair. "I already feel the same. And it's only going to get worse, and before much longer."

I nodded, then sighed. "How soon do you want to engage the Dasnarian navy?"

Ursula glanced at Harlan, who looked up, face calm and resolute. He tapped a blunt finger on a set of calculations. "Ideally—depending on you—we'd like to open a hole for the initial battles by midday tomorrow. Er, today. We don't want them to have time to assimilate the barrier change and alter their strategy. If all goes as planned, we'll keep supplementing our side with fresh ships over the next several days. We already began sending our ships to the barrier, and we'd like to send another wave on the dawn tide in a few hours."

So soon, but it made sense.

"I wanted to wait to check that you'd be ready to do this," Ursula said, turning that penetrating gaze on me again. "That's why we only sent some of the fleet so far."

"I'll be ready," I answered immediately.

"Don't answer too fast," Ursula warned. "This is going to be a sustained effort, which I expect will be draining for you. If you need a day to rest then—"

"I don't." *Dragons are tireless.* "I only seem tired at the moment because I've been awake all night. Using the Heart and the Star made moving the barrier relatively easy. Monitoring that portal won't require much from me." Not entirely true, but here I could lie with abandon.

Except I couldn't fool Ursula, who narrowed her eyes, the color steely. "Once we engage, we likely won't be able to back off," she said.

"I can always seal the barrier again. Give our side a breather." And myself.

She looked doubtful. "Maybe. But since we plan to execute the n'Andana plot simultaneously, won't you need all your strength for that?"

I raised my brows at Ursula, uncertain if she'd informed Dafne of our plan to strike at the high priestess.

"Dafne knows. I filled her in on everything," Ursula replied. "That's going to require a great deal of you—both timing and sorcery."

"I'm laying the groundwork for the effort, and it will be a balancing act to do both, yes, but taking her out will be less a blast of power than a precision strike."

She narrowed her eyes. "That doesn't answer my question."

"Isn't it your job—to push us to our limits, and beyond?" I asked coolly. "After all, it's necessary."

She sat back in her chair, assessing me. "Point taken," she said, dipping her chin to acknowledge she recognized her own words that I'd thrown back at her. "But it's also my job to make sure I don't squander our resources through careless disposition." She held my gaze, making it clear she'd deliberately chosen to treat me as a soldier, not her sister.

"I know what I'm doing," I replied. "This is the timing we have to work with. Every day, every hour that passes plays into her favor with whatever she has planned."

"I agree." She made a note on a checklist. "As an additional argument to move quickly—as if we needed another—we received an official message from Hestar, regarding my marriage."

"*Our* marriage," Harlan inserted quietly.

"As anticipated," she continued without pause, "he is angry and refused to acknowledge Harlan as his brother."

"I'm sorry," I said to Harlan, who shook it off.

"I was not eager to claim him as brother, so it's something of a relief," he replied. "Think of the excruciating family dinners."

Ursula threw him an unamused look. I tried to smile at his joke, but the deep sadness in him sapped the effort. A keen grief there, and not for his brother Hestar. For his sisters? No, for a particular sister, decorated lavishly with diamonds and pearls, her ivory blond hair trailing to the floor. A familiar face...

"What do you see in my mind, Sorceress?" Harlan asked quietly.

"I apologize," I replied quickly. "Sometimes the thoughts come to me. I won't invade your privacy further. Please continue, Ursula."

She didn't right away, looking between us. Deciding something, she went back to business. "The result, unfortunately, is that Hestar is calling in all the empire's forces to send against us, to smash us like a particularly displeasing insect, I believe was the translation."

Harlan nodded. "A *festilt*, a parasite in Dasnaria that is much reviled."

"I'd take that as the bluster it sounds to be," Ursula said, nodding to Dafne, "except that we've also heard from Akamai, and through him, Inga and Helva."

Dafne extracted a scroll written on in an elegant script, giving me a concerned look. "They also mention Hestar's rage. More important, there's a cloaked warning that the Dasnarians may have a way to compromise the barrier. There are hints that Hestar, deprived of an alliance, will seek help elsewhere, at the peril of his soul."

"Then there is certainly no question," I said, "that we continue with the plan to act on both fronts. If anything, we have more reason to handle the two simultaneously. I'll keep a close watch on the barrier. Hestar must be counting on Deyrr to do the compromising. Though it could be that this is old information, that they're still relying on that Deyrr incursion, but I won't assume."

"Yet another responsibility for you," Ursula noted.

"Another facet of the same one. I'm aware of what I'll be fielding on multiple fronts. I don't understand why we're revisiting this discussion." I was tired of talking about it, tired of all of it. I wanted it over and the high priestess banished from the world.

"Because *you* will bear the brunt of confronting multiple enemies at one time." Ursula tapped a scroll on the table in an impatient rhythm that gave lie to her carefully parsed words.

"One enemy," I corrected. "This is all *her*. The rest are just her tools."

"I suppose that could be true, but—listen to me, Andi— don't let this become a personal vendetta."

I laughed, and it came out cracked. "Why not? That's what this is: a very personal battle that happens to have a massive war with worldwide complications attached. Speaking of which," I continued over her as she began to argue, "I'm not waiting any longer. I'm going to rid Rayfe of Deyrr's control." I threw that out there like a gauntlet in an old tale. A challenge, not a request for permission.

"No." She leveled a steely stare on me. "Not yet,"

Magic lifted my hair, stirring it around my shoulders, bared by the simple shift I wore. As the righteous anger filled me, I watched the caution light in Ursula's eyes, Harlan's posture going wary. Little Salena, sensitive to magical shifts already, wailed and Dafne shushed her.

"You don't command me," I said softly.

A muscle in Ursula's jaw flexed, then she held up her palms. "You're right. I don't." She smiled, wry, rare exhaustion showing through. "Believe me, I'm very well aware that this is your war, that our mother planned it this way. But you can't do this alone. I'm only saying what you know is true."

I sagged, releasing the magic, letting it settle back into my personal reserves. "I know."

All three of them relaxed, and I wished I could find it in myself to be sorry that I'd frightened them. They weren't the ones who deserved my fury.

"Only one more day," Ursula urged. "Just long enough to make sure our plans remain a surprise. Then what you and Rayfe have suffered will at least be redeemed by what we gain." She slid a goblet over to me. "Have a little wine. It's yours, after all, and an excellent vintage. Then go sleep a few hours."

I gazed back at her, bemused. "Is that an order, Your Fucking Majesty?"

"In this case, yes." She tried a smile, though it faded quickly. "Hatred and anger can tear you apart, little sister."

I drank from the goblet, the rich wine a welcome taste, then eyed Ursula over the rim. "I disagree. My hatred and anger will tear *them* apart. I'll worry about the state of my soul after we win." And my heart.

She smiled in truth. "That's my girl. Now get some rest."

"I could sleep," I admitted. If Rayfe hadn't returned to our chambers, ready for another battle. Or worse, if he wasn't there because the high priestess had led him to someone else's bed. The prospect made my gut curl with dread. "Where is Rayfe— does he know yet about the barrier shift?"

"According the Hawks I have watching him, he's sleeping," Ursula said, keeping her voice very neutral.

"The effects of the barrier shift haven't been felt here yet," Dafne said, "if we feel them at all. All the reports so far have come from where the barrier meets ground or water. Recall that when you three initially expanded the barrier, no one in Annfwn noticed anything—it was only where the barrier scraped over this reality that it caused friction."

I nodded. "Friction" was such a gentle euphemism for the damage it caused. If I did have to execute my last resort, I'd have to make sure the barrier remained as permeable as possible while still containing magic. If I could do that. A headache for another day. I had another swallow of wine and pushed the goblet back to Ursula.

"All right—I'll sleep a few hours, then meet you all back here for breakfast." I stood, then arched my back against the ache, the baby kicking a little in protest or approval, I wasn't sure which. Dafne gave me a sympathetic grimace as she rocked Salena, peacefully sleeping again.

"On that note," Harlan said, standing and tugging Ursula to her feet, "we should get a few hours sleep, too."

"I'll stay here and field messages—and I'll wake you if any-thing critical occurs," Dafne said.

"Don't you need sleep too?" Ursula sounded dubious.

"I slept all afternoon and part of the evening," she replied, looking bright eyed indeed. "And if you want these ships out on the morning tide, I need to reconcile some of these supply redistributions. It will only take a bit longer. Plus, I'd like to wait up for Nakoa." A soft, secret smile crossed her lips.

I smiled at her, trying to make it genuine and hoping I didn't reveal the sour pang I felt. How lovely would it be to look forward to seeing my own husband, to seek out Rayfe, and to be certain of a warm reception. I'd once had that, even in the beginning when I refused him at every turn, and I hadn't realized how much it had meant to me. *She is doing this to you on purpose, so you'll feel alone, isolated, and in despair*, I reminded myself.

Ursula put a hand on my arm, squeezing a little. "You'll purge him of the taint and everything will be good again," she reassured me, as always discerning just a little too much.

I kept my smile frozen in place and nodded. Even if—no, when—I purged Rayfe of the high priestess's control, even if we both survived this war, the fractures in our marriage would remain. After all we'd done to hurt each other, I wondered if the rifts between us could ever be truly mended.

And if not, what I'd do then.

*What do you owe them besides duty to a mother you barely remember? You could live a life that* you *choose.*

I shook off that haunting suggestion. Time enough to decide what I'd do *after* we survived.

If I had anything left of my heart and soul.

# ~ 16 ~

I STRUGGLED OUT of a deep sleep that churned with the cries of people injured and dying, of angry magic raining fire, and ships capsizing as the barrier ground over them, sea monsters feasting on the drowning sailors and passengers.

And me, laughing maniacally, blood dripping from my hands.

"Good morning, Andromeda." Rayfe's icy voice brought me fully awake.

Fully dressed, he stood next to the bed. He wore his formal black, flowing and severe at once, his equally dark and glossy hair loose, his expression remote. Beautiful and unreachable.

And so very, brutally angry.

Groaning mentally, I sat up, pushing my hair back and rubbing my hands over my face, the covers falling away. The sun had barely risen, still long away from clearing the cliff rim, and the room remained cool from the night breezes, my nipples crinkling in response. Rayfe's blue eyes flashed hot as they ran over my nakedness. Then cooled as he averted his gaze, staring stonily past me instead.

"So," he said. Then took a breath. "You moved the barrier last night."

"Yes." I searched for something else to say and came up empty.

"Imagine my surprise when I was informed of something my own wife—my co-ruler—hadn't seen fit to mention."

"Rayfe, I—"

"Something," he continued remorselessly, "that you knew you planned to do when you rejected me last night."

"I didn't reject you. I said that—"

"That you had to consult with Ursula. Yes, I recall clearly how you lied to my face." His voice remained cuttingly cold, but emotion destabilized it. Fury, betrayal, grief.

"I did consult with Ursula," I protested weakly. "It wasn't a lie."

He laughed sounding bitter, wrapping his fingers into fists at his side. "You deliberately misled me, to keep me from knowing what you were about. Didn't you? At least respect me enough to admit that."

I had no excuse, no ready soothing lies to offer. "Yes, I did."

His remote expression thawed into bewildered hurt, and he stared at me like he didn't know me. "Why?" he asked starkly.

"I…" I had no answer. So easy to be angry at Ursula, to pin the guilt on her, but I'd been the one to do this to him.

"I know I've been distant," he continued. "I admitted to that last night. And that I'd made mistakes, but I tried to make up for that, to mend things. Now it seems I'm the only one trying here. I don't understand how you could treat our marriage—and me—with such utter disregard."

"I didn't do that, I—"

"Lied. Misled me. Failed to trust me," he spat. "I've never given you cause to distrust me, especially with something that so profoundly affects Annfwn. *Our* kingdom. Even if you don't trust me as a man, even if you no longer want me as your lover—do you also think I'm a weak king?"

"No!" Moranu take it, I couldn't sit in bed for this. I flung aside the covers and stood, the polished stone cool on my bare feet. Pulling on the green silk dressing robe I'd dropped on the floor when I crawled exhausted into bed a few hours before, I tied the sash. My lack of a waist meant I had to snug it over the protruding round of my belly, which then made the lapels sag open obscenely over my heavy breasts. I glared at Rayfe, the irritation with my swollen body at least prodding me out of despondent guilt. "I've never thought you're a weak king. I do trust you as a man, and I never stopped wanting you as my lover. How many times have I asked, even begged you to touch me these last months?"

"Until last night," he hissed. "And now I know why you changed your mind."

I set my teeth. "I wanted more than anything to say yes, but we'd made the plan. People—many people—were waiting for me, counting on me to do my part at the time I'd promised I'd do it. Would you want me to put a personal relationship, even with you, above my duties as queen?"

"No," he replied in an even voice, the lethal predator in it. "I'd want you to tell me what's going on in my own kingdom. To include me in this plan." His voice had risen to a near shout, and he broke off and wiped a hand over his brow. "It would've been so simple to explain. You can't imagine I would've objected. No, I would have *helped* you, but you had to shut me out of even that. Why didn't you tell me?"

"I…" Moranu curse me to the deepest ocean, I couldn't give him the real reason. "I couldn't."

He stared at me, waiting. Finally he set his jaw. "Is there more explanation or is that all you're going to say?"

"The reasons I couldn't tell you last night are the same reasons I can't explain more today."

"Even though I already know what you did."

"Yes."

He glared at me, frustration, insult, and stark heartbreak warring in him. "I don't understand you at all. You can't possibly believe I'd do anything to betray Annfwn or the Tala. Nor would I do anything to hurt you."

When I didn't have a ready reply to that, either, he shook his head. "I guess you don't believe even that."

"Rayfe." I reached out a hand and laid it on his lean chest, the tension and rage vibrating through him. It seemed that the high priestess would win her gambit either way—I could keep him from knowing our plans, but then she'd drive us apart. I had to try to suture this wound. I looked up at him, letting him feel my pleading, my earnest apology. "I'm so sorry that I hurt you, but I'm asking you to trust me in this. I'm doing the best I can in a very difficult situation."

"We all are," he bit out, but he unclenched one fist enough to cover my hand with his. "All those years I waited for you, Andromeda, that I dreamed of what you'd be like, how our marriage would be—I never imagined that you would turn on me."

"I haven't turned on you. That's not what's going on."

"Then what is?" he asked, half demand, half plea.

"It's complicated, and I'm asking you to trust me, for just a little while longer."

"I thought you and I, we made a good team. We might argue, but we agreed on the important things. Has that changed?"

"No." I didn't know how to prove that, so I stood on tiptoes, leaning both hands on his chest, and brushing his unresponsive lips with mine. "We still agree. If I could tell you, I would, and you *would* agree. Everything I'm doing is for Annfwn, for you, and our people. Please believe me. Please bear with me."

He relented, at last, returning the kiss, though perfunctorily, without passion. He ran the fingers of his other hand through my hair, sorrow creasing his face. "I'll try, Andromeda, I really will."

"Thank you," I whispered. "I love you so much."

"Then give me something, *anything*."

I tensed, sensing the change in him. The high priestess hadn't been speaking through him before this. I hadn't sensed her, and Rayfe's outrage and hurt had been too real. She'd slipped in, from one moment to the next, like a disease. "Give you something?" I asked, managing to keep the smile from freezing on my face.

"Why did you compress the barrier only for a few leagues?"

"What do you mean?"

"Did you hope to make it much smaller, but then the high priestess stopped you?"

Oh yes, definitely *her* asking that question. I'd told nobody that I'd encountered the high priestess out there. This was an opportunity, the kind Ursula would've crafted if she could. I had to master the turmoil of emotion to feed her the most useful lies, and to keep her talking so I could assess how she occupied his mind. I might not be able to free him now, but I could be ready to do it at a moment's notice.

"To prove myself to you, I'll tell you what happened with the barrier," I said, making a show of grimacing ruefully.

I had to think like a warrior, like a sorceress, in this very personal battle, to let go of worry about the effects on Rayfe, on our relationship and marriage. I must remember that I spoke to my enemy and nemesis, not my husband and lover. *You're not doing this to* him.

Except that he'd remember every word of this, and my heart broke for that. Nevertheless, I invaded Rayfe's mind again, extending those tendrils of thought as I'd done before, tasting and testing with a delicate touch.

"I started to shrink the barrier, but she stopped me, and I dropped it in a random place," I continued saying as I explored.

This was different from what she'd done to Karyn. That had been encompassing, the vile stench of Deyrr wound all through her heart and mind. This was far more subtle, probably all the better to fool me—and to keep me from wresting control back, as I'd done with Karyn. That process had been brutal and painfully wrenching. I could only guess how much worse it would be extracting Rayfe from these many tentacles digging deeply into him. The high priestess was skilled and clever.

I would have to be better.

"She's so much stronger than I am, Rayfe," I added, just to lure her in a bit more.

He nodded, expression sharp and eager. Her face, showing through his. Revolting and infuriating. "I've tried to warn you that you have no chance of defeating her."

"She's so powerful, and she knows so much that I don't."

"It's true." He stroked my hair and I had to restrain the shudder of revulsion. "It's not fair of everyone to expect you to stand up to her."

"She doesn't have the Star of Annfwn, though," I said, watching for a reaction, planting my seeds carefully. "That's an advantage she doesn't have."

"Do *you* even know to use it though?" he demanded. "The n'Andanans destroyed so much information."

"I just know that the Star could make all the difference between victory and defeat." I shrugged, pretended to restlessness and paced away, tugging my robe tightly closed. It was too awful, touching him while the high priestess spoke through him, looked at me through his eyes. "She offered to teach me," I confessed, then bit my lip as if torn. "If I'd come to her side, she'd instruct me in sorcery, things I could never learn anywhere else."

"What did you say?" he asked.

"I said no, of course. My duty is here. To you, and to Annfwn."

"If you think about it, though, the Tala, the n'Andanans, and Deyrr were once all one, all on the same side," he pointed out. A dangerous gambit of hers. Rayfe would never say anything like that. A miscalculation born of her disregard for the Tala, the way she thought of them as mindless animals.

There was another key difference in this possession. With Karyn, the high priestess had cozened her, warped her wants to fit with Deyrr's cause. What she'd done with Rayfe was both subtler and more straightforward. She'd taken over his will as she did with the more active sleeper spies, using him like a puppet. I could sense the strings clearly now. What I didn't know was how much Rayfe was an impotent bystander. From what he said when he was himself, he experienced her control like a dream, half-forgotten. Too much remembered.

"If Moranu created us all," Rayfe continued, "maybe we should all be one again, not fighting each other."

"I just don't know. Everything is so confusing."

"We could stop many deaths by surrendering," he said. "I've been thinking about that more and more."

"Ursula would never agree to a surrender," I replied, nearly holding my breath in anticipation of what the high priestess might reveal.

"Your sister has bigger problems with the Dasnarians," Rayfe confided. "If the Twelve Kingdoms ships fall to them, we might have to reconsider our stance with Deyrr. There's no shame in yielding to inevitability. We could save ourselves, even if she won't."

I nodded, trying to seem both reluctant and eager. "Maybe so. I'll think about it. Maybe we can suggest that at the strategy meeting. You're coming?"

"Of course. What is the backup plan, since moving the barrier failed?"

"We'll have to discuss that. I should clean up and get dressed."

"Good idea." He looked me over. "I'm sure you'll feel better if you do something with your hair."

I nearly rolled my eyes at her. Rayfe had never once complained about my hair, unless it was to encourage me to grow it longer. Her ambition, enormous ego, overconfidence—and enormous vanity—made her careless. I simply had to find a way to use that against her.

THE NEXT WAVE of ships had gone out on schedule, well before we convened the strategy session that was mostly an elaborate play for Rayfe and the spy inside him. Ursula turned out to be excellent at that sort of subterfuge—no surprise there—making it seem as if our navy had been deployed to attack n'Andana. All that remained, she declared, was for us to determine the remaining details of the attack.

I affected careless confidence about the barrier, emulating the high priestess's ego and attitude, assuring them all that the Dasnarians posed zero threat, and we could safely ignore them. Mostly Ursula and the others argued about how big of a force to send by air, which would arrive ahead of the ships, and how soon to follow up with foot soldiers.

Using that cover, hating myself for the paranoia, I scanned

each of them for the markers of the high priestess's influence. I nearly sagged with relief when all but Rayfe came up clean. Even Karyn showed none of the markers of the high priestess's passage—though I could detect the shadow of her past occupation, a stain that Karyn would likely carry forever, along with the black thorns inked into the skin of her arm.

Ursula adeptly adjusted to the points Rayfe insisted on— Dafne noting them down in a special column—appearing to defer in the moment, so that we could be sure to do the reverse. All in all, it didn't take long. Fortunate, as we had real battle plans to make, and as a hole wore its way through my stomach every time I helped lie to my husband. Occasionally I caught glimpses of his true self, but for the most part the high priestess kept the upper hand, growing increasingly careless in her certainty that she'd fooled us.

Once we had Rayfe convinced we planned to begin sending aerial troops that afternoon to commence a slow, three-day journey with many rest and refueling stops, we pretended to adjourn.

It was Ash's turn to keep Rayfe occupied, so they went off to rally the ground forces. He'd report to us on what the high priestess did to undermine us there. As we wouldn't be truly moving them any time soon, we should be able to repair any damage.

Once Ash reported via Djakos to me that Rayfe was safely away, we crept back like traitors to finalize our true plan. They wouldn't need me to open a portal in the barrier for the first of the Dasnarian ships to enter until later in the afternoon. Harlan and Ursula were still debating how many to string through the opening to begin with. He wanted to allow more to enter unhindered, to appear to lose to them, so that more ships would commit. She, of course, wanted as few intact and active

Dasnarian battleships inside the barrier as possible. Kral—via staymach message—had weighed in with Harlan, and that made Ursula dig in even more as she didn't trust Kral's motives still. Knowing her as I did, I suspected appearing to lose went more against her grain than she'd admit.

I gave them an edited version of my conversation with Rayfe earlier in the morning, then left them to argue about the battle with the Dasnarians, and went to the Heart to retrieve the Star.

Though I'd only left it hours before, it felt good to enter the depthless silence of the Heart, to absorb that life-giving magic. *All the power of the Star and the Heart at your command… and you lack the knowledge, the skill to use the tools you have.* She wasn't wrong. I had the ability to tap into both, could catch a glimpse of the potential there, but I didn't have more than surface understanding.

*You've only scratched the surface. You are a danger only to yourself— and to the people too stupid to get out of the way.*

The high priestess's analogy of the toddler with a broadsword was uncomfortably apt. I knew enough to recognize the potency of the weapon, and that I lacked the strength and skill to wield it. She was dead wrong, however, that the people around me were too stupid to duck. They wouldn't protect themselves because loved and trusted that I wouldn't harm them.

That meant it was up to me to master my fearsome weapon, and quickly.

I had no time to grow up, no sword master to teach me the necessary skills. But I wouldn't fail to use my best weapon, and not only because the high priestess clearly wanted that. She wanted me so afraid that I'd hesitate to use the power at my hands. I couldn't worry about cutting myself. After all, a toddler without a sword was defenseless.

Holding the Star in the palm of my hand, I lingered a while

on that abalone throne where so many sorceresses before me had sat. Back when I'd been ostensibly heir to the High Throne after Ursula, I'd thought that having my butt on a throne would mean the world would have fallen apart beyond repair. Funny, that. Though, even then, untrained and living in a land starved of magic, I'd had some of my native abilities. I'd glimpsed the future without knowing what it was.

Perhaps it was true that I'd only scratched the surface of a world of magic so immense and rich that I couldn't comprehend it, but I still understood worlds beyond what I had before. I'd been born to this, and my mother had known exactly what she was doing. Perhaps that's what that vision had meant, when Moranu showed me Salena looking down the years at us with pride and satisfaction.

I might not have learned to wield that sword like a master, but I *could* lift it. Because it was mine, and it was in me to do this thing.

Studying the Star, I reinforced my connection to it, following my intuition. My inner teacher was the only one available to me, and I knew who that was. Ami had said it and Shaman had confirmed it: Moranu would guide me. The goddess of shadows and magic would be the greatest teacher.

I would do what was required, but one thing I was certain of: I would only sacrifice myself. I wouldn't give her my child.

I waited for the goddess to argue otherwise. Or to give any sign at all. How do you try to listen? That had to be the most unhelpful advice ever. When Moranu offered no insight, no demands or gripping visions, I tested the futures surrounding the Star, recoiling at the many scenarios where I failed to strike the high priestess effectively and she used it to amplify the power of Deyrr with devastating results. And yet... I could also see futures where our plan worked.

There: the high priestess crumpling to ash, becoming the corpse she should've been centuries ago.

There: the high priestess directing an army that clogged the seas, skies, and land, the Star in her triumphant clasp.

It began to bother me, the differences between the scenarios. Could I be seeing successive futures? Something wasn't right.

In the end, I took the Star with me, but when I took on human form—and human dress—I stowed the Star in one pocket and the high priestess's lesser jewel in the other. Hopefully Moranu would eventually guide me to the right choice. The goddess's silence was not reassuring.

The four going to n'Andana awaited me on the beach, Zynda and Zyr in human form. Karyn and Marskal wore fighting leathers, along with plenty of weapons. Karyn sported at least two bows that I saw. Their supplies sat nearby in orderly piles, ready to be strapped on to Zynda as soon as she took dragon form. That would allow Zyr to carry only Karyn and no other weight. I considered arguing again that it would spare his lighter gríobhth form if Karyn also rode Zynda, but one look at him, at the wildness of his First Form riding high beneath his skin, and I knew he'd never allow Karyn to be so close to Marskal.

That animal nature had kept Zyr from being king, as it would always override his better judgment. Rayfe, on the other hand… surely he had become king because he had been able to control the wolf. He'd had the intelligence, resolve, and cunning to come after me, to bring back a queen for Annfwn. The high priestess might have a leash on his will, on Rayfe's mind and heart, but he was a man to be reckoned with. I would trust in that.

They all greeted me, their excited anticipation humming in the air, and I used the flurry of conversation to check them all once more for the high priestess's strings. Just in case. Fortunately, they remained untainted and we didn't need to alter the plan. I hadn't had an alternative for what we'd do if any of this team had been compromised. Send only one pair, I supposed, which could've explained several disasters I'd glimpsed.

Not something to I needed to worry about now.

"Are you all clear on the plan?" I asked.

They exchanged glances.

"There's an actual *plan?*" Zyr made a shocked face. "I thought we were to fling ourselves upon the dark waters of destiny and sacrifice our very lives for the greater good."

Karyn poked him. "I apologize, Your Highness," she said. "And for Zyr."

He tugged her braid and she winced.

Marskal cleared his throat, presenting me with a somber expression. "I have to agree with Zyr that the term 'plan' is overstating things."

Zynda rolled her eyes expressively. "That's because this is very simple. We fly straight to the high priestess's palace, pretend to be surprised that she's expecting us, briefly engage in a pitched battle as if attempting a suicide strike, lose the Star in the process, and flee."

"Oh, is that all," Zyr muttered.

"You volunteered," Karyn scolded him. "In fact, you pushed for this particular gambit."

"Gambit or gamble?" he retorted, then ducked in to kiss her before she could reply.

I held up a hand, commanding their attention. "All joking aside, this effort is a risky one. It *is* a gamble, and the odds are against us." My gown and hair stirred as the magic gathered to me, Moranu's hand settling over me with palpable intensity. I welcomed Her presence. Finally. "There's a strong possibility you all could die, and in the process hand our enemy the very weapon she's sought." I withdrew the Star from my pocket and held it on my palm, where it glowed like a smaller sun.

"We're sending the dragons with you, and all of our shapeshifters capable of taking winged forms—plus those riders who've previously drilled—but their job will be to lure the high priestess into using the Star to attack them, to distract her enough that I can strike. No one will be helping you."

"Good thing we don't need help," Zynda commented.

"Yeah, the wonder twins have this," Zyr added, and they exchanged cocky grins.

Marskal rubbed a hand over his face and Karyn muttered something in Dasnarian. I gave them all a moment. "There's no shame in changing your minds. We can come up with another, less risky plan."

Zynda gave me a long look. "You would tell us not to go if we didn't have a chance of succeeding. I'm in."

"Where my lady goes, I go," Marskal replied simply.

"Zynda isn't going to hog all the glory," Zyr answered. "I might not have dragon form yet, but a gríobhth in battle is a fearsome thing."

Karyn gazed at him with amusement, and obvious love. I doubted she'd have volunteered to do something so dangerous if not for that.

"Karyn," I said. "You can stay here. This is arguably not your battle to fight."

She returned my gaze calmly. "Apologies for my impertinence, Your Highness, but you're wrong there. This *is* my battle." She took Zyr's hand and he laced his fingers with hers. "We set out before to do this very thing, destroy the high priestess in her stolen nest, and Zyr and I expected to die then. Zynda and Marskal rescued us, at their peril. Now the four of us will go back to finish it. This is what heroes do, yes?"

They all nodded gravely, then all bowed to me, even Zynda

and Zyr. Surprised and deeply moved, I returned the bow. "Zynda?"

She held out her palm and I pressed the round of the topaz there, wrapping her fingers around it. Her gaze briefly met mine, then she nodded. "We all trust you, Sorceress Andromeda."

"May Moranu go with you and watch over you," I replied, feeling the rush of the goddess's presence as I invoked Her. *May that mean I'd made the right decision.*

We stepped back to give Zynda room, and she became the dragon, immense and sapphire dark on the white sands of Annfwn. Zyr and Karyn helped Marskal load their supplies onto her harness. Farther down the beach, Kiraka and Djakos gleamed bronze and silver, the paired fighting teams and other aerial fighters assembling.

Marskal climbed the harness, swift and agile, strapping himself on while Zyr changed to gríobhth form. Black as night, with the muscular body of a lion and the head and wings of an eagle, the sight of him sent an audible murmur from the watchers. He didn't often reveal his First Form publicly, and it always caused a stir.

Karyn climbed on, she and Marskal giving me the Hawks' salute. Then the dragon and gríobhth leapt into the air, Zyr staying low to the waves as he gradually gained altitude. It wasn't easy for him to take off from the ground, but he and Karyn had been practicing.

The waves of our flying forces followed, a stirring sight. I watched them disappear into the perfect blue sky, rolling the Star of Annfwn in my pocket, hoping and praying I'd made the right decision.

## ~ 17 ~

RAYFE MET ME on my way up the beach, striding toward me with his lethal grace, his glossy dark hair kissed with blue as the breeze tossed the long strands. His eyes caught the light in that uncanny way of the Tala, like a predator's reflecting at night, something I should've grown used to by now, but that never failed to give me chills. I searched his face for signs of his mood, who he might be at the moment, hoping to avoid having to touch his mind.

Behind him, Ash stopped, giving me a wry salute before heading over to the next wave of aerial attackers mustering to depart. Babysitting duty duly handed off. Moranu how I hated this.

Rayfe stopped before me, searching my face also, then looked at our people vanishing into the distant sky. "I should be leading them," he said. "In all the time I've been King of the Tala, even before that, I've always led my people into battle."

From those words, I knew he was himself, if only for the moment. Though he hadn't posed the words as a question, I understood his doubt and confusion as if they dwelled in my own heart.

I bridged the space between us, standing on tiptoe to wind my hands behind his neck, fingers tangling in his silky locks. The taut round of my belly made it awkward to lean against him, but

I managed—and sighed with relieved pleasure when his arms came around me to embrace and steady me.

I turned up my face, brushing his lips with mine, and—after a brief hesitation—he took me up on the invitation, gradually intensifying, then sinking into a kiss that heated my body, and my heart. I opened to him and his tongue touched mine, tasting and tentative, his hands tightening on me, the kiss becoming hungry, his mouth demanding. We'd always had this, the physical connection, the midnight bond that tied us together. For once I didn't chafe against the destiny that bound us together. I was profoundly grateful for it. Fate would keep him mine, no matter how carelessly I trampled his heart.

It might make me as ruthless as my nemesis, but I would use every weapon at my disposal in this, too.

Rayfe drew back to gaze at me, eyes hotter than blue flame. "What was that for?" he asked, with a quirk of a smile that wrung my heart.

*For all the ways I've lied to you, violated your trust, put you second to duty.*

"I've missed you," I said.

"It feels like forever since we've been just us," he replied, extracting a hand to stroke my cheek with a gentle caress, gaze on my mouth.

"Has it *ever* been just us?" I asked lightly, though my voice scraped a little. "Even that first time we met, when you kissed me, your wolfhound guard stood around watching."

"There was the cabin," he returned. "Our wedding night—that was only the two of us."

"That was a good night." I smiled at the memory, how nervous I'd been and how determined to make a real marriage of it, to change the destiny of both our realms. I'd been so innocent, in more than body.

"We've had other good nights," he reminded me, smile going sensual. "And days." He paused, searching my face again, hand cupping my cheek. "I've missed you, too, and I don't know why. You're right here and yet I feel like I've lost you."

My heart grabbed, my throat dry. "You haven't lost me. We've argued is all. We can come back from that."

He nodded, eyes a muddled blue of troubled emotions. "I feel sometimes like I'm in a dream I can't wake from. Are we truly attacking n'Andana?"

"Yes. A surprise attack," I added, just in case the high priestess reviewed his memories. "And you're not going with them because Annfwn needs you here. You're king for more than the warriors. The fighters can take care of themselves. The rest of the people here rely on your protection. The non-combatants, the children, the elderly, those who can't or won't fight—they need you."

"And you, my queen?" he asked softly. I caught my breath at the welcome endearment. The high priestess would never understand how Rayfe calling me his queen spoke so intimately of his regard for me. "What do *you* need?"

"I need you to love me," I whispered, my heart aching.

He kissed me, and oh, it was sweet. "Done. What else?"

"We should go check in with Ursula to find out."

He tucked a windblown lock of my hair behind my ear, smile going grave. "That's not exactly what I meant."

"I know." I gave him another kiss, lingering over it, savoring the taste, scent, and feel of him, the welcome harbor of his arms. "But anything else has to wait until we get to the other side of this."

He withdrew, physically and on every other level. My senses flared, detecting the change. Now that I'd taught myself to watch for it, the advent of the high priestess had become as obvious as a cold wind snuffing a candle flame. "Yes, let's attend your sister's war council," he said, stiff and haughty. "Though I greatly fear we'll be crying surrender before the sun sets."

I rolled the Star in my pocket. We would see.

RAYFE ACCOMPANIED ME to the council chambers, transformed into a bustling strategy center. I anxiously scanned the visible materials for anything that might tip off the high priestess as to our true intentions, but Ursula and the others had done a masterful job of disguising the working charts and messages regarding the Dasnarian battle front. Everything I could see pertained only to sailing to n'Andana. We updated each other and speculated on the triumph of our surprise attack on the high priestess while Rayfe smirked.

Ash had departed with Djakos, leaving Ami determinedly cheerful and obviously worried out of her mind. She'd taken over distracting Rayfe's attention as much as possible. Fortunately the high priestess seemed to be coming and going, her attention divided, leaving Rayfe confused in her absence—and bemused by Ami's mild flirtations and rambling conversation.

When Ursula passed me a note to commence contact with Jepp, I pleaded fatigue from having been awake most of the night—not a lie, though my declared intent to take a nap was—and I left for the Heart.

Once ensconced in the abalone throne, I checked the time, mentally coordinating with the staymach bird that had become Jepp's companion on the *Hákyrling*. Hardening my nerve, I made the mental leap to enter Jepp's mind.

Though I'd spoken to her before, this was the first time that

I occupied her fully enough to perceive the world through her senses. I'd learned a great deal from observing how the high priestess possessed Rayfe. It was a heady sensation, and really so very easy.

The skies had cleared far out at sea, and through Jepp's long-seeing eyes—and with her permission—I clearly saw the shimmer of the barrier, and the innumerable Dasnarian ships amassing beyond. I'd thought I'd been prepared for the scale of the Dasnarian attack, but no amount of bracing could've steeled me against such a sight.

Jepp stood on the deck of the *Hákyrling*, Kral in full armor beside her. And, on the other side of the barrier, the sea crawled with ships, all the way to the horizon. The Dasnarian warships looked even larger and more menacing from a human perspective. When I saw such sights in visions, they tended to be on a broader scale, from far off, rarely from the height of a person. I didn't know why except that I wondered if the visions came from Moranu's perspective.

A trio of warships had advanced, well past the line of the previous boundary. The Dasnarians had clearly discovered that the barrier had moved. One ship belched flame, a boom lagging behind the bright flash, and something collided with the barrier, bouncing off again.

"Are you listening, Andi?" Kral said to Jepp. I felt suddenly, and deeply uncomfortably, like the high priestess lurking in someone's mind. No surprise there. I asked the staymach perched on Jepp's shoulder to duck its head in its bird-approximation of a nod. I could listen and see through the staymachs to some extent, but a human mind and senses worked far more cleanly and accurately. Appalling that I had the high priestess to thank for this discovery.

*Use the weapons you have*, I reminded myself.

"That's so creepy," Jepp muttered, and I had to agree.

"This is war," Kral retorted. "Don't be missish about a sound communication technique."

"I'll show you missish, General Lunkhead," Jepp said as she twirled a dagger in her hand, a sensation I could oddly feel with my own fingers, and I marveled at the man's courage. "And I notice you didn't invite Andi into *your* head."

"For good reasons, too," he replied with a cocky grin. "Welcome, sorceress. Your timing is excellent. As you can see, they've begun testing the barrier. They're using a standard Dasnarian fleet search pattern, so it's clear from their technique that they're expecting there to be a hole they can exploit. We're as ready for them as we can be, and have identified a spot for them to unexpectedly encounter a portal." His voice dripped with sarcasm and anticipation. "Jepp will show you."

Jepp shifted her gaze from the scout ships to a place farther down the barrier. One conveniently free of our ships. In fact, from what I could see, very few of our ships seemed to be nearby. "Oh, look!" Jepp exclaimed with a thick Dasnarian accent. "I bet there could be a weak spot in the barrier down that way. And those stupid *festilts* aren't even guarding it."

"Can you do that, sorceress?" Kral asked.

*"Yes,"* I whispered in Jepp's mind, feeling her flinch as I startled her anyway.

She didn't show it on the outside though. "She says yes," she reported crisply.

*"Checking something,"* I told her, then moved my consciousness out to the barrier. They'd indicated a fairly wide swath, so I could take my pick. Ursula wanted it about three ships wide, which was less easy to figure, with only sea and sky all around. Dafne could probably measure it, but without a point of reference, I had trouble. I'd also have to make it go deep enough

under water to allow the deep drafts of the Dasnarian warships to sail through and high enough for their masts to fit.

When I'd moved ships through the barrier before, I'd been physically present, and I'd been able to alter the permeability of the barrier selectively as the ships moved through. Jepp had done the same thing using the Star, but the artifact itself had been physically present, too. Making a hole that would persist when I took my attention away posed a significant challenge.

Since the barrier seemed to operate on the principle of circles, I tried creating a small circular hole near the waterline. Then if I expanded it equally outward, it should be as high above water as below, with the same width. I could make the hole and stabilize it easily enough—but the barrier kept nudging me with that information, as if it thought I needed to be alerted. I reassured it that I'd intended to make the hole and it subsided. Then, a moment later, it nudged me with the information again. This would get old—and draining—quickly.

Back under the sea, the crabs gathered, scuttling in schools like fish shifting direction, tapping their claws to get my attention. They formed a sort of very basic intelligence using their group mind. It had been clever of the ancient n'Andanans, as the crabs minded the barrier without sorcerous intervention— a critical safety back up—but they possessed a limited understanding. I could convince them to let me change the protocol in the moment, but as soon as I stopped intervening, they reverted to normal maintenance. Which meant they'd keep telling me over and over about the hole. And trying to get me to fix it.

Sure enough, as soon as I stepped back and let go of the barrier, they immediately mended the hole. I'd have to hold it open for each ship. Far from ideal, especially when I'd need all of my attention to strike at the high priestess. We'd have to do this non-simultaneously. I'd have to allow as many ships through as I could, but when our team reached n'Andana and I needed my full concentration there, I'd have to let the barrier revert. I couldn't afford to divide my attention during our gambit in n'Andana.

An excellent rationale against the simultaneous dual attacks, but too late now. Moranu take me if I'd admit to Ursula that she was right.

I went back to Jepp's mind, startling a little at the sight of Kral's handsome face snarling through the opening of his helm.

"What do you mean you can't tell if she's listening or not—don't you know your own brains?"

"Why don't you let the scary sorceress into *your* head," Jepp replied sweetly, "and then you'll understand. It's very strange. It felt no different when she said she was listening and when it seems she isn't."

"I'll pass," Kral said, lip curling. "That kind of thing smacks too much of Deyrr."

Too true, my friend. I asked the staymach to flap its wings, but neither of them was paying attention. Besides which, I needed to explain the change of plans. I couldn't linger until the searching ships reached the chosen spot—that looked to be an hour or more away—so I'd have to inform Ursula, so she could reframe the battle strategy. I'd "return" to the *Hákyrling* in an hour or so. All far too complicated for even my staymach's songbird brain to relay.

Another line to cross, but this was war and all.

"This is Andi. I'm here now," I had Jepp say. She jumped, nearly throwing one of her daggers, before she realized, then gripped it tightly. "I take it back," she said. "*That* is totally fucking creepy."

"I apologize," I had her say, "but I needed words."

"Are you talking as you and as Andi?" Kral peered at Jepp,

poking her forehead with a big finger that she batted away.

"Yes. And it's as unsettling as you'd think, so let's get it over with. Talk away, Andi."

Was that how Rayfe felt, hearing words that weren't his coming out of his mouth? No—the high priestess must do something to dull his awareness so he didn't know what was going on. I startled Jepp because she was fully aware. I was purging Rayfe as soon as possible, I didn't care what Ursula said.

"I have to hold the portal open," I explained quickly. "I can't just open it and leave—I have to be present. I'll update Ursula and will be back in an hour. Yes?"

Kral scrutinized the search pattern, picked up an instrument and measured against the sky. "Make it two hours, and we'll be ready. Tell Her Majesty to trust us to make decisions here. She can't control every Danu-cursed thing."

I felt Jepp roll her eyes. "Leaving now," I said through Jepp's mouth, as it felt like the right courtesy. As I withdrew, I heard her spit over the rail. "If I never have to do *that* again, it will be too soon," she declared.

Apparently I didn't need to defect to Deyrr to become just like the high priestess. No time for guilt, however. I ran a quick check of the barrier, as I mentally travelled away. All good. I drew my consciousness back over the waters, past n'Andana, then scanned for the null spot that would be Zynda. I found her quite easily. That was a concern as the high priestess no doubt could do the same. I touched Zynda's mind in greeting, a sort of knock on the door I could do with a sister telepath that didn't work with someone like Jepp.

Zynda welcomed me in with a mental embrace.

*"How's progress?"* I asked.

*"Sea and sky, sea and sky,"* she answered with a mental shrug. *"Zyr is holding up well, as are the reinforcements. No trouble so far. If*

*they're expecting us, they're letting us come all the way in, which makes sense for an ambush. I estimate we'll arrive in about three hours."*

I mentally groaned. How long would it take a warship to sail through the portal? Some time to verify they'd found it, then to alter course. Then time to actually pass through. For multiple ships to come through and make the battle worth it... The timing couldn't be worse.

But if the high priestess was helping Hestar, we needed the distraction of that battle to divide her attention. We'd deliberately set up this timing to coincide. I really hated that Ursula might be right about too much depending solely on me. I refused to be the weak link.

*"All right, I'll be back before then,"* I promised.

*"Careful what you think at me—*she *might be able to listen in."*

Good point. This began to feel very bad, the balance shifting in the wrong direction. Back in my own body and senses, I gazed out at the dark ocean beyond the glow of the Heart. The crabs winked glossy blue as they scrabbled over the dome, doing their work.

So tempting to look through the future visions, to see how the next few hours would fall out. But what good would that serve? I'd committed to several courses of action—we all had—and knowing one way or the other at this point wouldn't give us time to change course. Or would it?

I rolled the Star in my palm, hoping I'd made the right choice not to send it with Zynda. I might not be able to strike at the high priestess as effectively through her smaller focus stone, but in the moment intuition—or Moranu?—had advised me not to send the powerful artifact into Deyrr's hands. *Moranu, I'm listening.*

Nothing. Just me, my thoughts, and the glow of the Star. I could wish that it held the power to guide me through this chain of decisions the way it had guided Ursula and Ami to rescue me when Terin and his gang had kidnapped Stella and taken me hostage. A foolish gambit of theirs, as it would've been years before Stella could get them into the Heart. I still didn't know what Terin's little rebellion had hoped to gain by—

I sat up straighter, the edge of realization creeping over me, a pattern emerging that I hadn't had the wit to recognize before.

Stella had been born with the Mark of the Tala, as I had. We'd assumed Terin had abducted Stella as a way to control the Heart, which was puzzling since she was only an infant at the time and wouldn't be able to access it until she matured into a young woman. But looking at the bigger picture—what else was going on at that same time? Illyria, minion of Deyrr and of the high priestess, had been in Ordnung, manipulating Uorsin, trying to locate and steal the Star.

She'd been unsuccessful because Ursula had brought the Star with her into Annfwn, chasing after Terin. Our late, unlamented Uncle Terin had been outside the much smaller barrier that at the time enclosed only Annfwn. He'd left after I demonstrated my ability to control the barrier, to become Queen of Annfwn in fact as well as in name. He'd been bitter that his brother— Salena's mate in their youth—had committed suicide, jealous, bent on revenge. Easy emotions to manipulate.

Could Terin have been mind-controlled by the high priestess to kidnap Stella? That would explain a great deal. It had made no sense, the way Terin and his people had holed up in that cave. A desperation move we'd thought at the time, going to ground, but what if they'd been waiting? I thought back to those few days I'd been held by them, mostly concerned with caring for baby Stella, confident that Rayfe would come for me, as he'd always sworn he'd do. Those hushed conversations, Terin watching impatiently, pacing. Protesting when his people had argued for surrender.

Refusing to leave that place.

I'd sealed the barrier a few days before that, right after Ursula and Harlan came through. I'd needed to admit them, but I'd known I'd be distracted by the search for Stella. I'd been still learning to sort the ever-changing visions of the future. So I'd made the barrier impermeable even to animals for those few days, as one less thing to think about. Had I inadvertently—and fortuitously—shut out the high priestess?

It could've been a two-pronged strategy in direct response to my taking my mother's place in Annfwn: get the Star and take control of the Heart using Stella.

Understanding unfolded like window after window opening into a brightly lit room. This was why Windroven had been under siege all this time—because of Stella. I'd seen visions of the storming of Windroven, the devastating attacks that tore the castle from its clifftop perch. I'd thought those visions had been due to Djakos, but then the visions hadn't changed when Zynda and Marskal liberated the slumbering dragon. Instead it seemed that Djakos might've been what held the Deyrr creatures at bay.

The high priestess wanted Stella. It was so obvious now, though she'd hidden that aim as deftly as a con artist sliding shells from one spot to the next.

The high priestess wanted the Star of Annfwn, too, which I'd nearly handed to her. Could she have been manipulating us into that move, one I'd thwarted only by last-moment instinct? But clearly she believed that Stella would give her something she needed.

And now Stella was in Annfwn, unprotected because we'd sent all of our warriors away.

Panic surging in me, I pocketed the Star, and flung myself at the Heart's barrier, shapeshifting into a deep-water fish first, then wriggling my way through. Painfully and ignominiously slow. After that, I ascended rapidly, shifting from one form to the next, then finally shooting into the air as the heron, arrowing my way toward the cliff city. My staymach guard swirled up, spun around me and, reading my mood, shifted into raptor form. The harbor and bay looked stark and empty, with so many ships out, the previously teeming cliff city nearly a ghost town with so many of the warriors departed on our oh-so-clever plan, leaving Annfwn virtually undefended.

I pumped my wings, cursing myself for being a fool. I'd said it to Rayfe myself, only hours before. *The fighters can take care of themselves. The rest of the people here rely on your protection. The non-combatants, the children, the elderly, those who can't or won't fight—they need you.*

They weren't only coming for Stella. This was it. The attack on Annfwn I'd seen a thousand times in my mind had nearly arrived. And we were woefully vulnerable.

I desperately wanted to call for Rayfe.

I didn't dare call for him.

This would be up to me. First things first. We could afford to lose this battle. If we lost Stella to them, we'd lose the war. I knew it as surely as if Moranu whispered in my mind.

I flew directly to the council chambers, landing in their midst and shifting back to human form with a thump to the floor that startled everyone. Rayfe wasn't there. Ursula and Harlan both leapt to their feet, swords drawn.

"What?" Ursula demanded.

"And who is watching Rayfe? Where are the kids?" I demanded in turn, and Ami surged to her feet also. "Stella—where is she?"

"At the new secret training ground." Ami had gone deathly pale. "Why—what's wrong?"

"*Where is it?*" I nearly shouted at her. Why, oh why hadn't I had someone tell me? This was what came of delegating.

Ami was already moving. "I'll take you there."

"Where's Rayfe?" I called as I ran with her.

"We're coming." Ursula and Harlan paced us. "I have two Hawks on Rayfe."

I spun back. Nakoa had stood, too, Dafne clutching the baby to her, eyes wide. "Dafne," I said, "call Kiraka to defend you. Nakoa, guard them. Don't trust *anyone* until we return." It burned my mouth to say it. "Not even Rayfe."

I hurried to catch up with Ami, who'd gathered her skirts to run, moving far more swiftly than I'd expected of her. Summoning more staymachs, I gathered them to us, sending a warning out to all the denizens of the cliff city. *Attack incoming*, I broadcast to anyone who could hear. *Wizards, seal the lower levels, close off the upper. Prepare to defend! Prepare for siege.*

With another thought, I activated the Gate of Annfwn, closing down access to the rest of the kingdoms. Annfwn might fall, but maybe we could restrict the doom to this place.

"Andi, explain." Ursula ran easily beside me.

"We fucked up. I did. We have to abort the attack on n'Andana. They're coming here. I'm sending the call to lock up the city and prepare for attack."

Ursula cursed viciously. "Can you tell Kral—can someone?"

"I have to get to Stella first. Then… No. Too late. They're already here."

"What—"

A roar interrupted the question as all around, serenity went to jagged chaos. The sea erupted into geysers typhooning at the cliff city. Sand clogged the air, and shrieks rent the sky. Deyrr's n'Andanan forces swarmed over the beach like swamp midges descending on bare flesh. Screams rang out, and the formerly empty harbor suddenly teemed with ships. Barely a tenth of them ours.

She'd fooled me. Completely and thoroughly.

Ursula hurled orders at a few of her lieutenants. Cursed. "I have to mount the defense."

"Go do that. I have to stop her from getting Stella," I bit out. Ami was racing for the lower caverns. Of course, of course. We'd learned the cliff heights were unsafe so we went down to protect the kids. So easily pushed this way and that. Right into her waiting hands. "Ami!" I yelled in sudden panic, realizing what she would run headlong into.

I shifted to heron form again. My staymach guard, now raptors with wicked beaks and lethal talons, flanked me, as I plunged into the shadows below. The lower levels were dark. The parts of the cliff city open to air and light started well above beach level, but inside they dug down deep. Though Tala rushed to obey my orders, all the portals—even the ones closed on peaceful days—all stood open to the beach. Rayfe. Only he could've issued that command. What... I turned a corner and found two of Ursula's Hawks, a woman whose name I didn't know and a man named Tays. Both dead, showing marks from Rayfe's wolfhound guard.

With our doors standing open, the Deyrr army poured into the cliff city, countless animals of all kinds, from gigantic to tiny, cascading through the arches in an unending wave. Ami slowed, aghast at the sight, then set her shoulders in her trademark obstinacy and started forward again. I winged ahead of her, circling to buffet her with my wings, herding her back.

She tried to bat me away, head down, but Harlan appeared just then, exercising the simple expedient of lifting Ami and tossing her over his shoulder, as she screamed bloody murder. I left him to protect her, knowing with a certainty that could be foresight or was simple logic where to find the kids.

I flew through and over the Deyrr attackers, masking myself with the high priestess's mind-control taint, one more bird among many. Taking a shortcut through the warren of tunnels, I quickly put them behind me, and followed the echoing ursine roars of Meg, and the shrieks of terrified children.

Reaching out wildly in a mental call, I risked a message to Zynda. *"Abort, abort, abort."*

*"What? I don't—Oh, Moranu save us,"* she swiftly followed as I showed her the scene. *"We're coming, but it will be hours."*

I knew. I knew all too well. *"Send someone to Kral. Warn the fleet."*

*"Warn them of what, exactly? What can they do?"*

I rounded the bend in the tunnel, the screams and roars no longer echoes, but immediate and terrifying to my sensitive ears.

*"Andi? Andi, what—"*

I shut out Zynda's mind-voice with ruthless resolve. All that mattered was in front of me: a wall of Deyrr creatures trapping the children in a cave. Landing and changing to human form—and fought off the wave of dizziness that came from shapeshifting so many times in succession—I brandished the Star, which glowed like a sun. Tapping into the fiery power of the heart, I hit the advancing creatures with a blast of magic.

It bounced off them, just as had happened with the warthog. They turned, far too alert and fast for the standard Deyrr creature, recognizing me now as the enemy, moving fast toward me.

I couldn't possibly fight them all. Instead, I swallowed the dizziness and changed to horse form, galloping with all speed for the children. If nothing else, I had to rescue Stella. We might be doomed to lose this battle—as I'd seen all along—but forfeiting Stella would be the absolute and final defeat.

I burst through, ignoring the bite of claws and teeth—and

came face to face with Rayfe, in human form. Meg lay collapsed his feet, and he pointed a bloody sword at a snarling bear cub, Astar. In his arm, he gripped a fiercely struggling, naked, and blood-smeared Stella.

# ~ 18 ~

ALL RIGHT. SO we were doing this.

All of those visions of the future, of this moment, telescoped into a concise present. I focused on this, and only this. I gathered the power to me, from the Heart, from the ambient magic of Annfwn soaked into the very stones around me, and my own native magic, wringing out the cells of my body for everything in me.

As I did, Astar lunged, swiping at Rayfe, and he—expression cold and somehow cruelly beautiful with the high priestess's visage—stabbed the sword into the bear cub's breast. Stella screamed like a person five times her size, the gut-curdling wail shocking Rayfe. Her clawed fingers raked down his face, gouging his eyes and making him jerk backward.

"You brat!" he howled, his voice a curious comingling of the high priestess's chill command and the wolf's howl. Power whipped out, fastened on Stella, and she went limp, unconscious.

Taking the opportunity Stella afforded me, I focused all my power through the Star and stabbed at him.

Or, rather, at the tether of her consciousness connecting to Rayfe. Like an oily black rope, it snaked from the distance, from wherever the high priestess physically was. I wasn't going for her, however, instead I concentrated on where the connection split into his mind, sundering into its many branching and countless small connections that needled into the smallest parts of his brain—tiny tentacles operating the levers that made him move, hear, speak. Betray.

Ruthlessly, I laid his mind open with my mental knife. I couldn't afford sentimentality or fear. Rayfe's mind was chaos. His will struggling to reassert itself. Deep panic. Overwhelming remorse and fury. And the multiplying threads of Deyrr magic, slamming the cage doors shut on him.

I felt *her*, turning her attention to me. Calling her minions to attack me.

I spared a thought to alert my staymach guard, but had no time for surgical precision with Rayfe. Throwing all of my intent behind it, I reached for the rope to the high priestess, biting back the instinctive revulsion as the Deyrr magic slimed into me as I gripped it.

She was there, and so was the god.

As I'd seen through Karyn's eyes, the remorseless golden face of the incarnate god—chillingly beautiful, unbearably cruel—stared into my very soul with His black, depthless gaze.

***You cannot defeat me, mortal daughter,*** He whispered chidingly. ***The gods are beyond your ken.***

"I don't have to." I probably said it aloud, too focused on sharpening and positioning my mental blade to bother with making my words mind-voice only. Thank Moranu I'd so carefully planned how I'd do this. "I only have to cut off your hands."

With superhuman effort, I sliced through the rope, holding on with everything in me to the end tethered to Rayfe's mind. I hauled at the other end, grimly delighted by the high priestess's agony thrumming down the taut length, then released it. It snapped back with a boom that resonated on physical and metaphysical levels. The high priestess screamed, the sound scraping across the timeline with horrifying resonance. She punched back at me, reaching into and through me, opening a hole in something deep inside. Stunned by the unexpected blow, I lashed back at her—and she vanished, Deyrr's presence going with her.

Though I held on as tightly as I knew how, the threads of Deyrr control still embedded in Rayfe's mind slipped from my grasp like water through splayed fingers. Rayfe sent up a howl of anguish, blood pouring from his eyes, ears and mouth. He fell, and, still unconscious, Stella went with him. Both collapsed over Astar's prone and bleeding body.

*No!* I lunged for them and—

Claws raked my back, teeth sinking into my neck. My turn to scream, the physical agony a shock after being so immersed in the metaphysical realm. I rallied my staymach guard, bringing them in to free me from whatever had me in its grip. Spending power recklessly, I spun out a blade of power and severed the connections of these creatures to Deyrr. It would leave their souls suspended, forever trapped in Deyrr's hold and removed from their undead bodies, but I couldn't do otherwise.

Us or them.

Bodies fell around me—furred, scaled, feathered, skinned—and I felt as if I waded through stone to reach the bleeding pile of my husband, niece, and nephew. I couldn't reach them, and yet I *must*. I struggled on, forced a step back for ever two I managed.

Ami's wail of horror penetrated my determined haze. How in Moranu had she gotten here?

Then, impossibly, Ursula strode past me, face stony, slashing through the Deyrr creatures in a ruby glow that had them falling away. Salena's rubies—I'd forgotten. Ami, blood-spattered and brandishing a dagger, followed in Ursula's wake. Then Kelleah, her fiery curls an odd combination of green and ruby light.

I lurched after them—and Harlan's bear hug wrapped me in place. "You're wounded," he grated in my ear. "Let them do it."

"Rayfe…"

"They've got him. And the kids. Let me help you." He released me and began tying a tourniquet around a wound on my upper arm I hadn't even noticed. I tried to see around him, but Harlan is a big man. Harlan knelt, grunting as he surveyed the cuts on my torso, enabling me to see more. It seemed more people had filled the cavern, bringing lanterns and torches. The sounds of fighting continued here and there, but lessened from before. I couldn't see Rayfe and the twins, walled behind a group of people, maybe a deliberate screen to protect me from the truth.

"Annfwn?" I asked, forcing myself to think about the bigger picture.

"We are overrun." Harlan sounded uncharacteristically dour. "Everyone is either in the upper levels or down here. The doors are sealed and our people are doing their best, but it won't be enough."

I could feel it, the steady hammering of the attack, the pitched roar of mental commands and calls for help. Calling for me, for Rayfe, for their queen and king to help them. A call Rayfe might never answer again. I couldn't face that possibility. What would my life be, empty of him?

"I should go. We have to fight."

"I'm under orders to keep you here." Harlan looked up from bandaging my leg, his normally somber face contorted. "You can't feel it, but you're bleeding in half a dozen places. You go now, you'll collapse from blood loss. Give me a few minutes. We're hunkering down here, reassessing."

The endless stream of Deyrr creatures had indeed diminished. Hawks and Tala fought some of the ones I hadn't yet killed, but no more arrived. Harlan took note of my returning rationality. "We sealed ourselves in. We're safe as can be for the moment, as long as that lasts."

"Dafne, Nakoa and the baby. We—"

"Can't help them right now. We can't even *get* to them. You told them to stay in the council chambers, remember? That's secure. Nakoa can handle it."

"Right." Maybe he could. Maybe he couldn't. But Harlan was right that they were on their own. "I can give us more time, if that will help."

"Absolutely. We need to regroup and plan."

I tapped into the Heart while Harlan bandaged the wounds on my back, using it to augment the doors the wizards had moved into place. I layered a new barrier into the stone, a mini barrier connected to the bedrock and the Heart of Annfwn that should hold for hours, at least.

"Done," I said.

"And that takes care of the worst of the bleeders until Kelleah can heal you," Harlan replied. "Can I trust you to stay put while I help clean up here?"

"Yes." I nodded, to assure him, putting my hands on his muscled arms to steady myself. He wore one of Salena's ruby necklaces, the dangling strands made into a choker around his thick neck. It should have looked absurd, but somehow it became heroic. "I have to go to Rayfe."

"I know." His eyes held compassion, the kind that showed he, too, feared the worst. "Where are the rest of the kids—do you know?"

"Back behind that door. Meg managed to shut most of them in."

"Any of these animals with them? So far we're just defending, but we need to deal with all the Deyrr in here."

Oh, right. "Probably. The Tala will know."

He nodded and let me go, waiting a moment to make sure I stayed on my feet. Then he brushed a hand over my cheek. "You did well, Queen Andromeda. Your very best. Keep reminding yourself of that."

His intended reassurance only reminded me of how abysmally I'd failed. I'd known all along that we'd be overrun, that none of the futures allowed for an alternative, and yet I'd still clung to a fragile hope that I could stop it.

I made my way to where Rayfe had fallen, staggering a little as my wounds and blood loss made themselves known. A Hawk guarding the little group nodded to me, expression grim, and stepped out of the way.

Ami sat on the ground, pink skirts arrayed as if at a picnic—but she clutched Stella in her arms, rocking her. She murmured a steady stream of quiet words, coaxing Stella to wake, all the while she had her gaze fixed on Astar, still in bear cub form. Kelleah knelt over him, deep into healing mode, her hands buried in his cinnamon fur. She wouldn't waste the energy on him if he was dead. Kelleah was far too practical for that.

And Kelleah was far too loyal to her king to ignore Rayfe in favor of Astar, so either he was dead, or he was less wounded than Astar. With anguish and dread, I reached out mentally—my legs sagging with watery relief when I found a low rumble of life in him still.

I sank to my knees, shifting Rayfe's gore-scarred head into my lap, smoothing his tangled, blood-snarled hair from his face. He'd gone so strengthless and limp, skin waxy pale against the angry wounds. With his face lax in unconsciousness, he looked far younger than his years, his habitual brooding expression erased, uncharacteristically vulnerable. I reached for a loose edge of my skirt to wipe the gore off his face—I couldn't tell if Stella had gouged out his eyes or simply torn the flesh around them—but I found my entire gown seemed to be soaked in blood.

"Here," Ami said, holding out a cloth. I took it from her, slightly bemused. "Comes of being a mother," she added tightly. "You have to be ready to clean all sorts of disgusting messes. You'll see."

With a pang of wistfulness and dread, I mentally checked in with my unborn child. Fortunately he seemed to be fine, riding along in his cushioned bubble. A relief to know that nature, or the goddesses, or whatever, handled some things for me. I cleaned Rayfe's face with care, using water from the flask Ami also handed me.

So odd to be sitting here in this island of light and relative peace, while the others prowled in the dimness of the caverns and tunnels around us, the scuffles of brief skirmishes and occasional calls and answers coming back to us. Every once in a while, a child's querulous voice rose, then faded under the murmurs of adult answers.

And outside a battle raged.

Exhaustion washing over me, now that I sat, I began to feel every one of those wounds Harlan had mentioned. I concentrated on cleaning Rayfe's wounds, with diligence and tender care. As if I could make up for everything by doing this one thing right. If I could just wipe all the blood from his many wounds, then he would be himself again. He didn't stir under my ministrations, his consciousness so deep I could barely sense him inside, though his body lived. Maybe that was just as well.

The way those Deyrr threads had snapped back into him... I wondered if I'd ever be able to root it all out of him, if he'd ever be completely free of it. That is, if his sanity survived. The chaos

I'd glimpsed in his mind while I rampaged through it… I didn't know how anyone could survive that. Or would want to. Reaching to the Heart, I fed its magic to Rayfe, encouraging the conduit to strengthen him enough for him to shift.

And I began purging him, seeking out the dregs of Deyrr's passage, lifting it into myself and dissolving it in the clean flow of the Heart's magic.

"Did Nilly get his eyes?" Ami asked tentatively, startling me a little.

"I think the eyes themselves are all right," I answered. An easy thing to assess and think about, his physical wounds. In the background, I kept searching and cleansing. "But she did a thorough job on the flesh all around."

"I'm so sorry." She sounded truly stricken, and I jerked up my gaze, astonished.

"Don't be sorry," I said, harshly enough that she flinched. I closed my eyes and tried to get a grip. "I'm sorry. *We* are sorry. He tried to abduct Nilly and she only defended herself."

"It wasn't him, Andi," Ami said firmly. "You know that."

I did know that—and yet it changed nothing. "I'm just glad that our Nilly is so fierce. She will be a force to be reckoned with someday."

Ami stroked her unconscious daughter's dark curls. "Is that prophecy?"

"Simple prediction of the future based on the present," I replied wryly.

"She won't wake up, and I don't know why. Willy is obviously wounded, but—" A hiccupping sob interrupted her words.

"The high priestess used her power over shapeshifters to put her out," I explained gently. "Nilly will be fine. They wanted her intact, so they wouldn't have done anything to harm her."

Both our gazes strayed to where Kelleah labored in intense

silence over a limp, very small bear cub. We knew the same wasn't true for Astar. He'd been expendable to Deyrr, and easily dispatched as such.

"How did you guess?" Ami asked in a hush, and for a moment I thought she meant about Deyrr's disregard for a small boy with no special destiny. "Or did you see it in a vision, that they'd come for my Nilly?"

"I'd like to know that, too," Ursula commented, coming into our circle of lamplight, then crouching. Her leathers were spattered with gore in shades from bright red to the black ooze of Deyrr. She still held her sword—too fouled for her to sheath—resting the tip on the bare stone.

"No vision," I replied with some bitterness. "Just simple logic that I failed to piece together for far too long. That's been the high priestess's aim for years: to secure the Star of Annfwn, and Stella with the Mark of the Tala, and thus control the Heart—and all the world."

"She doesn't want to destroy Annfwn," Harlan said, joining us, dawning realization on his face. "She wants to own it."

"And all the shapeshifters within," I agreed.

"Then why didn't she try for you?" Ursula wanted to know. "She could've grabbed you long ago, and the Star, too, after Mother died. You were a child not much older than Stella, and we were unprotected, living outside the barrier at Ordnung, unprotected by the barrier."

I smoothed Rayfe's hair back from his forehead, my fingers snagging in the snarls, sticky with dried and drying blood. There wasn't water enough to wash, that, too. When—if—he woke, he could shift to heal his wounds and be his usual self: sensual, powerful, and so beautiful to my eyes. He'd always seemed so invulnerable to me. *Oh, Moranu, please that be so.* "I had the Mark, yes, but it wasn't...active. I was asleep," I said, partly to myself, "until Rayfe wakened me with a kiss. Blood to blood, and the Mark came to life." I remembered how our blood had mixed, flying off as tiny dark birds.

"So," Ursula said, and by her neutral tone I imagined I'd sounded daft, "the high priestess had also been inactive until then?"

"I'm not sure, but that makes sense. She was starved of magic, like the others, we know that. It could be she hibernated, sleeping like the n'Andanan dragons, awaiting the return of magic."

"But she was outside the barrier, how could she have awakened before we moved it? Nothing about her access to magic changed until then."

"Didn't it?" I glanced up at Harlan. "The seraglio at the Imperial Palace is magically maintained, yes?"

He nodded thoughtfully. "After my—After I left forever, the events of that time disrupted many of Hulda's plans, and also Hestar's. Hulda might've reached out to Deyrr for power. Or Hestar did, to secure the throne. Or both did. A great… upset happened in our family around that time."

Looking at him, I saw again the ivory blonde, draped in diamonds and pearls, a whirlwind of light and grace as she danced. I saw pain, and blood, sex used as a weapon, so cruelly. Inga and Helva weeping. Hulda raging. Then a casket, a desiccated figure inside, being brought to the tropical lagoon of the seraglio.

"I think they did bring the high priestess to the seraglio," I murmured. "Some time after the ivory blond girl left."

Harlan went rigid, a wave of grief and anguish rolling off of him, and Ursula went alert. Had she been a cat, her ears would've flattened, tail lashing. I looked from one to the other. "Do you know who she is?"

Ursula looked to Harlan, but he seemed to be unable to speak. "Yes," she said. "Have you seen where she is?" She asked with such measured care that I felt my own skin prickle.

"I've seen how she was, then," I temporized. "She was dressed all in shades of ivory and cream, diamonds and pearls. So young. Long ago. So much suffering." The loss of innocence to such uncaring brutality made my heart throb. "And," I added carefully, watching Harlan, "I've maybe seen her after that, much later. I think it's the same woman."

"*Later?*" Harlan asked with hushed intensity. He flexed his fingers, as if he wanted to reach for me, to drag the information out.

I shook away the vision. Knowing how the high priestess had been resurrected confirmed our speculations, but I didn't see how it was otherwise helpful to our current predicament. "*Maybe.* The visions don't come with helpfully labeled dates. And what I saw could be garbage. Not everything I see is relevant."

"Would you…" Harlan's voice cracked, and he squeezed his eyes closed. When he opened them, they glittered with rare turmoil from the stalwart former mercenary. "Would you tell me anyway?"

"Please, Andi," Ursula added with unusual fervency, given our circumstances. Usually she'd be all about focusing on critical decision making, not distant players in a drama that didn't involve us. "As a favor, to me. To us," she added, setting down her sword and reaching up to take Harlan's hand. He crouched beside her, both of them watching me with serious—and hopeful expressions. Though they both had gray eyes, I'd never thought they seemed the same, his so pale and hers so steely, but in that moment they looked so much alike that it seemed impossible they'd ever not been joined together.

"I've seen the part I just told you," I said gently. "A young woman, barely out of girlhood, with very long hair of an extraordinary ivory color. She's dancing, wearing a kingdom's treasury of jewels."

"An empire's," Harlan put in softly, and I began to understand.

"She was brutalized, hurt badly. I see Inga and Helva crying over her. But she's not dead. She's gone."

"And *later?*" Harlan urged.

"I'm not sure it's the same woman," I cautioned, and he nodded, much too eagerly. "She's tanned, substantially older, the hair the same, but her face a mature woman's. In these visions I can see that her eyes are an intense blue. However, she is not anywhere that I recognize as Dasnaria."

"No, she wouldn't be," Harlan inserted, excitement infusing him.

I waited a moment, but he said nothing more. Who was this woman? "It's a hot place, with a large river. Everyone but her is much darker skinned, and there are elephants."

He blew out a breath in choked sound part exclamation, part sob, startling even Kelleah out of her concentration. "It's her, it has to be."

Ursula gripped his hand, rising to her feet to look him in the eye. "We don't know that."

"*I* know it," he replied unequivocally, and she put her hands on his shoulders as if restraining him from going somewhere. As if any of us could go anywhere. Though we couldn't stay trapped down here forever.

"Even if it is her," Ursula said, very reasonably, and I recognized the tone she used, the same as when she thought I might charge off to do something crazy, "we can't go look for her now."

"I know that," he bit out, not at all his usual patient self.

"But there has to be a reason Andi is seeing these visions."

Ursula looked pointedly at me and I shrugged a little. "Not necessarily. As I said, I see a *lot* of things, and part of the challenge for me is to winnow out what's relevant from what's simply carried along by attachment to people who are critical elements of events."

"There," Ursula said. "Besides, Kaedrin said she knew where she is."

"And then Kaedrin disappeared again without giving me the information as she'd promised," he replied with some vehemence, then put a hand over hers. "I know we couldn't have gone to look for her yet. My loyalties aren't conflicted. You come first. You always have."

"Not *always*," she replied wryly, but she lifted her other hand to cup his cheek. "I know this is hard for you. I just don't want you distracted by this information."

Ami cleared her throat delicately. "Are we to know *who* under Glorianna's gaze you're talking about?"

"Danu's gaze," Harlan replied gruffly. "She became a priestess of Danu."

Ami gave me a wide-eyed look. "Gosh, I understand everything now!"

I snorted, not a laugh, but close to it. "You know as much as I do."

"Another of Harlan's sisters," Ursula told us. "Lost, long ago." She nodded to me. "Under terrible circumstances. Harlan made vows to reveal nothing about her—some things he literally cannot speak aloud—in order to help her escape her mother, who we fondly know as Hulda, and the wrath of the Dasnarian Empire. Her name is Ivariel now."

Ami and I absorbed that. "She actually managed to escape the seraglio?" I clarified.

Harlan looked overcome with emotion—or perhaps struggled against the *geas* that bound his words—but nodded.

"She did, with Harlan's help," Ursula said, almost more to him than us, reassuring him of something. "And I'm entertained that's the only question you have."

"Yes, well. A lot of pieces fall into place, knowing all that." I contemplated that, smoothing my fingertips over Rayfe's brows and cheekbones. He'd grown some stubble, too. Unusual for him. His puppet-master hadn't been tending to him. No surprise, but I had to wrestle back the sudden burst of rage. "Perhaps this Ivariel is connected somehow, I don't know. In the vision, when I saw her with her family and the—"

"Family?" Harlan burst out, spinning away from Ursula, but retaining her hand.

I blinked at him, reassessed my vision, and how much every detail meant to him. "Remember that I'm making assumptions. They spoke a language I don't know, and I have only the context of what I saw and heard, but the man seemed to be a lover or husband, and there was a young woman who seemed to be her daughter."

"A husband and daughter," he repeated reverently, seeming unaware of the tears tracking down his hard warrior's face.

"Possibly," I warned him, but Ursula shook her head slightly, so I let it go. Clearly he had a great deal of old emotion tied up with this lost sister. "Anyway, when I saw her with her family," I tipped my head at Harlan, "they were working with elephants, and the magic wave passed over."

"When the wave passed over last night with the barrier shift?" Ursula asked, frowning.

Had that been only last night? It felt like ages ago. I traced the lines of Rayfe's lips, so soft within the sharp stubble, wishing he'd wake. I glanced at Kelleah, all of us determinedly not hovering over her, all of us waiting for the verdict. "No, when we moved it the first time. It expanded to cover wherever they are. I couldn't understand why those people and that place, of all the people and places affected by that first barrier shift, mattered all that much. But, this Ivariel, if she left Dasnaria a long time ago…" I left a pause for them to fill in.

Ursula glanced at Harlan. "Twenty years ago," he said.

I nodded, paused midway. Oh. *Oh.* "This makes sense. This is what I saw from back then: in the wake of her departure, a casket arrived in the seraglio. There was a desiccated body inside. If we presume that it was the high priestess, then they brought her to the seraglio to absorb magic and awaken. It could be that the seraglio was first created as a reserve for magic, much like the Heart, and only later made into a dwelling."

"A prison," Harlan corrected, voice hard, and Ursula dipped her chin in agreement. "Dasnarian legend says the seraglio existed first, and the palace was later built around it."

"Would it have been sunk under water?" I asked.

He cocked his head, intensely curious, a bit taken aback. "Deep beneath a lake, yes."

That made sense. "Here's the interesting part. If—"

"We're only just now getting to the interesting part?" Ursula said drily, but she finally released Harlan's hand and picked up her sword, using the water and cloth beside me to clean it.

"The timing," I said to her. "If Ivariel left twenty years ago, I would've been about three years old, and Ami not yet born. Let's figure it takes a couple of years for the high priestess to absorb enough magic to awake, then—"

"Danu's freezing tits!" Ursula snarled. "Our mother died right when the high priestess awoke?"

"The timing is awfully coincidental," I agreed.

"Then maybe I'm not wholly at fault for her death?" Ami

asked in a small voice.

Ursula whirled and crossed to her in one great stride, crouching down and looking Ami in the eye. "You were never at fault for our mother's death. *Never.* She loved you and she was so happy to bring you into the world."

Ami was weeping, but she smiled through the tears, holding Stella close. "I would give my life for Nilly and Willy…" Her luminous violet eyes strayed to where Kelleah finally straightened.

"Thank Moranu we were so close to the Heart," Kelleah said. "He's fully healed."

A sigh of relief blew out of us, the shifting of a welcome breeze after the raging storm.

"I'll go triage our remaining wounded," Harlan volunteered, and Kelleah nodded her gratitude. She lifted Astar, now in boy form, and brought him to Ami, who moved Stella over to make room.

"Let me," Ursula said gently, slipping Stella from Ami's arms and cradling our niece in her own. Ami took Astar, running her hands over his smooth, healthy skin, marred only by blood and no wounds, but checking nevertheless.

Unoffended—probably accustomed to mothers wanting to be sure for themselves—Kelleah turned to me and sank to her knees. "How is our king?" she asked gravely.

I'd been keeping myself together fairly well until she asked that. In the face of her sympathy, I crumpled. "I'm not sure. He's very deep inside. If only he'd wake, he could shift and then—"

Her warm, moss green eyes held sympathy. "I'm low on healing energy and there are others wounded I should see to before I have to sleep this off. What if you and I together wake him? I can use small amounts of healing as the tool, if you can power it, then you force him to shift."

"I don't have that ability." The high priestess did, and I'd already crossed so many ethical lines. If I pushed Rayfe to shift, then all that remained would be for me to resurrect the dead by enslaving their spirits to my will.

"The king and queen have that ability," Kelleah was assuring me, "so you have it within you."

"But I'm not a real queen, because—"

"Nonsense." She gave me an impatient look worthy of Ursula. "You are Queen of Annfwn, daughter of a long line of queens and sorceresses. Stop whining and act like it."

I gaped at her, and I thought I heard a snorting sound from Ursula, but when I gave her a narrow look, she seemed intent on cuddling Stella.

Kelleah gazed back with a long, expectant stare, not without compassion. "Sorceress Andromeda, remember that you are also the hand of Moranu, of the many faces. What is in Her is in you."

*Whether you want that or not,* she didn't have to say aloud. I looked down at Rayfe, his face so bloodless and still that he might be a corpse. If not for him, then…

"All right," I conceded with a sigh. "Though I worry about his state of mind when he awakes." Again, I looked to Ursula.

This time she gazed back, Danu's clear light in her eyes. "Whatever it is," she said, "we'll handle it. Take care of Rayfe, and we'll go from there."

Kelleah lifted my hand and laid it over Rayfe's heart, placing both of hers on top of it. Her green healing light grew slowly, and I pulled on the Heart to augment her power. She hummed in gratitude, the light strengthening. "Lead the way, my queen," she murmured.

I slid into Rayfe's mind, the pathway as familiar as a kiss, leading Kelleah with a mental hand. She reacted with some shock when she encountered the Deyrr residue I hadn't yet cleansed, like discovering the rotting remnants of a flood in a closed closet. Where we passed, I cleansed it, having gotten rather proficient at the skill.

Deeper and deeper we passed, through levels of his wounded mind. I saw myself in there, and others. Longings and memories, anger and love. Bitter betrayal and doubt. Kelleah would see it all, too, and I tried to let that go. Would she see how bad things had gotten between us? Not that she'd ever violate confidentiality by saying so, but I found myself ashamed and exposed.

Nothing like Rayfe was, though, so I made myself stop being selfish and let it go.

We found him, the wolf sleeping in a deep cave, secure in his den. Kelleah hung back and let me go forward. Hesitantly—honestly afraid he might bite me, either because he didn't know me, or because he did and hated me for what I'd done—I brushed my mental fingers through his fur.

"Call him." Kelleah's mind voice whispered in echoes.

"Rayfe," I called. "My king. My love." I bent and pressed a kiss to his wolf's muzzle, the metaphysical fur silky under my lips. "Come back to me. Please."

His eyes popped open, wolf bright, snarl rising—and I nearly flinched. Then stopped myself. This was Rayfe, and from the very beginning he'd promised never to hurt me.

"Time to wake up, my love," I told him. And he calmed.

In the outside world, Rayfe stirred under my hands. My heart leapt with joy—and trepidation. He moaned deep in his throat, and I soothed him, feathering my fingers over his brow, taking care to avoid the angry furrows left by Stella's claws. Kelleah nodded at me, then abandoned me to go treat her many other patients.

I was on my own.

"Andromeda?" Rayfe gazed up at me, confused, and in pain. But him. Sounding dazed and uncertain, but at least all himself. "I'm hurt."

"Yes. You need to shift."

He frowned, then winced. "It's not there."

"It is," I soothed him, desperately covering my fear that he might never be the same again. "You're just a little weak is all. Shift and all will be well."

Lifting a hand, weakly, but enough to reach a trailing lock of my hair, he wound his fingers in it. "Why do you weep, my queen?"

I hadn't realized I was. "Happy tears, my wolf."

He blinked at the blood in his eyes. Stella had gotten them, after all, the blue marred and leaking. "I can't see very well."

"A minor injury. Just shift into First Form, and you'll be fine."

"If you say." He stilled. Frowned. "I can't. I must be badly hurt, but I don't remember…"

"You can remember later. Try one more time, and if you can't shift, I'll call Kelleah to heal you."

"No, Queen Andromeda," Kelleah called out from another part of the cavern. "Handle it."

I caught Ursula's grimly amused expression when I lifted my head to deliver a scathing command to our recalcitrant healer.

"You have your marching orders, Your Highness," Ursula said.

"Someday you'll have to teach me how you make your subjects actually follow your orders instead of issuing them."

She snorted. "When I figure that out, I'll be sure to let you know the trick. In the meantime, quit stalling."

All right. I could do this. Surely I could. I slipped into Rayfe's mind again, looking for the wolf. He paced eagerly now in the more surface levels, greeting me with lavish affection that made me want to weep again—or more—even as it gladdened my heart. How to do this?

I hesitated to use what I knew of shifting, since I'd always been so backward and amateurish with it. So hopelessly mossback. But… that was all I knew.

And my mother had made me who I was. Moranu, too. I clung to that belief.

*Concentrate. Focus.*

Coaxing the wolf along, I pulled him through. Rayfe shivered under my hands.

And became the wolf.

# ~ 19 ~

"WELL DONE, SORCERESS," Ursula said gravely.

Rayfe, now a massive black wolf, leapt to his feet and shook his coat vigorously. He regarded us with intact, sapphire blue eyes, then lifted his nose, taking in the scent of all the violence around us.

"I think he did it on his own," I replied, shaken by how easy it had been—and by the heady rush of power it brought. Deep in the dark of my mind, I thought I heard a murmur of the goddess laughing at me.

Ursula rolled her eyes, and Ami—apparently satisfied with Astar's health—gave me a stern look. "Give yourself credit, Andi. You're an amazing sorceress. Better than our mother was."

I opened my mouth to protest… Then closed it again. I didn't know how I compared to Salena. But I did know that comparisons are invidious. Time to stop thinking about what my mother could have, or would have done. She was gone. Maybe the high priestess had a hand in her death, which would absolve our father of that crime, at least.

In that case, avenging her would be up to me, among vengeance for so much else. That bitch had a lot to answer for.

Rayfe padded over to me. Then became the man—fully healed, wearing fighting leathers in glossy black, his hair tumbling wildly around his gorgeous face. His fulgent eyes shone sharp with sane intelligence, and I went boneless with relief at the sight. He held a long-fingered hand down to me and I took it, leaning on his strength as I rose. His winged black brows spiked as he looked me over.

"You are covered in blood, my queen," he said hoarsely, then pulled me into his arms, holding me in a fierce embrace. "Dare I ask how much is yours?"

"Some," I answered honestly, very much feeling the injuries and blood loss—and that I'd never lie to him ever again.

"Why has no one tended you?" he demanded, turning the frown on Ursula.

"Don't start on her," I cut in. "There were people worse off, including you."

He turned back to me, expression intense as he cupped my face in his hands. "I felt you in my mind."

"I know," I whispered, too wracked with guilt to say the words any louder. "I'm so sorry. I had to."

"You misunderstand, Andromeda," he replied with a soft smile, so full of love my heart tripped over it. "I was drowning and yours was the hand that pulled me from the deeps. Like Moranu Herself, you lit up my night and brought me home. I know we've been… I don't know what we've been, except that I've failed you in so many ways." He frowned, lines of pain around his eyes.

"No," I insisted. "You never once failed me."

"I know I did. I can't remember it all, but I hurt you. I'm so sorry."

"Don't be. There's nothing to be sorry for."

"You came for me," he said, talking over my words. "That gives me hope that, somewhere in your heart, you might find a way to love me again."

"Oh, my wolf," I breathed, my voice as ragged as my heart. "I never stopped loving you. Not once."

He smiled, a quirk of his sensuous mouth, and bent his head, bringing his mouth to mine. The brush of his lips and breath were bare whispers of contact, until I breached the distance, flinging myself against him, deepening the kiss and drinking him in. He responded with fervor, hands bold on my body, a possessive growl in his throat, consuming and treasuring me. Our tongues, thoughts and emotions twined, desire blooming like blossoms on old wood thought dead. Life remained inside the husk, ever ready to be brought to new growth with a bit of nurturing.

Someone cleared their throat pointedly, and I became aware of our surroundings again. So did Rayfe, and he broke the kiss with a laugh, leaning his forehead against mine. "What did you say about us never being alone?"

A rush of gladness filled me that he remembered that conversation. At least his memories from when he'd been himself were intact. He seemed sane enough. "When this war is done," I replied, "you and I are going away somewhere, just the two of us."

"Or three," he answered, pulling back to search my face. "Yes?"

"Yes," I agreed with fervor, gripping his hands before turning to face our audience.

"Sorry to interrupt that touching reunion," Ursula said, her tone acerbic, her gaze soft with emotion. "But Nilly here is waking and we weren't sure if we needed to be prepared for anything."

Like the high priestess in her mind. That was all we needed. "Good thinking."

Rayfe looked around, perplexed. "Why are we in the tunnels?

What's going on?"

I grimaced, not at all looking forward to telling him that he'd betrayed his own people. I should be the one to tell him, but as I was learning the hard way, with every passing moment, I couldn't do everything. No one else could look into Stella's mind, but someone else could tell Rayfe about our current predicament. I wasn't being a coward by delegating that uncomfortable task. At least, that's what I told myself.

"Harlan?" I called, and the big Dasnarian entered our circle of light. "Would you catch Rayfe up on our current circumstances? I need to tend to Nilly."

"What's wrong with Stella?" Rayfe asked, not letting me go.

"Harlan will fill you in," I said. "Trust me?"

He cupped my cheek, stroking in a subtle, sensual caress. "Always."

Moranu take me, I nearly wept—again—at that. I smiled and turned my face to kiss his palm. "Thank you." Hopefully he'd still feel that way about me once he learned what had happened—and what I'd done.

"But you're getting healed next," he reminded me.

"I will," I promised, if only to make him smile at me one more time.

I went to Ursula and Harlan stepped up, gripped Rayfe by the shoulder. "Good to see you in fine form, Your Highness," Harlan said. "Let's walk over here and I'll explain." Harlan tipped his head at me reassuringly, and I knew he'd feel his way gently around the holes in Rayfe's memory.

I sat next to Ursula, Stella blinking sleepily in her arms, sucking on a thumb as she hadn't done in some time. "Should we call Kelleah to heal you?" Ursula asked.

"No." I shook my head in emphasis, and immediately regretted it when dizziness swamped me. "I'm all right for now.

You're wise to consider we need to clear Nilly here first. Hi, baby girl, want to come cuddle with Auntie Andi?"

She looked from Ursula to me. Then held out her arms. I brought her into my lap, her little body so soft and warm, her silky curls tumbling over my arm.

"I'll go help Harlan explain to Rayfe," Ursula said, standing and brushing herself off, sheathing her sword. "We have things to sort anyway."

Hopefully the swords would stay sheathed, but I said nothing. I needed to focus on my niece.

"Is my Nilly all right?" Ami asked anxiously. Astar sprawled over her lap in boneless abandon. With his rose-gold curls and lavish lashes on his round-cheeked face, he looked like a painting of one of Glorianna's baby angels.

"Of course she's all right," I replied firmly, coaxing Stella to sit up more. "Isn't that so, Nilly?"

She gazed at me soberly, so much more subdued than when I saw her on arrival. I scanned her for traces of Deyrr, but with so many Deyrr creatures all around—and having waded through so much of the residue in Rayfe's mind—it had become levels more difficult to detect subtle taints. Stella popped her thumb out of her mouth and I braced myself. If she began spewing with the high priestess's vitriol, I'd have to mute her fast, or Ami would go Glorianna as vengeful mother in a heartbeat.

"That mean lady with the dead eyes came back," Stella complained to me. "You promised you'd stop her, but you didn't. She hurt me."

Ami gasped and started to say something, but I held up a hand. "I'll make Essla sit on you," I warned, and she subsided, burying her face in Astar's golden curls.

"I know I promised, and I apologize that I let you down," I told Stella.

She shrugged a little, then reached out to play with my ruby necklace. "That's all right. Can I have this?"

"Stella Andromeda!" Ami cried, not silenced for long.

This time I ignored her. "Someday, yes, when you are older. If you study hard and practice your magic."

Her gaze returned to my face, curious and thoughtful. "With you?"

"If you like."

She turned to look at Ami. "Mommy, can I?"

Ami managed a smile. "Yes, Nilly mine. When you are older."

"Yay," I sang out, and Stella grinned at me.

"Everybody is very upset," she confided. "That hurts, too."

"I know. Would you like me to help with that?"

She nodded vigorously. "Yes!"

"Yes, *please*," Ami inserted. I rolled my eyes and Stella giggled.

Then I gave her a serious look. "This is an important thing I'm asking. To help you shut out all the emotions of people being upset, I have to go into your private thoughts. I won't do that without permission."

She considered that with a maturity far beyond her years, even for a precocious shapeshifter child. "Will it keep the mean lady away?"

I ran a hand over her long hair, so like my own, I realized. "I hope so. I'm also learning new things."

"We can practice together," she said, slipping her hand into mine. "You're hurting, too. Want me to fix it?"

I glanced at Ami, who gave me a wide-eyed look. "Her healing ability is amazing. She healed Ash's arm after the sleeper attack like it was nothing."

Children rarely possessed much healing ability, as it usually appeared with maturity. I didn't want to strain Stella, but healing me would keep her occupied while I worked on her mental defenses—and sniffed around for the high priestess—while also allowing me to evaluate her abilities.

"I would love that, thank you," I told Stella, then nearly gasped as green healing energy, vital as springtime, filled me. She held nothing back. With all the uninhibited honesty of a child, bursting with the vigor of her young, fresh body, she poured the healing into me almost faster than my own strained body could absorb it. "Whoa, pull it back some, baby girl," I managed.

Her face crumpled, and the healing cut off abruptly. "Did I hurt you?" she asked anxiously. She shimmered slightly, a sign she might shapeshift, so I hastily grabbed mental hold of her current form. Now that I'd embraced the ability, it came reflexively.

"Stay with me, Nilly. It's fine." I waited for her to relax. Shapeshifter children were both like and unlike non-Tala children. All children had something of a feral nature to them, much closer to their animal instincts. But shapeshifter children, especially those who found their First Form early, tended to be as much that beast as human child. Or more, as in Astar's case. Rayfe might have a point that we needed to intervene and push Astar to spend more time as a boy.

"Better," I told her with a smile, that she returned tremulously. Clearly I had a lot to learn about being a teacher. "Softly, like petting a kitten, with gentleness, so you don't frighten it."

Her healing energy slipped in quietly. "Lovely," I told her. "Concentrate on keeping that the same. I'm coming into your mind now. This is me knocking to say hello, I'm here."

I knocked mentally, like I did with Zynda, and Stella's eyes flew open wide. *"!!!"*

I nearly laughed at her wordless mental reaction, her

thoughts scrambling and spinning like a kitten chasing its tail. *"Hi Nilly. It's Auntie Andi."*

*"!!!"*

*"Try to say hello."*

"Hi Auntie Andi!" she exclaimed, startling Ami.

"I'll never get used to this," Ami muttered.

*"See if you can say it without your voice. Think the words at me."*

**"Hi Auntie Andi. This is weird. You tickle, but inside my head!"**

I covered my wince at her volume. Better for her to be loud than too quiet. *"Hi Niecey Nilly,"* I said. *"Now you know how to reach me. You don't have to knock. If the mean lady returns—or if anything bad happens—you call me."*

**"I will! I hate that lady."**

*"Me too."*

**"You do? Mommy says it's wrong to hate people, that we should love everybody, no matter how bad."**

I managed not to roll my eyes. Ami *would* say exactly that. Being the avatar of the goddess of love came with a certain onus. Looking to Moranu came with advantages that way. The followers of the goddess of shadows and dark arts could hate just fine—and I planned to use that. But how to handle this with Nilly? Ami wouldn't thank me for interfering.

*"It can be our secret,"* I told Stella. *"I'm going to destroy the mean lady, so she can't bother either of us again."*

Stella's eyes widened more. **"Can you do that???"**

*"Yes."* I infused that with all the confidence I didn't feel.

**"Good. She tried to kill Willy."**

*"You knew it was her and not Uncle Rayfe?"*

**"Of course."** Her scorn rolled through with disbelief. **"He doesn't feel at all the same when** she *is making him move and talk."*

Ah, if only I'd done this sooner. *"You are so powerful and clever."* I let her see the truth of that in my mind, carefully walling off anything she shouldn't see. *"I'm going to look around now, to be sure the mean lady didn't leave any bad things in you."*

**"Yesyesyes! Please,"** she added with a mental giggle. **"I'm healing you. And talking to the baby."**

I startled at that, pausing in the careful scan I'd already begun. *"You can talk to him?"*

**"Yes. Kind of. He doesn't have words though. He loves me already. But not as much as he loves you. I told him his mommy is the most powerful sorceress in all the world!"**

Faintly embarrassed, I set that aside and resumed checking Stella's mind. Searching a child's mind felt so different than what I'd done before. With fewer memories and complex ideas, in some ways she was more open. But that feral nature extended to her mind, so that communicating with her was more akin to talking to Fiona, or the staymachs in some ways—all formless thought, emotion, and unleashed impulse. Perhaps that's why she could talk to my unborn child.

Another riddle for better days.

And one I forgot about immediately when I found the hook in Stella's mind. That's how it seemed—like an anchor embedded deep in her still forming brain—and one that felt like it had been there for quite some time. Probably since Terin stole her from her cradle at Windroven.

It was so deeply embedded, in fact, that I didn't dare remove it, for fear that I might permanently damage Stella's mind. *That fucking bitch.* The rage filled me clear and cold, with a sharp and bitter edge.

*"Is something wrong with me?"* Stella's mind-voice came more tentative now, and I greatly regretted that she'd felt my anger. I also considered reassuring her. Such a baby still, to be confront-

ed with this kind of tampering. And yet… this was her mind, her sovereignty of will, and she deserved to know. Also, she'd be the one who'd know if the high priestess attempted to use it.

"You *are perfect in every way, Nilly love.*" I poured all my conviction into that thought. *"But the mean lady left something in you."*

**"*Get it out!!!*"** she boomed in panic, and this time I couldn't help the flinch. *"Sorry,"* she said more quietly. A soothing balm flowed over my own mind. *"Didn't mean to hurt you."*

Remarkable, this small child's gifts. *"I think only killing the mean lady will get rid of this thing,"* I told her, baldly and honestly.

*"And you're going to kill her, right?"*

*"Yes, I am. But meanwhile, I want you to see this hook, so you'll know if she tries to use it. It's what she uses to talk to you."*

*"Show me."*

Why her imperious command reminded me of Kiraka, I couldn't say. I took Stella by the hand and led her mentally to the hook deep in her mind, showing it to her.

*"That's always been there,"* she commented.

*"It shouldn't be."*

*"Oh."* She was quiet a moment, and I could feel her exploring it. *"Can I stop her using it?"*

*"Try building a wall around it."*

I watched with fascination as she made several attempts—and I didn't interfere as her ideas were far more creative than anything I'd have suggested. A pang of nostalgia assailed me, as it occurred to me that I might've worked with my mother this way, learning from her, had things gone differently.

*I wish it, too.*

The voice crossed my mind, so like my own thoughts that I almost didn't hear it as different. But immersed so deeply, with Stella's bright green magic suffusing me, I mentally spun, looking for the source.

*"That's Grandmother Salena,"* Stella told me in an absent tone. She was creating a mental version of some toy blocks in colorful shapes and assembling them into a little castle that looked very much like the walls of Windroven. So absorbed was she that she didn't note my astonishment—and stab of grief.

*"Grandmother Salena talks to you?"* I asked it quietly, hesitant to disturb her concentration.

*"Sometimes. She's dead though, so it's like talking to the baby. Not clear, like you are."*

Amazing and wonderful and terrible. I didn't know what to make of that. Old stories always implied that children were more open to hearing the voices of ghosts, some said because children had taken only a few steps from that other realm, others said it was because their minds were more open and malleable. I'd love to talk to Zynda about it.

*"This is working,"* Stella mentally stepped back and showed me her castle.

*"Excellent job."*

*"It needs more though."*

*"All right."*

"Andi?" I heard my name called in the outer world. "I don't know—they've been like this for some time."

*"I should go talk to everyone."*

*"Can I keep working on this?"*

*"Yes. And sleep. You'll be tired from this good work, and from healing me. Thank you."*

She yawned mentally, the kitten stretch of her mind agreeing sleepily. *"All right. Love you."*

*"I love you, too, Nilly mine."* Gently I extracted myself from Stella's mind, erasing the traces of my passage as I went. As I came back more fully into my own body, I became aware that the pair of us had slid down, cuddled together, and someone had put a blanket over us. Taking one more moment, I inhaled the

sweet scent of her hair, delighting in the warmth of my niece tucked against me. The baby stirred and I sent him a loving thought. If only all the world could be this way, all the time.

"Well, if they're sleeping, I hate to wake them, but…" Ursula, her voice strained.

"Andromeda would want us to wake her," Rayfe declared, and he knelt beside me, brushing my hair from my face with tenderness that wrung my heart. "My queen," he murmured, and whispered a kiss over my cheek.

I rolled onto my back, making sure to tuck the blanket around Stella as I turned. I lifted a hand to Rayfe, winding my fingers in his hair, tugging him down to me for a kiss. He obliged with heat, and I gloried in it. I wanted to savor every good moment left to me. "I'm awake," I said against his lips.

I felt him smile. "All appearances to the contrary."

"No, I really am." Then I remembered, saw the pained knowledge in his eyes of all that had occurred. "How are you?"

He sobered. "Not a question I can answer for myself with any certainty, it seems."

"Rayfe…"

He kissed me again. "We will talk. Later."

Blowing out a breath, I nodded and sat up, warmed that he slipped an arm around me to help me lever up. I scrubbed my hands over my scalp, pushing back the tangled mess of my hair. Everyone had gathered round again, tension riding the air. "What's going on?"

A silly question, with many answers, but no one gave me grief for it.

"The doors to the tunnels," Ursula said. "They're digging through. Only the barrier you erected is stopping them and I assume we can't rely on that indefinitely. Besides, we can't just hide down here. We need to make a plan."

## ~ 20 ~

WE TUCKED THE sleeping Astar in with Stella under the blanket, their twin heads, bright and dark, immediately leaning together. I reassured Ami that our Nilly would be fine—and did *not* tell her about the hook the high priestess had embedded in her daughter's mind. A favorite aunt could keep some secrets, I decided—especially when her mother would only worry.

"We're seriously hampered by not knowing what's going on with everyone else," Ursula fretted. "We need to go out there and meet the Deyrr forces head on, but who knows what we might encounter? Still, we'll be at a worse disadvantage if we wait for them to breach the doors."

"I can find out how things stand," I said.

Rayfe nodded. "Andromeda is, of course, far more powerful than I, and she can extend her mind farther, but I can track the movements of our people. Between us, we should be able to find out everything you'd want to know."

Ursula gave us a look of astonished disgust. "Why didn't you say so before this?"

I shrugged, making it Tala elaborate, just to poke at her a bit. "We had other priorities."

Rayfe laughed softly, then turned to me. "Speaking of which—are you all right? I don't smell fresh blood anymore."

His concern no longer felt so prickly and smothering, and I leaned against him, glad for the shelter of his arms and the lean strength of his body. "Yes, Nilly healed me completely. I feel better than I have in weeks."

"Is that so?" He eyed our sleeping niece with the same surprise I'd felt.

"How are you," I asked tentatively, unwilling to look in his mind for myself, "with… everything?"

His brows slanted down, and he lowered his voice. "I feel very strange, like I've been asleep. And there are things I'm wondering about. Traces of you in my mind. You didn't—"

Ursula cleared her throat pointedly, tapping her fingers on the hilt of her sword. Grateful to postpone the inevitable confession to Rayfe of how I'd violated the trust between us, I gave her a look of polite attention.

"Yes," Rayfe said, facing her. "Speaking of which, I owe you apologies and amends, for the Hawks I apparently murdered."

She gave him a long look. "Are you going to apologize for every person killed by Deyrr? Because that would be a *lot* of amends."

He frowned. "Well, no, but—"

"No buts," she said, cutting him off. Never had I been so grateful for her decisiveness and clear, bright lines.

I touched his cheek. "No one blames you."

"Enemy," Ursula said pointedly, and loudly. "At the doors. About to descend upon us. You can canoodle later."

"*If* we survive," Ami quipped, then looked sorry she'd said it. But she straightened her spine. "I'd like to point out that you all are together with your partners in life, whereas Ash is…" Her musical voice broke and she lifted her chin defiantly at me, as if I'd criticized her for the lapse. "If you can tell me how he is, I'll forgive you not finding out and telling me before this."

Chagrined, I nodded at her. "I recalled the n'Andana attack team before we retreated down here, but I'll check with them first."

"I'm surveying our people now," Rayfe murmured.

I heard his call to the Tala, a bone-deep sounding like the howl of a wolf on a full-moon night, summoning, asking for answer. I'd felt something similar before when he called the Gathering. The King of the Tala, rightful alpha of them all, asserting his leadership and requiring their attention. Even I quivered to respond, though I was able to set the urge aside and focus on my own task.

I reached out to Zynda, knocking first. No reply.

Dread chilling my heart, I tapped more loudly. Nothing. I widened my call, looking for traces of any of their minds. Zyr I could usually at least hear, but no. I zoomed out my mental scope, scanning for the null spots that would be Zynda and Djakos's dragon-shaped holes in the world. Nothing nothing nothing.

Increasingly panicked, I cast about for Kiraka, not bothering to politely tap for attention this time. *"Kiraka!"* I sent.

*"So the queen emerges from hiding,"* the old dragon replied. There was a sense behind her thoughts of a battle raging, of a minute pause between each word like a person puffing for breath.

*"I can't feel Zynda or the others."*

*"I'm sorry for you, but I'm busy. The cliffs out here are overrun."* She slammed me into the view from her eyes, as if she'd grabbed me by the throat and mashed my face against a window. We *were* entirely overrun. Kiraka perched on the ledge outside the council chambers, the little table Rayfe and I had once shared in happier times now shattered. I might not have recognized Annfwn, the way smoke clogged the skies. Once colorful silk banners flamed or flapped in rags. Screams rent the air. And the sea boiled with

ships.

A phalanx of Deyrr creatures arrowed in on Kiraka. She blew out a wide swath of flame, ashing them from the sky. The dust cleared and another took their place.

Profoundly shaken to see my visions a reality, I asked, *"Dafne, Nakoa, and the baby?"*

*"Doing all I can to protect them. Wish I'd taken them out of here."*

*"Do it now."*

*"Can't. Dafne won't leave you all, even if I could get them out. We're trapped."*

*"We're coming to help,"* I promised recklessly.

*"Better make it soon."*

Hoping against hope that at least we didn't have to deal with the Dasnarians yet, I expanded my mind out to the *Hákyrling*. Not wasting any more time, I tapped directly into Jepp's mind. Then reeled in astonishment at what I saw through her eyes, unable to wrap my mind around it: it looked like the entire Dasnarian navy indeed streamed through the barrier.

Jepp was fighting. I felt her moving in a whirlwind of blades, my phantom hands tracking with hers. Fishbirds flew in pieces as she spun.

"Andi, tell me if you're there," she panted. Then she repeated it, like a chant.

"I'm here," I said with her mouth.

"Thank fucking Danu," she snarled. She spun and ran for a door, hissing as something sliced her arm. She vaulted through and paused in the dark interior, slowing her breath. "The barrier is breached. We're doing our best here, but the Dasnarian ships are pouring through, and moving fast. They'll be at Annfwn before long. Tell Ursula I'm sorry."

"Do you need help?" I asked, though I didn't know what I'd offer if she said yes.

"We're playing it safe, holding back or else we'll be decimat-ed. We can't stop them, but at least we can come in behind them. One of Nakoa's storms would be handy. Any other magic tricks, too. Though you might need all of that there. Good luck."

"Good luck to you," I said back, though numbly. She thumped a fist to her heart in the Hawks' salute, then plunged out the door again, knives at the ready.

The barrier breached. Just as I'd known it would be, but how had it happened? I reached for the Heart, finding the cobalt crabs going about their business… except for one side. They'd opened up a hole in the barrier, sea water now filling my dome, the abalone throne knocked onto its side by the force of inrushing pressure. I remembered with a visceral stab how the high priestess had punched at me when I freed Rayfe from her leash. She'd been ready for me to do that very thing—and I'd been connected to the Heart, pulling as much power as I could to augment my own.

No matter what I did, I seemed to be dancing to her tune. Well, that was going to change.

I commanded the crabs to repair the barrier, but they—impossibly—ignored me. I reached into the barrier itself. For the first time since I first infused it with my will, it failed to respond. I tried again, but it was like dashing my power against an impervious wall.

Just like when I tried to blast that Deyrr warthog.

At least the true Heart—the font of magic buried beneath the ocean floor, still responded to me, a flood of power surging through me with uninhibited fire. The high priestess had compromised the barrier itself, but she didn't have the Heart. That was mine.

Furiously I jammed my hand in my pocket, finding the Star, not the high priestess's focus stone, but I used it nevertheless to wrench a door open to her mind. I startled her—she recovered fast, covering it up—but I took savage satisfaction in catching her that much by surprise.

She hastily formed a featureless bubble around herself, but not before I caught a glimpse of a serene aquamarine sea— unmistakably the Onyx Ocean near Annfwn—and the spars and masts of a sailing ship with billowed sails. Not clad in her usual semi-naked sensual attire, she wore a version of Dasnarian armor, though in her trademark gold instead of silver. It also fit her feminine curves and petite frame, clearly custom-made for her in an empire that not only never armored its women, but went as far as possible in the other direction, denying them even shoes. A delicately wrought helmet perched on her head, framing her lovely face with sharp metal thorns that emphasized her beauty while protecting her face.

She'd learned from the time she'd attacked Ursula, and lost both eyes in the process. I didn't know how she'd regrown them—if those dark pits even required regrowing—but she was clearly taking no chances with a repeat injury.

"Oh, Andromeda! I'm afraid you've caught me at a busy time," she chirped, as if I'd stopped by for a neighborly chat at an inopportune moment. "Can we talk later? After I've finished conquering Annfwn and enslaving the Tala will work for me. I know *you* will be at your leisure, with no people and no king-dom."

I'd lashed out without a plan of what to say, but I wasn't backing down now. "What have you done?" I snarled.

She simpered prettily. "Catching on now, are you? Really, it's been dreadfully dull waiting for you to see past a few simple diversions. I'd rather thought you'd be smarter but..." She lifted a shoulder and let it fall. "I've realized I expected far too much of you. Unfair of me, as I knew you couldn't amount to much, poor untrained, untalented little thing. Such a pity your mother died before she could teach you anything useful."

"You certainly saw to that, didn't you?" The rage had a grip on me.

She raised her brows and fluttered her lashes, a gesture that on Ami looked charming, but became grotesque with those dead black eyes staring out. "I can't imagine what you mean, Andromeda, darling. You'll really have to try to be more specific with your questions."

It didn't matter if she'd killed Salena or had a hand in her demise. I shouldn't let it sidetrack me. *Don't let this become a personal vendetta. Hatred and anger can tear you apart.* No, I reminded myself, my hatred and anger will tear *them* apart.

"In answer to your question," the high priestess said with some impatience, and I realized my pause had spurred her to keep talking. "What I've done is win. Again, unless you'd like to be more specific. Or, perhaps you're rethinking your curt refusal of my patronage. There's still time to pledge yourself to me. Just say the word. I've outmaneuvered you in every direction. Give up now and you, at least, will have a good life."

Tempting, to spit out all the things I knew—but also foolish. I needed to be smarter. All the things I wanted to ask—what had happened to the strike team, how close was she to Annfwn, how she'd taken control of the barrier—would reveal what I did and didn't know. If the high priestess didn't know about Zynda and the others, then they might be hiding, and I'd betray them by asking.

"Perhaps I was hasty." I tried to sound contrite. "Let's meet and discuss."

She laughed, a gay twinkling sound appropriate for a glass of wine with friends. "Silly little baby sorceress. We're talking now. Pledge yourself to Deyrr. Otherwise I can't possibly trust you.

Surely you understand that."

"How would I go about doing that?"

"Oh dear, that is a conundrum." She pouted, then a reptilian smile crept through, cold and without a shred of compassion. "I suppose you'll have to wait like a good girl. Surrender and I might take you to Deyrr. But that will have to wait until we meet." She made a moue, adding that fatalistic shrug, then laughed. "Which is fortuitously quite soon!"

She waved a hand and cut the connection with a vicious backlash that had me physically reeling. Rayfe caught me, steadying me in his warm embrace. Utterly grateful for his strength, I burrowed against him.

"Andromeda." He drew out my name like a warning, but I sensed no anger from him—and I clung to that small comfort. "Were you… You were talking with the high priestess."

"Yes. Yes, I was. And not for the first time."

"Is that wise?" Ursula asked.

"Every weapon at my disposal," I answered.

Rayfe frowned. "I don't understand what you're doing."

"No, I know that," I replied quietly. "Will you trust me any-way?"

"Yes," he answered simply, no uncertainty in it, and I drew strength from that. I needed it for this next bit. "Ami—I'm sorry to say I couldn't make contact with any of the n'Andana team. They're not answering, and I can't sense the dragons like I usually can."

Ami, who wept over the death of a baby bird, firmed her chin and studied me with dry eyes. "Ash is dead then? Along with all of them."

"I don't know. This is what I do know." I gave them the rundown of everything I'd seen, heard, and learned.

"That verifies what I discovered," Rayfe added. "The cliff

city is overwhelmed, but we cannot hide down here any longer. We can fight or surrender. I say we fight."

"Kiraka can hold awhile longer, but not much," I said. "I can pass a message for Nakoa to brew a storm, but we need to get to them."

Rayfe growled deep in his throat, likely not even aware of it. "We have to get ourselves out of *here*."

I swallowed against the knowledge that we'd at last run up against the wall. This was the moment that everyone I loved would throw themselves into that endless onslaught of monsters, with only a spinning fragment of chance they'd live through it.

"This is what I propose," Ursula said. "We bust out our forces, seal the tunnels with the vulnerable inside. Rally the outside troops, secure the cliff city, repel the high priestess, then we should have a short breather to prepare to repel the Dasnarian navy."

It sounded so easy, put that way.

"I'm with you," Rayfe declared, body singing with energy, eyes glittering with feral excitement.

"Our ships, even the ones we've recalled, won't reach us until tomorrow at the soonest," I reminded them. "And our aerial forces might be trapped, or destroyed. We can't count on any help."

Ursula actually looked excited. "Then we'd better step up and handle this ourselves."

Rayfe nodded at her, expression the twin of hers. Never had they seemed more alike to me, to my great love and everlasting despair. "Agreed," he said.

"We need a temporary strategic retreat," she said.

"Behind Kiraka," he said.

"Perfect," she said. "We'll need to clear a path and rally everyone to the cliff city. Abandon the beach."

"Won't we risk being trapped there?" Harlan inquired mildly.

Rayfe grinned, the wolf in it. "We can always go up and over."

"I see." Harlan nodded thoughtfully. "A small rear guard can defend us from pursuit."

"And Andromeda can lock the gate to the road, so they won't be able to follow that way," Rayfe added.

"You can?" Ursula raised her brows at me.

"Already done," I said. "I'd intended it as a final measure to keep any forces that defeated Annfwn from invading the other twelve kingdoms." Rayfe watched me with calm knowingness in his eyes, and I realized he'd known this, too, about me, all along.

"How long can you hold it?" Ursula asked cannily. "And be honest."

"Honestly? I don't know. I've never had to hold a fixed enchantment against a high priestess of Deyrr and a god, while fighting to regain control of the larger barrier and maintain several other battles at once," I replied, trying not to snap at her and failing.

"What's this?" She made an astonished face. "The great and powerful sorceress Andromeda is recognizing her limitations at last."

A retort hovered on my tongue, but I swallowed it. "You have no idea," I finally said, feeling the sag in my shoulders. I straightened them and my spine. "But I'll hold it as long as I can."

"That's all we ask," she said, giving me a smile before she moved on. "All right. We make a concerted push to get every able-bodied fighter out of the tunnels, rally our people to the cliff city, leadership meeting back at the council chambers. If we cannot hold until our reinforcements arrive, we evacuate the cliff city and reconvene at Ordnung."

"Abandon Annfwn to Deyrr?" Rayfe said the words like a question, but I knew he was testing the truth of that possibility within himself.

"We always knew we might have to," I said softly, leaning into him so he'd feel my shared sorrow. "Annfwn was always temporary. A toehold clawed out of a desperate effort to recreate what had already been lost."

He looked down at me, holding my gaze. "I know. It just … feels like defeat."

"Lose the battle to win the war?" I asked, attempting a brave smile.

"We can hope. All right, agreed. I'm telling the Tala." Rayfe closed his eyes, the song spinning out.

"Andi—can you relay to the staymachs with our lieutenants?" Ursula asked me.

"Yes." I opened my eyes. "Done."

She acknowledged that crisply. "Are you going to the Heart?"

"Not enough time to get there." They didn't need to know the Heart had been compromised. I would fix it. "I'll be on the promontory. I can access the Heart from there and still see everything." I thought Rayfe might object, but he dipped his chin at me, his confidence bolstering.

"All right. Ami—would you stay here to guard the children and others?"

"Of course," she replied, her face set in cool reserve. "And I shall pray to all three goddesses to intervene on our behalf."

"We'll clear the doors and send reinforcements," Harlan told her.

"I can put up the shield again," I offered. "Though it will keep us from communicating with you. You'll be on your own with your people here."

"Not entirely," she replied with firm conviction. "No mortal shield can thwart Glorianna, Danu, and Moranu. The sisters will be with me."

Ursula glanced at me, an unreadable look in her steely gaze. We'd come so many years from spoiled little Ami trotting out Glorianna's wishes as justification for her childish whims. "All right with you if I call on Danu's attention and assistance from time to time?" she asked. Though she'd phrased the question with some amusement, a core of sincerity rode in it.

"You are Her avatar, Essla," Ami replied seriously, exactly the way her daughter did. "May Danu protect you and guide your blade."

It might've been the emotion of the moment, the certain dread that this might be the last time I saw some of them alive—or all of them—but Ursula seemed to take on a light, banishing the shadows. And Ami… she wore the face of love.

"And you, Andi," Ami said, turning to me. "Moranu goes with you. She is yours and you are Hers. There is nothing for you to fear in letting Her will fill you."

I shivered at her insight, and the compassion in her violet blue eyes, so lovely, and so knowing. How had she known of the fears that plagued me? Such a narrow line for me to walk between fighting the high priestess—and becoming her. Unable to voice any of that, I simply nodded.

But Ami—or Glorianna—didn't let me off so easily. She canted her head slightly, the stern mother shimmering in her. "Remember that Deyrr is Moranu's ancient nemesis, more than any other of the sisters. You have been Marked by Her from the beginning. Don't refuse Her will now, when all hangs in the balance."

A midnight wash of silver flame licked through me, as if the many-faced goddess set her hand on me, indeed. I tried not to resist it, but I also flinched at the darkness so like Deyrr's. *I never asked to be Marked.*

"But you did," Ami said, making me jump. The numinous echoed in her voice, and I knew Glorianna spoke directly to me.

"Before you were born, you asked for this," Ursula said crisply, Danu in her eyes.

A firm hand at the small of my back kept me from retreating. I looked up to find Rayfe watching me with that same ruthless compassion as he had from the beginning. "There's choosing and there's *choosing*," he said.

I smiled at him, knowing it to be tremulous. Then I faced the goddesses, all three of them—the two in Ami and Ursula, the one flickering around me with the beating wings of night—and said, "I accept my destiny and will do my utmost."

The immediate, crushing presences of the goddesses withdrew, and I took a full breath.

"You handle the barriers and the high priestess," Ursula said. "Trust us to deal with the rest."

"Nothing will get through me to harm the children, or anyone down here," Ami vowed. "You have my word."

I almost didn't say it, but felt I should. I'd placed trust in Stella and she in me. I would honor that. "Nilly will tell you if the high priestess approaches."

Ami paused in surprise, then dipped her chin, not questioning.

Ursula embraced Ami, then crouched to kiss the sleeping twins, Harlan following suit. "We'll organize our forces and get the doors cleared," she told us.

"We'll be right behind you," Rayfe replied, following me as I hugged Ami and also kissed the children goodbye. "Be strong, heart-sister," he said gravely. "I trust no one more with the children of Annfwn."

Her eyes filled, but the tears didn't spill. "Andi—Ash is alive. I'd know it if he wasn't."

"I believe you. We'll find him, all of them. I promise."

Rayfe and I walked together, ascending the long tunnel more slowly as Ursula and Harlan jogged away, calling commands. He took my hand, weaving his fingers with mine, and it felt so familiar, so necessary that I shuddered inside. "Harlan explained everything," he said quietly. "There's so much I don't remember. Stretches of time gone from my memory."

"Yes," I whispered into his expectant silence, though he hadn't posed it as a question.

"I understand now why you lied to me," he said. "Though I imagine I don't know all the lies you told me."

"It probably doesn't change anything, but I want you to know I really hated lying to you. I can't express how much."

"I don't know whether that changes anything," he said slowly. "I don't know what to think or feel."

"I understand that." I bit down on my lower lip, wanting to tell him more, but it felt selfish to tell him how hard this had been for me.

"It's a very strange thing, not to be able to trust one's own mind."

"You can now. You're free of her. I made sure of it."

He paused at the last turn—Ursula and Harlan's orders echoing from around the corner, preparing our people to push through—and turned to face me. Rayfe searched my face, his eyes shadowed in the flickering lamplight. "You went into my head, like she did, and some of those missing memories, they're gone because of you, not her. It's very odd, though—I can't really tell you apart. What you did and what she did, they're the same, aren't they?"

"Yes," I whispered. "I'm so sorry."

"Are you?" He canted his head slightly, the wolf sensing vulnerability, considering the danger he might be in—and how to attack. "Why?"

"I never wanted to become like her, to do that to you. I don't expect you to forgive me, but I—"

"Andromeda." He stopped my tumbling words with a little shake. "There's nothing to forgive. If your power is the same is hers, then it's good that Annfwn has you on our side, that I have you."

"But that kind of ability, to alter someone's thoughts and memories, their very will—I never wanted that. To be that kind of person is…" I trailed off because he smiled, amusement lighting his eyes. "What?"

"You will never be like your father, Andromeda."

My lips parted, but no words came out. "I…"

He cupped my face in his hands. "Yes, *you*," he murmured. "This is about *you*. Not your father, not your mother, not the high priestess, or any of them. The power is there for you to use, in all of your compassion and wisdom. You used it to save me, and I will be forever grateful for that. I only regret that I have not been the husband to you that you deserve. I promised you a long time ago that, though you didn't have a choice in marrying me, I'd make you happy you did. I let you down, I know."

I loosened my hand from his and put my arms around him, laying my cheek against his chest. He put his arms around me without hesitation, and it was as if nothing between us had ever been otherwise.

"I want you to know," I said against him, "that I love you with everything in me. I know that we were forced together, that I'm not someone you… chose, but I *did* choose you. When I found a way to sneak out of Windroven during the siege, it wasn't only to stop the war. I wanted you. Not out of duty or because of destiny, but for myself. I wanted you from that first day in the meadow, and there's never been anyone else. Could never be anyone else." *There's choosing and there's* choosing.

He made a pained sound, and I braced myself for him to brush off my words, or to say something unintentionally cutting. With my cheek still pressed against him, the sound of his heart thudded under my ear, and I closed my eyes in misery, for the past, for our terrible present, and the doomed future.

"Andromeda." Rayfe eased me away from him and I firmed my lips, really hoping I wouldn't cry. He slipped a finger under my chin, coaxing me to look at him. "Is that what you think—that I didn't choose you? I could've made a hundred, a thousand other choices. After that first day in the meadow, I could've gone back to Annfwn and never given you another thought."

The leap of hope, of longing, was nearly painful. "But Annfwn needed me, you kept saying—"

He shook his head, an impatient gesture, and he firmed his grip on my chin. "Annfwn survived nearly thirty years without a queen to manage the barrier. We could have found a way. I made myself a bargain that if I didn't like what I saw, I'd go home and never breathe a word to Salena's daughter about our betrothal. Instead, I waged a war for you. I risked everything for *you*. Not out of duty or because of destiny, but for myself." A slow smile curved his lips and his fingers gentled, stroking my jaw, his thumb feathering over my lower lip.

I gazed at him, feeling, knowing the truth of that. "Then it wasn't only for Annfwn?"

He bent his head, brushing a kiss against my lips so sweet and full of answering longing that I almost couldn't bear it. "It was never about Annfwn," he murmured against his lips. "Or not only about Annfwn. If it had been, I wouldn't have married you."

I frowned. "We were married for a lot of reasons, by representatives of several goddesses and cultures, for the peace treaty."

He shook his head slightly. "I mean when I married you in the Tala way. That night in the cabin. Blood magic to bind us together for all our lives."

I stared back, shuffling the memories of that night, the bits and pieces of things I'd heard referenced since. Of course I knew not all Tala performed that particular ritual—not many Tala opted for monogamy at all—but I supposed I'd thought it had to do with being queen. "It wasn't necessary?"

"Not even a bit." He looked both chagrined and hopeful. "I told you before—you didn't need me at all. You could've reigned as Queen of Annfwn without me, certainly without marrying me."

"No I couldn't," I replied with fervor. "I wouldn't want to."

His smile turned rueful, and he lifted a hand to caress my cheek. "It was unfair of me not to tell you before the ceremony. I know that, and yet...I was driven. I couldn't risk losing you. Then afterwards... I hesitated to tell you. Nothing can break our marriage bond. Wolves mate for life. I've warred with the wolf in me over it. The man knows I tricked you, but the wolf doesn't care. You were mine from that first kiss, and I was unwilling to let you go."

"I see." I did see, suddenly understanding so much that I hadn't.

"I was a coward," he confessed quietly. "I didn't want you to be angry with me. To maybe leave me because of it."

"I'm not angry," I whispered.

"You're not?" He asked the question in a wondering tone, a hesitant smile blooming on his lips.

"No. I'm glad to know you love me, that *you* wanted me.

That we aren't simply dancing the steps destiny forced upon us."

He kissed me, softly. "You are far too fierce to be forced to dance to anyone else's tune, my queen."

Except that I had been, bowing and skipping along to the yank and pull of Deyrr's strings. No more.

"Rayfe, Andi—time to do this, people!" Ursula shouted.

"Time to say goodbye," I said, tipping up to kiss my husband one last time.

His hands tightened on me with a possessive ferocity I'd missed like I'd lost a part of myself, and he took the kiss deeper. Not sweet or soft at all, but ravenous, consuming, all encompassing. He broke off as suddenly as he'd taken control, leaving me shaken.

"Not goodbye," he grated. "Because we cannot be parted. And I categorically refuse to let them win. You do what you must to stay alive."

"You too," I managed, overcome.

"Would it be wrong…" He hesitated. "I've missed so many opportunities, but could I say something to our child?"

Tears sprang out and rushed down my cheeks. "It's not wrong at all. He'd love to hear his father's voice."

Rayfe's face transformed, luminous with a joy I'd rarely glimpsed in him. "We're having a son?"

"It seems so."

Rayfe sank down onto one knee, expression reverent, smoothing his hands to cup my belly. He placed a kiss there, murmuring something I couldn't hear, laying his cheek against the taut round, just as I'd listened to his heart. I ran my fingers through his long hair, impossibly moved. He reached up and took my hand, twining my fingers with his, then looked up at me, his face ravaged. "I've wasted so much time. Out of fear. Childish worries."

"I've been afraid and worried, too," I told him.

He turned his gaze to the bloodstone ruby I wore. "You've never taken this off."

"Not since the day you put it on my finger. I never will." I realized I'd once promised to give him a ring, too, and had never quite gotten around to it. So many lost opportunities.

"Is there a future for us?" he asked somberly, and I remembered the first time he asked me what I saw ahead of us, back in that cabin on our wedding night.

"There is always that possibility." I said the words as firmly as I knew how, hoping I didn't speak a lie.

"There has to be, because I can't let it end here."

I squeezed his hand. "Then we won't, my wolf."

He grinned at me, sharp and feral. "Together?"

I raised him to his feet. "Together."

## ~ 21 ~

Ursula's face held the same sharp-edged and glittering anticipation as Rayfe's. The battle lust brought out her Tala blood—as did Danu's hand, silvering her with the light of the just cause—and never had she looked more like a child of Annfwn.

Harlan stood at her side, ready to guard her back and flank. With all the solidity of his height and bulk, he epitomized the granite fatalism of Dasnaria, grimly somber, steadfast and unflinching. The Hawks and Tala lieutenants ranged behind them, backed by former Vervaldr, more Tala, and soldiers from the Twelve Kingdoms. Many more of them had made it down to the tunnels than I'd realized—and all were warriors to the bone.

I was not a warrior. I'd never felt that excitement that shone on all their faces. Before I met Rayfe, all I'd wanted was to spend as much time riding Fiona as possible. I'd never wanted to rule, to battle anyone. I'd only wanted to be left alone.

And I had been. I'd been hiding away behind my shield of quiet invisibility. Not being bothered, but also not alive. *I've wasted so much time. Out of fear. Childish worries.*

I could understand now, something of what they felt, ready to fight. Better to act than to dread. We'd go out there and we'd fight until we won or died. There was a simplicity in that.

Ursula read it in my face. "Ready?"

I looked to Rayfe, holding my hand still, and he nodded. "Yes," we said together.

Ursula nodded to Rayfe and stepped back, yielding to his authority. With a glance at me, he tugged me forward, then released my hand. I pulled the Star of Annfwn from my pocket, holding it up for all to see. It glowed in the dimness of the tunnels with the light of the moon, sun and stars all in one. The assembled warriors made a sound greater than several hundred throats. I rarely displayed the artifact, but now it shone for all to recognize. Drawing on the Heart, I poured power through the focus stone, making it shine even brighter.

"The Star of Annfwn!" Rayfe roared, and they all cheered.

*A star to guide you.* Ursula met my eyes and I knew she remembered our mother's words also. Rayfe nodded to me. My cue to act.

Ursula raised her sword and I amassed more magic behind the building wave, poised there. Rayfe let out a howl, becoming the wolf, and all around us reality shuddered as hundreds of shapeshifters shifted form at once.

Ursula dropped the sword.

I released the magic. The giant stone wheel rolled aside.

Our people surged forward. Their people fell in, abruptly losing the wall they'd nearly chewed through. As planned, I shifted into heron form, taking the Star with me, and my staymach guard made a tight formation around me of fierce raptors. Anticipating me, they flew ahead of and around me, shepherding me above the onslaught.

It was endless, a churning sea of Deyrr creatures, as far as I could see. I tried not to look back, but an attacking Deyrr eagle forced me to duck and wheel as my guard savaged it. Coming around, I saw Kiraka high on the cliff face, her fire turning the blue sky white with the heat of her flame. Ash floated like snow from the creatures she'd burnt. And below me…

Ursula, sword shining like Danu's truth, wading into the mass of surging creatures, Harlan huge at her back. I couldn't spot Rayfe at all among the masses of animals, though usually his wolf form stood out in size and sheer power. Ursula advanced, blade a blur of ruby and silver, Harlan doggedly one step behind. The wave of attackers billowed in cresting surf of fur, scales, and feathers, then overwhelming them both. She vanished beneath, gone from my sight.

Exactly as I'd seen over and over. It took everything in me not to fly toward her. I nearly did, my bird body following the prod of my emotions. But a wolf's howl penetrated my mindless panic, the king's summoning rattling through my blood and bones.

I saw him then, the huge black wolf poised on a rock outcropping, head thrown back in the wolf's cry to rally. From all over the cliff city and beyond, the Tala answered, the cries from tens of thousands of voices carrying audibly and inaudibly.

We are Tala and we will defend Annfwn.

Determination renewed, I flew directly to my promontory, dodging the toothy jaws of the sea monsters that leapt to seize me from the air. One of my staymach guard screamed at its wing was caught, abruptly silenced as it was dragged under the shining, bloodied sea.

Badgered from above and below, my guard fought fiercely, protecting me with their lives as I made for the shelter of my outpost. I landed there, shifted back to human form, and snapped into place the magical barrier I'd layered into the very rocks. At least foresight had done that much—the time spent creating these protections had been worthwhile.

Replete with power, feeling fully healed and surging with magic from the Heart, I'd manifested back in human form wearing the red velvet gown, my crown, and Salena's jewels. If I had to face the high priestess and her pet god, I'd do it as Queen of Annfwn.

I'd have been more powerful inside the Heart—or rather inside the dome that had protected the Heart—but I was fiercely glad that circumstances and timing kept me above. It would've been much worse to be far below the sea in my silent bubble, only able to witness events from a safe remove. No, I wouldn't be that person again. I'd live and fight with immediacy, no matter how painful.

I had a job to do: hold the gate and regain control of the barrier. Relatively simple compared to what I had been doing. Still two things at once—and neither of them included watching over Rayfe or Ursula as I truly wanted to be doing—so I firmly made myself look at one thing at a time. I checked the gate, hoping that would be simpler, hoping the Deyrr forces would be focusing elsewhere for the time being.

To my dismay, the Deyrr seemed to be taking advantage of our forces withdrawing from that area to answer the rally call. A team of large animals—a rhino, two hippopotami, an elephant, and three oxen were taking turns battering at my barrier. So far several had bloodied their heads against it, but that didn't deter their mindless efforts. Hopefully mindless and not personally directed—and protected—by the high priestess.

Summoning power from the Heart, I tried blasting the lot of them, steeling my heart against the throb at destroying the innocent lives trapped in those bodies.

My blast bounced off. "Moranu curse that bitch," I snarled. I really needed to figure out how to get around that defense of hers, fast. Reaching through the Star, I metaphysically yanked her hair.

"Ow." The high priestess popped into illusory being in front of me. She wore her armor as before and smiled gleefully. "Is someone having a temper tantrum? Seems sacrilegious to take your goddess's name in vain. Yes, I heard that. Though I suppose such a weak and distant deity could hardly be of concern to you."

"Moranu certainly seems to be of concern to *you*," I retorted, diverting my attention to reinforcing the gate while the high priestess was occupied with talking to me. I sent a mental tendril toward her mind, seeking a way in to find that protective shield she used. It would probably look like mine. "You mention Her often enough. Maybe you're jealous that my goddess is more powerful that your little demigod of death."

"Yours is the false deity!" she spat, tempting me to ask who was having the temper tantrum now. "I wouldn't have her—and believe me, She tried. But I gave my allegiance to Deyrr and He is truly powerful. Once you join me you'll understand."

"Eh, I don't think so. Why take second best?" I wormed another tendril into her mind, using it in tandem with the first to make a crack, then a wedge. She didn't seem to be aware of my intrusion, but I went carefully, wary of yet another trap.

"You, my darling Andromeda, won't have a choice," the high priestess was saying as she made a show of examining her nails. "By now you've realized I've outmaneuvered you. All will be mine—in service to Deyrr, of course. This brave defense is charming, but ill conceived. You have a lovely view to watching them all die, however." She turned to look beside me. "I hope some of them survive. I'll need more bodies to handle all the dreadful cleanup."

Still diligently prying at the crack I'd opened in her mind, I made a show of turning my attention to the cliff road. I knew the cliff city as well as the corridors of my palace. Unable to help myself, I scanned for Rayfe, knowing he'd be at the forefront of any key points.

There: a phalanx of Deyrr bears blocked a narrow turn, the black wolf leading the charge. Rayfe and our people would take them out if she didn't shield the bears. The high priestess had skill and knowledge, but she didn't have power to spare, and she still had a mind as human as mine. Or once human. Regardless, she couldn't possibly be protecting all of her creatures simultaneously. With my finger on the pulse of her power, maybe I'd feel her shift that protective barrier from one group to the other.

I sent a light blast of power at the team attacking the gate. As she deflected it, I pivoted mentally, hitting the group of bears. The high priestess paced me, leaping to block, and I trapped a delicate tendril of power around the muscle she used to make that shield.

Then I pulled the blast and reversed the power, cutting the cords that bound the bears to Deyrr. The empty husks of the creatures collapsed, the bodies beginning their immediate and precipitous decay. The technique no longer gutted me as it had before. This time it felt only like a solid punch to the gut. I managed not to audibly gasp for breath, pulling on the Heart's power and the Star to fill the hole. Was it an illusion that it felt like the Heart's power flowed more freely?

Rayfe howled a rallying cry and the horde of Tala shapeshifters hurtled over the decaying bears, heading higher to reach Kiraka and the Tala barricaded above. A few in human shape stayed behind to clear the road. Though cutting the tether left the souls of the Deyrr creatures unanchored, unable to either live or pass on to whatever afterlife there was and consigned the spirits of those people to eternal slavery to Deyrr's consuming hunger, at least we didn't have to worry about hacking them apart or the ashes eternally attempting to coalesce.

Small comfort there.

The high priestess spun on me. "You dare try to take my creatures for yours! I will—" She paused, brow furrowed, then she burst out laughing. "Oh you fool! Really, Andromeda, you make things too easy. Your soft heart will be your undoing. You don't have what it takes to fight me. Just admit it and give up."

Ignoring her, I tested her reaction by reaching to cut the cords on the team battering the gate. Making a knife of my will, I sliced and—there. She flexed that muscle, and my blade met with nothing.

"Tsk." The high priestess frowned prettily. "I'm wise to you now. You won't be interfering that way anymore. And look!" She pretended to shade her eyes, turning to point at a ship coming into view, followed by a dozen more. "Here we come. I'll see you in the flesh momentarily. This will be such fun. I *love* winning!" She gave me a saucy wink and a salaciously blown kiss, then vanished, never guessing I had the key to her trick now, and would save it for the perfect moment. Another thing I'd learned from her.

I surveyed the approaching ships with a sinking heart, then resolutely turned back to assess our status. Too many of our people fought on the beach still—at least half of our remaining fighters. Whole groups had been cut off from access to the cliff roads. Those able to take avian forms had retreated to the higher levels. They dove and soared in fighting formations, neatly ducking Kiraka's flame, but unable to help the Tala below.

The sight gave me an idea, though. I could set aside restoring the barrier as the less immediate problem. And, if I could stop paying attention to the gate, and not reveal my secret weapon to the high priestess by blasting the creatures there that she'd only replace, I could help with the battle on the beach.

*'Kiraka. There's a group attacking the gate to the road out of Annfwn—can you go fry them?"*

*"No."*

*"I can remove the high priestess's shielding. They'll be vulnerable."*

*"No."*

I paused, not at all ready for such a firm refusal. *"You mean, you can't?"*

*"I mean I won't. What care I for gates and roads when my Daughter and my Daughter's Daughter's lives are at stake?"*

*"If we fall to Deyrr, your human companions won't be worth anything to you!"* I shot back in frustration.

*"If the gate falls and Deyrr invades your other kingdoms, they might leave here. If I abandon my defense, I might lose them. On balance, my chances are better staying. Leave me be, sorceress."*

A snarl worthy of Rayfe rose in my throat as Kiraka broke contact. I looked again, and the situation had only worsened. More ships appeared from downcoast, moving swiftly towards us in shallow water, clearly intending to land on the beach. I couldn't stop them from landing, but I could try to clear a path for our people to get out of the way. If our troops were caught between the Deyrr army blockading them from the cliff access and the arriving attackers, they'd be decimated.

I left the gate to its fate. In some ways Kiraka was right—if the gate went, that would relieve the pressure on Annfwn. I thrust aside the images—all too real and seen far too many times—of the endless Deyrr army of foul undead creatures descending on the peaceful farms and villages of Mohraya. For it was my birthplace that lay at the other end of that road, full of people who'd never be able to comprehend the dark magic unleashed upon them.

But I couldn't do everything.

Concentrating on the scene on the beach, I flung my mind outwards, hopping from eyes to eyes to assess the worst threats. The high priestess couldn't divide her attention so much as to shield each individual, and with the increased flow of magic from the Heart, I seemed to have plenty of ability to cut the attachments to Deyrr. I barely felt the impact anymore as, ruthlessly and selectively, I pulled the cords on one Deyrr creature after another. The large and the fierce fell as I found them. Their souls howled in agony as I severed them, shrieking in terror as they snapped back into the god's greedy maw.

Part of me longed to take the reins of their will for myself. Moranu's silver black presence flowed in me, reaching for that control, drawn to it. It was the nature of the goddess to want to reclaim Her children, for even these abominations of shapeshifters were Hers.

And it would be easier. Tempting, even, to justify it as at least wresting those souls from Deyrr.

But then they'd be mine, and that was a bridge too far for me. Just as the high priestess had scorned me for flinching from doing it, I couldn't let myself take control of another's will, not even for Moranu. What I'd done to Rayfe had been bad enough, and even though he'd forgiven me, one more step over that line and I'd become a monster. I couldn't let that happen, if only for the sake of my unborn child, who deserved to be born to a mother with at least a shred of humanity.

*Even if that means your child won't be born at all?* The small voice whispered its insidious doubts. It was true, I thought, as I cut another soul from its mortal tether, destroying lest I be destroyed. If I died, my son would die with me, and he'd never have a chance at anything at all. Death ended possibility. Only life held hope. Maybe better to become a monster and allow my child a chance at life.

Or was that the high priestess influencing my thoughts? *I don't know what's real anymore.*

I found a trio of Deyrr jackals harrying a small group of Tala wizards who'd been reinforcing the spells on the stone gates to the tunnels below, and blew through them like the icy winds of winter at Ordnung, leaving decaying bodies behind. Maybe if I took the reins of their wills instead, I could find a way to later free them, save all this destructive waste…

Or was that her again, tempting me to throw in with Deyrr's corrupting power?

The ships had reached the beach, extending gangplanks into the shallows to unload more Deyrr creatures to crush our own. I couldn't move fast enough to free our people in time. Would wresting control of Deyrr's slaves be any faster? And where had Ursula gone? In all my scanning and hopping, I hadn't glimpsed her.

Of course, I'd been focusing on the beach and maybe she and Harlan had already begun climbing.

The sails of the new ships snapped, the sound carrying over the water and the raucous sounds of battle. Dark figures scrambled in the rigging to tighten the ropes and steady the vessels being thrown about in close quarters. Odd that they'd come in so fast, at full sail, into such shallow water, especially with the battle so clearly going their way. These ships must have far shallower draft than ours, but even so—

A scream of fury wrested my attention away. It echoed through my bones and blood, and I frantically scanned for the source. A dragon dove from the sky, ruby red and glittering like fresh blood, blazing with fire.

*Not* one of our dragons.

Kiraka roared at it again, a sound I'd never heard any of our dragons make before, a cry of anger and despair. A friend of hers, perhaps, taken by Deyrr. It flew directly at Kiraka and I reached to sever its ties—

*"Don't you* dare!*"* Kiraka screamed it so loud in my head that

I physically reeled, nearly pitching into the sea when I set my foot down on patch of gravel. *"I'll handle this."*

With that she took wing, bronze form the color of the sun just as it sinks into the sea, and she hurled herself at the red dragon, meeting it midair and engaging it in a tumble of wings, lashing tails, and wayward spires of fire and smoke. The two pitched in the sky, an impossible tangle, then dropped like stones. Time seemed to spin endlessly as they fell… Until they hit the water with a *boom* and massive splash that sent water and steam mushrooming into the sky.

The wave of reaction rippled out, boats—theirs and ours—rising and falling, some capsizing. The wave rolled huge toward my outpost and I braced myself, slipping the Star deep into a pocket, and using my connection to the Heart to anchor myself to the rocks. Saltwater, surprisingly cold for Annfwn's gentle sea, pounded and poured over me. It left me drenched, shivering, and dazed—and it took me a moment to clear my eyes to survey the aftermath.

Sadly, the new ships hadn't been budged. They sat unnaturally stable in the water, all with gangplanks out to the shore. And, to my astonishment, elephants galloped down those ramps—way too fast for even Deyrr creatures being directly puppeteered by the high priestess or her minions.

Also, these glittered with armor strapped on to protect their vulnerable joints and other soft spots, the sort of rigging a Tala shapeshifter would scorn to use. People rode the elephants, war cries harmonizing with their mounts' trumpeting. These were decidedly not any of our human/shapeshifter fighting pairs. The people bristled with foreign weapons, like ours and not. Some employed long spears and javelins, decorated—or ballasted—with exotically colored feathers. Others standing on deck had bows as tall as a Dasnarian, using them to hurtle huge arrows to clear the way, while their elephant-mounted brethren galloped headlong onto the beach, hanging on to the harness with acrobatic daring, scything with long swords.

And they were killing the Deyrr creatures.

I blinked, focusing my physical eyes and zoomed in with metaphysical sight. A huge elephant led the charge, a lithe man on its back, a long queue of hair flying behind him. Right behind them a woman whose ivory hair shone in the light rode a smaller elephant with white scars on its gray hide. The vision tunneled through me, coring my heart and leaving me gasping and empty.

Could this be Harlan's lost sister? It must be and yet... how could they have come to Annfwn?

Then I saw Danu's warrior, her flying braid as silver as her sword. Kaedrin the wanderer. She cleaved through the walls of Deyrr fighters with like tornado of steel. The elephant-mounted warriors charged and spun in tight formation, superbly trained and clearly well-accustomed to working together. They did what we'd been unable to do, sending the surging masses of Deyrr creatures into chaotic disarray.

Gathering my scattered concentration, I gratefully pulled my attention back from the battle of Annfwn's beach to our surprise rescuers, taking a moment to check the gate. Not much had changed there except that several of the attackers had dropped to the ground, having apparently battered themselves brainless against the immovable barrier. More unfortunate creatures had taken their place, however, renewing their assault.

Worse, additional Deyrr forces had begun working on the barrier on either side of the gate. The high priestess was no fool and she'd no doubt correctly surmised that I had devoted most of my effort to reinforcing the gateway itself. Farther along on the one side, the forest became too dense, and the hills too steep for easy passage. On the other, of course the cliffs rose sheer and difficult to scale.

But for several lengths on either side of the massive gateway, the barrier could be breached—with considerable effort, but still possible—and the wide road to Ordnung was relatively accessible beyond. I reinforced those sides, also, throwing more magical energy into the gate itself, and then extended the reach of it all farther into the ground, as some of the Deyrr creatures had begun to tunnel. If that didn't work, I'd have to blast them all and risk the high priestess being on to me and changing her tactics.

A flash of pain brought me back to my body. A Deyrr-controlled octopus had crawled onto the rocks and wrapped several arms around my legs, dragging me toward the water. I'd reflexively gripped the rocks, and the pain of my nails breaking and fingertips shredding had alerted me. My staymach guard divebombed it with beaks and talons, but the bulk of the creature lay safely below water, glaring at me with a mad, violet eye.

I blasted the tentacle gripping me most tightly—and was completely unsurprised when that bounced off. I wouldn't kill the shielding yet, not until I'd exhausted my other tools. I reached to cut the creature's tethers to Deyrr instead—and shockingly enough, I found another consciousness inside. Not the high priestess. This was an even younger woman, one who looked to be about fifteen, with the round full cheeks and creamy skin of barely blossoming womanhood, looked back at me. Ringlets of rose-gold hair bounced prettily around a face that would've been the portrait of lovely innocence—if not for her cruel smirk and dead dark eyes.

She must be one of the junior priestesses Karyn had mentioned. How short-sighted of me not to realize she'd have her minions operating some of the key attackers. The red dragon must be similarly piloted. And this one had been specifically targeted to capture me.

Unlike her mistress, this one spent no time taunting me. Instead her expression sharpened with vicious triumph as she batted away my attempt to cut the octopus's body off from Deyrr's animating force—and renewed her puppet's grip on my leg, snaking out several more tentacles to fasten on my other leg and increase the leverage. My body slid, and I released my hold on the rocks, for fear I'd break my fingers. A bad idea, as I now skidded and bumped over the rough rocks, bruising and skinning the front of my body.

Including my belly and my precious passenger.

Incensed and panicked, I hacked at the octopus with magical blows, desperately trying to sever its hold—or Deyrr's hold on it. To no avail. Throwing caution away, I circumvented the shielding and blasted—only to have my magic bounce off again. Clearly an individual thing. Just wonderful.

One of my staymachs had taken the form of a flying reptile, landing on one tentacle and digging in scaled claws, its scissoring beak sawing at the purple-gray fresh, sending the oily black blood of Deyrr spattering. Another tentacle seized my stalwart guard from behind, wrapping around the staymach's throat, lifting it away and tossing it into the water.

With a final yank, it pulled me off my clawhold, and pulled me down into the drowning deeps.

# ~ **22** ~

WATER BURNED UP my sinuses and swamped my brain, the heavy red velvet gown dragging me down. Forgetting in my instinctive panic that I wasn't a fish, I gasped for oxygen, only making things worse. A shapeshifter raised in Annfwn would've instinctively shifted the moment she hit water.

Not me. I had to think it through. Not easy with a giant octopus swimming out to sea faster than a galloping horse and dragging me along behind it. Besides which, it still had me by the legs, pulling me feet first, which meant the skirt of my gown billowed up and over my head, tangling me in the heavy folds, making it even more difficult to get my bearings. I needed to shift—and soon—or I'd drown. Or I'd shift so far out to sea that it would take hours to return, and there might not be anyone left alive—or mentally free—by the time I got there.

I shook my chattering thoughts into sense. The octopus wasn't taking me out to sea—we were likely headed straight for the high priestess's flagship. I could only guess at why she'd gone to the trouble to physically grab me, but I knew for certain that was a place I decidedly didn't want to be. Better go for porpoise form. I wasn't sure what octopuses ate, but probably any aquatic form smaller than it would be fair game. I could do this.

*Concentrate. Focus.*

Nothing.

Something—no, someone—had blocked my shift. An impression of a girlish laugh filled my head, the rose-gold ringlets bouncing. Of course. The priests and priestesses of Deyrr could force shapeshifting. Or block it.

And my vision was going crimson black. Maybe Deyrr didn't want to abduct me. They might just want me dead. They'd killed my mother, a far more powerful and experienced sorceress. Now I'd die, too, and without a fight.

Silvery moonlight edged out the crimson black of impending death. The pounding panic faded, replaced with the comforting shrouds of night shadows. An impression of many faces whirled around me. Feline, fox, ursine, avian, aquatic, insectile, fabulous, prosaic—the many forms of the wildlife of all the world whirled through my mind.

Moranu, goddess of night, walked through me in serene beauty. And offered me Her hand. I knew what the price would be.

*Moranu goes with you,* Ami whispered in my memories. *She is yours and you are Hers. There is nothing for you to fear in letting Her will fill you. You have been Marked by Her from the beginning. Don't refuse Her will now, when all hangs in the balance.*

All certainly hung in the balance. Even if I didn't die immediately, I'd lose consciousness soon. If the high priestess laid hold of me in this vulnerable condition… It didn't matter so much what happened to me, but for the sake of my child, for Rayfe, for everyone depending on me, for the entire world, I had to do it.

I took Moranu's hand, braced for what she'd ask of me, of my son.

She swept into me and my illusions broke like glass before the onslaught of the deity's presence. I became like one of the dolls Salena left for us, a limp collection of rags and dead hair, tossed about. This wasn't like Zynda's vision, where she'd seen Moranu and spoke with the goddess. I'd become a vessel for the goddess—emptied of everything that I was to make room for Her.

But I couldn't be that, couldn't be like Shaman, with no connections to the world of people. I had a husband, a child coming, sisters, friends. I wouldn't be like my mother, giving myself for the cause and abandoning the ones who loved and needed me most. I would never be invisible again. Neither would I be an unthinking tool of the goddess.

*So you do have spirit, Daughter. I'd begun to wonder.* Moranu's voice shimmered around me, wordless and timeless, and yet I understood her meaning and her infinite amusement and compassion. Maybe "amusement" was the wrong word, but there was a joyfulness in her, a core-deep love that I would've ascribed to Glorianna.

*We are three and We are one. Individual faces of one being. Just as all of Our children spring from one source, though you wear different faces. You are all Ours, all one.*

*"Even the high priestess? Even Deyrr?"* I didn't precisely think the question, but she understood my doubt.

*Even so.* And now the joyfulness became subdued. Not sorrow exactly, but a tolerant impatience. *Just as you have flaws in yourself that you seek to excise, Deyrr is an aspect of Us that We lost control of and need to correct.*

*"And here I thought the gods and goddesses were perfect."*

*Perfection is a human ideal that does not exist. How can it? Perfection is static by definition and the universe is in a state of constant change.*

I glimpsed Moranu's many faces again, the whirling mélange of animal and human forms, morphing out into plants, rocks, stars, and planets. Liquid to gas to solid to time to light to vacuum.

**Change.** The goddess showed me the concept as much as she spoke the word, and I comprehended in a way I never had before.

*"But if Deyrr is part of you, is it true that Deyrr is your ancient nemesis?"*

**Yes. You should understand this, as you have been at war with yourself, Andromeda. All your life. You've been unwilling to truly embrace your gifts.**

With Her voice flooding every aspect of my being, I could hardly ignore the truth of this. *"I like to think of them as flaws I'm trying to excise."*

She laughed, the sound of a midnight river under moonlight. **Were you anyone else, you might have that luxury. But you do not.**

*"Then I am bound by fate."*

**The perversion of the cycle of life and death must be stopped. The imbalance grows and threatens to topple the universe into entropy and chaos. The tipping point is nigh. Call that fate if you like, but this is the time and you are the one.**

*"I don't know how to stop them."*

**So stubborn. It is your gift and your curse.** The goddess sounded amused again. **You know what to do. You simply resist the knowledge.**

Hmph. In that case I was resisting it so well that I didn't know what it was.

**True.**

Nothing like having a goddess possessing my mind to read even the thoughts I hadn't articulated. It would be helpful if She would just come out and tell me what to do.

*That presupposes that* I *know what you should do. If I could act for you, I would. I cannot.* You *must be the one to decide, to act.*

"This isn't at all how I thought receiving the word of the goddess would be."

Again that amused compassion. *No, it never seems to be.*

"Any hints? I assume you've taken possession of my being for a reason."

*You were about to die. That would have been inconvenient timing.*

So flattering.

*Yes. Death is, of course, simply another change, but We need you alive in your current form. The timing has become critical. So I am here to encourage you to live.*

"Great, so You can keep me from dying here and now?"

*No. You must do it yourself. Use your gifts. They come from Me, and I wouldn't give you anything you shouldn't have.*

"And the price?"

*You already know that.*

"I can't give you my child! I won't make that choice."

*Andromeda, My daughter. Your son is Mine, as you are Mine, as Stella is Mine. He will be born with the Mark. The choice was never yours to make. Or his.*

"But what about the required sacrifice?"

*Oh, child of Salena. You should know this: the sacrifice was made long before you were born.*

Oh. Oh, I should have realized that. Salena had given everything so all of this could come to pass. *"I understand now."*

*Good. Now go.*

Abruptly I was back in my drowning body.

And the knowledge was there—what I needed to do, what I

could do, and had been practicing—as if Moranu had put it there for me to find. Or maybe, as She had said, I'd known it all along.

I reached past the octopus to the puppeteer, the cruel sweet-faced junior priestess, and slipped into her mind. It was brutally easy to follow the threads of involuntary control, the shapeshifter she'd forced into octopus form, murdered, and harnessed to Deyrr through her own will. It was an inherently corrupt connection, and I followed it straight to what remained of her humanity. A brief shock of surprise from her. And her will was my own.

Tucking her will in my pocket, I became a porpoise. The octopus followed along, belonging to me now, too. I swam faster, leaping out of the water and into the air, becoming the heron on the wing.

Vigor and health suffused me, and I felt better in that form than ever before. Never had I shifted so easily, or into a form with such perfect health. So this was how it was supposed to feel. Amazing how accepting yourself without fears or reservations could change everything.

I wheeled on wing tip, and winged at top speed back toward the white cliffs of Annfwn, like clouds on the horizon. We'd come far, indeed, and I cast my long sight about as I flew, finding the Deyrr flagship not far away at all.

I raced ahead of it, not in the least tired, and soon met my avian staymach guard who'd been struggling to follow after me. They swirled about me in a dance of greeting, shifting colors in ways decidedly unlike the animal forms they'd chosen to imitate. Seeing if I could, I reached for Rayfe's mind. Perhaps my mindspeaking skills had also improved.

*"Rayfe?"*

*"Andromeda!"* He grasped my mind's touch in a mental em-

brace, strong, warm, as if he'd never let me go. *"Where are you?"*

*"Coming back."* I sent him a story bubble of what had happened to me, though I left out Moranu's intervention. I understood now why Zynda hadn't liked to speak of it. The encounter had been as intimate and deeply moving as it was improbable.

*"You're so strong and clear,"* he replied. *"Something changed."*

*"Yes, for the better. What's the status there?"*

*"Better, for the moment, though the next battle is imminent. You won't believe who's here. You'll have to see for yourself."*

*"All right. I'm nearly there."*

*"Were you able to restore the barrier?"*

I hesitated. Restoring the barrier seemed pointless at the moment. The Dasnarian navy was inside already. The high priestess was about to land right here, and the barrier couldn't stop her. Besides, more and more it felt like the Heart's power flowed more freely with the dome broken. I'd relied on that barrier so much, fixated on it, but maybe now was the time to let it go.

*"Rayfe, my wolf, what if I pull the barrier down altogether?"*

I felt his shock, then a thoughtful pause. *"What is your idea?"*

This. This was what our marriage had been and should be. I'd lost sight of it in all the pain and moving of shells, but this… This felt like coming home.

*"The barrier no longer protects us from Dasnaria,"* I said, thinking it through. *"It no longer serves its original purpose, to starve Deyrr of magic. It's become a thing that restricts people, harms them, and divides them. If I take it down, magic will return to all the world, which—isn't that how it should be?"*

*"And what about Deyrr?"*

*"Either we defeat them or we don't—but how is the barrier a factor in that, either way? Starving them didn't work because there will always be*

*pockets of magic, exceptions that people seek out. Because people need magic—and it's the right of everyone in the world to have it, not just the greedy who stole it or those lucky few who hoarded it."*

*"You make an excellent argument. Will you want to consult with Ursula? She hasn't convened with us yet."*

She hadn't? Danu preserve her then. I set that worry aside. *"No. This isn't her decision. The barrier belonged to Annfwn. It's Annfwn's decision. Yours and mine."*

*"Truly just yours, as the barrier has been yours to hold—or not."*

*"No,"* I replied firmly. *"We are a team and we decide together."*

The wave of love he sent filled and bolstered me. The high priestess had been devastatingly accurate in undermining this foundation of my life. Without Rayfe, I could survive, but with his love, I exceeded what I'd thought I could do.

*"In truth, then,"* he said softly, with some regret, *"the barrier never belonged to the Tala at all. We were those thieves and hoarders. Annfwn flourished at the expense of others. It's time we shared that wealth."*

*"Thank you, my wolf. You're a good man and a better king."*

*"Because of you, my queen. Do it, and come home to me."*

Folding my wings, I dove into the sea, and went to the Heart one last time.

The crabs had been busy trying to follow their embedded instructions to repair the barrier, even though they hadn't heard me. They massed all along the open hole, like a necklace of lapis beads, gleaming in the glow of the remaining shield around the dome. More light streamed out from the Heart below, illuminating the water in a narrow beam, like the sun breaking through clouds.

This would be my first test of the high priestess's shielding: I would confirm my ability to circumvent it, and also very likely alert her that I could do so. I readied myself—and a huge shadow passed over my fish form, nebulous and threatening. I whirled to confront it, and realized my octopus had followed me. It waited patiently, apparently expecting instructions.

Which reminded me I had that junior priestess bound to me as well. It might not fool the high priestess for long, but if I could masquerade as her minion, that might be enough to confuse her for a short time. Slipping inside the junior priestess's magic, I used her like a glove, extending her consciousness to the high priestess's shielding, and using that to vanish it.

Moving fast, I released the crabs from their onus, freeing them to return to whatever deep ocean lives they'd lived before the ancient sorcerers of n'Andana conscripted them. They scuttled off into the abyss, singing a silent and joyful song of freedom. After that it took me only moments to take hold of the dome and its larger cousin, draining both back into the Heart from which they sprang. The task required very little of me— nothing like manipulating the barrier had—as I simply guided the magic back to its origin.

The Heart drank the magic in, reabsorbing it into its own, all light vanishing.

And in that darkness, the primordial magic of the formless and faceless time before creation radiated out through the world. Moranu smiled, silver edged in the blackness that held all of life, as balance began returning to the universe.

# ~ 23 ~

WHEN I FLEW into the cliff city, a great deal had changed.

The battle on the beach still raged, but the tide of it seemed to be turning. Even more warriors on elephants had landed, and they worked in impressively effective teams to isolate Deyrr's creatures and turn them back into the sea. There was no sign of Kiraka or the red dragon, so I sent my octopus to search for them. It seemed surprisingly pleased to have a task—though I had no other clear sense of the person who'd once occupied that flesh. More N'Andanan ships ringed our harbor, making a path for the high priestess's flagship to approach. She would land in another hour to my eye. We'd have to decide how to handle her.

I landed on the breakwater and cast my mind over the battlefield that had once been our paradise. Scanning the Deyrr creatures, I examined the mental leashes controlling them. A few belonged to the high priestess, and I left those alone for the time being. Others were the mindless variety, trudging ever onward with their basic instructions. But I found individuals—usually the larger, fiercest animals—and groups with connections to Deyrr's magic like bundles of ribbons gathered into a bouquet, all leading back to various junior priests and priestesses.

I took a moment to look through their eyes and listen through their ears. They had all gathered in a great council chamber, one I recognized from Karyn's memories as being in the old palace in n'Andana. They sat around a long table. Dozens of them, so deep in trances that they looked like the pale statues from the courtyards at Ordnung. I spotted the priest and priestess I'd already taken, verifying that they looked no different from the others—should anyone awaken enough to take note.

One by one, I plucked them from the withered vine they'd adhered to, taking their minds and wills for my own. I'd already defeated the two most proficient sorcerers among them, so I worked my way down the chain, selecting the ones I wanted, those piloting the beasts attacking the beach at Annfwn. I would deal with the rest later, if they survived the destruction of the high priestess.

As I gathered their wills in my own dread bouquet, I directed them to pull their creatures back from the fighting. To disengage and wait.

Then I flew to the council chambers, now guarded entirely by our own people—a welcome sight—and they recognized me, cheering my return. Nakoa, Dafne and a crying little Salena stood to the side. All appeared to be unharmed, Dafne giving me a wave and smile of relief. Nakoa stood off to the side, face a mask of concentration. He was brewing the storm to slow the Dasnarian navy then. Excellent.

Two strangers stood with Rayfe. Shifting back to human form—in full Queen of Annfwn mode, complete with jewels and crown—I surveyed the new arrivals with considerable bemusement. *Ah, Moranu, you trickster.*

Rayfe, resplendent in formal black and, to my surprise wearing his own crown, strode to my side with a wolfish grin. Lifting my hand, he kissed it, lips passing warmly to my skin. "My queen, may I present our saviors."

My eyes went straight to the tall, ivory-haired woman with

the extraordinary blue eyes. Now that I knew to look, I picked out the bone structure so like Harlan's—and the same gentle nature within. I gave her a gracious nod. "Imperial Princess Ivariel, I presume?"

She glanced at the dark-skinned man beside her, a wry smile on her lush mouth, and he grinned widely. "Your Highness, Sorceress Andromeda," she replied, her Common Tongue stilted and colored with a Dasnarian accent, "I left the rank of my birth behind long ago, and with great gratitude that I could do so. Please call me Ivariel. And this is my husband, Ochieng."

The man I recognized from the visions bowed to me with a flourish, dark eyes sparkling with humor both odd for the tense circumstance and most welcome. "Forgive my bemusement, Your Highness," he said in flawless Common Tongue, "it's not every day one meets a heron that becomes one of former High King Uorsin's daughters. Dragons, wizardry, shapeshifting! I'm still assimilating this wondrous land of yours. So much here that seems more out of an old tale than real."

Ivariel made a face. "He talks a lot," she confided to me. "And we have pressing matters of war to discuss, Your Highness."

"Indeed. And call me Andi." I turned to Rayfe, catching Dafne's eye, too. "Still no Ursula and Harlan?"

"Harlan?" Ivariel jumped on his name with breathless alacrity. "Harlan Konyngrr?"

"Your brother, yes," I replied. "He is here somewhere." I hoped. "Though I believe he would lay no more claim to your family surname than you do. Rayfe?"

He shook his head. "No report of either of them. I have people looking."

"I must go to him," Ivariel demanded, eyes flashing. She hadn't left the imperial princess too far behind. "Ochieng, we must find him and help. I can't come this close and—" She broke off, unable to speak the worst.

Ochieng took her hand. "Give them a moment. Take a breath."

She calmed instantly, an impressive skill that he could affect her so quickly. Ivariel turned a beseeching look on me. "You must help find him. I care deeply about this."

"Ursula is my sister, so I care deeply also," I replied in a dry tone, already casting out my senses to locate them, and realizing as I said it that these relations made Ivariel my heart-sister. Just what I needed: another hard-headed sister who liked to give orders. She opened her mouth and I held up a hand to stop her. "While I'm looking, we need to make plans. The high priestess will make landfall in an hour."

"Dafne and I were just explaining the situation when you arrived," Rayfe said. "You look. We'll discuss."

I threw more effort into scanning for Ursula, knowing our long history and shared blood would make her show up to my mind's eye more easily. Where would she be? Wherever it was, Harlan would surely be by her side. Not on the beach. Not in the tunnels. I leapt from mind to mind, eyes to eyes. Then I knew where she'd be.

Aha! Sure enough. She and Harlan faced down an army of Deyrr creatures at the gate. Of course she wouldn't be able to stand aside and let them attack her other kingdoms. Scanning those animals, I found most belonged to the high priestess. Some looked to other, still active junior priests and priestesses, so I didn't dare take them just yet, lest I tip my hand. Ursula and Harlan were holding their own, but we needed to extract them. I threw more magic into the gate, and the invisible walls around it, the power of the Heart flowing hot and fast like blood from an artery.

"They're at the gate," I announced, coming back to the room. "They need help."

"I'm going." Ivariel turned to dash out, but Ochieng caught her hand again.

"La," he chided. "I will go, too, but let's plan to take a force with us."

"Yes," I said, nodding in thanks to him, and turning to Rayfe. "We need to get everyone together—including Ami—for when the high priestess lands."

He cocked his head, invisible wolf's ears pricking with interest. "You know what you're going to do now."

"Yes. Yes, I do."

The wolf showed in his smile. "I knew you would."

IVARIEL CHAFED WITH impatience, but within minutes we had a plan. After giving me an impassioned kiss that had Ivariel and Ochieng raising their brows, Rayfe flew to marshal our forces fighting at the tunnels. I gave Ivariel a staymach bird—which she immediately passed to Ochieng, commenting that he was the one gifted with animals—to guide them to the gate. They'd gather their people on the way. Once they retook the gate and freed Ursula and Harlan, they'd all meet us on the beach before the cliff city.

My octopus found Kiraka, hanging well back from the superheated water around her and red dragon as they spun in a death grip of talons and flame in the deep sea.

*"I'm taking control of the dragon's puppeteer,"* I warned her after a brief knock.

*"About time you figured that out,"* she snapped, not in the least

gracious. But then, she wouldn't be Kiraka if she displayed gratitude.

*"You could've suggested it."*

*"You're too stubborn. My Daughter,"* she demanded.

*"All are well, and the battle is turned in our favor, since you didn't ask,"* I replied absently as I slipped into the mind of the priest piloting the red dragon. He flinched in shock at my invasion, then lashed out with a mental whip.

Kiraka snorted in amusement at my rebuke, and helpfully clamped her jaws over the red dragon's sensitive muzzle. The priest tried to pull out of dragon, abandon his puppet to its fate, but I already had him in an unrelenting mental vise. His will became mine—a lifetime of vile cruelties bursting into my mind as if I'd bitten into a bile-filled sack—and the dragon stopped fighting, going limp in Kiraka's grip. I spat mentally, ridding myself of the priest's memories, stripping away what I didn't need from him. I didn't want to know, and who he'd been, what he'd done, didn't matter anymore. All he needed to do was serve me by piloting the red dragon. I gave him his instructions.

*"See you both up top,"* I said. *"We're going to need you."*

*"What else is new?"* Kiraka grumbled, but she began stroking for the surface with great sweeps of her wings as if she flew through the dense water, the red dragon steadfastly pacing her.

I became the heron again. With the Heart's magic flowing freely—and having slipped the restraints of my own fears about who or what I might become—I shapeshifted with glorious ease.

Heading to meet the others at the gate, I cast my mind outward, seeking the null spot that would be Zynda. They had to be out there, just hidden by the high priestess's shielding. Both dragons erupted from the water below, the red dragon already farther out toward the horizon. I tracked with him, keeping a piece of my attention inside the priest's mind. He would tell me when he and the dragon found my people.

I jumped to Jepp's mind. No longer fighting, she stood at the wheel of the Hákyrling, Kral beside her, watching from peaceful, sunlit seas as a lightning storm plagued the Dasnarian fleet.

*"This is Andi,"* I said, trying not to startle her, but also not wanting to lurk in her mind without her knowing. Either I was getting more proficient or she'd gotten more accustomed to my intrusions, but she didn't jump this time.

"Glad you're here, Andi," she said aloud, Kral turning to look at her with a wide grin. "Nakoa's storm is a thing of beauty. The entire navy is stalled."

"Thanks for clearing the Deyrr creatures out," Kral added. "They abruptly vanished a quarter of an hour ago. We're able to think straight now—and we figure we have you to thank."

Clearing out the Deyrr creatures? But I hadn't... oh. I re-examined the impression the priest had left, the shadow image of his many tentacled magic, before I'd pared him down for my purposes. All of these creatures in this region had been his. When I'd peeled him down to a single use, all of those tethers had been cut from the source. His creations still "lived" in their way, carrying out their simple instructions, but without focus or strength. Hmm.

*"Do you need anything more?"* I asked Jepp, unwilling to use her mouth unless necessary.

"She asks if we need anything, but I don't think so?" Jepp said to Kral.

He shook his head, pulling off his helm to wipe sweat and blood from his brow, running a big hand over his pale hair. "The question is, what do they need? I only regret that we can't get to you. How fare things in Annfwn?"

I laughed, realizing they didn't know, and felt Jepp's lips

curve in response to my amusement. *"We may yet win this thing. Tell Kral that his sister is here with elephants, and they've probably saved the day."*

Jepp relayed the message, incredulity in her voice, and Kral looked thunderstruck. "We need to get there," he growled.

"There's a touch of bad weather twixt here and there," Jepp pointed out.

"As if I needed reminding."

"Seems as if you did."

He glared at her. And my heron body had arrived at the gate. *"If you're good, I need to go."* I showed Jepp what I saw.

She whistled, long and low at the sight of the vast, unending column of Deyrr creatures pressing up against the gate, some trampled beneath their fellows' uncaring tread, others mounding up from the pressure behind. Trees had fallen, breaching my invisible wall, with creatures of all kinds trudging like ants along the bridges they made. More looked to be tunneling beneath, throwing up dirt and rocks into piles.

And, from the beach side, an army of elephants cut through the mass of Deyrr-animated animals. The mounted warriors stabbed and sliced, cutting some down, but the real threat came from the elephants. They trampled with fierce and meticulous attention, swinging trunks like blunt weapons that swept anything in their path aside. Using their mass with skill, the elephants worked together in an unstoppable siege engine. Tala and Hawks filled in the gaps, working with our new allies with seamless skill.

*"Tell Kral this is what his sister has wrought,"* I said, before withdrawing.

"Danu go with you," she called as I left.

I'd spotted Ursula and Harlan, back to back, fighting to keep a space before the gate itself clear. I threw up a barrier around them, landing inside of it, dodging when Ursula swung reflexively and nearly took my head off.

She glared at me. "Danu! Don't laugh, you reckless brat."

Harlan lowered his sword, seeming to realize at the same moment that no more assailants came at them. Both were covered in blood and breathing hard. She took the momentary reprieve as an opportunity to survey the larger situation. "We've held the gate, but we don't have the means to stop them from going over, around, and under. I can't estimate how many are already on their way to Ordnung."

"I can stop them before they get close," I assured her.

She wheeled on me with an astonished expression. "Since when are you so confident of that?"

"I figured out a few tricks."

"Some trick."

I laughed, the feeling of hope returning like the scent of rain after drought. "Yes."

"I hope you didn't have to sell your soul to Moranu for it," she commented, steely gaze upon me.

I shrugged in the elaborate Tala style. "I wasn't using it anyway."

She caught my arm as I turned. "Andi…"

"That was a joke!" I protested, then sobered. "Seriously—what better purpose for my immortal self than to serve a goddess? I've always been Marked for Moranu. I just accept the truth of it now."

Narrowing her eyes, she swore under her breath. "You're hysterical."

"No, Essla," I said gently. "I'm finally at peace with myself."

*"Andromeda, my queen,"* Rayfe said in my mind. *"We are gathered on the beach, and the high priestess's ship approaches."*

*"I'll slow her down,"* I replied, *"but we'll be there soon. Ami is with*

*you?"*

*"Yes. Go carefully."*

I blew him a mental kiss, then turned to Ursula. "I'm ready to kill the high priestess, and I need you there. Ready to go?"

She surveyed the press of creatures, and Harlan barked out a laugh. "We can't fly over the top of this, so…"

"Oh, there will be a path out," I replied with confidence. "Give it a minute. Harlan, I think you'll like this."

They exchanged looks as if they doubted my sanity. But after a moment, the wall of Deyrr creatures mashed against my invisible wall began to shift. They moved, squished to the sides, then some farther back flew through the air.

"What in Danu?" Ursula breathed, and I grinned at her.

Harlan stilled, a granite-carved giant of a man, and squinted at the gleam of Ivariel's ivory hair flashing through a break and quickly gone. "Can it be?" he said, barely speaking the words in his low rumble.

"Yes," I said to him, because I couldn't bear the straining hope he tried to contain, so afraid of being disappointed that he nearly broke its wings.

Then the beasts directly before us were shouldered aside by the biggest elephant I'd ever seen, Ochieng perched on her shoulders far above our heads. Beside her a smaller elephant wedged in with nimble strength. I dropped the barrier as several other elephants made a wall around us. Ivariel leapt to the ground and launched herself at Harlan.

He caught her reflexively, wrapping the tall, slender woman in a bear hug that looked bone cracking. Ursula glanced to the side, wiping away some tears, then smiled wryly when she caught me looking. I slid my arm through the crook of hers, heedless of the blood and gore. I'd clean up before facing down the high priestess.

"It's good," I murmured. "We need good things."

She nodded, firming her mouth, clearly unwilling to trust her voice.

Harlan set Ivariel down, holding her by the shoulders, scrutinizing her with astonishment. "Jenna," he said. And the world shivered, the bonds of an old vow falling away. "I swore I'd never speak your name until I held you again. And here you are."

"Here I am," she answered, tears streaming down her face. "Though you've grown a bit since last I saw you."

He grinned through his own tears, unworried about them. "So have you. But how are you here?"

"I heard my baby brother needed rescuing," she replied saucily. "I figured I should return the favor."

"Oh, Jenna—" He broke, catching his breath on a sob. "I'm so sorry. I—"

"Hush. There is nothing to be sorry for," she answered with ferocity. "You saved me. And I go by Ivariel now. She's the woman you set free to live and become so much more. I want you to meet my husband and children."

"This is my wife, Ursula," Harlan said, reaching for Ursula and drawing her close.

I let her go, taking a moment to check on my octopus friend, who'd wrapped two arms around the breakwater and the rest around the underside of the high priestess's ship. She was trying to take hold of its will, with no success. Still we needed to get moving.

"Your Majesty." Ivariel curtseyed in a formal Dasnarian style I'd only seen Karyn use. "I heard my favorite brother gave you the *Elskathorrl.* Do you deserve it?"

"I…" Ursula didn't seem to know what to say, uncharacteristically flustered.

"Usually this is my hard-ass sister's line," I inserted, "but I hate to interrupt a touching moment with matters of war. We need to get to the beach."

"Ride with me?" Ivariel suggested to Harlan. Her elephant mount stepped forward, curling her trunk as if holding the hand Ivariel held out. "This is Efe, my special friend." She looked to Ursula. "If you'd like to ride Violet with Ochieng, he'll give you a hand up."

Ursula looked dubious, but soon all four were mounted again. Our elephant escort cleared a path for us, and I shifted to lion form, pacing alongside Efe and Violet. I chose that form partly to stay with them, and just in case I needed my claws. After a brief bout of curious snuffling, the elephants calmed, eyeing me as if they understood I wasn't *that* sort of lion.

Our warriors closed ranks around us, and we withdrew. Let them hammer at the gate. If all went well in the next hour, we'd have no more need of it.

*Please, Moranu, let my plan work.*

The goddess didn't reply, not in words, but her silvery glide sifted through me. And the priest piloting the red dragon reported tonelessly that they'd located the null space in the sky. Using him like one of Kral's armored gauntlets, I smashed through the high priestess's shield.

I knocked politely, and Zynda pulled me in with the equivalent of a mental tackle hug. Looking through Zynda's eyes, I took in the small island. It seemed all our people were there. Zyr, in gríobhth form with Karyn at his side, Djakos and Ash nearby, Marskal already climbing the harness to Zynda's back. Beyond them, all of our aerial forces, lolling over the small patch of land in various reclining poses. All rose to their feet at Zynda's alert, weapons ready, wings flexing.

*"Thank Moranu,"* Zynda said. *"What took you so long?"*

*"This and that. Have you been here the whole time?"*

*"Pretty much. We stopped for water and the high priestess grounded us. Nothing I could do could break through the shield she put over the island. I'm so sorry."*

*"Don't be sorry. Those shields were a major problem. Almost impossible to breach."*

*"Were and almost?"* Her hopeful tone made me smile.

*"Yes. I can take her down now. How fast can you get here?"*

*"Fast."*

*"Good. Have that focus stone ready."*

*"We'll be there before you know it."*

To prove it, they all leapt into the sky.

## ~ **24** ~

---

B Y THE TIME we returned to the beach, a great deal had changed. A few Deyrr creatures fought here and there, but the majority had retreated to orderly ranks, waiting off to the sides in obedient patience. My octopus had slowed the vessel enough, so I let it stop fighting. It hung in the water, waiting for instructions. When this finished, I'd have to figure out what to do with all these beings I'd leashed to my will. They weren't a burden—indeed, it seemed the force of their suspended lives flowed into me, which was no doubt a perk for those serving Deyrr—but they did depend on me for instruction. A responsibility I did not want.

In the back of my mind, dark silvered laughter chuckled past. I ignored the goddess's sarcastic reaction. I'd never asked for detailed instructions on what to do and how to live.

*Didn't you?*

At least Moranu's voice was back to sounding like my own conscience, rather than a booming entity shattering my skull.

Rayfe's wolf form paced to greet me, rubbing his jaw along my muzzle, his scent speaking to the animal part of me of mate and home and safety.

Soon that would be true.

We both shifted to human form, both in our formal regalia, and turned as one to face the approaching vessel as King and

Queen of Annfwn. A united front.

Harlan and Ivariel, then Ursula and Ochieng joined us, along with others of their family, including their elephants ranged behind. Dafne held Salena, sitting with Nakoa on Kiraka's back, where she could protect them. Kaedrin, her shining armor blood-spattered, strode up and exchanged Danu's salute with Ursula.

"You brought the Nyamburans here," Ursula said, with dawning realization.

"We were already on our way," Ivariel said in her accented Common Tongue, "but yes, my old teacher found us and guided us to be here at the correct place and time."

"You were on your way?" Harlan repeated, dumbfounded.

"Danu guided my steps," Ivariel told him somberly.

"And we all jumped at the chance to miss the rainy season this year." Ochieng grinned back at their family, who returned the smile with enthusiastic nods.

"I like the rains," Ivariel protested.

"You'll have to tell me about them," Harlan said. "And the elephants."

She smiled softly. "I will like that."

Ami, skirts gathered so she could run, but billowing around her like a glorious pink sunset, dashed up to us.

"Ash is alive, whole, and on his way here," I told her before she could ask.

She came to a halt, a tumult of rose-gold abruptly stilled in utter relief. "Thank Glorianna," she breathed, drawing the goddess's circle in the air.

"I think Moranu gets the credit this time," I replied wryly, and Rayfe slid me a sparkling glance.

"Thank Moranu," Ami replied dutifully, drawing her crescent moon, then bisecting it with Danu's diagonal sword. "And

Danu, too," she said to Ursula. "I knew you all were fearsome warriors, but I can't believe how fast you turned the tide on this battle."

"I suspect credit for that goes to Moranu, also." Ursula's gaze rested thoughtfully on me. "Or to her avatar."

Ignoring her, I spoke to Ami. "Willy and Nilly—are they all right?"

"Yes, safe in the tunnels. Who are all these people?"

"No time for introductions now. Are you wearing your rubies?" I glanced to see that Ursula wore hers, bright on her ears and gleaming like fresh arterial blood against the leathers protecting her chest.

Ami sighed dramatically. "Under my gown."

"Let's see."

"I'm wearing them!"

"Prove it."

"You don't *wear* rubies with pink," she grumbled, but dragged at her lace-edged neckline and pulled out a large, heart-shaped ruby pendant on a long chain.

Ursula eyed it. "I don't remember that one."

"I helped myself to it a long time ago," Ami replied sweetly, with a flutter of lashes. "Obviously it was meant to be mine, being a heart and all."

"Obviously," Ursula muttered, shaking her head.

I nearly laughed, so filled with love for them, and for the good things that never changed, no matter how terrible things got. "This is how it will go," I told them, raising my voice. "Ursula, I need you ten paces to my right. Ami, the same distance to my left. Rayfe will take my back, and Harlan to Ursula's. Ivariel and Ochieng, would you guard my youngest sister's back?" When they nodded, I asked Rayfe to distribute the remaining warriors at his discretion.

They all moved to their places with grave alacrity and without argument. I realized the winds of magic had begun to lift my hair and whip the heavy red velvet skirts of my gown. I pulled the Star of Annfwn out of my pocket and held it loosely. It glowed and hummed, the rubies I wore taking up the harmony in bloodred thirst, echoed by those Ami and Ursula wore.

The high priestess's vessel stopped at the shallowest point possible. I expected a small boat or punt to bring her ashore, but that wasn't dramatic enough. She stood at the rail, blinding gold as the sun struck her armor, then she floated to the water, where a pair of large porpoises rose. She stood with one foot on each, taking up a harness they held in their mouths. Lifting a hand like a general, she pointed them toward shore. Gliding over the spray like a triumphant golden goddess, she zoomed through the gentle surf.

"Tacky," Ami proclaimed with a sniff.

I smothered a smile, but Rayfe, just off my shoulder laughed darkly. "She is a little much," he murmured.

"You haven't seen the half of it," I replied under my breath.

No joking came from Ursula and Harlan, but they'd both suffered horribly at the high priestess's hands—or claws—and they were doing well to stand firm. Speaking of that incident, a wave of magic poured ahead of the high priestess, like a shimmering squall sweeping in from the sea, an enchantment to freeze us all in place as she'd done to them.

I batted the spell aside, taking it by the root and feeding the magic to the Heart. It burped a little, chewing hard, then digested the tainted magic in chunks, taking it back and making it clean again.

*Good woman,* my conscience murmured.

The high priestess's porpoises brought her to the shallows and she stepped off with a bounce, prancing a few steps, before pausing to frown. Another wave of magic blasted us, a lashing storm this time. I funneled it all to the Heart, which devoured it with relish this time. The others didn't seem to notice much, but the high priestess fixed her dead-black gaze on me. I allowed a smile and shook my head.

She lifted her chin in regal arrogance and strolled toward me. "Andromeda," she crooned. "So kind of you all to gather to greet me. Easier to surrender all at once. You will kneel as you do so."

Rayfe's low growl breathed hot over the back of my neck, and I shivered with the savagery of it. Yes, we would tear her limb from limb. But first, we would strip her of everything.

"Silly little baby sorceress," I replied in the same tone. "No one is surrendering to you. We're all here to witness your total annihilation. Once and forever."

Kiraka breathed a tongue of flame, lifting her wings with it. The high priestess rolled her eyes. "Dragon flame cannot harm me. None of you can do a thing to even touch me. You cannot defeat me. You're so stupid you don't know I've won!" She clapped her hands together and laughed.

"With what army?" I asked politely when she finished.

"Fools!" she hissed, and lifted her arms dramatically. The thousands of strands of her power pulsed, yanking on her creatures. Using the Star, flush with the power I'd channeled to the Heart, that it freely shared back with me, I ripped away her shielding, slipped down to the root of her control, and took them all for my own.

She flailed, groping for the sudden loss, staring at me in flummoxed astonishment.

*Shout your loyalty*, I sent to all of them, including the creatures I held through her junior priests and priestesses. They did. All the Deyrr creatures near and far sent up a thunderous hue and cry, shaking the earth and sky with the sound.

"They said, 'all hail Annfwn,'" I explained seriously. "I thought you might not be able to understand, since they're no longer yours."

"Well, well, well." The high priestess recovered her aplomb, though her fair cheeks burned angry red within the spiked helmet. "Our girl has grown up. Learned a trick or two, did you? But I'm still a few steps ahead of you. You see," she smiled thinly, "you forgot that I am not the only acolyte of Deyrr."

Her mind lashed out with furious commands. I let her do it, so she would feel the lack of answer. While she'd been talking, I'd taken over the last few of her minions. She called them, one by one, then *en masse*. The silence strung out, then I instructed them to answer her.

***"All hail Annfwn!"*** they shouted mentally at once, and the high priestess flinched, turning wild eyes on me.

"Maybe I forgot to mention, but they are all mine now, too," I informed her softly. "You're alone."

She quivered. Drew herself together. Then laughed. The gay, silvery sound rippled over the now silent gathering, all the people and animals listening to every word we spoke. "Oh, dear, sweet, stupid Andromeda! Have you listened to *nothing* I've told you? I am not alone. I have my god, and He is all powerful. Did you think I came back to life from nothing on my own? When Empress Hulda brought me to her, fed me the milk of Dasnaria's ancient magic, Deyrr was there to lift me up."

Off to my side, I saw Ivariel start, daggers leaping to her hands. Before I could tell her to stand down, Ochieng had his hands on her shoulders, whispering in her ear, and she relaxed. But kept her daggers at hand.

The high priestess was continuing in full rant, and I used the time to gather magic.

"I had nothing and no one," she sneered. "I was a withered mummy thanks to them!" She shot a finger at Kiraka, who blew disgusted steam out her glittering nares. "But Deyrr kept and carried me. I rose from death! And I rebuilt an empire. I created those junior priests and priestesses; I can do it again. For I have Deyrr. Watch, and be afraid."

She waved her hands and a crack shook the sky.

The golden god Deyrr stepped off the boat. Three times the size of a man, carved naked and with a protruding erect cock the length of my arm, it walked across the water toward us with long, angry strides.

"Well," Ivariel commented archly, "he's certainly overcompensating."

The high priestess glared at her, then looked again. "Who are you?"

Ivariel replied in Dasnarian, something I didn't understand, but her words made the high priestess pale.

"Andi?" Ursula said in a mild tone, as the god closed on us. "You have a plan?"

The high priestess laughed. "No, she doesn't. And now you all will die to feed Deyrr's hunger."

*"Are you in position, Zynda?"*

*"Yes, I'm directly above and behind. Ready to dive."*

*"Then go."*

I felt her plummet, and I reached to the focus stone she carried, then connected the Star with the rubies I wore and then out to the rubies my sisters wore. I poured magic into the triangle we'd created through the stones. Ami and Ursula both staggered as the lines connected, but the people at their backs caught and held them. Rayfe steadied me, his heartbeat loud and wild in my blood. Zynda dropped from the sky to level the three-sided trap—a line going straight from her to the god through the high priestess to me.

"Sorry to disappoint," I said, "but I made a promise to a two-year old. Time for you to die."

"There is nothing you can do to me, for I am immortal!" she shrieked, body arching as the power lanced through her. She lashed out with her own magic, but it bounced off the warding of Salena's rubies.

"Oh, honey," I said, feeling sorry for her at last. Putting her down would be a mercy to the twisted, insane creature she'd become. "I told you before. Only the gods are immortal."

"Yes!" she screamed as she writhed under the searing whip of magic. "And Deyrr will devour you all. Behold your doom!"

The golden figure had slowed his stride, close enough to see the glitter of those depthless eyes. I drilled through the metal casing, filling him with heat. And the metal began to melt.

"A false idol," I informed her. "The gods are immortal, yes, but they cannot take physical form for long, for it makes them vulnerable. See?"

I released my grip on her just enough for her to turn and look. The idol had shuddered to a stop, sinking to its knees in the water, the great cock drooping as beads of gold ran down in giant tears. The high priestess wailed and waded to him, all grace lost. "No! He cannot die! I can't and won't."

"Death is simply another change," I told her, not without sympathy. "One you have avoided for far too long. This unnatural extension of life has twisted you into a perversion of who you used to be."

She turned back, eyes wild, face distorted in a snarl, screaming at me in her native Dasnarian. I raised a hand, making the sign of Moranu, Ursula and Ami echoing the movement with the signs of Danu and Glorianna. When I dropped my hand, the red dragon and Djakos—Ash on his back—dove from above, flames searing.

The idol of gold and the flesh of the sorceress went up in flames together.

A great cheer of triumph roared from the assembly, but I held up a hand. "We're not done yet." Magically amplified, my voice rolled over them, and they fell into an expectant rumble.

I could see what most of them could not—how the high priestess's truly immortal aspect, her spirit, clung to Deyrr. The god easily abandoned the metal slag he'd briefly occupied and cradled his erstwhile servant in his arms. We often spoke of the dead as returning to the bower of Glorianna's arms. The sight before me became, as so often happened with Deyrr, a perverted mirror of that metaphor.

The disincarnate god billowed black and bilious against the sky, the many tentacles of his insatiable hunger reaching restlessly to drain magic from the pores of the world. The shade of the high priestess turned her attention to me.

*"See?"* Her numinous voice echoed in my very bones. *"Even now I am more than what I was. He has raised me up. You pitiful mortal. You cannot defeat a god."*

"I don't have to," I replied, and gave myself over to Moranu.

Her silver-edged darkness filled me, almost painfully so, but Her blackness was a relief in its fullness. She was the new moon, the dark that is full of all existence. The opposite of the void of Deyrr, the starvation that could never be sated.

Moranu stepped through me, many forms and faces flashing like lightning and thunder in a vast storm. Her sisters joined her. Danu, unbearably bright and sharp-edged, the clear-eyed warrior brandishing her lethal swords of justice and wisdom. On the other side, Glorianna swept in a cloud of ferocious love. Mother, maiden, crone, she was all in one. As Danu wore Ursula's face, so Glorianna wore Ami's. Or perhaps we'd been born in their images.

I couldn't say, and I didn't have to.

It was over in a moment: the Three embraced Deyrr and his burden, containing and shrinking him. The divine magic threatened to shiver the foundations of the world, building to an unbearable intensity.

And then They were gone, leaving nothing but the physical world behind.

I opened my mouth to pronounce it done.

*Not quite.*

Whether Moranu Herself, or my own conscience, I acknowledged the inner voice. Taking the leashed wills and lives beholden to me, I gathered them together and sent them into the Heart. It welcomed them in, all the lost souls, opening like a portal that moved in all directions.

All around, bodies fell as the unnatural magic that animated them fled. The red dragon fell from the sky, becoming a rain of ash that sizzled into the water.

I sagged, going boneless as the thousands of lives left me empty. Distantly I knew that Rayfe caught me and held me close.

Knowing I was safe, I looked up at his face, his eyes fulgent with triumph and worry. "Andromeda?"

"It is done."

And it was.

# ~ 25 ~

"THERE'S STILL THE Dasnarian navy," Ursula said.

Not much time had passed. I recovered my equilibrium fairly quickly, though I could tell it would take some time before I felt right being alone in my own skin again. By the time Zynda and Zyr had landed and shapeshifted to human form, and Ash had jumped straight from Djakos to embrace a freely weeping Ami, I could stand without Rayfe's support.

He stayed close, however, a hand resting on my lower back so I'd feel him near.

"I hate to interfere with the celebrating," Ursula added, as no one had mustered an answer for her. She gestured at the spreading jubilation outside our circle. "But the navy will be here before long and we're nowhere near ready. And we have yet to deal with all the Deyrr creatures that made it past the gate. The winged ones could be reaching Ordnung even now."

I shook my head. "I can set your mind at ease there. No Deyrr creatures will reach Ordnung, or anywhere ever again. I took over every last one of them. That's part of how we defeated the high priestess."

Her eyes glittered, the flash of a sword's edge in a victory blow. "Then you can marshal that entire army. We'll use them against the Dasnarians."

"You can't do that," Ivariel burst out. "I'll be the first in line to kill Hulda, but there are good people in Dasnaria, too. To turn those monsters upon them." She clutched Harlan's arm. "Think of our sisters there if no one else. Don't let her do it."

Harlan gave her a grave smile, patting her hand. "I do not command Ursula's actions."

"But she—"

"It's an irrelevant argument," I said, cutting her off, then turned to Ursula. "I let them all go." I swept a hand at the carcasses and corpses littering the beach and sea, decaying rapidly or slowly, according to how long ago those bodies had died.

Zynda, who'd joined our circle, studied me with hopeful interest. "Then all those spirits trapped by Deyrr…"

"Are free," I confirmed, feeling weary enough to lean back against Rayfe, who set warm hands on my shoulders, bracing me. "They're all free," I repeated with some wonder, assimilating the truth of it.

"But still dead," Marskal asked, looking from Zynda to me.

"Lost to the living," Ash echoed sorrowfully.

"Yes." I nodded, understanding they grieved for all those lost. They hadn't seen what I had, and what Zynda had, the horror of those spirits enslaved to Deyrr's hunger for all eternity.

"So many people," Karyn said, leaning against Zyr. "All those n'Andanans. Millions of dead, maybe."

"But free, gréine," he reminded her, tucking a lock of her buttery hair behind her ear. He met my gaze. "You did right to set them free."

"Restoring the balance." Zynda nodded thoughtfully.

"It's the natural order of things," Ami said, mostly to Ash. "Once Deyrr had them, no one could restore them to their bodies. But Andi returned them to the eternal wellspring of the universe."

I thought of the Heart, and how it had inhaled the magic as well as exhaled it. An eternal wellspring, indeed.

"What about Nilly?" Ami wanted to know, rounding on me, and fluttering her fingers at her own head. "The thing that bitch put in her mind."

"Gone," I promised. Though I made a mental note to check later and be certain all trace had gone.

Ami sagged against Ash with relief, and he kissed her warmly.

"That's all well and good," Ursula put in, tapping her fingers on the ruby in the pommel of her sword, "and I don't mean to be insensitive to the moment, but there *is* still the Dasnarian navy."

"My Essla is quite single-minded," Harlan said to Ivariel. "Especially when it comes to her royal responsibilities."

"As a queen and warrior should be," Ivariel replied, inclining her head in respect to Ursula. "I will also say that dealing with Dasnaria is my responsibility. Especially Hulda. This is my war."

"As you say, your imperiousness," Ochieng replied in a teasing voice. "It is still the rainy season at home. And we brought the elephants all this way."

"Forgive my impertinence." Karyn, who'd been staring at Ivariel with fascination, dropped into a formal Dasnarian curtsey, "but are you her Imperial Highness, the lost Princess Jenna?"

Ivariel lifted a shoulder and let it fall. "I was, once upon a time, and lost indeed. Until I was found." She gave Ochieng an intimate smile before she turned back to Karyn. "And you, how is a Dasnarian woman of noble birth here?" She glanced dubiously at Zyr who was caressing the inner curve of Karyn's elbow. "With no family."

"A long story," Karyn confided. "Suffice to say for the moment that you have been an inspiration to me."

"Very difficult to imagine," Ivariel mused. "Regardless, though I claim neither that name nor that title, I cannot deny that Hulda is my mother. We have testimony from that foul sorceress's lips that Hulda conspired to unleash Deyrr upon us. She must be brought to justice. As she owes me other debts, I shall be the one to make her pay in full." As she spoke, she shone with Danu's light. Ursula and Kaedrin gave her Danu's salute in response.

Harlan frowned thunderously. "You cannot mean to go back to Dasnaria."

"I can," Ivariel replied evenly. "Besides, I made a promise to Inga and Helva, if they still live, that I would return."

"They live," Ursula told her, when Harlan said nothing. "We are in contact with them at the Imperial Palace."

Ivariel looked to Ochieng, who took her hand. "I remember," he told her quietly. "And we stand ready to go with you."

"You can't go," Harlan burst out. "You forget what it's like for women there."

"I forget *nothing*, Harlan." Her voice, her very carriage, had gone to ice. "Not a day has gone by in all these years that I haven't faced the pain of what they did to me. But they no longer rule me. I refuse to be afraid."

Harlan nodded, deflated and resigned. "I understand."

"Besides," she said more softly, stroking his arm as if to soothe a difficult beast, "my children want to see the land of their ancestors."

He blinked at her. "Your children. Yes. You mentioned, but..."

"But there wasn't time. Children!" She said something more in the Nyamburan language. Dafne, who'd also joined our circle of conversation, listened with fascination, clearly making mental notes.

A number of the warriors dismounted. Tall, lithely muscled, the shining adult "children" leapt off their elephant mounts and strode over to join us with eager smiles. All had their mother's extraordinary bones, and their father's warmth.

"May I introduce your uncle, Imperial Prince Harlan Konyngrr, who—"

Harlan cleared his throat. "I, too, no longer claim the rank or family name."

She smiled ruefully. "Good, though they are poorer for it. These are my children. My eldest daughter Kajala, my son, Shaharlan." She paused there, smiling at Harlan's thunderstruck expression. "My younger daughters, Ingalaika and Helvalesa."

Harlan, overcome, embraced each one, Ivariel and Ochieng watching proudly. Another young woman, quite a few years older than Kajala, stood nearby, a hesitant smile on her face, her black eyes full of bright curiosity. Ivariel drew her forward.

"And, lest I forget, my niece Ayela. She wishes to become a priestess of Danu," she said to Ursula.

"May the goddess treat her kindly," Ursula replied in a dry tone.

"Why?" Kaedrin broke in with a rare grin. "She never has any of us. I have begun Ayela's training—where Ivariel left off— on the journey here. Ayela will make a fine priestess."

"This is all well and good," Ursula raised her voice over the laughter and babble of remarks in several languages, "but there is *still* the Dasnarian navy on its way here."

"Then let's go turn them around," Zyr said cockily. "Karyn and I have been deprived of our heroic battle, after all."

"Zynda and I, also," Marskal remarked.

"I can keep the ships going in unfortunate circles for some days with my storms," Nakoa said, startling everyone. The

Nyamburans eyed the Nahanaun king's tattoos with interest.

"And we do have several waves of our ships going that direction," Dafne added. "Plus our aerial forces are rested and ready to go."

"I can fly a few of us to the *Hákyrling*, to consult on strategy," Zynda said.

"Is that a land?" Ivariel inquired. "It sounds Dasnarian."

Harlan cleared his throat. "Er, it is our brother Kral's ship."

She stilled, going to ice again. "Kral. He is emperor now?"

"No…" Harlan rubbed a hand over his short hair. "Hestar is."

Ivariel's expression grew blacker. "Too much to hope he wouldn't be. And Kral leads the navy for him?"

"He actually left Dasnaria," Harlan explained. "And he's fighting for us."

Her icy demeanor melted into sheer astonishment. "How the world turns and times change," she murmured. Then she lifted her gaze, her blue eyes clear and determined. "Perhaps Kral will also like to help cut off the head of the beast."

"You would forgive him so easily?" Harlan seemed sincerely surprised.

"Forgive?" Ivariel pondered the word, then sighed. "I don't know. You have."

He looked back at her, lips parting. "How did you know?"

"Oh, baby brother, your goodness is writ all over you. I hear it in your voice." She asked him something in Dasnarian and he replied slowly. She nodded crisply. "I shall allow him to grovel and we shall go from there."

"That I'd like to see," Ursula commented.

"Do you want to go with them?" Harlan asked.

"I cannot." She shook her head. "I must return to Ordnung. There's a great deal to do." Raising her brows at me, she added.

"Apparently I have an extraordinary reign yet to conduct."

I tipped my head at her ruefully. "I'm sure you'll think of something."

"Indeed. It will be interesting to finally settle down to the business of actually running the realm. And I trust my people to handle this Dasnarian aggression. Will you go with them?" she asked Harlan in a carefully neutral tone.

"No." He lifted his still-bloodied dagger to his forehead in the *Elskathorrl*. "My place is with you. Always."

She nodded in acknowledgment, but I read the relief in her. "Whatever supplies you all need, just ask." Pausing, she looked to Rayfe. "With your permission, of course."

Rayfe rubbed my shoulders. "Of course. We are all in this together."

So good, to feel the balance returning. "Will you take the elephants to Dasnaria, though?" I asked Ivariel and Ochieng.

"It will start getting quite cold there before long," she replied, then turned to Ochieng. "Will you be able to keep the elephants warm enough?"

"For that matter," Dafne broke in, "how did you keep them warm enough on the journey here? I've been wondering about that, since everything I've read about elephants indicates they couldn't withstand the temperatures around the Crane Isthmus."

"Well, it is still summer, so it wasn't awful," Ivariel replied, her eyes sparkling with mischief. "But it turns out that, with the return of magic to Nyambura, the D'Tiembo family's natural gifts with elephants extend to quite a few supernatural tricks."

Ochieng grinned easily. "We can keep the elephants warm, yes. Besides, Violet tells me they long to see the land that birthed our Ivariel. And perhaps stomp on a few people."

The matriarch elephant, Violet, along with Efe and several others, lifted their trunks, trumpeting in apparent agreement.

Frowning, thinking through the logistics even though she'd claimed she was handing over the problem, Ursula added one more thing. "You'll be sailing there from here then, and eventually you'll need Andi to get you all through the barrier if you want to get to Dasnaria."

"Oh." I straightened, and Rayfe chuckled in my ear. "I forgot to mention. I took the barrier down. It's gone. Forever."

They all stared at me with varying levels of incomprehension. Then everyone started shouting questions at once.

The universe might be in a state of constant change, but some things stayed the same. I leaned back into Rayfe's arms, and laughed.

## ~ EPILOGUE ~

"A BLINDFOLD SEEMS ridiculous," I protested to Rayfe. "You know I can see using other means."

"Yes," he replied, laughter in his voice as he steered me from behind, hands firm and warm on my hips. "But you promised you wouldn't."

"Hmm." I hadn't exactly *promised.*

"A sacred vow," Rayfe intoned, saying it the way the Shamans chanted to Moranu. He caressed my hips, lightly kneading the muscles of my lower back.

I groaned in appreciation. "Keep doing that and I'll promise anything you want."

He chuckled, low and sensuous. "Deal. And we're here."

Slipping the blindfold from my eyes, he swept a hand at the scene before me. A decidedly *not* exciting sight. I'd known we were climbing the path to the cliff top, but I hadn't expected to see Fiona there, arching her neck in greeting, and lightly pawing the gritty soil with a dainty hoof. I went to her, stroking her gleaming neck and accepting the horse nibbles against my arm. Had I known I'd be seeing her, I would've brought a treat. I squinted at her companion, also saddled and bridled. That alone would've tipped me off, even if I couldn't see staymach magic. "That's a real horse," I informed Rayfe.

"Can't get anything past a sorceress like you," he agreed.

I just gave him a look. "You prefer staymach horses, and..." I scanned the area. "Where's your wolfhound guard?"

"I told them to stay away." He looked from me to Fiona. "Would I be insulting your abilities as a rider if I offer to help you up?"

I sighed, running my hands over my distended belly. "I'd like to be offended, but I know I need the help. I take it we're riding to wherever we're staying overnight?"

"So clever," he murmured, ducking with a wicked grin when I snarled. He settled hands on my hips. "You don't have much of a waist anymore."

"You don't have to tell me, but you're also not winning any points here."

He slid his hands lower to cup my bottom, smile widening. "Ah, now there's a better grip. Ready?"

"Are you sure you can lift me?" I braced my hands on his shoulders. The ocean breeze tossed his gleaming dark hair, sunlight picking glints as blue as his eyes and as the deep sea beyond.

"Forever, my queen," he murmured. And with shapeshifter strength, he lifted me onto Fiona's back, holding me steady with casual ease while I found my seat.

"I never thought I'd have to ride sideways again," I griped.

"Kelleah said you'd have an easier time of it, and I've promised to go slowly," Rayfe said, swinging onto the back of the other horse with enviable grace. "I also promised you wouldn't fall off."

"I never fall off my horse," I retorted.

"You did that one time."

"That was entirely your fault. And, as I've told you a hundred times, I didn't fall: Fiona did, and I went with her."

He held out a hand, twining his fingers with mine. "Then make sure Fiona doesn't fall. She's carrying the two most important people in the world to me."

I smiled mistily, blinking the tears away. "You can't say stuff like that to me right now. I've cried three times today already, and once was at the sight of a cup of milk."

"It doesn't bother me," he said, squeezing my hand. "Shall we? It's not that far, but we do have to go slowly."

"We could've shapeshifted," I pointed out as Fiona glided into her smooth stride.

"Yes, but you love to ride, and you always complain you don't get to do it enough."

True enough. And it was a beautiful day. Peace had returned to Annfwn, magic filtering through everything with abundance, making the sky more blue, the light more golden, and the sounds of laughter, bird song, and the buzzing of pollinators a quiet harmonious symphony. The flowers of Annfwn bloomed with redolent splendor.

And the love of my life held my hand, smiling over at me, as he rode by my side. "This is good," he said. "Quiet."

I nearly mentioned the virtual din of sound, but I knew what he meant. No screams. No clashing of weapons. No demands. "Oh," I realized. "We're *alone*."

"Except for the horses," he agreed, "but you're catching on now."

"Do I get to know where we're going yet?"

"Not to *that* cabin, though I considered it. That's farther than Kelleah would agree to. She wants you close enough for her to attend, should you go into labor."

"I'm still weeks away."

"Nevertheless."

"Besides," I teased, unable to resist poking at him, "I'd have you with me."

He didn't laugh or rise to the bait. Instead he tightened his grip on my hand. "Yes. As long as I live, I'll be with you.

Nothing can change that."

"My wolf," I said softly, hating the haunted look in his eye, "I know that. Nothing ever will change that."

His sensuous lips curved, but his eyes were suspiciously bright, and he cleared his throat. "That said, I'd just as soon not be wholly responsible for helping you deliver our son."

"Wise." We'd climbed some ways into the foothills above the cliff city, following a winding path that rose through the dense forest, then ran parallel to the sea. "I don't think I've been this way before."

"There didn't used be much this way to see," he allowed.

Something about the way he said it made me raise a brow. "And now?"

"You'll see."

Indeed, around the next bend, we came through a break in the trees, and out onto a promontory jutting high over the ocean. A lovely house sat on the point, with open windows on all sides. A meadow in back beckoned to the horses, who pricked their ears at the scent of the emerald velvet grass, studded with brilliant buttercups.

"Oh, Rayfe," I sighed. "It's just so pretty. How did I not know this was here?"

"Because it wasn't." He brought his horse to a halt and swung down. Coming over, he held his hands up to me, helping to lever my ungainly self to the ground. "I had it built for you. For us. They just finished yesterday. There may be a few rough edges yet, but I didn't want to wait to spend a night here with you."

I gazed at the quiet place, then up at him. "Alone."

"Alone," he confirmed. A wry look crossed his face. "Not that they can't find us if they try, but I left Ami in charge. She knows that it better be an act of war before they interrupt us."

I mock shuddered. "Don't even say it. I've had enough of war to last the rest of my life."

"You're the one with Moranu's ear. Tell Her so."

"She knows." I leaned against him as best I could with my belly between us. "I think all the goddesses agree we deserve some peace."

"Yes," he replied fervently, then kissed me on the forehead. "Why don't you go inside and explore while I take care of the horses?"

"If we're replicating our wedding night, then I should help you."

"We're not tied together this time."

"Not with rope," I replied, "but in every other way."

"In every way that matters," he agreed, dropping his mouth to mine, lips soft and heated. I hummed, the need rising in me. "Go inside," he breathed, "I'll be right there with the bags."

"All right, but only because I need to pee," I agreed.

"Didn't you right before we left?"

"Rayfe, my love, when our son is born, I'll have him sit on *your* bladder all day and you can tell me how it feels."

His laughter followed me as I walked through the velvety soft grass, glad of being in Annfwn where I could simply go barefoot and not try to wedge shoes over my swollen feet. The last few days since the Battle for Annfwn, I'd mostly slept. That seemed to be the best thing for me to recover, and I felt fully restored. A good thing, too, as Kelleah had utterly depleted herself healing people and had been asleep for the last week. Same with Ash, Vanka, and everyone else with a smidgeon of healing magic.

I entered the open doorway of the cottage, the cool ocean breeze wafting in from the graceful balcony that overhung the sea. It wasn't large, consisting mainly of the one open room with a wide porch ringing it on three sides. A large bed with fluffy pillows took up most of one corner, and various lounging spots for reading, napping, or simply lying in the sun took up the rest of the space.

Rayfe came in and set the saddlebags down. I turned, smiling at him. "Is that a bed like the one from the wedding night cabin?"

"The same bed," he confirmed.

"You brought it here?"

"I had it brought here," he clarified. "In pieces. Sometimes it's good to be king, and although we didn't spend much time in the actual bed"—his smile widened salaciously—"I thought it brought us good luck."

"True. As I recall, most of the sex occurred on that white fur before the fireplace."

"Yes, which is why I had that brought, too."

I followed his gaze to the white bear fur in front of the fireplace on the one wall without windows. "A fireplace—in Annfwn?"

"We can make a fire without heat, for ambience." He ran his long fingers over my bare arms, eyes going lambent with wicked intent. "I loved the way the firelight flickered over your skin, the way it brought out the red in your hair. You glowed from within, Andromeda. You took my breath away and I kept wondering what I'd done to deserve such a beautiful, magical, and brilliant woman to be my wife."

"Rayfe," I breathed, unutterably moved. "The brutal foreign king who waged a war to capture me… a romantic?"

His expression went determined, and he combed the hair back from my face, threading his fingers through it. "I once told you that I would've wooed you properly, had I been able to. And I'd thought to do it after, to give you romance and win your love. Then I somehow forgot."

"'Somehow,'" I echoed with a smile. "We've been a little busy. Besides, you didn't have to win my love. You've had it all along."

"But I won't take it for granted, ever again," he replied with somber intensity. "I hate that anything I did ever led you to believe I found you ugly, or anything but the most admirable person I know."

"It wasn't you," I reminded him. "She—"

"No," he interrupted, then kissed me, an edge of desperation in it. "I let my fears open the doors to doubts. Never again. Will you lie with me, my queen?"

"Yes. Oh, yes." I glanced down at my round, taut belly. "Though we'll have to figure out a way."

"I have some ideas." He smiled, sensual and confident, the wolf in his eyes. "Come over here."

He started to lead me to the bed, but I resisted. Turning back with quick concern, he looked me up and down. "No?"

"The rug." I tugged his hand in that direction. "Like the first time." With a flick of a thought, I made a fire burn, flickering ruby flames without heat.

"Beautiful," he murmured, but he was looking at me.

"It will be pretty when night falls," I said, smoothing my hands over his leanly muscled chest, untying the laces that held the black silk together. Separating the sides, I pushed it off of him, following the carved lines of his arms, chest and abdomen. So gorgeous, my husband.

He slipped the light straps of my gown from my shoulders, letting the simple light shift pool at my feet. I hesitated, feeling decidedly unbeautiful, with stretch marks on my breasts and belly. I could've shapeshifted to erase them, but it seemed a waste of energy when the marks simply reappeared overnight.

And that did nothing about the enlarged blue veins tracing spider webs over my breasts, belly, and thighs—or the rest of me being so swollen and just… so large and ungainly.

But Rayfe's expression was rapt, his hands greedy on my skin as he cupped my breasts, running thumbs over the engorged areolae. His hair veiled his face, but not the smile of wicked delight at my sharp intake of breath, followed by a guttural moan at the shock from my sensitive nipples.

"Your body is different now," he murmured, lowering his mouth to delicately kiss one nipple, then the other.

I clutched at his shoulders, unbalanced by the intensity of the sensation. "In so many ways," I agreed.

He lifted his head, eyes brilliantly blue under black winged brows. "Next time, I will follow every change, every day will be a new discovery, together."

"Next time?" I hadn't thought that far ahead. I'd been so consumed with premonitions of annihilating war that it hadn't occurred to me to imagine life beyond that. But here we were: living the rest of our lives.

"If you want to?" Rayfe asked, concerned by my shock.

"I want to," I assured him. "I want a dozen children. More." Especially since our son would belong to Moranu. Time enough to face that day when it came.

"Two dozen?" Rayfe suggested.

"We do have a race of shapeshifters and wizards to rebuild," I pointed out.

"Very true." His mouth took mine in a kiss full of wild emotion, the charge of it surging between us, his thoughts—full of love and optimism—twining with mine as his hands roamed every curve of my body, learning it anew.

He lowered me to the rug, helping me arrange my graceless body upon it, moving my hair out from under me as he knew I didn't like lying on it. Kneeling beside me, he traced the round of my belly with reverence and desire. "You are as beautiful as mother as you were as maiden, my Andromeda," he said in a quiet voice. His eyes rose to meet mine, showing me the honest emotion.

"Let's hope you can say the same when I'm a crone."

"I look forward to seeing you as matriarch," he replied with a mischievous smile, "though shapeshifters and wizards are long-lived and tend to be well-preserved."

"A happy thought that—" I broke off on a gasp as his fingers slid into the folds of my sex, preternaturally sensitive, throbbing with such need that I arched, nearly climaxing right then. He backed off the intensity just enough to keep me from going over, but gently insistent, making me writhe with pleasure, unable to quite catch my breath. He knew me so well, understood exactly how to torment and delight.

"You should see yourself," he said, a soft growl under his words. "With your dark hair spread over the white fur, the firelight gilding you. Andromeda, you are bloodred rubies and midnight fire. My sorceress, my queen, my wife." He brushed his lips over mine, his hair falling silky over my face, the firelight and sunlight dancing through the blue-black strands.

I wound my fingers in his hair, tugging him down and drinking him in. "I need you inside me."

He slid a finger into me, watching my face. "Is there room? You're so tight."

I laughed a little, then moaned at the shivers his clever fingers sent through me. "A fine question. Let's find out."

"I've always loved your curiosity," he murmured with another kiss. "Turn on your side."

He helped me roll over so I faced our fire. And it was like that night, in that snowstorm in the mountains above Windroven. Just the pair of us, two strangers from different worlds, forging something new and beautiful between us. A vision flashed into my mind of another snowy night, another fire—though this one in a shadowed cave. A much younger Salena and Uorsin sealed a bargain between them. And my mother's voice echoed over time.

*You made sacred Annfwn safe again, and you gave the Tala what I could not: a future. One of infinite possibilities.*

I closed my eyes against the welling tears.

"Andromeda?" Rayfe brushed a kiss on my shoulder. "Are you all right?"

"Yes." I took his hand and pressed a kiss to his palm. "Everything is so good, I almost can't bear it."

"You'd best learn to, because this is how our lives will be."

He coaxed my upper leg to bend, creasing at the knee and opening me from behind. Then he entered me gently, excruciatingly slow, his breathing ragged.

A moan tore out of me at the keenness of the sensation, and he stilled. "Too much?"

"Not enough," I panted. "Keep going. Oh, please."

"Thank Moranu." Bracing himself, he pushed into me to the hilt, and our groans of knife-edged pleasure twined together, dark and light, shadow and flame. "This might be over fast."

"Good," I said, "because I need to pee."

"Again?" He laughed.

"You have no idea."

"I want to know. I want to know everything." He licked my ear and bit it lightly, rocking inside me so I went boneless.

Sliding one arm beneath my head to make a pillow, he reached over me to caress my breasts. I caught his hand, interlaced his fingers with mine and held our clasped hands against my heart. He began moving, rocking his hips, so the need built soft as snowfall. His breath hot on my neck, he kissed me there, in those intimate spots that melted me and made my heart race.

It was fast. And it was glorious. A meteor of blazing delight that burned hot and consumed us both. Our skin slicked together, our bodies joined, our thoughts wound together, we found ourselves in each other again. The most profound coming home possible.

Afterward, I did have to pee—and it gave me an opportunity to get what I needed from my bag—and when I came back, he lay there waiting for me. A bounty of masculine beauty, a feral, leanly muscled man reclining on the white fur, blue eyes blazing like the wolf in the dark. I slid into his arms, where I belonged, and he smoothed the hair back from my forehead, kissing my closed eyelids.

"I suppose we've sanctified the fourth way now," he said, the words whispering over my lips as I lifted them for a kiss.

"The fourth way?" I asked, perplexed. Then I remembered. "Oh, as on our wedding night."

"Yes. The first way for the human, and the second way for the animal, for we are both."

"Thank Moranu of the many faces," I replied quietly.

"Though I seem to recall that you consecrated a third way," he continued, a smile in his voice. "I don't think you named it, however."

I flushed with heat at the memory of how I'd pushed him to his back and straddled him, the wolf tamed to my hand. "The queen's way," I informed him loftily.

He chuckled. "And so it is."

"What shall we call this fourth way?" I asked after a contented pause.

"The marriage of hearts, minds, and bodies," he replied.

"A mouthful," I said dubiously, but I pressed my lips to the hollow of his throat, tasting the salt of his skin, drinking in the scent of him, and reveling in his embrace. "But, speaking of which, I have something for you." I leaned up on one elbow, unfolded my fingers, and showed him the ring resting on my palm.

He frowned at it in puzzlement, then realization dawned. "For me?"

"You once told me you'd be delighted to accept a token like this from me."

Taking it from my palm, he held it to the light, then dropped his gaze to mine. I'd touched him, more than I'd imagined. Bringing the bloodred ruby to his lips, he kissed it, eyes still on mine. "'Delight' is a weak word for how I feel now," he whispered. "One of Salena's rubies?"

"Yes." I took the ring from him and slid it onto his finger. "And the silver from the dagger I once stabbed you with. I thought that might be fitting."

He admired the ring briefly, then wound our fingers together, pulling me down again. "Most fitting. Thank you." He ran his hand down my hair. "Does this mean we're really married now?"

I laughed. "Many times over, in more ways than we'll ever be able to name."

"Let's just call it love."

And call it love, we will.

# TITLES BY JEFFE KENNEDY

## FANTASY ROMANCES

### A COVENANT OF THORNS

Rogue's Pawn
Rogue's Possession
Rogue's Paradise

### THE TWELVE KINGDOMS

Negotiation
The Mark of the Tala
The Tears of the Rose
The Talon of the Hawk
Heart's Blood
The Crown of the Queen

### THE UNCHARTED REALMS

The Pages of the Mind
The Edge of the Blade
The Snows of Windroven
The Shift of the Tide
The Arrows of the Heart
The Dragons of Summer
The Fate of the Tala

**THE CHRONICLES OF DASNARIA**
Prisoner of the Crown
Exile of the Seas
Warrior of the World

**SORCEROUS MOONS**
Lonen's War
Oria's Gambit
The Tides of Bára
The Forests of Dru
Oria's Enchantment
Lonen's Reign

**THE FORGOTTEN EMPIRES**
The Orchid Throne
The Fiery Crown
The Promised Queen

# CONTEMPORARY ROMANCES

Shooting Star

**MISSED CONNECTIONS**
Last Dance
With a Prince
Since Last Christmas

# CONTEMPORARY EROTIC ROMANCES

Exact Warm Unholy
The Devil's Doorbell

**FACETS OF PASSION**
Sapphire
Platinum

Ruby
Five Golden Rings

## FALLING UNDER
Going Under
Under His Touch
Under Contract

# EROTIC PARANORMAL

## MASTER OF THE OPERA E-SERIAL
Master of the Opera, Act 1: Passionate Overture
Master of the Opera, Act 2: Ghost Aria
Master of the Opera, Act 3: Phantom Serenade
Master of the Opera, Act 4: Dark Interlude
Master of the Opera, Act 5: A Haunting Duet
Master of the Opera, Act 6: Crescendo
Master of the Opera

## BLOOD CURRENCY
Blood Currency

# BDSM FAIRYTALE ROMANCE

Petals and Thorns

# OTHER WORKS

Birdwoman
Hopeful Monsters
Teeth, Long and Sharp

Thank you for reading!

# About Jeffe Kennedy

Jeffe Kennedy is an award-winning author whose works include novels, non-fiction, poetry, and short fiction. She has won the prestigious RITA® Award from Romance Writers of America (RWA), has been a finalist twice, been a Ucross Foundation Fellow, received the Wyoming Arts Council Fellowship for Poetry, and was awarded a Frank Nelson Doubleday Memorial Award. She serves on the Board of Directors for the Science Fiction and Fantasy Writers of America (SFWA) as a Director at Large.

Her award-winning fantasy romance trilogy *The Twelve Kingdoms* hit the shelves starting in May 2014. Book 1, *The Mark of the Tala*, received a starred Library Journal review and was nominated for the RT Book of the Year while the sequel, *The Tears of the Rose* received a Top Pick Gold and was nominated for the RT Reviewers' Choice Best Fantasy Romance of 2014. The third book, *The Talon of the Hawk*, won the RT Reviewers' Choice Best Fantasy Romance of 2015. Two more books followed in this world, beginning the spin-off series *The Uncharted Realms*. Book one in that series, *The Pages of the Mind*, was nominated for the RT Reviewer's Choice Best Fantasy Romance of 2016 and won RWA's 2017 RITA Award. The second book, *The Edge of the Blade*, released December 27, 2016, and was a PRISM finalist, along with *The Pages of the Mind*. The next in the series, *The Shift of the Tide* and *The Arrows of the Heart* came out in August, 2017, and October, 2018. A high fantasy trilogy, The Chronicles of Dasnaria, taking place in *The Twelve Kingdoms* world began releasing from Rebel Base books in 2018. The novella, *The Dragons of Summer*, first appearing in the *Seasons of Sorcery* anthology, finaled for the 2019 RITA Award.

She also introduced a new fantasy romance series, *Sorcerous Moons*, which includes *Lonen's War*, *Oria's Gambit*, *The Tides of Bàra*, *The Forests of Dru*, *Oria's Enchantment, and Lonen's Reign*. She's begun releasing a new contemporary erotic romance series, *Missed Connections*, which started with *Last Dance* and continues in *With a Prince* and *Since Last Christmas*.

In September 2019, St. Martins Press released *The Orchid Throne*, the first book in a new romantic fantasy series, *The Forgotten Empires*. The sequel, *The Fiery Crown*, will follow in May 2021.

Her other works include a number of fiction series: the fantasy romance novels of *A Covenant of Thorns*; the contemporary BDSM novellas of the *Facets of Passion*; an erotic contemporary serial novel, *Master of the Opera*; and the erotic romance trilogy, *Falling Under*, which includes *Going Under*, *Under His Touch* and *Under Contract*.

She lives in Santa Fe, New Mexico, with two Maine coon cats, plentiful free-range lizards and a very handsome Doctor of Oriental Medicine.

Jeffe can be found online at her website: JeffeKennedy.com, every Sunday at the popular SFF Seven blog, on Facebook, on Goodreads and pretty much constantly on Twitter @jeffekennedy. She is represented by Sarah Younger of Nancy Yost Literary Agency.

jeffekennedy.com

facebook.com/Author.Jeffe.Kennedy

twitter.com/jeffekennedy

goodreads.com/author/show/1014374.Jeffe_Kennedy

**Sign up for her newsletter here.**

jeffekennedy.com/sign-up-for-my-newsletter